Dedicated to:
The both of you.
Travelers, finally where they belong.
Welcome home.

Y039420

The item should be returned or renewed by the last date stamped below.

Dylid dychwelyd neu adnewyddu'r eitem erbyn y dyddiad olaf sydd wedi'i stampio isod

To renew visit / Adnewyddwch ar
www.newport.gov.uk/libraries

PRAISE FOR J. R. WARD AND HER
BLACK DAGGER BROTHERHOOD SERIES

'Frighteningly addictive'
Publishers Weekly

'J. R. Ward is a master!'
Gena Showalter, *New York Times* bestselling author

'J. R. Ward is the undisputed queen ... Long live the queen'
Steve Berry, *New York Times* bestselling author

'Fearless storytelling. A league all of her own'
Kristen Ashley, *New York Times* bestselling author

'J. R. Ward is one of the finest writers out there – in any genre'
Sarah J. Maas, No. 1 *New York Times* bestselling author

'Ward is a master of her craft'
New York Journal of Books

'Now here's a band of brothers who know
how to show a girl a good time'
Lisa Gardner, *New York Times* bestselling author

'This dark and compelling world is filled with enticing
romance as well as perilous adventure'
Romantic Times

'The Black Dagger Brotherhood owns me now.
Dark fantasy lovers, you just got served'
Lynn Viehl, *USA Today* bestselling author of *Evermore*

J. R. Ward lives in the South with her incredibly supportive husband and her beloved golden retriever. After graduating from law school, she began working in health care in Boston and spent many years as chief of staff for one of the premier academic medical centres in the nation.

Visit J. R. Ward online:

www.jrward.com
www.facebook.com/JRWardBooks
@jrward1

J. R. WARD

LOVER UNVEILED

PIATKUS

PIATKUS

First published in the US in 2021 by Gallery Books
An imprint of Simon & Schuster, Inc.
First published in Great Britain in 2021 by Piatkus

13 5 7 9 10 8 6 4 2

Copyright © 2021 by Love Conquers All, Inc.

Interior design by Davina Mock-Maniscalco

A CIP catalogue record for this book
is available from the British Library.

Hardback ISBN: 978-0-349-42053-0

Printed and bound in Great Britain by Clays Ltd, Elcograf S.p.A.

Papers used by Piatkus are from well-managed forests
and other responsible sources.

MIX
Paper from
responsible sources
FSC® C104740
FSC
www.fsc.org

Piatkus
An imprint of
Little, Brown Book Group
Carmelite House
50 Victoria Embankment
London EC4Y 0DZ

An Hachette UK Company
www.hachette.co.uk

www.littlebrown.co.uk

GLOSSARY OF TERMS AND PROPER NOUNS

ahstrux nohtrum (n.) Private guard with license to kill who is granted his or her position by the King.

ahvenge (v.) Act of mortal retribution, carried out typically by a male loved one.

Black Dagger Brotherhood (pr. n.) Highly trained vampire warriors who protect their species against all harm. As a result of selective breeding within the race, Brothers possess immense physical and mental strength, as well as rapid healing capabilities. They are not siblings for the most part, and are inducted into the Brotherhood upon nomination by the Brothers. Aggressive, self-reliant, and secretive by nature, they are the subjects of legend and objects of reverence within the vampire world. They may be killed only by the most serious of wounds, e.g., a gunshot or stab to the heart, etc.

blood slave (n.) Male or female vampire who has been subjugated to serve the blood needs of another. The practice of keeping blood slaves has been outlawed.

the Chosen (pr. n.) Female vampires who had been bred to serve the Scribe Virgin. In the past, they were spiritually rather than temporally focused, but that changed with the ascendance of the final Primale, who freed them from the Sanctuary. With the Scribe Virgin removing herself from her role, they are completely autonomous and learning to live on earth. They do continue to meet the blood needs of unmated members of the Brotherhood, as well as Brothers who cannot feed from their *shellans* or injured fighters.

chrih (n.) Symbol of honorable death in the Old Language.

cohntehst (n.) Conflict between two males competing for the right to be a female's mate.

Dhunhd (pr. n.) Hell.

doggen (n.) Member of the servant class within the vampire world. *Doggen* have old, conservative traditions in service to their superiors, following a formal code of dress and behavior. They are able to go out during the day.

ehros (n.) A Chosen trained in the matter of sexual arts.

exhile dhoble (n.) The evil or cursed twin, the one born second.

the Fade (pr. n.) Non-temporal realm where the dead reunite with their loved ones and pass eternity.

First Family (pr. n.) The King and Queen of the vampires, and any children they may have.

ghardian (n.) Custodian of an individual. There are varying degrees of *ghardians*, with the most powerful being that of a *sehcluded* female.

glymera (n.) The social core of the aristocracy, roughly equivalent to Regency England's *ton*.

hellren (n.) Male vampire who has been mated to a female. Males may take more than one female as mate.

hyslop (n. or v.) Term referring to a lapse in judgment, typically resulting in the compromise of the mechanical operations of a vehicle or otherwise motorized conveyance of some kind. For example, leaving one's keys in one's car as it is parked outside the family home overnight, whereupon said vehicle is stolen.

leahdyre (n.) A person of power and influence.

leelan (adj. or n.) A term of endearment loosely translated as "dearest one."

Lessening Society (pr. n.) Order of slayers convened by the Omega for the purpose of eradicating the vampire species. Past enemy.

lesser (n.) De-souled human who targets vampires for extermination as a member of the Lessening Society. *Lessers* must be stabbed through the chest in order to be killed; otherwise they are ageless. They do not eat or drink and are impotent. Over time, their hair, skin, and irises lose pigmentation until they are blond, blushless, and pale-eyed. They smell like baby powder. Inducted into the society by the Omega, they retained a ceramic jar thereafter into which their heart was placed after it was removed.

lewlhen (n.) Gift.

lheage (n.) A term of respect used by a sexual submissive to refer to their dominant.

Lhenihan (pr. n.) A mythic beast renowned for its sexual prowess. In modern slang, refers to a male of preternatural size and sexual stamina.

lys (n.) Torture tool used to remove the eyes.

mahmen (n.) Mother. Used both as an identifier and a term of affection.

mhis (n.) The masking of a given physical environment; the creation of a field of illusion.

nalla (n., f.) or *nallum* (n., m.) Beloved.

needing period (n.) Female vampire's time of fertility, generally lasting for two days and accompanied by intense sexual cravings. Occurs approximately five years after a female's transition and then once a decade thereafter. All males respond to some degree if they are around a female in her need. It can be a dangerous time, with conflicts and fights breaking out between competing males, particularly if the female is not mated.

newling (n.) A virgin.

the Omega (pr. n.) Malevolent, mystical figure who has targeted the vampires for extinction out of resentment directed toward the Scribe Virgin. Exists in a non-temporal realm and has extensive powers, though not the power of creation. Eradicated.

phearsom (adj.) Term referring to the potency of a male's sexual organs. Literal translation something close to "worthy of entering a female."

Princeps (pr. n.) Highest level of the vampire aristocracy, second only to members of the First Family or the Scribe Virgin's Chosen. Must be born to the title; it may not be conferred.

pyrocant (n.) Refers to a critical weakness in an individual. The weakness can be internal, such as an addiction, or external, such as a lover.

rahlman (n.) Savior.

rythe (n.) Ritual manner of asserting honor granted by one who has offended another. If accepted, the offended chooses a weapon and strikes the offender, who presents him- or herself without defenses.

the Scribe Virgin (pr. n.) Mystical force who previously was counselor to the King as well as the keeper of vampire archives and the dispenser of privileges. Existed in a non-temporal realm and had extensive powers, but has recently stepped down and given her station to another. Capable of a single act of creation, which she expended to bring the vampires into existence.

sehclusion (n.) Status conferred by the King upon a female of the aristocracy as a result of a petition by the female's family. Places the female under the sole direction of her *ghardian*, typically the eldest male in her household. Her *ghardian* then has the legal right to determine all manner of her life, restricting at will any and all interactions she has with the world.

shellan (n.) Female vampire who has been mated to a male. Females generally do not take more than one mate due to the highly territorial nature of bonded males.

symphath (n.) Subspecies within the vampire race characterized by the ability and desire to manipulate emotions in others (for the purposes of an energy exchange), among other traits. Historically, they have been discriminated against and, during certain eras, hunted by vampires. They are near extinction.

talhman (n.) The evil side of an individual. A dark stain on the soul that requires expression if it is not properly expunged.

the Tomb (pr. n.) Sacred vault of the Black Dagger Brotherhood. Used as a ceremonial site as well as a storage facility for the jars of *less-*

ers. Ceremonies performed there include inductions, funerals, and disciplinary actions against Brothers. No one may enter except for members of the Brotherhood, the Scribe Virgin or her successor, or candidates for induction.

trahyner (n.) Word used between males of mutual respect and affection. Translated loosely as "beloved friend."

transition (n.) Critical moment in a vampire's life when he or she transforms into an adult. Thereafter, he or she must drink the blood of the opposite sex to survive and is unable to withstand sunlight. Occurs generally in the mid-twenties. Some vampires do not survive their transitions, males in particular. Prior to their transitions, vampires are physically weak, sexually unaware and unresponsive, and unable to dematerialize.

vampire (n.) Member of a species separate from that of *Homo sapiens*. Vampires must drink the blood of the opposite sex to survive. Human blood will keep them alive, though the strength does not last long. Following their transitions, which occur in their mid-twenties, they are unable to go out into sunlight and must feed from the vein regularly. Vampires cannot "convert" humans through a bite or transfer of blood, though they are in rare cases able to breed with the other species. Vampires can dematerialize at will, though they must be able to calm themselves and concentrate to do so and may not carry anything heavy with them. They are able to strip the memories of humans, provided such memories are short-term. Some vampires are able to read minds. Life expectancy is upward of a thousand years, or in some cases even longer.

wahlker (n.) An individual who has died and returned to the living from the Fade. They are accorded great respect and are revered for their travails.

whard (n.) Equivalent of a godfather or godmother to an individual.

LOVER UNVEILED

CHAPTER ONE

Trade Street and 30th Avenue
Downtown Caldwell, New York

Forty-eight minutes before Ralphie DeMellio got murdered, he was living the life.

"You got this," his buddy was saying as he rubbed Ralphie's bare shoulders. "You fucking *got* this, you're a monster, you're a mother-fucking *monster!*"

Ralphie and his crew were on the sixth level of a parking garage that was all about the oil stains and litter, rather than any Oldsmobiles and Lincolns. The abandoned facility was just a fucking concrete bureau with nothing in its drawers, and in this part of Caldie, any kind of structural on-its-lonesome didn't last long. Hello, BKC. Bare Knuckle Conquests was the only legit underground fighting circuit in the southern part of New York State, and the bout held tonight was the reason why he, his bros, and five hundred clout-chasing Insta-famers were here.

Any more selfies and it'd be the driver's license lane at the DMV.

BKC was big-ass business, and Ralphie, as the reigning champ, was making big-ass fucking bank—provided none of these dumbasses with the camera phones gave their location away. And like, what were the chances of that.

"Where's the coke."

He put his hand out, and when the brown vial was slapped into his palm like a surgical instrument, he went to town. As he honked two kilos of powder deep into his sinuses, his eyes went jumping bean over the crowd. Down at the other end of the level, they were antsy, drugging, and putting their bets in with the organizer's bookies. Nothing but three rounds of bare-knuckle minutes between them and the killing they expected to make.

Ralphie was a very good bet.

He hadn't lost a fight yet, even though he had Slim Jim muscles and smoked a lot of weed. But here was the fucking thing. The bouncer-types with the boulder biceps and the jelly bellies were only impressive when they were standing still. Get them moving and they had no balance, no speed, and follow-throughs like they had double vision. Long as Ralphie kept buzzing around like a fly on shit, he was unhittable as his right hook went to work.

"You good, Ralphie. You fucking good!"

"Yeah, that's right, Ralphie, you the best!"

His crew was five guys from the neighborhood. They'd grown up together and were all related, their families having come over on the boat to Ellis Island a couple generations ago and gotten out of Hell's Kitchen soon as they could afford it. Little Italy in Caldie was little different than the one in Manhattan, and as his father always said, don't trust someone you don't know and don't know someone if you can't walk to their house.

And there was one other person on Ralphie's team.

"Where is she." Ralphie looked around. "Where is—"

Chelle was back by the G Wagon, posed like a Pirelli girl, her elbows on the hood, one heel stabbed into a tire rim. Her head was back, the purple ends of her black hair licking the metallic paint, her pink lips parted as she stared up at nothing. The night was chilly because April was still a bitch in this zip code, but she didn't give a fuck. Her bustier was all she had on up top, and the bottom half of her wasn't covered much better.

Fuuuuuuck. Those tattoos on her upper thighs were showing. And the ones on the swells of her breasts. And the sleeve on her left arm.

She'd always refused to get one of his initials.

She was like that.

As if she caught his drift, Chelle slowly turned her head. Then she licked her lips with the tip of her tongue.

Ralphie's hand went to the front of his jeans. She was not the kind of woman you brought home to mother, and at first, that was the reason he'd fucked her. But she was smart and she had her own hair salon. She didn't check his phone. She didn't care if he went out with the boys. She had her own money, she never asked him for a goddamn thing, and she had options, lotta options.

Men wanted her.

She was with him, though. And no matter what she looked like, she didn't come on to his crew. She was not a pass-around, and anybody rubbed up on her? She was one slap away from knocking their fucking teeth out.

So yeah, after a year, Ralphie was way into her.

To the point where he didn't care about what anyone else thought, including his traditional Italian mother. As far as he was concerned, Chelle was wifey material and that was all that fucking mattered.

"—got this, Ralphie—"

To kill the ass-kissing all up in his face, Ralphie put his hand on the center of his boy's chest and pushed the guy back. "Gimme a minute."

His crew knew what was up, and they turned around and faced the crowd, closing shoulder to shoulder.

And Chelle was well damn aware of what he was after.

The G Wagon was parked ass in, with a couple of feet of space between the rear bumper and the garage's nasty concrete wall. Chelle went around and assumed the position, leaning back on the Benz's boxy rear door and arching her shit. In her heels, she was as tall as Ralphie, and as her lids lowered and her breasts strained against the lace trim of the bustier, she met him right in the eye.

Ralphie's heart was going fast, but his smile was slow as he put his hands on her little waist. "You want it?"

"Yeah. Gimme it."

Ralphie unzipped his jeans and stroked himself as he kissed her throat. 'Cuz she wouldn't want him to mess up her lipstick. That kinda shit would come later, after he beat the ass of whoever was going to try him tonight. But he wasn't about to drive his truck through mud, and he wasn't about to mess up his female in public.

Chelle moved her thong aside, and as she put a stiletto against the concrete, he pumped into her while she grabbed onto his bare shoulders.

The sex was hot as fuck. Because it turned out that if he respected the female? It made everything hotter.

As Ralphie lifted her up so she could put both her legs around his hips, he closed his eyes. The pre-fight rush, the coke, Chelle, the new G Wagon from the cake he was earning at BKC, it was all power in his veins. He was the man. He was the monster. He was—

Ralphie started to come, and he would have yelled out, but he didn't want people catching his girl like this. Instead he gritted his teeth and held on tight, dropping his head into Chelle's perfumed neck and squeezing out curses through his locked jaw.

And then he had to say it.

"I love you, I fucking *love* you," he grunted.

He was so into his girl, so into the coming, so into the feel of her coming with him . . . that he didn't notice who was watching them from the shadows about twenty feet away.

If he had, he would have packed up his true love and his crew, and left rubber on the road as he got the fuck out of the parking garage.

Most of destiny was on a need-to-know basis, however.

And sometimes, it was best that you didn't get a heads-up on the inevitable that had your name on it.

Way too fucking horrifying.

CHAPTER TWO

2464 Crandall Avenue
Eleven Miles from Downtown

Mae, blooded daughter of Sturt, blooded sister of Rhoger, pulled on her coat and couldn't find her purse. The little ranch didn't offer a lot of hidey-holes, and she found the thing—with her keys, bonus—on the washer by the door out into the garage. Oh, right. She'd brought in her necessaries the night before and had lost control of so many bags. Her purse had thrown up on the tile floor, and she'd only had the energy to put the Humpty back in her Dumpty. Carrying the Michael Kors knockoff into the kitchen had just been too much.

The lid of the Maytag was as far as she'd gotten.

Grabbing the thing, she checked that the broken strap was still hanging on by the safety pin jury-rig she'd managed. Yup. Good to go. She supposed she could head to T.J.Maxx and buy a replacement, but who had time for that. Besides, "Waste not, want not" had always been the mantra in her family's household.

Back when their parents had still been alive.

"Phone. Need my . . ."

She found the iPhone 6 in the pocket of her jeans. Her last double check? The mace canister she always had with her.

Pausing by the back door, she listened to all the quiet.

"I won't be gone long," she called out. Silence. "I'll be right back."

More silence.

With a sense of defeat, she lowered her head and slipped out into the garage. As the steel door slammed shut behind her, she locked the copper dead bolt with her key and hit the opener. The overhead light came on, and the cold, wet night was revealed inch by inch as the panels rolled up the tracks.

Her car was eight years old, a Honda Civic that was the color of a winter cloud. Getting in, she caught a faint whiff of motor oil. If she were human, instead of a vampire, she probably wouldn't have noticed, but there was no avoiding the scent. Or what it meant.

Great. More good news.

Putting things in gear, she hit the gas and eased forward onto the driveway. Her father had always told her to back in, so she was ready in case she needed to get out in a hurry. In the event of fire, for instance. Or a *lesser* attack.

Oh, the sad irony on that.

Looking into the rearview, she waited until the garage door was locked back in place before hanging a right on her quiet street and speeding off. All the humans were settling into their houses for the night, hunkering down for the dark hours, recharging before work and school rearrived with the return of the sun. She supposed it was strange to be living so closely around the other species, but it was all she had ever known.

As with beauty, weird was relative.

The Northway was a six-lane byway running in and out of downtown Caldwell, and she waited until she was on it and cruising at sixty-one miles an hour before she got out her phone and made her call. She kept things on speaker and in her lap. There was no Bluetooth for her old car, and she was not going to risk getting pulled over for using a handheld—

"Hello? Mae?" came the frail, wobbly voice. "Are you on your way?"

"I am."

"I really wish you didn't have to do this."

"It'll be okay. I'm not worried."

The lie stung, it really did. Except what else could she say?

They stayed connected without talking, and Mae had an image of the old female sitting beside her in the car, the embroidered housecoat and pink shuffle slippers like something Lucille Ball would have worn around her and Ricky's apartment. But Tallah was barely mobile, even with her cane. There was no way she had the gumption for what was coming.

Hell, Mae wasn't sure she could handle this.

"You know what to do?" Tallah asked. "And you'll call me as soon as you're back in the car?"

God, that voice was getting so weak.

"Yes. I promise."

"I love you, Mae. You can do this."

No, I can't. "I love you, too."

As Mae hung up, she rubbed her stinging eyes. But then she was all about the exits. Fourth Street? Market? She got nervous about missing the one she needed, and ended up leaving the highway too soon. Making an inefficient box pattern around a basket weave of one-ways, she found Trade Street and stayed on it, the numbers on the avenues going up through the teens and into the twenties.

When she entered the thirties, the commercial property values plummeted, the old-fashioned office buildings all boarded up, any restaurants or shops abandoned. The only cars around were either passing through or dead and picked clean, and forget about pedestrians. The cracked and debris-strewn sidewalks were empty, and not just because April remained inhospitable in upstate New York.

She was losing faith in the whole plan when she came up to the first of several packed-full parking lots.

And Jesus, it was about what was in them.

The vehicles—because they sure didn't look like regular sedans and hatchbacks—were brilliant neon unless they were black, and they were styled like anime, all aerodynamic angles and scooped bumpers.

She was in the right place—

Scratch that. She didn't belong here, but she was where she needed to be.

Mae pulled into the third lot on the same theory she'd bailed early on the highway: If she went much farther, she might overshoot things. And once she was inside the one-block boundary of rusted chicken wire, she had to go all the way to the back row to find a space. As she rolled along, humans who matched the fancy drag racers, versions of Jake Paul and Tana Mongeau, looked at her like she was a librarian lost at a rave.

This made her sad, although not because she cared about a bunch of humans' opinions of her.

The fact that she knew anything about human influencers was courtesy of Rhoger. And the reminder of how things used to be between them was a door she had to shut. Falling into that black hole was not going to help her right now.

When she got out of her Civic, she had to lock the door with her key because the fob was dead. Tucking her bag against her body, she lowered her head and didn't look at the people she passed. She could sense their stares, however, and the irony was that they weren't eyeballing her because she was a vampire. No doubt her jeans and her SUNY Caldie sweatshirt were an offense to all their Gucci.

She wasn't exactly sure where to go, but a trickle of people was funneling into a larger tributary of humans, and the lot of them were heading toward a parking garage. As she joined the eventual river of twenty-year-olds in all their hot-and-sexy, she tried to see up ahead. The entrance to the multi-leveled concrete stack was barricaded, but a line had formed outside a door that was off to one side.

As Mae took a spot and kept to herself, there was a good forty feet of single file going on and things were moving slowly, two men the size of semis growling at the chosen who were allowed in—and they did turn people away. It just wasn't immediately clear what the data screen was, although no doubt Mae was going to be on the "yeah nope" list—

"You lost or something?"

The question had to be repeated before she realized she was being addressed, and as she turned around, the two girls—well, women—who were making the inquiry were looking as impressed as the bouncers were going to be when they tried to deny Mae entry.

"No, I'm not lost."

The one on the right, who had a tattoo under the eye that read "Dady's Girl" in cursive, leaned in. "I think you're fucking lost."

Her pupils were so dilated that her irises were invisible, and the eyebrows had been plucked to such a thin wire that they—no, wait, they'd been tattooed on, too. Fake lashes were tipped with little pink dots that matched the pink-and-black ethos of what was more costume than clothing, and there were piercings in places that made Mae hope the woman never had a runny nose or food poisoning.

And FWIW, one had to wonder whether the missing *d* had been intentional, or if the masterful work had been sold by the letter and someone's pocket change had run out.

"No, I'm not," Mae replied.

The woman stepped forward, breasts out like Barbarella, even though she probably had no idea who Jane Fonda was now, much less who the actress had been in the sixties. "You need to get the fuck out of here."

Mae looked down at the cracked sidewalk they were all standing on. Weeds had muscled their way in through the seams, though everything was dried and dead thanks to the winter.

"No, I don't."

Next to the aggressor, the other woman lit up a cigarette and looked bored. Like maybe this happened a lot and her buddy's drama had long lost its appeal—

"You fucking get out of here, fuck."

Dady's Girl punched both her palms into Mae's shoulders with such force that it was ass-over-teakettle, the landing on the packed ground hard, the only good news that her purse's broken strap held and nothing fell out. As stunned disbelief consumed most of the air space in Mae's brain, she looked up.

Dady's Girl was standing over her prey, all superhero-superior, hands on hips, high heels planted in a wide stance, the invisible cloak of her sadistic joy at having bullied someone waving over her shoulders.

The rest of the wait line was looking over, but no one was coming to any rescue, and nobody seemed as impressed with Dady's Girl as she herself did.

Mae braced a palm on the concrete and pushed up back to level, rising to her full height—which, compared to the high-heeled GLOWer, was underdog status and then some.

"Get out of here," the woman hissed. "You don't belong."

Those hands came out a second time, hitting the same place, like it was a well-practiced shot, a perishable skill that was kept in tip-top shape. But Mae had also just had some relevant practice. As she stumbled back, arms flapping, feet tap-dancing, her body better prepared for the tilting scramble, she had a moment of profound numbness. She felt nothing, not the bad balance, not the momentum-created wind in her hair, not the quick draw of cool air in her lungs.

It was a surprise that she managed to catch herself.

Dady's Girl didn't give her much time to recover. The woman rushed forward at a steep angle, like she was a linebacker—

Mae's arm shot out of its own volition, the limb going tree limb. And the human female ran right into the open palm with the front of her throat. The instant contact was made, Mae's fingers closed tight.

After which, the pushback came.

Mae started walking forward, escorting the woman off the sidewalk. And when Dady's Girl struggled to accommodate the backward movement, those spiky heels catching on the ground, Mae helped things by lifting her up by the neck so that those shapely legs dangled. Meanwhile, long-taloned nails decorated with diamantés and swirls of pink clawed at the hold on that windpipe and got nowhere, the tips snapping off, one of them hitting Mae on the chin and rebounding into thin air.

Not that she cared. Not that she really noticed.

The parking garage was constructed of concrete that had been poured properly—so its walls offered a whole helluva lot of buck-stops-here. As Mae banged the woman against the slab, the body habitus was what gave way, breath exploding out of the lungs, those pink-tipped lashes flaring.

But that didn't go far enough for Mae.

She put her free hand on the sternum and laid increasing pressure on the front rib bones . . . which translated to the lungs . . . and finally to the fiercely beating heart inside its cage of calcium and collagen bars.

The human woman's eyes bugged out. Her jugular went from pounding to flickering. Her coloring became florid as barn siding.

In a low voice, Mae said, "You don't tell me where I belong. Are we clear?"

Dady's Girl nodded like her life depended on it. Which was the truth.

Meanwhile, on the periphery, the wait line had reoriented from its forward-to-back formation to a horseshoe around Mae, and there was chatter, dim but excited—

"Jesus Christ, y'all know you can't be doin' this shit!"

Members of the crowd were tossed aside like stuffed animals as one of the bouncers came forward. And when Mae took her eyes off Dady's Girl to give him the once-over, he stopped short and blinked. Like he wasn't sure he was seeing this right.

Like maybe a houseplant had turned out to be marijuana.

Or a man-eating species.

"Lady," he said in an um-well-so tone. "What the hell are you doing here?"

Mae decided to follow the guy's example with the onlookers. With a casual flick of the wrist, she empty-chip-bag'd Dady's Girl and then primly retucked her shirt and straightened her jacket.

Staring up at the bouncer, she cleared her throat. "I'm here to see the Reverend."

The bouncer blinked again. Then he said in a low voice, "How do you know that name."

Mae moved her purse in front of her torso and covered it with both arms—even though the likelihood of her getting pickpocketed had just gone seriously south. Then she walked up so close to the guy that she could smell his fresh sweat, his faded cologne, and the hair product he'd used to make sure his high was high and his tight was tight.

Narrowing her eyes, she dropped her voice. "That's none of your business and I'm done talking. You will take me to him right now."

Another blink. And then, "I'm sorry, I can't do that."

"Wrong answer," Mae gritted. "That's the wrong fucking answer."

CHAPTER THREE

The Commodore Building, Luxury Living at Its Finest™
Downtown Caldwell

Balthazar, son of Hanst, had shoes that were soft as lamb's ears on his feet. His skintight clothes were black. His head and most of his face were covered with a skull cap. His hands were gloved.

Not that vampires had to worry about leaving fingerprints.

As he lived up to all the silent, creeping myths about his species—or at least the ones the humans made up—he was a shadow among shadows, whispering through the high-ceiling'd rooms of the largest condo in the Commodore, cataloguing all manner of goodies that were on display in dimmed light.

The fucking triplex was like a museum. For someone who watched a lot of *AHS*.

Coming around another corner, and entering yet another small room with a theme to its objects, he stopped short. "What the . . ."

Like the other capsules he'd ghosted through, this one was filled with glass shelves. It was what was on them that was a surprise—and considering he had sauntered through an entire room full of Victorian surgical instruments, that was saying something.

Oh, and then there'd been the bat skeletons.

"You went and bought a bunch of rocks," he murmured. "Really. Like you didn't have anything better to do with your money."

Through the darkness, Balz drifted over the fancy parquet floor to something that looked like a loaf of pumpernickel bread that had been overproved. The thing was egg-shaped with a semi-solid core, its outside limits full of holes, the whole production set up on some kind of Lucite stand. A little nameplate that was brushed gold read: *Willamette Fragment, 1902.*

Each of the hunks seemed to be named for a place: *Lübeck, 1916. Kitkiöjärvi, 1906. Poughkeepsie, 1968.*

None of it made any sense—

Dover, 1833.

Balz frowned. And then, before he could do any conscious math on the date and place, the past slammed into him: Instantly, he was sucked away from the luxurious, weird condo, teleported by memory back to the Old Country . . . where he and the Band of Bastards had been living on their own in the forests, scrounging for food, for weapons, for *lesser* kills. Ah, those rough and exciting earlier years. They'd been the very opposite of where they were now, aligned with the Black Dagger Brotherhood and the First Family, crashing in a great gray mansion on top of a mountain, safe, sound, protected.

He missed some parts of the good ol' nights. He wouldn't change a thing about the present, though.

But yeah, back in March of 1833, in the Old Country, the bastards had been just rousing from the shallow cave they'd taken refuge in to avoid the sun during the day. Suddenly, overhead, a brilliant flash of light appeared to streak across the entire night sky, burning bright as a star and growing larger by the heartbeat, its tail a streamer of sparkling jewels.

They'd raced back into the cave and crouched down, arms over skulls to protect heads and faces.

Balz had thought that maybe the world was coming to an end, the Scribe Virgin finished with pussyfooting around with the species—or perhaps the Omega had discovered a new weapon against the vampires.

The explosion had been close by, the sound of the impact earsplitting, the ground quaking, stone particles falling on their shoulders as the structural integrity of the cave was challenged. After that . . . several minutes of waiting. And then they'd filed out and sniffed the air.

Iron. Burning iron.

They'd followed the metallic stench through the trees . . . to find a smoking burn pit with a small rock in the center. Like an odd, mystical bird-creature had laid a toxic egg.

Balz came back to the present and looked around again.

These were meteorites. All of these craggy chunks of God-only-knew-what had traveled through space and landed with fanfare on the earth. Only to be corralled here by a collector with a lot of money and an arguably clinical case of OCD.

"Fill your boots," Balz muttered as he continued through.

It had taken him a couple of weeks to scope out this target—said research and stalking the anticipatory foreplay before the felonious orgasm. Husband was a hedge fund manager—which to Balz conjured up images of a man in a suit safeguarding $27.94 in bush trimmers. Wife was a former model—which meant she was still hot, just not photographed professionally now that she had a ring on it. Unsurprisingly, there was a nineteen-year age difference between the two, and given the life spans of humans, that wasn't going to matter so much now when it was a case of late fifties vs. late thirties. Ten years from now? Twenty?

Hard to imagine that wife with the good bone structure and the superior posterior was going to find dentures and a walker worth rolling over for.

But whatever, when you were a manager of hedges that had funds, you needed a hot wife. You also required some real estate flex. Or six properties, as the case was. Here in Caldwell, the guy had purchased the top three levels of half the Commodore, and the layout of the triplex was logical. First floor was made up of big public spaces for entertaining— you know, for when you had to throw checks-for-canapés events to support local philanthropies. The second level was this rabbit warren of little rooms with their curated collections of space pebbles, nineteenth-century poke-and-tickle nightmares—and oh, yup, those three dozen bat skeletons that were like model ships only with wings.

Balz actually almost respected the guy's taste.

As for the third floor? That was what he was after, and when he came up to the staircase, he ascended those marble steps on a whisper. Oil paintings by Banksy marked the curving wall, and up above, a chandelier strung with lead crystal prisms gleamed quietly, like a rambunctious debutante that had been told to pipe down at the ball. Up on the penthouse level, the wall-to-wall carpeting started, and there was a change in scents here, a flowery bouquet tinting the air with lavender, honeysuckle, and the lilting freedom that came with big fat bank statements.

Balz followed along the runner, the pile so thick it was like walking on Wonder Bread, the trail taking him by a lineup of arched windows that let in a glowing view of the skyscrapers and linking roadways below. The sight of the streaming lines of white headlights and red taillights, coupled with the glowing, graceful arches of the twin bridges, was so captivating he had to take a moment to appreciate the urban landscape.

And then he was on the move again.

The security system had been as expected, a high-level, integrated set of belt-and-antiburglar-suspenders that had been a fun challenge to disarm.

Hey, Vishous wasn't the only one who was handy with the IT shit, 'kay?

It had been a moment of pride for Balz that he hadn't had to consult the Brother with the Mensa membership about disarming all the motion detectors, door contacts, and laser-sighted sensors in the place. And the fact that Balz did the strip job all on his own was part of the rules he set for himself. These humans with their portable objects of value were sitting ducks for a thief like him: For all intents and purposes, in any conceivable house, condo, apartment, yacht, bunker, whatever, he could just dematerialize in through a plate glass window, put the inhabitants to sleep mentally, and use the five-finger discount to take what he wanted, when he wanted.

But that was like sitting down to Monopoly with a set of brass knuckles. If you could just knock out your opponent, grab all the hotels and houses, all the paper money, and all the properties? Well, congratulations. You just roll those dice and move your little shoe around the board for the next seventy-five thousand rounds, playing with yourself.

The challenge was in the constrictions. And in his case, he applied all human limitations to himself: He was not allowed to do anything that those rats without tails couldn't. That was the one rule, but it had many, many implications.

Okay, fine. He also cheated on occasion.

Just a little.

But he was a thief, not a priest, for fuck's sake.

Going along, he wasn't interested in the lineup of empty guest bedrooms. In fact, the entire condo, including the panic room(s) he was heading for, was vacant. He'd intended to get in when the happy couple were clocking time on the premises—because homeowners were much more of a challenge when they were actually, you know, home—but he was on rotation with the Brotherhood and the Mr. and Mrs. traveled a lot of the time. He was done waiting for the stars to align.

The animal charity he was giving the cash to needed to rebuild after that fire. Fortunately, none of the dogs or cats had been killed, but their medical wing had taken a hit—

What. So he was a sucker for four-legged things. Besides, he didn't need the money and having a purpose to the taking was what made everything more than just a robbery hobby.

The master suite was an apartment within the condo, a localized concentration of super-fancy and ultra-private that included a separate kitchen area, its own terrace, and a bathroom/closet combo the size of most people's houses. And they'd totally followed Jodie Foster's 2002 example. The whole thing went on lockdown in the event of an infiltration by someone with a net worth of less than $40 million or, if it was female, a waist-to-hip ratio lower than 0.75.

Standards, doncha know.

As he crossed into the Big Man Zone, he stopped and listened to all the quiet. God, how fucking boring was this. He really would have preferred to wait for the Mr. and Mrs. to be in res.

Coming up to an archway, he glanced into the kitchen. It was barren as an operating room and just as cozy, everything stainless steel and professional. Then again, it wasn't like there were any family dinners happening. The Mr.'s original Mrs. and attendant offspring, generated prior to his making his first billion, had been jettisoned like a bad investment. No further use for cozy things.

Sleek and beautiful, cold and state-of-the-art.

Like the new wife, the new life.

Balz kept going. The dressing room had two entrances, one through the bedroom and one through a shallow hall for the servants. It seemed only polite to choose the latter considering he was committing a burglary on the premises, and he was surprised to find things locked. No problem. Taking out his picklock kit, he was in like Flynn in under a minute, and as he entered the Neiman-Marcus-worthy collection of suits, ties, dresses, and accessories, he breathed deep. Ah. So this was the source of the fragrance that permeated the upper floor, and yeah, if money had a scent, this would be it. Heady, strong enough to be noticed, yet not overpowering . . . flowery, but with the serious weight of sophisticated men's cologne.

And shit, it was a wonder the Mr. and Mrs. had anything left in the bank considering all these threads.

Behind glass panes, just like the display cases downstairs, hanging rods were set at all levels, as if the hundreds and hundreds of thousands of dollars of clothes were perishable if left out to the open air. There was also a thirty-foot-long center aisle of double-sided bureaus, his and hers.

Party time.

Whistling through his front teeth, he tap-danced along as he zeroed in on the compartment holding the man of the condo's array of tuxedos. Opening the glass, Balz pulled a Moses and Red Sea'd the shoulders of the fine silk jackets. The wall that was revealed was smooth—except for the square outline that, if you didn't have vampire eyesight or the details of the safe's location, you wouldn't tweak to.

Outing a CPU the size of a venti latte, he typed a couple of commands on the BlackBerry-like keyboard. Then he put the unit against the wall. There was some whirring sounds, a clunk and a hiss . . . and then the panel retracted to reveal a three-by-three-foot safe face with an old school dial—which had been a nice surprise when he'd hacked into the alarm system to check on the how-many's and where-are's of its contacts.

He respected the analog choice. Because, hey, you couldn't break into the damn thing over the web, and as he gave the dial a little spin, he acknowledged that he would have had a hard time getting inside even with a blowtorch and a couple of hours.

So yeah, it was time to fudge his rules.

As he triggered the non-copper lock with his mind, the easy capitulation of the internal bolts made him feel like he'd been sitting in a BarcaLounger eating Doritos for two nights straight: He felt bloated by the ease and dulled by the lack of challenge.

There would be other nights to be tested, he told himself.

When the safe door opened, a little light came on inside, and it illuminated the kinds of goodies he'd expected. The interior also had—wait for it—see-through shelves, and everything on them was separated into—surprise!—like kind: There was cash in stacks that were banded together, reminding him for some reason of bunk beds. There was a case full of watches rocking back and forth, jet-setters line-dancing to some unheard song. And there was a whole bunch of leather jewel cases.

Which was what he was here for.

On that note, he picked off the top one. The thing was bigger than his pretty damn big palm and covered with red leather embossed with a gold border. Digging into the release with his thumb, he popped the lid.

Balz smiled so wide his fangs made an appearance.

But the happy-happy-joy-joy didn't last as he counted the cases still left inside. There were another six, and for some reason, that half dozen of further opportunity exhausted him. In another time in his life, he would have gone through each one and picked the most valuable. Now he just didn't give a shit. Besides, what he had was Cartier, and the diamond weight was in the forty-to-fifty-carat range with superb cut, color, and clarity. Like he needed more?

And no, he wasn't going to scoop them all. His rule was one thing, and one thing only, from any given infiltration. It could be an object, a bunch of things in a container, or a set that was somehow loosely, but tangibly, linked together.

Back in the Old Country, for example, he'd stolen a carriage with four perfectly matched grays under that little loophole.

So he was sticking with the Cartier, and leaving the rest behind.

Getting to his feet, he willed the safe door closed and relocked. And just as he was wondering if he was going to have to get out his trusty little 007 whammy-box again to close the panel, the wall section came down and clicked into place automatically.

For a moment, all he could do was stare at the vacant white Sheetrock between the parted sea of the tuxedo jackets. Closing his eyes, he felt an emptiness that—

"What are you doing?"

At the sound of the female voice, Balz spun around. Standing in the doorway that led in from the bedroom, the Mrs. of the triplex was directly under one of the ceiling fixtures—which meant her diaphanous nightgown was utterly translucent.

Well, Mr. Hedge Fund Manager, Balz thought, *you certainly did well for yourself at the altar.*

"What are *you* doing here?" Balz tossed back with a slow smile. "You two are supposed to be in Paris."

CHAPTER FOUR

As Ralphie zipped up his pants and Chelle reorganized herself under her skirt, he was razor-alert but not buzzing, the orgasm having taken the edge off the coke. Locking his molars, he curled up his arms and tightened all the muscles in his upper body, the torsion curving his spine forward, his lips coming off his front teeth, his bones bending.

The sound he made brought his crew's faces around.

"He's ready! He's the monster!"

At that moment, like the "officials" had been waiting for him to bust his nut, the air horn sounded down at the far end of the garage level.

His crew started chanting, and Chelle came up and leaned into him. He kissed her forehead and said ILY quietly enough so no one but her heard. Then he walked forward, his boys forming a spear of bodies ahead of him, Chelle bringing up the rear. When they penetrated the crowd, people got out of their way, the cheering reaching volumes that would have attracted attention—if anyone had been anywhere near this shitty part of town.

Inside, Ralphie was smiling. Outside, he was all about the fuck-you.

The Reverend had arranged this bout three days ago, with some out-of-towner who had no record and a name no one had heard of. So this was going to be a piece of fucking cake.

"Monster! Monster!"

His crew was chanting his name, and the crowd picked up on it and carried the ball. And even though he knew she was watching, he had to glance back to make sure Chelle was checking this out. She was. Her chin was down, but her eyes were on him, and she had a secret smile on her face that made him feel taller than he was. Thicker than he was. Stronger than he was.

She was his source of strength.

'Cuz he wanted to see that little happy on her face all the time.

Ralphie pulled himself together and refocused on the bodies that were getting out of the way for him. As he closed in on the fighting area, he entered a field of sallow illumination thrown by the running lights of the few cars that had been allowed through the barricades down at street level. The crowd started to go even nutserer when they got a better look at him, and he pretended that he was in the WWE and about to crack a skull in the ring.

Even though all he had was a red circle spray-painted on the stained concrete.

There were two circles, actually, the inner about fifteen feet across, the outer providing a five-foot buffer that the crowd was not supposed to get into—but always did by the ends of the matches. At the start, they followed the rules, though, so he left his crew behind as he alone went into the punch zone.

Beneath his boots, the dried bloodstains from last week's fight were the color of mud, and he cracked his knuckles as he paced around, his heart pumping as he remembered breaking that nose and knocking out those teeth. As he psyched himself up, the crowd—even his boys and Chelle—disappeared from him. Everything went goodbye. He was in himself and of himself. In himself, of himself. In himself—

As the mantra began to repeat and repeat, a train catching at its tracks, the momentum creating its own kind of surge, he sank his weight into his knees and went from boot to boot with his lean. Fists up, biceps curled, eyes barely blinking, he focused across the circle, at the ring of bodies that had yet to part to reveal his opponent.

Bouncing.

Breathing.

Bouncing.

Breathing . . .

After a minute and a half of that shit, Ralphie got pretty fucking impatient. What the fuck. Where was the motherfucker? Fucking pussy-ass, out-of-town fuck—

All of the sudden, people in front of him started vibing like they were uncomfortable, heads ripping back and forth like some kind of shit was going down. And then they were moving too quick, a few tripping in the scramble.

Jesus, no one better be outing a goddamn gun—

A thirty-foot-long chute was formed by the hyping bodies, the messy aisle running from the fighting circle to the far breezeway. At the end? A fighter who stood alone, facing away from everything, from everyone, his heavy shoulders silhouetted against the city's cold steel glow.

Ralphie's jumping stilled. His heart skipped a beat.

But then a woman dressed like a Karen stumbled into the safety zone and looked around with bug eyes, as if she had no frickin' clue where she was.

Ignoring her, Ralphie kicked his own ass. What the *fuck*. Was he the pussy here? That guy was no different from any other big-ass idiot. The bastard turned around? He was probably fatter than Uncle Vinnie.

Fuck him—

The lightning came from out of nowhere, the flash so fucking bright, it turned the inside of the garage into noontime. And as people in the crowd, and even his crew, put their arms up over their heads and crouched down, Ralphie did neither.

He just stood there.

And measured the tattoo that covered the other fighter's massive, muscle-ribbed back. The black-and-whiter was a huge fucking skull, the crown of bone up at the nape, the jaw with its sharp teeth down at the waist. And even though the eyeballs were gone, all death-rotted out, evil radiated from those pitch-black sockets.

Slowly, the fighter turned around.

Ralphie flushed and could not breathe. As his opponent smiled like he was a serial killer staring down his next victim, his teeth seemed way too long. Especially the canines.

I am going to die tonight, Ralphie thought with an absolute conviction that had nothing to do with coke paranoia.

It was more like the Grim Reaper's bony hand had landed on his shoulder . . . and closed its claiming grip. Forever.

What was about to come at him was an *actual* monster.

◆   ◆   ◆

Mae got past the bouncers at ground level. Of course she did. And she managed it without resorting to a replay of Dady's Girl tactics—although she would have gotten physical if she'd had to, and as a vampire, she could have knocked the block off of any of those barrier-to-entry men. It was more efficient, however, to just flip switches in those human brains and slip inside like she belonged, a pimento among Swarovski crystals.

And now she was up here, packed into a thicket of humans dressed for show, their shoulders bumping into hers, their scents invading her nose like stabbing fingers, their excited chanting a tangible, noxious smoke thickening the air and clogging her lungs. Assaulted by the miserable sensory overload, her brain tried to rise above, but her awareness was like a snow globe, all swirling agitation that obscured the centerpiece.

Where was the Reverend?

Forcing herself to calm down, she tried to send her instincts out. She had no idea what the male looked like, what his real name was. But vampires could locate vampires, and she was not leaving until she found him—

The crowd abruptly shifted, the humans moving like spooked cattle in the concrete acreage of the parking garage—and as she tried to get away from whatever commotion was happening, she suddenly found all kinds of space around her. She was standing totally alone.

Looking down, like maybe there was a bomb in a briefcase she'd somehow missed, she saw two red spray-painted lines. And when she glanced back up, she discovered she was at the head of a long break in the cram of bodies . . .

Mae lost all breath in her lungs.

Time slowed. The people disappeared. She wasn't even sure where she was anymore.

The vampire down at the parking level's far end, who was facing out into the night, was extraordinary . . . and terrifying—

Before she could form any further thought, blinding light erupted everywhere.

The night sky flooded with an illumination so bright, so vast, it was as if the Scribe Virgin had turned her wrath upon the earth itself. And then came the explosion. Whatever impact occurred was so devastating that an even more intense flash permeated the parking garage, the white light barging in on all sides and taking over as a distant thunder reverberated throughout the city.

Yet in spite of all this, Mae only had eyes for the male.

That tattoo of death across his broad back was a thing of horror, and she had a feeling so was he—

The fighter turned around and she gasped. He had great shoulders bulked with muscles and thighs that were set more solidly than the concrete he stood upon. His bare chest was likewise tattooed, the black-and-gray-inked landscape over his pectorals and abdominals depicting a bony hand reaching out of his torso. As if he were the conduit through which *Dhunhd* claimed its due.

"Get back!"

Once again, Mae spaced on the fact that she was being addressed. But then a hand grabbed her arm—and for a split second, her brain told her that it was that claw of the fighter coming for her. With a scream, she jumped—and before she could reassemble reality, she was dragged back.

"You're in the fucking safety zone," the man snapped. "And trust me, you're going to want to get out of the way of *that.*"

There was no question what the guy was talking about, and Mae tucked her arms around her middle, even though she was not anyone's target. And whether the vampire's opponent was ready or not, whether the crowd could handle what was about to happen, the male started to come forward, a menace in heavy boots that landed like he was dominating all of Caldwell. With his chin down and his nasty stare straight ahead, his heavy brow and his brutal expression made it impossible to tell what color his eyes were, but in the marrow of her bones, she knew they were black. Black as the depraved soul that dwelled within that awesome and powerful body.

As a sick sense of dread rippled through Mae, she tried to get away even farther, but the bodies behind her were too packed in. And then it dawned on her. Who the hell was fighting the male?

She shifted her head in the other direction. "Oh, God . . ."

The human who was about to get eaten like a meal stood inches shorter and a hundred pounds lighter, and it was clear, going by the naked expression of fear on his lean face, that he knew he was in trouble. He, too, had tattoos, but they were a hodgepodge of different scripts, symbols, and ink colors, the random collection no more coordinated than what had fallen out of her bag the night before. And she imagined, going by his wide, dilated eyes, that his thoughts were no more organized than his markings.

Mae wanted to tell him to run. But he already knew escape was in his best interests. He was checking behind him like he was assessing his flight path—yet for some reason, he sank down into a semblance of a fighting stance, and raised his bony fists up to his cheeks. As his head and shoulders leaned forward, the rest of his body arched back on his hips—like his vital organs wanted no part of this.

And still the vampire kept coming.

The male stopped only when he was inside the wobbly inner circle that had been spray-painted on the concrete—and unlike the human, he didn't brace for aggression. He just stared at the man with his arms down at his sides and his spine straight as an oak. No fists were made. No lunges hinted at or initiated.

Then again, he was a predator so deadly, he required no defenses and no offenses. He was a law of physics, undeniable and inevitable.

As the crowd went silent and the two fighters became an on-the-verge tableau of a beatdown, Mae found herself staring at the male's bare chest. There was something captivating in the way the bony hand moved as he breathed with controlled, calm inhales. Meanwhile, across the circle, the human waited for an attack with a jittery series of hops and skips. When nothing came at him, his eyes wilded around. The crowd was becoming restless, and the man seemed to be compelled by their impatience. He approached with caution, the male not moving in response. And then the human threw the first punch, the angle upward and seeking that heavy jaw—

The male caught that knobby fist in his much larger palm, and he twisted the arm like a rope. As the human let out a scream and fell to his knees, the crowd gasped and then went silent again.

"Stop," Mae said under her breath. "Stop this . . ."

The vampire's expression never changed. Neither did his breathing. And both made sense. He was a killer who was not exerting himself.

Without a care in the world, he forced the human onto his back and then straddled the prey. The man seemed momentarily incapacitated by terror. That changed. Some gear clicked in his head and he began kicking, his leg small enough that it could bend in and punch his foot out into the crotch area. The vampire jumped out of range—and came back down with a set of face-targeting knuckles that were barely avoided with a roll. The concrete cracked under the force of the punch's impact and the human jumped back to his feet. His balance was bad, and his greater opponent took advantage of this, grabbing the other arm, spinning him around, and yanking him back against that huge chest.

Don't bite him! Mae thought. *Are you crazy? With this many humans—*

Except the human was the one sinking canines through skin, his flat-topped teeth locking into the forearm. That didn't last long. The vampire ripped the bite free even though flesh went away with that mouth, and then he threw a punch for a second time.

The impact to the side of the skull knocked the human out cold, the thin body going boneless to the concrete, a pool held together only by that sloppily tattooed bag of skin.

The vampire's smile returned.

Slow. Evil. Deadly.

With only a hint of fang.

As the human began to move his arms and legs like he wasn't sure they were still attached, the male bent down and waited for consciousness to be fully resumed. Because, clearly, it was not enough to kill. You had to murder your victim only when they were aware you were taking their life—

Suddenly, all Mae could see was her brother. Rhoger was the one lying beneath the menace. Rhoger was the weaker of the two about to be struck. Rhoger was about to die—

"No!" she yelled. "Don't hurt him!"

Given the shocked silence of the crowd, her voice carried throughout the parking garage's level, and something about it—the pitch? the tone?—made the vampire jerk to attention. Then that terrifying face turned to her, and those horrible eyes narrowed.

Mae's heart stopped.

"Please," she said. "Don't kill him—"

From out of nowhere, the human's fist struck out with a flimsy punch that once again missed the mark of that prominent jaw.

Except then came the blood.

A trickle. A gush.

A geyser.

From the throat of the vampire.

Confused, Mae looked to the hand that had done the flimsy swipe—and something silver was glinting in the human's grip. A knife.

As the red rain fell on the man's throat and chest, five hundred pairs of shoes and high heels went on a bolt, the crowd racing for the stairwell. Meanwhile, the human seemed shocked at his success. As for the vampire? His expression still had not changed, but not because he was unaware of his mortal wound. He touched the second mouth that had been opened at the side of his throat and then brought his glossy fingers into his field of vision.

If anything, he was merely annoyed as he listed to one side. Fell to his knees. Propped a hand on the concrete to keep from totally collapsing. Meanwhile, clearly unsure whether he was free from danger or not, the human wriggled out from under and took off at a dead—natch—run.

Mae looked at the vampire. Then glanced at the stairwell, which was choked with bodies trying to get out of the parking garage, out of the neighborhood, out of the state.

"Shit," she muttered as gurgles rose up from the male.

Do not get involved, she told herself. *Your first and only concern is Rhoger.*

Except she wanted to help. Hell, she felt responsible because she'd distracted the vampire—and that was the only reason the human had survived, the only reason why the male wasn't going to.

But her brother needed her more than this violent stranger.

The male made a sound.

"I can't help you," she said in a cracked voice.

The male was struggling to speak, and as he coughed up blood, she looked around . . . and then went over to kneel down beside him. There was no 911 equivalent for vampires, and even if there were, he was losing blood too fast for any kind of ambulance—or even a healer who could dematerialize to him. Besides, who could she call?

Maybe the King's Audience House number?

No. There were rules against fraternizing with humans, ones that she was very certain precluded underground-fighting in a sea of *Homo sapiens* and trying to kill members of that species in front of hundreds of those rats without tails. If she called the King's people, both she and this vampire were going to be in huge trouble.

And Rhoger had to come first.

"Is there someone I can get for you—"

"Go," he said between labored breaths. "You must leave me. Save yourself!"

His voice was very deep and really rough, and when she didn't respond, his eyes focused on her with a glare that shot right through the back of her skull.

"For godsakes, female, take care of yourself."

It was the very last thing she expected him to say, and when he repeated the strained words, Mae got to her feet and stumbled back. As she moved away, his hard stare tracked her, even if she wasn't sure he was seeing her.

"Go," he ordered in spite of the blood coming out the side of his neck. "Go!"

"I'm sorry—"

"Like I give a shit!"

Trembling from head to foot, Mae closed her eyes and tried to concentrate.

When she was finally able to dematerialize, the gurgling sounds of the dying vampire haunted her. But she had her own problems, and he was right. She had to take care of herself. Her brother was depending on her.

Besides, if you lived by the fight, you died by the fight.

It was a fact of fate, and not something someone like her could try to change.

CHAPTER FIVE

H ow do you know we were supposed to be in Paris?"

As the triplex's Mrs. presented the quite reasonable question to Balz, he found himself totally distracted by what she looked like under that ceiling light. Those breasts of hers were . . . tight-tipped because it was a little chilly . . . and that thin, ever-so-slightly-see-through silk was almost better than completely naked.

Because it gave a male a job to do. Slowly. With his tongue.

While he made a short film of the two of them together in his head, the Mrs. started talking to him again, her mouth moving, her expression expectant but not alarmed. Courtesy of the images in Balz's mind, however, all he heard was the Teri Hatcher line from that *Seinfeld* episode: *They're real and they're spectacular.*

". . . you?"

"What?" Balz murmured. "I'm sorry, I was distracted."

"Are you taking that." The Mrs. pointed to the Cartier jewel case. "In your hand."

"Yeah," he said with a nod. "I am."

"Oh." Her expression grew remote. "My husband bought that necklace for me a year ago. For our anniversary."

"You want me to snag something else, then?"

After a moment, she shook her head. "No. That's fine."

Balz smiled some more. "You think you're dreaming, don't you."

The Mrs. smiled back. "I would be terrified otherwise."

"I'm not going to hurt you."

"But you're a thief, aren't you?"

"Thieves steal objects." He tapped the jewel case. "We don't hurt people."

"Oh, that's good." Her eyes drifted to his mouth. And then continued down across his chest. His abs. They lingered on his hips . . . like she was wondering exactly what was behind his fly and how well he could use it. "That's really good. Yes."

"Tell me something, is your husband here?" Balz murmured as he felt his body stir in places that had been woefully underutilized of late.

"No. He's in Idaho."

Balz blinked. "Idaho? Is that why you didn't go to France?"

"Idaho is more important. Even though it's our anniversary tonight."

"I can't fathom that math."

"He has a company that's headquartered there. It's a manufacturing firm. They need a lot of space, and the land value is very reasonable. He has his own plane and they have a runway for him." Abruptly, her eyes lowered. "But business is not why he's really going there."

"Why's he going?"

"He has . . . a friend. In Idaho."

"What kind of friend." When she didn't elaborate, Balz muttered, "That man is a fool."

Those pretty dark eyes returned to his own and her hands, graceful and worried, went to the bodice of her nightgown. "Do you think?"

"Think what. That he's missing out, not being with you? Fuck yeah—" Balz put his free hand forward. "'Scuse my French."

As the Mrs. blushed faintly and looked down again, it was beyond sad that this beautiful woman needed reassurance from a thief. Then again, who better to ascertain value?

"So he's in Idaho." Never had Balz liked a state more. "How nice, especially this time of year."

The Mrs. lifted her eyes. "Oh, no, the weather is awful in the early spring."

"I disagree. I think the weather is perfect for him." May the bastard get frostbite on his pecker. "Just like things are better for you here in Caldwell. Much, much . . . better."

After a moment, she nodded slowly. "It is very nice here. This time of year."

Funny, he reflected, how two strangers could ask and answer things using words that had fuck all to do with what they were really talking about.

"And I think you're wrong," Balz said as he popped the lid on the necklace box. "If your husband bought this for you for your anniversary, you should definitely keep it."

Her eyes went to the jewelry case. In a hard tone, she muttered, "It's insured. So he'll get his money back. He always gets his money back."

"Still, there should be a sentimental attachment to it." He freed the collar of diamonds from its velvet nest with his pinkie and tossed the case over his shoulder. "Something to make you smile when you wear it."

"You think so?" she asked.

Balz nodded. "I know so. And I'll prove it to you."

"Will you?"

"Yes." He walked over to her. "Right now."

The scent of her arousal totally got him going. But like his erection needed help considering her body?

Balz unclipped the clasp and then he turned the diamonds around so they faced front and reached across the electric air between them.

"What are you doing?" she whispered.

"I'm putting your husband's necklace around your neck." He lowered his lips right next to her ear as he refastened the clasp. "So I can fuck you with it on."

Her gasp was erotic as hell. "Why . . . why . . . why would you do that?"

Balz eased back. Her heart rate was flickering at her jugular, and as she breathed fast, the silk of her nightgown moved up and down over her nipples. Fuck, he was hungry all of a sudden. Ravenous.

"It takes more than just diamonds to make a woman feel beautiful." He trailed a fingertip over the skin at the base of her throat, following the necklace's contours. "It's something that husband of yours should remember. And since he doesn't care, I'm going to give you all kinds of memories to go with these cold, icy stones."

"But I thought you're stealing this." She put her hand up and touched him as he touched her. "I thought you were—"

"Let's just focus on you for a little while."

Leaning down, he pressed his lips to the hollow between her collarbones. Then he moved to her sternum, nestling in between her breasts. As she let out a sigh, he felt her fingers dive into his hair, and that was when he moved to where he had wanted to be from the moment he'd seen her.

Balz extended his tongue and licked at one of her nipples, moistening the silk. Inching back, he took a moment to admire his handiwork, the fine barrier disappeared, the nightgown clinging to her delicious flesh. When he blew across her breast, she shivered and her scent got louder in his nose.

"Oh, God, do that again," she breathed.

"My pleasure, Mrs."

With that, he scooped her up into his arms . . . and carried her to her stupid-ass husband's bed.

◆   ◆   ◆

Seven floors below, homicide detective Erika Saunders stepped off the elevator and looked left and right. She knew where she was going, but it was an old habit. You always checked both ways before you crossed the street. Or entered a hallway.

Or headed down the aisle.

She really should have minded that last one.

The Commodore was urban luxury living at its finest—or at least that tagline was part of its newly registered trademark. And from what she'd seen, from the concierge service at the front desk to the views of the bridges over the Hudson to what she'd heard the condos were like, everything had been freshly renovated to the standards of the very best co-ops on Manhattan's Upper East Side. The place even had a fitness facility and a swimming pool now, and the hotel corporation that had bought it a year ago was talking about add-ons like a gourmet restaurant, a spa, and a yoga studio.

Plans, plans, plans.

Ah, but there was a monkey with a wrench, she thought as she started walking. At least with attracting new owners.

Wait, was that the saying? Or was it . . . a wrench in the works? No, that wasn't right, either.

Goddamn, she needed some sleep.

About six doors down, she came up to a uniformed CPD officer standing at attention, and he immediately opened the door for her.

"It's in the bedroom, Detective." Like he was a museum docent.

"Thanks, Pellie," she said as she slipped a pair of flimsy blue booties over her black Merrells.

Inside the condo, her first impression was all iGen new money. There were digital picture frames all over the place, the images showing the same couple in the same cheek-to-loving-cheek, super-happy pose with different Instagram-worthy backdrops: tropical, mountainous, desert, stream. The sofa-and-chair setup was natural fiber, the knobby rug was clearly hand-loomed, and speak of the downward dog, a pair of lavender yoga mats were laid out side by side in the open area by the galley kitchen.

Kitchen was nothing special, except for the drug paraphernalia left out on the granite countertop next to a juicer the size of a bathtub and a bowl full of no-doubt-organic fruit.

Looked like the pair were not as faithful to the body-is-my-temple stuff as their social media might suggest.

MDMA was definitely not sold at Whole Foods.

Following quiet voices down a thin hall, she started to smell the rot, and the death bouquet really bloomed as she came up to the open door of the bedroom.

Three or four days, she thought as she snapped on nitrile gloves. *Maybe close to a week.*

Over on a queen-sized bed, the man and woman from the photographs were laid out naked on their backs, their heads on the pillows, their gray faces angled toward each other. There was extensive blood loss from both, due to centralized wounds in their chests, and the bedding underneath had soaked up the moisture.

They were holding hands, their loose, unresponsive fingers locked in place by what looked like dental floss around their wrists.

Detective Andy Steuben, who was taking notes by the headboard, looked at Erika. "I don't have the heart to mention how sad this is."

Erika rolled her eyes. "We're good without the commentary. Thanks."

Striding across to the bodies, she got a good look at the mutilations. Both the man and the woman had had their hearts removed, and not in a neat-and-tidy surgical fashion. The cavernous wounds were ragged on the edges, and fragments of bone dotted their abdominals and the bedcovers. It seemed like whoever had done the extractions had reached in with their hand and ripped the cardiac muscle out.

Except that was impossible.

"CSI is on the way," Andy announced.

Erika already knew this, but just as Steuben had a reputation for being a smartass, she was the division's resident cold bitch, and she didn't feel the need to stoke that gossip by one-upping the guy on a not necessary.

Running her eyes around the room, she noted the bureau had all its doors closed. There was a laptop and camera equipment out on a desk. Wallet and purse were next to them. Bedside table on the left had a silver dish with a bunch of gold jewelry and a heavy watch in it.

Erika rubbed her aching head. "I gotta go make a phone call."

"You pulling in the feds?" Andy asked.

Erika walked up to the rough wood headboard. Above it, in cursive, a four-letter word had been screwed into the wall.

LOVE.

"This is the third set of victims," she said grimly. "I think we've got a serial killer."

CHAPTER SIX

B ack at the moment Sahvage's throat was slashed, he had one, and only one, thought going through his brain: Maybe he was finally getting off this fucking train.

That's what he was thinking as he went down on his knees and felt the warm pump of his blood breaking through his fingers and falling free to soak into his pants and pool on the concrete. As the fight crowd bolted, his brain started slowing down—so he had some hope, some optimism that finally, after all these years—

Who knew that human had it in him.

And speak of the stupid, the skinny guy with the knife in his hand scrambled out from under and tore off like his life depended on it. Sahvage let the fucker go. The quick bastard deserved the bid for freedom given that slick move with the hidden blade. Although if that female hadn't been such a distraction—

Before he lost consciousness, Sahvage's brain ordered his head to turn to where she'd been standing. But things were draining rapidly, energy, awareness, cognition. So he didn't make a lot of headway with that. Instead, the world went on a whirl, spinning around him.

The funneling sensation ended with a clapping impact, something cold and hard hitting the side of his face—and he wondered who had swung a frozen salmon at his jaw like a baseball bat. Except no, it wasn't a pescatarian assault. It was the concrete floor he'd been standing on rushing up to grab his body and hold it down.

Wait, that didn't make sense.

And wasn't that great, he thought as his vision tapped out, even though his eyelids were still open.

Maybe this time, he thought with an exhausted anticipation. *Maybe . . . this . . . time . . .*

He was momentarily surprised as his vision got back with the program, but then he recognized that another brilliant, blinding light was calling him to attention. At first, he thought it was the Fade, but no. The source of it swung away. And then there was another. And another—

The cars that had lit the fighting area were getting out of Dodge.

And someone was standing over him.

That female . . . the one who had shouted at him. And even as he bled out, he took note of her.

Which was so much better than having his life flash before his eyes.

She was tall, and dressed simply, her jeans and thick sweatshirt out of place with the elaborate, revealing shit that the humans wore. Her hair was pulled back, so it was hard for him to tell what color it was, and her face was angular, the cheekbones high, the jaw strong, the hollows between the two suggesting she was hungry some portion of the time.

What the hell was she doing in a place like this?

As another car took off, its blue-bright headlights streamed over her and her wide, scared eyes.

"Go," he told her. "Leave me."

When she didn't move and didn't acknowledge his words, he wondered if he'd only spoken in his head—

Sahvage started to cough, but it was weak because there wasn't a lot of air in his lungs. And goddamn, his mouth was full of copper.

The female looked around, and that was when he saw her ponytail.

Dark hair, but with blond streaks. Then she was down on his level and her mouth was moving.

What the hell was she doing? She needed to take care of himself—

Herself. She needed to take care of *herself.*

Just as he was getting ready to stand up and push her over the side of the fucking parking garage, she straightened to her full height and took one last, long stare at him. She seemed pained. He wanted to tell her not to bother.

Even if they'd been intimates, he wasn't worth that. And they were strangers.

Eventually, she disappeared into thin air, the space she had inhabited vacated, the last of the cars that had been used to light the fight, a boxy black SUV, squealing its tires and passing right through where she had been standing.

The thing nearly ran him over. He wished it had finished the job for him.

As the last of the lights faded, and the sounds of the humans became silence, and the temperature of the night grew colder and colder, Sahvage smiled in the pool of his own blood.

Finally, a female who did what he told her to when it really counted. As opposed to . . .

✦   ✦   ✦

Old Country
1833

"You cannae save me."

As his charge, Rahvyn, spoke the words, Sahvage was struck with a terrible temper at the female who sat before him in the meadow grass. Verily, had his first cousin laid her open palm upon him, she could not have offended him more.

"What say you," he growled deep within his chest. "I am your ghardian. 'Tis my honor and duty to ensure you—"

"Stop." She placed her pale hand upon the rough leather of his sleeve. "I implore you. There is no more time."

Determined not to let loose his tongue at her, he thus looked away from where they were sitting across from one another. In the midst of the quiet meadow just awakening unto spring's warmth, beneath the splendor of a clear, starry night with a partial moon, it was unseemly to argue. It was ever unseemly to argue with Rahvyn. Yet his nature was what it was.

And she was alive because of that.

"Sahvage, you must let me go. It serves no betterment for you to fall before—"

"It serves ev'ry betterment! Have you no sense, female—"

"Let them have me," she whispered. "You shall survive, thereafter. I promise."

Sahvage fell silent. And could not return his gaze unto her. He stared forth whilst seeing naught, his blood seething, his urge to fight unserved with a target, for he could never hurt her. Not by deed. Not by word. Not even by thought.

He cursed. "I gave my vow unto my uncle, unto your sire, to protect you. You have already insulted my black daggers, now shall you move on to my honor?"

He glowered at the tree line and the distant cottage in which the two of them had lived ever since her side of the family had been left for dead by lessers. His sire and mahmen had already died off. Without Rahvyn, he had no other in his direct bloodline.

When she did not say aught, he had to look upon her once more. Her hair, as black as the wings of her namesake, curled outside of the hood she had drawn up upon her head, and her pale face gleamed in the moonlight. Her eyes, black and mysterious, refused to lift unto his own as she twisted her hands in her lap, and her preternatural concentration upon the nervous movements stiffened his spine.

"What have you foreseen?" he demanded.

In response, there was only a silence that braced his resolve even as it threatened to break his heart.

"*Rahvyn, you must tell me.*"

Her stare finally rose to meet his own. Tears, luminous and tragic, trembled on her lower lashes.

"*It will be easier for us both if you leave. The now.*"

"*Why.*"

"*The time of my rebirth is nigh. The trial I must go through is prepared for me by destiny. To find my true power, there is no other way.*"

He reached out and wiped the one tear that fell. "*What madness do you speak.*"

"*The flesh must suffer so that the final barrier may burn away.*"

A chill went through Sahvage. "*No.*"

Off in the distance, there came a clamor of hooves upon the packed dirt road that skirted the open field. Torches, held high and much agitated by the driven gaits of powerful horses, came 'round at a war-like speed.

It was a guard bearing Zxysis the Elder's colors.

"*No!*" *Sahvage jumped to his feet, outing his black daggers and facing the attack.* "*Save yourself—I shall hold them!*"

The count of the males upon those steeds was a dozen. Perhaps more. And behind them? A horse-drawn cage of steel.

"*Rahvyn,*" *he barked.* "*You must go!*"

When she said nothing, he glanced over his shoulder—

Sahvage lost all track of thought. A glow had coalesced around his cousin, and as his eyes adjusted, he was confused, for he saw that stars had eschewed their placement above for an orbit about her as their sun. How was this possible—

No, not stars. They were fireflies. Except . . . 'twas the wrong season for them, was it not?

Sitting in their midst, in her black hooded cloak, her ashen face lifted unto the moonlight, she was a living virtue, purity vested within mortal confines.

"*No . . .*" *Sahvage's voice cracked.* "*Do not let them take you.*"

"*It is the only way.*"

"*You do not need power.*"

"Thereafter I shall be responsible for myself, Sahvage, no longer a weight upon you that prevents you from serving your duty unto the species."

Sahvage reached through the glow, grabbed hold of her arm, and dragged her up. "Leave! Now!"

Her eyes met his own. And she shook her head. "This is the way it must be—"

"No!" He checked on the horsemen who had cut off from the road and were barreling o'er the long grass, honing in on the light that gathered 'round her. "There is no more time—dematerialize!"

Rahvyn shook her head slowly, and as he closed his eyes, his chest burned.

"They will tear you asunder," he choked out.

"I know. It is the way it must be, Cousin. Now, go, and allow me my destiny."

"Rahvyn, blooded daughter of Rylan," came the shout. "You are bound by Zxysis the Elder's authority upon this land!"

As broadswords were unholstered and raised high, Sahvage forced his cousin behind him and prepared to engage. In his years of combat, he had killed more than this lot by himself, and for his cousin, he would see their blood run as a river 'cross the meadow.

"Why must you be so stubborn!" he barked at his charge.

Before he could look back at her again, the first of the arrows whistled by his ear. The second went between his braced legs. The third? Hit him in the shoulder.

And they came not from those setting upon him with those broadswords.

'Twere from the east. From . . . behind the trees that offered stout protection: The archers had stayed hidden and waited for their assistance to arrive upon those thundering hooves and with those frothing torches—

The arrow that killed him was the fourth that was sent his way, its steel tip and honed shaft penetrating his heart, the leather layers meant to protect him in the event of a knife or punch offering no resistance to the deadly rush of the sleek projectile. And even after that mortal strike, brethren of his conqueror continued to strike through his torso, the muscles of his legs, his back.

There had to be more than one archer, for the bows were reloaded too fast for merely a singleton.

"Go!" he cried as he fell to his knees. "You must take care of yourself!"

As Sahvage fell upon his side, his vision departed him, though his wits stayed live at least for a moment. In truth, he had always prayed unto the Scribe Virgin that he would be taken in battle, a cloak of honor and bravery the funereal draping that covered his body as it grew gray and cold.

He did not want to go like this. Failing in his service unto his charge, knowing that they would set no arrows upon her, for she would be taken alive unto Zxysis and given over to him.

For pain. Degradation. The pits of fire from which she believed she would surface, a phoenix rising out of suffering unto a seat of power.

"Do not hurt him!" Rahvyn screamed from up above, as if she were shielding him with her body. "You mustn't kill him!"

As her voice registered in his ears, pure terror nearly animated him. But his failing heart was too far gone, and the resurgence in power and awareness lasted not nearly long enough.

Goddamn it, she was still with him . . .

That was the last mortal thought that came upon him prior to Sahvage finding himself in a vast white landscape, the door unto the Fade rushing up to him, as if he'd had an assignation with it that was long, long overdue.

Lo, his heart was done. And not merely in the mortal sense. For that which was going to be done to his beloved cousin . . . he was broken as he died.

CHAPTER SEVEN

I t wasn't lightning."

As Nate, adopted son of the Black Dagger Brother Murhder, continued to hammer at the framing board in front of him, his buddy leaned forward and spoke louder, like maybe he hadn't been heard.

"Not lightning." Arcshuli, son of Arcshuliae the Younger, shoved his phone in Nate's face. "See?"

After one more hammer strike, Nate lowered his weapon of construction and took the nails out of his mouth. "Okay. That flash wasn't lightning. So?"

"So what *was* it." Shuli popped his arching brows. "Doncha wanna know?"

In his khaki cargo shorts and his t-shirt, Shuli looked like just another member of the construction crew—as long as you ignored his bone structure, the Hublot on his wrist, and the rumors that his sire was the head of the underground *glymera*.

"Come on, don't you want to know?" he repeated.

"No, I want to finish framing this out. Then I want you to help me with the Sheetrock. After that, we can—"

"But you saw that thing. It lit up the whole sky. And my brother says it wasn't lightning."

"Now he's a meteorologist? I thought he was a Ph.D. candidate in a human chemical engineering program."

Shuli disappeared his iPhone into his ass pocket. "Exactly. He's the smart one, I'm the pretty one. And FYI, he's better-brained than the two of us put together."

Wait for it. Just . . . wait for it—

"Of course, I'm better looking than all three of us."

Bingo. "That makes no sense."

"Have you seen this face?" Shuli made a circle around his puss. "Seriously. I'm hot—"

"You are ridiculous."

A rhythmic chirping had Shuli re-outing his cell. "Oh, my God, it's break time." He flashed the phone again, like the alarm going off might be subject to misinterpretation if there wasn't a visual confirmation. "Guess we have to put our hammer and nails down and—jeez, I don't know. Go for a walk in the woods over thataway?"

"Break time," came the foreman's voice from inside the farmhouse they were remodeling. "Take thirty!"

Nate looked out of the open garage in the direction Shuli was pointing. The two of them had been assigned the work in here because they were newbies, and if the holes left by the windows' removal weren't patched with total perfection, who was really going to care?

Well, Nate cared. Shuli? Not so much.

"Come on." Shuli took Nate's Black+Decker and put it down on a table saw. "Let's go for walkies."

Nate shrugged and played follow-the-leader, the pair of them heading across the driveway and onto the lawn. When they got to the fence, they each threw a leg over the bottom two rails while they ducked under the top one. After that, it was all open field, although given that it was only late April, there wasn't much grass growth. Little bit of mud, though—their steel-toed boots mucking through the slop.

With a frown, Nate glanced at his friend. "Why are you wearing shorts?"

"I'm hot-blooded, my friend."

"You're a virgin."

"So are you. And do not conflate my lack of experience with a paucity of enthusiasm."

"Big words," Nate said with a laugh.

"Dad's a psychiatrist, remmy."

"And that relates to you how?"

"I know all about conflation." Shuli leaned in and lowered his voice. "As well as other things that end in '-ation.' And start with the letter *M*. And have a 'bruh' without the *R* in the middle—"

"What's that smell?"

Shuli jumped ahead and walked backward. "So . . . have you?"

To avoid a sneeze, Nate rubbed his nose like he was buffing its end to a high shine. "Can you smell that?"

"Stop avoiding the question. You're three months out of your transition, and a fully functioning male. Which means—"

Nate looked past the other male's shoulders. "It smells like burned . . . iron."

Shuli stopped dead in the path of progress. "Have you made yourself come yet."

"None of your business." Nate stepped around the living, breathing, incredibly classy but horny obstacle. "There's smoke, too."

"I don't see what the big deal is. I'd tell you."

"You already have." Nate shot a dry look at the guy. "Many times. Don't you have hairy palms and blindness by now?"

"That's just for humans, and I'm trying to inspire you by leading through example."

"I'm not interested in that kind of leadership." Nate clapped a hand on the back of the guy's neck and gave him a shake. "Enough. Let's concentrate on your bright idea. Now will you look at all that smoke?"

To help ADHD focus, he turned Shuli's face toward the plume rising up out of the tree line and into the night sky.

Shuli stopped again. "What the fuck is that?"

"It's not on account of your hotness."

"Well, duh, or it'd be right above us."

The good news was that courtesy of whatever they were walking toward, the guy left the left-handed business alone. The bad news was that whatever was steaming in those woods, and smelling like someone had lit a cauldron on fire, was likely . . . well, bad news.

"Should we call someone," Nate wondered.

"Like who?"

"My dad?"

It still felt a little weird using the d-word, but not because Murhder wasn't his father. He'd just never expected to have one. Life wasn't supposed to grant you a true family just because you'd wanted one. Just because you needed one.

Nate frowned. "Hey, are there people in there?"

"You know, maybe this isn't such a great idea—"

"No, I want to—"

"Nah, I made a mistake. Let's turn around. Break time's done."

When Nate felt his arm get taken in a hard grip, he shot Shuli a glare. "You're kidding, right."

His best friend's face was more serious than Nate had ever seen it. "I made a mistake."

"No, you're being a pussy—wait, is that a gun? What the fuck are you doing with a gun!"

"I'm protecting you."

Nate blinked and shook his head at the weapon in his buddy's hand. "Who are you and what have you done with Shuli?"

"I can't let anything happen to you."

With sudden dread, Nate said, "What did my father tell you."

"It has nothing to do with your dad."

Nate glanced at the plume and the people he could see moving in and around the forest. Then he decided, *Fuck it.*

"Well, I'm not your problem, and I'm going over there. If you have another opinion about this? You can shoot me in the ass."

He didn't make it far before Shuli caught up. "Nate, this is dangerous—"

"Put that thing away, will you? Christ. You'll just end up popping yourself."

As they hit the tree line, they were arguing about all kinds of things—guns, idiots with guns, idiots who wanted to go investigating stuff when it wasn't safe, idiots who suggested investigations and then bailed on them—although at least the nine millimeter was out of sight.

And boy, they were not alone.

At least a dozen people had gathered about a hundred yards in, but fortunately, going by the scents, they were all members of the species. Then again, there weren't a lot of humans out here in the sticks, which was precisely why that farmhouse was being worked on by their crew.

It was best to stay far away from those rats without tails.

Nate had learned this firsthand. In that lab.

As the metallic stench got worse, his sinuses revolted, kicking out sneeze after sneeze. To help, Shuli pounded on his back, which added a round of coughing to the party.

Nate was slapping his buddy's palm away, and worried that the Heimlich maneuver was coming next—or maybe, God forbid, CPR—when they stepped into a clearing.

Talk about the scene of a crime. The earth had been violated by something big enough, traveling fast enough, to backhoe out a good thirty or forty square feet of dirt. And in the hole? Steam. So it was hard to see much.

Nate and Shuli closed in, joining the males and females who were tilting forward and trying to eyeball whatever had landed.

"This belongs in a Stephen King book," Shuli muttered.

Blinking away the sting in his eyes, Nate looked up to the sky. "Meteor. And assuming that's what it is, he already wrote about one."

"Or space junk." Shuli elbowed Nate's arm. "Hey, do you think if I go lick the meteorite, I can go viral?"

"I think you'll *get* a virus."

"I'm serious."

"I know, and now I'm scared." As the wind changed directions and swept the smoke away, Nate muttered, "And no, I'm not going to film it . . ."

His voice drifted off, losing track of the words his brain promptly forgot.

Across the hole, at the side of the crowd, a lone figure stood by itself. Herself. It was a female. At least, he was assuming it was a female, going by the long, gossamer lock of pale blond hair that had slipped free of the hood that was up on her head.

"Hello?" Shuli prompted. "I said lightning doesn't strike the same place twice. So we're safe."

Nate turned away from his buddy, and mumbled, "I thought your brother told you it wasn't lightning."

As he started to walk toward the female, Shuli called out, "Where you going?"

"I'll be right back."

CHAPTER EIGHT

Mae's brain was tangled with recriminations as she dematerialized out of the parking garage. Re-forming in the shadows down at ground level, she rubbed her face and took note of the streams of humans pouring out of the stairwell and peeling away from the open-air lots. As cars skidded into a traffic jam, and people scrambled free of the door where the wait line had been, she told herself to just ghost out and go back home. Or maybe to Tallah's. She could return for her car in a half hour when the crush was gone.

Well, that was assuming the place wasn't flooded with human cops by then. Even in an abandoned part of town, this kind of commotion could get noticed, and frankly, she was surprised they got away with the fights at all.

"Damn it . . ." She looked up to the sixth level.

But this isn't about him, she told herself. *He is* not *my problem.*

Horns blared. Someone tripped and fell right in front of her— recovered, took off again. Up on the open floors of the garage, headlights were flying around, the three or four cars that had been used to throw light on the fight now funneling out the drain of the exit route at a bolt. When she glanced at the heavy concrete barriers that had been moved into place to block the entrance, she wondered if there was another way out—

The question was answered as a truck ran right into one and shoved it out of the way with its front grille.

So someone already has troubles with the law, she thought as the Ford cut across onto the sidewalk to circumvent the jam.

You must leave me! Go! Save yourself.

That was the right advice. That was—

Suddenly, Mae looked up again in a panic. What if the vampire who organized the fights . . . was the vampire who was *in* them?

What if that male who lay dying was the Reverend? She'd scoured the crowd with her instincts, searched all the scents and presences, and there had only been one vampire in that whole lot of humans.

"Fuck!"

As her heart started pounding, she closed her eyes and tried to take slow, deep breaths. When she got nowhere with that, she shuffled her feet, rolled her shoulders—and gave herself a big fat lecture about how she needed to chill the hell out RIGHTTHISVERYMOMENT.

Which was, of course, *so* conducive to calming things down in order to dematerialize.

She might as well have air-horned her own face—

As her body dissolved into molecules, she flew upward in a scatter, skating back into the open-air level. Re-forming by the fallen fighter, she had a thought she should check his pockets for ID.

Yeah, sure. 'Cuz he went around with his "I Am the Reverend" card in his wallet for just this sort of thing.

And crap, to save him only for her purposes struck her as inhumane. Invampiric. Whatever.

"Goddamn it," she muttered as she dropped her purse by his head and got onto her knees.

The huge male was sprawled on his back, one arm thrown out to the side, the other flopped across his heavy pecs. The pool of blood under him was three times the size it had been when she'd left only moments before, and she could swear that there was a pulsing to the flow leaving the open vein at the side of his throat—although that was the good news. It meant he still had a heartbeat. Not for long, though. His coloring was bad and getting worse, his face as gray as the concrete he was lying on, and that bony hand tattooed on his torso wasn't moving much—which meant he wasn't breathing much.

"Sorry," she said as she shoved her arm under his head and lifted him up. "Holy—good God, you're heavy."

With a grunt, she pulled him into her lap—or tried to. It was like moving a house, so she had to scoot under him. And oh, jeez, the blood. It was warm, it was slippery, it—

He smelled really good.

"You're thinking that about a dying man," she muttered. "Classy."

When Mae had him at least slightly elevated, she pushed her hair over her shoulder, even though it was still pulled back in a ponytail, and focused on that wound. It was like someone had taken a garden hoe to the side of his throat, and for a moment, she got woozy staring at the ruined anatomy. But like her passing out was going to help either of them?

"Sorry, I know this is a little . . ." Forward? What, like they were at a dinner party and she was reaching across his plate for the saltshaker? "It's just, um . . ."

Shut up, Mae.

Swallowing hard, she took a deep breath. And then she lowered her lips to the wound. There was only one way she could help him, and it was a long shot. But vampires had to feed from veins, and when they were done, they had to seal up the puncture marks.

With a gentleness that seemed like a waste of discretion, given the situation and the power in his body, she put her mouth to the slice—

The taste of him ricocheted through her on a tantalizing shock wave: That dark wine merely touching her tongue was the kind of thing she felt down to her marrow, and as a trembling hunger overtook her—

No, no, no, this is not a feeding, she told herself. *Totally and completely not the point.*

He was half drained already, for godsakes. And if he was the Reverend and she killed him because she couldn't control herself? That wasn't good for anybody.

Still, some sucking was inevitable, and therefore, so was some swallowing. But even though it caused her to break out in a sweat, she did not take a draw against that clean-cut vein. Instead she sealed it up. It took her some time, her lips and her tongue running up and over the deep wound and all its damage again and again—and she had a feeling things weren't going to heal right, at least not for a while. Like that mattered?

If he was the Reverend, she needed him to live. He was necessary.

When she decided to call it done, because she was just getting echoes of his taste in her mouth, she lifted her head—and studiously ignored the way her tongue swiped over her lips and not just to clean up. She savored his taste—and as she did, she stared down into his face properly. His hair had been cut with a buzzer down close to his skull, but she could tell it was dark, maybe black. His lashes were thick and rather beautiful, and that seemed like a frivolous thing to notice—so she moved right on to his mouth.

Bad idea if she were looking to keep things on the level.

Because it was . . . really pretty amazing—

She didn't meant to. It wasn't a conscious thing . . . but she stroked his face.

"Don't die on me," she begged in a voice that cracked. "I need you."

For some stupid reason, she expected him to stir at that. Maybe have those lashes open so he could peg her with his obsidian gaze.

At which point, her prince/Reverend would come around and be captivated by her makeup-less face, her messy ponytail, and her utterly unsexy clothes—and vow to give her what she had come here for.

Yeah, right, because real life was always scripted by Disney.

But come on, she'd saved him.

"Hello?" she said. "Um . . . hello?"

No, really. She'd saved him. Right?

His coloring was still bad, his breathing hadn't improved, and just because the blood puddle—or rather, pond—beneath them both wasn't getting any bigger, didn't mean he was out of the woods.

Like that wound closing was going to go far enough, though? He required proper medical attention.

"I need you to live through this," she muttered as she dragged her sleeve up.

Scoring her own wrist with her fangs, she waited for her blood to well and then she extended her lower arm out over his mouth. The first drop to hit his lips did nothing but give her a really bad comparison between his pasty skin and what a living person's was like. The second did nothing. The third—

The gasp that came out of him was so loud, so abrupt, so violent, that she jumped and nearly dropped his head off her lap. And then those eyes opened, but not in the dreamy way she'd fantasized.

That hostile glare was right out of his playbook, however.

And then he slapped a hold on her wrist.

As her bones were crushed in his grip, pure fear had her jerking back—or trying to. There was no freedom to be had, not until he chose to give it to her.

The male sat up, his torso curving, the musculature bulking as his chest contracted to lift the weight of his shoulders. And then his head ripped toward the open vein at her wrist.

The growl that came out of him was that of an animal.

Now that tattooed bony hand was reaching for her. Claiming her. Dragging her into the hell he kept in his black soul—

"No," she commanded. "You may not take more than you need. You may *not* hurt me."

As the words left her, strong and steady, Mae had no idea where the conviction came from. But she wasn't going to argue with it.

She needed to be alive for her brother.

That was just the way it had to be.

✦   ✦   ✦

As Sahvage's brain came back online, his first awareness was the smell of the female's blood. Even with so much of his own all around them, as well as on her hands, her sweatshirt . . . her mouth . . . her scent managed to overpower everything. She was a fresh meadow, on a starry night, just after a warm spring rain.

Captivating. Nurturing. Clean.

And he needed more of her in his nose—

With a frown, he focused on her pale and frightened face. She was beautiful, he thought, in a non-flashy kind of way, her even features un-slathered with makeup, her eyes naturally lashed, her hair pulled back in a simple way. And her lips were moving. She was talking to him. Probably telling him to let go. Not to hurt her. Maybe she was begging—

Fuck.

He was still alive.

Goddamn it.

With a numb, enduring frustration, he looked at his hand as it squeezed her forearm. Thanks to a fresh bite mark on her wrist, her blood, red and glistening . . . rivered down onto his grip.

That was the taste in his mouth, the heavenly taste that had lit him up, called him back, brought him to her like a dog summoned by its master.

And now? He had a decision to make. Kill her and take everything in her veins. Or let her go and leave right away. Because if he stayed and she was alive? He was going to fuck her while he drank her dry.

As Sahvage mulled over the polar opposites, he supposed the fact that he had to weigh the choice to let an innocent survive didn't reflect well on his character. But after all this time, he had no character left. There was no part of who he had once been remaining. He was a death machine roaming the earth, and the tragedy for the female was that she had chosen to stay with him instead of run away with the crowd.

"Are you the Reverend?" she asked in a husky voice.

Or at least he thought that was what she was saying. He was distracted by that scent of hers, that taste . . . the fact that he was now fully erect.

"I need to know," she said. "And you need to live. Take what you need, but no more."

With that, she put her wrist against his mouth, pressing the puncture wounds to his lips—and instantly, he was as lost as he had been while dying, his mind floating on a sea of compromised senses, his body no longer his to order, his heart skipping beats, his lungs freezing.

He couldn't swallow fast enough. He was a bottomless pit.

As Sahvage reclined back into her lap, he stared up at her as he drew against her vein. She wouldn't meet his eyes, and he wasn't surprised. He was not the kind of male a female like her should have had anything to do with voluntarily—and not because she was an aristocrat. He could tell by the clothes she wore and that handbag that she was a civilian, but that wasn't the divider between them.

He knew very well what he was, and anything living shouldn't be alone with him. Male or female.

And yet here she was helping him. For reasons that defied explanation.

I will not kill you, he vowed to her.

It was the minimum courtesy he owed her, wasn't it.

On that note, Sahvage retracted himself from her vein, her wrist . . . and, with a grunt, her lap.

On a messy shuffle, he flipped himself over onto his stomach and then he dragged himself away from her, his palms and his heavy arms doing the work, his legs scraping along the concrete, his boots a pair of dogging cabooses. When he was outside the giant blood puddle he'd left behind, when there was a good six or seven feet between him and the female, he let himself collapse again.

The cold floor of the garage felt good against the hot side of his face, and he had a thought that his arousal was getting seriously crammed at a bad angle in his combats. But like he was going to worry about his goddamn dumb handle? As he panted and tried to get his bearings, his hand went back to the side of his neck.

The wound was sealed up. She must have—

"I, ah . . ." The female cleared her throat. "I tried to help close it."

He looked over at her. "You shouldn't have bothered."

"Well, I did."

Those eyes of hers couldn't seem to light on anything, but really, what were her good options? Her bloodstained clothes? The pool of blood he'd left? The empty garage they both needed to get out of?

"How are you feeling?" she asked him.

"Fine. Just great."

"Do you, ah, want to go see a doctor?"

Sahvage laughed harshly. "Sure. Great idea."

That stare met his own directly. "Are you the Reverend?"

"Who?"

"Don't lie to me. We're not strangers anymore."

Down below on the streets, the sounds of sirens wailed in the distance, and Sahvage wondered how many cops were on their way. Humans were like that, always showing up where they weren't invited.

The female glanced away toward the noise, her brows lowering like she was attempting to count the number of blocks the police were covering per second. "They're coming closer."

"Yup."

"I need your help." She looked back at him. "I don't have a lot of time."

He narrowed his eyes. "You sure you want the kinds of things I can do?"

"If I had another choice, trust me, I would take it."

With a groan, he sat up and tried to brush the dirt off his pecs. But drying blood was like glue. "That I believe. What do you need?"

"Are you the Reverend."

Lowering his chin, he regarded her from beneath his lids. "Do I look like a religious figure to you?"

"Don't toy with me."

"I'm not, sweetheart."

"This isn't a game to me," she spat. "I need to know if you're the Reverend."

As she jumped to her feet, Sahvage measured her up and down—and had a thought that she would look good naked. Those loose clothes did nothing to emphasize her assets, but she had plenty of them—and he liked the fact that she wasn't the kind to put herself on display.

"And I need a Motrin," he muttered as he put his bloody palm up to his aching head.

What the hell did a male like him have to do to die? Wait . . . he didn't want the answer to that. Some things were best left to the hypothetical. And hey, at least he wasn't thinking about sex anymore.

"Are you the Reverend!" she said again, her voice echoing around the empty garage level and overriding the sirens.

All of which were zeroing in on this bloodbath involving a pair of vampires, one of whom was on the hunt for some kind of Protestant with fangs, and the other of whom had made it a point to never, ever again get involved in other people's drama.

Why had he bothered to swing through Caldwell again?

Oh, right. He'd been bored.

CHAPTER NINE

A re you the Reverend!"

You'd think Mae'd be yelling to be heard over the approaching police cars, but no, she was just pissed. And meanwhile, the huge male she'd given her vein to—yeah, 'cuz *that* had been on her list of things to do during this little adventure into downtown—was staring up at her with that bored expression of his, a twin trail of blood streaking from where he'd nearly died to where he'd dragged himself away from her.

The layout of it all looked like he was a rocket going into space, the big pool the explosion of liftoff, the streamers from his boots like the contrails of his fight.

Not that that made any sense at all.

And FFS, she could do without that tattoo on his chest pointing at her.

"My goddamn skull is pounding," he groaned.

So don't bare-knuckle fight with humans who have no honor, she bitched in her head. *What did you think was going to happen—*

"Whatever," the male snapped as he glared up at her. "*You* were the one who distracted me."

Shoot, she'd spoken that out loud. But *whatever* was right.

"Haven't you heard of the no-fraternizing rule?" she gritted. "You shouldn't be here in the first place."

"Says the female who was also in the crowd."

Mae put her hands on her hips and leaned down at him. "I'm allowed to go where I please, it's not the dark ages of vampires anymore."

"Oh, so you have freedom, but I don't because I'm a male. How convenient—"

"I wasn't bare-knuckle fighting with them!"

"So you only came to bet? Then, oh, yeah, you're *totally* aboveboard in all this."

Mae ground her molars—and thought seriously about walking over and kicking him in the leg. Or maybe the ass. Either way, she'd love to give him something to worry about other than his aching head.

"I did *not* come to gamble—"

"Was it for sex, then? 'Cuz you might get further if you showed some skin. You look like you could be someone's mother."

Mae rolled her eyes. "Oh, sure, I'm going to take sartorial advice from a three-hundred-pound walking ad for death. Haven't you ever heard of false advertising, though? 'Cuz last time I checked, you were getting sliced open by a human—"

The male threw up his hands. "Because *someone* we know was telling me not to kill the sonofabitch!"

"You shouldn't be killing anybody!"

"Well, aren't you two the happy couple."

At the sound of the dry male voice, both of them looked to the shadows where a large figure loomed in the darkness.

Without missing a beat, she and the fighter both spoke at the same time:

"We're not a couple—"

"We're not a couple—"

The chuckle that emanated from that corner was a yeah-sure if Mae had ever heard one—but then she was suddenly more worried about her life and safety than whether she was linked with Skeletor over here.

And P.S., survival should have been her priority in the first place.

As her hand dipped into her purse for her mace, the source of the voice stepped into a patch of ambient glow. "I'm going to request that you keep your weapons where they are, thanks. And that includes you, Shawn."

Shawn?

She looked over at the fighter. And then refocused on what had come to join them.

Okay, this male was . . . nothing like what she would have expected to see in a decrepit part of town. He was tall, he was big, and his face did belong in a lineup of people who'd murdered their enemies in very messy ways. So yes, all that fit the bill—as did his cropped Mohawk. But he was wearing a floor-length fur duster, and the gold cane that was aiding him with his balance made him seem like he was on the way to the opera—

On that note, "Shawn" got to his feet and moved the mountain of his body in front of her. Like he wanted to protect her.

"Relax, big man, I'm not going to hurt her," the other male said dryly.

"Damn right," Shawn shot back. "Because I'm not going to give you the fucking chance."

Mae leaned to the side and looked around a set of bulging arm muscles. "Are you the Reverend?"

The male in the mink's expression didn't change. Yet she sensed a shift in him, though she'd have been hard-pressed to pinpoint why she recognized it.

"What do you want the Reverend for, female?" came the slow drawl. "You're not his type."

"She's not yours, either, asshole," Shawn snapped. "So how 'bout you fuck off—"

"She's not talking to you, my guy—"

Okaaaaay, she was so sick and tired of big, swinging dicks.

Mae stepped out from under cover and stared at the newcomer. "Tallah sent me. To find the Reverend. And something tells me I'm looking at him."

Both males shut up, like they were surprised she wasn't willing to play wallflower to their thumping-chest routines.

"Just be real with me," she said with exhaustion. "I was so over to-night even before you waltzed in looking like Liberace and Hannibal Lecter had a love child."

As the male in the mink narrowed his eyes, Shawn barked out a laugh.

"Oh, come on, Reverend," he said, "you gotta admit that was a good one."

Mae was too busy measuring the stare of the other male to pay at-tention to Shawn's compliments. She had a feeling his irises were dark purple—which was something she had never seen before. And God, that weird sensation was going through her again. It wasn't attraction—no, no, she seemed to be reserving that for killers who had more ink than a Bic factory and tasted like heaven. No, what she was feeling was something else—and whatever it was, she just wanted to run from the coiling uneasiness.

"I'll ask you again, female." The male's drawl didn't change. "What do you want with the Reverend—"

"Oh, cut the shit," she interjected. "And I don't want you. I want the Book. Tallah said you'd know how to find it."

As tires screeched down below, and car doors started opening and closing, the male stopped talking. And stayed that way.

"So you know what it is," she said with hope. "You know what I'm looking for—"

"Sure, I know what a book is. It's two hard covers with some flimsy stuff bound in the middle. Words are written on the pages in even lines, unless it's illustrated. And sometimes they have cuss words in them, like what the *fuck* are you talking about."

The growl that rolled out of Shawn made it seem like maybe his name was short for something like Shawn-ado. And she wheeled around and pegged him with hard eyes.

"I do *not* need your help." When his nasty stare stayed locked on the other jackass in the parking garage, she batted at his chest. "Hey, Shawn. You can leave now—"

Annnnnnnnd that was when a bunch of human cops burst out of the stairwell, guns up and blinding flashlights pointed straight ahead.

As Shawn dropped another f-bomb, and the vampire in the mink coat threw up his hands, Mae shielded her eyes with her arms—and was very clear on the fact that, probably for the one and only time in all of their lives, she and these two males were in complete agreement.

Fuck was right.

✦   ✦   ✦

As Rehvenge was hit with a retina-busting beam of LED, he was *so* not feeling the female with the bright ideas about something she needed to avoid like the plague. He was also totally annoyed by Shawn and his he-man posturing—although that was mostly because the fight had been forfeited and now Rehv had twelve kinds of headaches to look forward to as he settled up with the bettors. But the police? Well, those boys and girls in blue ticked him off.

He had enough problems without them interfering.

On that note, he froze the trio with the shields where they stood. As a *symphath*, reading their emotional grids was both irresistible and a blink-of-the-eye kind of thing: The woman on the left was highly anxious, a new trainee still getting her feet under her; the man in the middle was completely calm, a veteran who had seen pretty much everything; and the guy on the far side was hiding something from everyone around him.

"Be of ease," Rehv commanded.

In a coordinated dance, they lowered their flashlights, turned off their body cameras, and reported to their shoulder communicators that there was nothing out of order on the sixth floor, nothing wrong, nothing going on. Whatever had been happening here had wrapped up. The call-ins had been incorrect or it was another case of a false report to divert resources.

Probably a bunch of kids, playing around.

Stupid kids.

One by one, they turned around, and they were chatting casually as they reentered the stairwell in single file: The woman had had a Reuben for dinner that wasn't sitting well with her, the guy in the middle was worried about the closing on his new house, and the man who was bringing up the rear was hoping to get his overtime approved.

Ah. He was saving up to buy an engagement ring for his girlfriend. That was what he was hiding—and how nice it wasn't kickbacks or some shit.

So fucking sweet.

As the steel door they'd come through slammed shut into its jambs behind them, Rehv looked at the pair of vampires. Who'd obviously just fed from each other. He could scent it in the air.

"Are you sure you two aren't together?" he said to the female to distract her. "Isn't he yours?"

"No!" She fiddled with her purse. The collar on her sweatshirt. Her left sleeve. "He's not—Jesus, we just met—I mean, we did meet. But I don't even know his name. Or didn't until you came—what was the question—"

While she babbled, Rehv went in and checked out her emotional grid—and what he saw was bad. Very bad.

"I don't know about any book," he said, cutting her off. "Sorry."

The female took a deep breath. "Tallah told me you did, and that you'd know where to find it. She was sure of this—she—"

"She's wrong." Rehv frowned. "How is she doing, by the way. I haven't seen her for years. She was a good friend of my *mahmen's*."

"But she said—"

"I'm done denying facts to you." Rehv smiled slowly and nodded toward Shawn, who was still steaming with aggression, a vampire clambake of possessiveness. "But you can answer me one thing. If he's not yours, why did you feed him?"

That stopped the female in her tracks. "He was dying."

Rehv laughed a little. "Let me get this straight. You come here looking for some kind of bestseller, run into this flyboy, and when he springs a leak"—Rehv indicated the oval blood carpet on the concrete—"you risk your own life to save his?"

"I did what anyone else would do."

No, Rehv thought to himself. *You had your own reasons for giving him your vein, and whatever they are, they're making you desperate.*

"No, you didn't," Rehv murmured. "Most would have left him to die. In fact, all would have. So he's yours now—"

"No, he's not—"

"He owes you his life. So he's yours—"

"I don't want him!"

Shawn—and by the way, who the fuck volunteered for a human name like that? Couldn't the bastard have thought of something else to disguise himself with?—suddenly looked offended. Like she'd passed on USDA-inspected meat fresh out of the refrigerator.

Yeah, because a male like him was such a prize. Especially for a nice female who was clearly out of her depth with whatever the fuck was going on here.

"Okay, fine, that's your business." Rehv shrugged. "And on that note, I'm out—"

"I need your help," she pleaded.

Rehv narrowed his eyes again. As she put her palms together and tilted forward like she was praying to him, the expression on her face would have been heartbreaking if he'd given a shit. But he couldn't afford to. Her grid, that superstructure that only *symphaths* saw, was glowing with a fierce, destructive illumination—that rose to the level of a five-alarm fire.

Especially given what she was asking about.

"What's your name?" he asked.

"Is that important?"

"Nah, not really—"

"You're my only hope," she begged.

After a moment, he shook his head. "That's a line from *Star Wars*, female. It's got nothing to do with me. Later, you two."

As he dematerialized, he had a thought that he needed to leave all this alone.

Unfortunately, given what she was after?

He was as involved as someone tied to a sinking anchor.

CHAPTER TEN

It was a good thing that the Reverend left. As that male with the fancy-ass coat had been flapping his gums, Sahvage had been wondering which way of killing the motherfucker would be the most satisfying. There were a lot to choose from, which was what happened when you'd spent a couple of centuries stalking the night and eradicating things. A lack of weapons, however, did limit some of his options—although bare-hands-only was hardly a deal-breaker.

In the end, the pick of the litter had been taking the guy's head and slamming it face-first into one of the readily available concrete walls—with the result being that the Reverend's skull cracked like an egg, and his brains broke out of their cranial prison like pigeons flushed from underfoot, scatter, scatter, splatter, splatter.

Oh, what a relief it is.

Unfortunately, before that happy little plan could be put into action, the fucker took off—

"No," the female hollered as she raced forward.

She was holding her hands out into thin air, even though her eyes must have told her there was no one there to catch, no one to hold. No one to help her.

Standing off to the side, Sahvage thought it would be interesting to be needed by her like that. Wanted like that. Determined to be necessary—

What was the *hell* was he thinking.

Been there, done that, and look at allllll the happy shit that had fallen on his head because of it.

"So what's this book?" he asked.

Damn it. No. He did not just open that door—

The female pivoted around. The utter defeat on her face was a shock—for absolutely no good reason at all.

"He was my last chance."

"For what?"

The female stared down at her shoes. When she finally looked back up at him, she tightened her lips and shook her head. "I have to go."

Sahvage crossed his arms over his chest. "If you want, I'll bring him back to you."

With raised brows, she cupped one of her ears, like she couldn't have heard that right. "What?"

"I'll find him and bring him back to you."

She let out a tired curse. "You can't do that."

"Watch me." He shrugged. "I don't mind carrying heavy loads with big mouths. Done it before, I'll do it again."

"He knows where it is," she murmured as she glanced back at where the other male had been standing. "Tallah would never lie to me. He knows where the Book is, but for some reason, he's pretending like he doesn't."

Sahvage went still. "What book are you looking for."

Absently, like it was an afterthought to everything else that was going through her mind, she said, "And you need to stop fighting."

Sahvage frowned and motioned around at all the empty space.

"With who? We're alone here, FYI, and this saucy repartee of ours can hardly be considered pugilistic."

For some reason, he felt like proving he knew some fancy words.

Her eyes returned to his. "You need to stop fighting with everything and everybody."

"Don't pretend you know me, female," he warned.

"I don't have to pretend. It's a billboard hanging over your shoulders for all to see." She shook her head. "Just stop fighting. It's a goddamn waste of energy. And I'm sorry I distracted you so that you got hurt. I think we're even on that score now, though—"

"You thought I was the Reverend," he said abruptly. "That's why you came back, wasn't it."

"It doesn't matter now."

"You're right." He took at step toward her. "But answer me something."

"I have to go—"

"If you'd known I wasn't him, would you have still tried to save me?" When she didn't reply, he lowered his lids. "Come on, be honest. What do you have to lose?"

"No," she said after a pause. "I wouldn't have come back."

"Good." As surprise flared in her face, he shrugged. "It proves you have half a brain, and something tells me you're going to need it, sweetheart."

The female took a deep breath. "If you call me 'sweetheart' one more time, I'm going to mace you."

Sahvage chuckled a little. "Sounds like fun. I'll even let you hold me down when you do it. I like the idea of you on top."

The flush started in her throat and rode up to color her face—and that wasn't the only heat that flared. The scent of her arousal traveled on the breeze to his nose, and he inhaled slowly, deeply.

"It's a shame you're leaving," he said in a low voice. "I have to take a shower and I could use some help with my back."

The female shook herself, as if out of a trance. "It goes without saying that I am beyond uninterested. You can keep your soap to yourself."

On that shutdown, she dematerialized so fast, he was astounded at her mind control. And then, as her absence properly registered . . . for a split second, he did as she had, and reached out into thin air.

Even though there was nothing in front of him.

Dropping his arms, an emptiness washed through his chest and was carried out to his limbs. The feeling of being nothing more than a void that breathed was a familiar one. It was who he'd been for a very long time.

Yet for some reason, that female made him conscious of his barren existence as if the weightlessness was brand-new.

Like anything mattered, though, he told himself as he dematerialized out as well.

Besides, he could reach his own goddamn back.

Always had, always will.

◆　　◆　　◆

Down below, at ground level, Mae re-formed in the darkness and studiously ignored the fact that she was panting. And there were all kinds of other things in her body she refused to acknowledge, but she wasn't going to dwell on them. Not that they existed. Because she was ignoring them.

"Fuck," she muttered. Even though she rarely swore.

Then again, this night was breaking allllll kinds of records.

Caught in her head, she started walking without bothering to see who was around. Fortunately, the cops were kibitzing on the other side of the parking garage, and all the other humans had already gotten out of Dodge, as the saying went.

Crossing the street, the random flashes of red from the lights on the squad cars strobed around the abandoned buildings, and there was absolutely no traffic on any of the roads in what seemed like a ten-block radius. Likewise, the parking lots that had been SRO for those flashy cars were now empty, nothing but trash and the occasional beater left behind—and overhead, the police helicopter was turning off its searchlight and paddling out of the area.

It was like the last scene in a horror movie, the scares over, the heroine safe, the lessons learned. Cue the credit roll.

Great analogy—metaphor, whatever.

Yeah, except this was always when Jason came back out of the pro-verbial lake and dragged the counselor down to the bottom with him.

Claiming his last kill, after all.

Her car was where she'd left it, and getting in, she cranked the ignition, put things in reverse, and k-turned around. As she headed off, in a direction that ensured she'd avoid the cops, she gripped the steering wheel, but sat back in the driver's seat.

God, this was not at all how she'd thought things would work out. And she needed to call Tallah.

Instead of getting her phone from her purse, she just drove out of downtown's Venn diagram of one-ways, finding an entrance ramp onto the Northway—

Shit, she was headed south, not north.

"Damn it," she muttered as she looked over her shoulder to merge.

There were no cars, just a couple of semis, and Mae got off at the next exit, tangled with a stoplight, and headed back onto the highway, going in the right direction.

Even as she kept the car in her lane, and stayed at the speed limit, and monitored the ascending numbers of the exits, she was mostly in her head, a slideshow of everything that had just happened flipping through scene by scene. As the start-to-finish came to an end and got ready for a replay, she glanced at the clock on her dash.

Holy crap. Only an hour had passed.

It felt like twelve.

Or maybe an entire week.

Yet for all that had transpired, the essentials remained unchanged, and the crushing reality of her situation made it hard to breathe. Cracking her window, she took some big inhales. Then she turned off the heater.

When she came to her exit, it felt as though her car got off on its own, and the same thing happened as she approached the Shell gas station she had been stopping at every night. As the Honda rolled to a halt in front of the shop part, away from the pumps, her head turned to the ice cooler.

For a moment, things got blurry, the cartoon penguins with their red scarves disappearing in the midst of their arctic landscape.

She held the breakdown off by opening her door and getting out with her purse. Heading into the convenience shop, the young guy behind the cash register looked up from his phone.

"Oh, hey." He stroked his scraggly beard. "The usual?"

"Yup, thanks."

As Mae got out two twenty-dollar bills, the human did his beep, beep, beep thing at the register and the cash drawer popped out. When he handed her back twenty-seven cents in change, she put the coins in the plastic dish for someone else.

"I kept it unlocked for you," he said as he resettled on his stool and went back into his phone. "You sure throw a lot of parties."

"You want me to pull the chain for you and put the lock on when I'm done?"

He glanced up in surprise, like a customer helping him had never happened before. "Yeah. Thanks."

"Take care."

"Yeah, you too."

Back outside, she went over to the freezer. It took her three trips back and forth to her car, and on her last one, she put her slippery, cold bundles on the pavement, ran the chain links through the pull-handles, and clicked the Master Lock in place.

Looking up into the security camera, she waved.

Through the glass wall, the man behind the cashier lifted his hand over his shoulder in response.

With a grunt, Mae gathered the final bags of ice and humped them over to the trunk. Tossing them in with the others, she slammed things closed and got back behind the wheel.

She cried all the way to her house.

To the house she and her brother had grown up in.

To the house that they now lived in together, following their parents' deaths.

The driveway seemed to rush up to meet the front tires of her car, and as her high beams washed over the face of the one-story ranch, she saw that one of the bushes by the door had died over the winter, and there was a branch down in the side lawn. She was going to have to deal with them.

As she waited for the garage door to open, she realized that she had been noticing that bush and that branch every night when she came back with the ice. And she made the same resolution each evening. Tomorrow night? She was probably going to repeat the whole thing.

Because nothing had changed—

"Crap," she muttered as she put things in reverse.

Out in the street again, she turned her car around, twisted to see over her shoulder, and backed the Civic in properly. Braking just before the Honda's rear bumper hit the back wall, she turned off the car and waited for the garage doors to descend and bounce into place. After that, it was a couple of minutes before she could bear to get to work.

She kept thinking of that fighter.

And no, she wasn't going to help him wash his back. Like she had any interest in staring at that skull while she Ivory-soaped his huge shoulder muscles and his tight waist and his—

"Do *not* go any further with that," she ordered as she got out of the car.

The ritual of propping the back door open with the trash bin and going back and forth from her trunk to the place where her purse had thrown up the night before was more exhausting than it should have been.

When she was finally done, she made sure the dead bolt was thrown, and then stood over the eight bags of ice cubes. Her palms were stinging and red, and she rubbed them on her pants. She couldn't breathe, but that wasn't from exertion.

When she felt like she could stand it, she walked down the narrow hall and passed through the kitchen. Out in the front of the house, the living room was dark, and the corridor on the far side of it, where the upstairs bedrooms and shared bathroom were, was likewise dim.

She and her brother had always crashed down there. But for the last two weeks or so, she'd moved to the cellar spaces.

Pausing at the closed door to the communal loo, she closed her eyes. Then she knocked. "Rhoger? Rhoger, it's me."

She waited, for no good reason.

When she opened the way in, she kept her eyes on the tile floor until she couldn't avoid it any longer. Shifting them to the tub, she felt a singing pain in the center of her chest.

Rhoger's body was submerged under a pool of ice water, the cubes she'd added the night before mostly melted. He was still in the clothes he'd been wearing when he'd come home and collapsed in the front hall, the bloodstains faded because of all the water, the shirt and its sleeves billowing out in the submersion, the worn jeans the same. There were no shoes, and his bare feet were the same marble white as his face.

His eyelids were open again.

Clasping her mouth with her hand, Mae started to hyperventilate, her rib cage working overtime, her burning lungs getting nowhere when it came to relieving a sudden smothering sensation.

"Rhoger, I swear . . ." She wiped her face and cleared her throat. "I'm going to get the Book. Somehow, I'm going to get it and save you."

Beneath the still water, her brother looked up at her with vacant, unblinking eyes.

She was well familiar with them. When she was able to sleep even a little, she saw them in her nightmares.

Stumbling back out into the hall, she wanted to fall onto her knees and retch.

Instead she pulled herself together . . . and went to get the fresh ice.

CHAPTER ELEVEN

"You were . . ."

As Balz waited for the Mrs. to finish her thought out loud, he smiled into the twilight of her and the Mr.'s majestic master bedroom. He'd been sure to keep the doors to the marble bathroom open so there was enough light for her human eyes to see what he was doing to her. And it had been a really good session, the kind of core workout that meant he was not going to have to hit the training center's gym when he got home.

Rolling to his side, he took his fingertip and ran it over the necklace of diamonds he'd put on her. "This was fun."

The Mrs. turned her head to him, her professionally tended hair spilling over the pillow, the brunette extensions tangled now, thanks to her orgasms and the way she'd arched back against the bed so many times.

"It was so much more than fun."

He trailed his forefinger up her throat and brushed her lower lip with his thumb. "I have to go."

"You can stay until morning—" Abruptly, the Mrs. looked away, her profile perfectly balanced, likely thanks to a little help from someone with a scalpel. "But you don't have to say it, I realize this is not . . . you know."

Balz pressed his lips to her bare shoulder. "You're incredibly beautiful, and any man would be honored to be in your bed. Trust me. I'm never going to forget this."

As her eyes returned to his, her smile was slow. "Thank you. I'm forgotten a lot."

"Never by me." As he told her what she wanted to hear, he took her hand and placed it on his chest, over his heart. "Right here, there's a place for you. Even though we won't see each other again."

The Mrs. nodded. "I am married."

"And you shouldn't feel bad about this. Especially when he's in Idaho. Promise me that, 'kay?"

When she nodded sadly, Balz kissed her on the forehead, and then extricated himself from her body, her sheets, her bed . . . her life. As he re-dressed in his black thieving clothes, she watched him, curling onto her side and holding the blankets to her breasts.

Which had, in fact, been spectacular. As well as real.

"You're not taking this?" she asked.

When he glanced over, she touched the diamonds at her throat and he shook his head. "No. You keep it. I don't want to take anything from you."

"Aren't you worried I'll call the police? I mean, I won't, ever, but—"

"No, I'm not worried about that."

And because it was time, because it was the way things had to be, he went into her brain and sent her off into a deep, healing sleep. Inside the file cabinet of her memory, he assigned everything they had done together to the figments of a dream state, the time they'd spent a wonderful, satisfying fantasy that would feel as real as it had when it was actually happening.

A banked fire to warm herself in front of in the midst of the winter of her marriage.

Before Balz left her, he pulled up the duvet so that as the sweat dried on her skin, she wouldn't catch a chill. Then he soft-footed it out of the boudoir and went back into the closet. Willing the double doors closed behind him, he made a second trip into her husband's formal wear section, and parted the tux-*sea*-dos again.

Balz snorted at his own funny as he reopened the safe, and there was no question what he was going to take this time. Picking up the case of rocking watches, he tucked the Mr's collection of timekeepers under his arm and reclosed everything.

What a fucking idiot the guy was. Had a good thing right at his side, but nooooo, he needed to go find some strange. In Idaho.

So stupid.

Back out in the hall, Balz had a thought about dematerializing through one of the double-paned windows. Instead, he found himself padding down the curving stairs just so he could go by the Banksy stuff again. Now *that* was art.

And he'd take one or two if he could. Unfortunately, masterpieces like that? You couldn't unload them for more than pennies on the dollar. Too much provenance, too much attention—and that was the thing about being a thief. It was all about the exit strategy, and not just in terms of getting safely away with somebody else's shit. You had to be able to liquidate—or you were just a felonious hoarder.

Down on the second floor, he pivoted toward the view and took a deep, calming breath—

The sound was quiet in the utter silence of the triplex, the kind of thing that, later, he would wonder how he'd heard.

It was a tap. Like on a window. But not quite.

Frowning, he pivoted and looked in the direction he thought it came from. That was when he heard it again.

Tap. Tap.

Like something was trapped and trying to get out.

Weird. In all his research on the Mr. and Mrs., he hadn't come across any pets. For one thing, the pair had the kind of travel schedule where you could hardly keep a houseplant alive, much less something that required food, water, and walks. For another? The Mr. was a nasty neat. Cat hair? Dog hair? He'd have a fucking coronary.

Well, whatever it was, there was no reason to—

Of their own volition, Balz's feet started walking, his body carried like inanimate luggage as they headed off in a direction, on a mission, that was utterly unconnected to his will: He wanted to leave. He wanted to head back with the watches to his room at the Brotherhood's mansion. He wanted to make a call to his black market guy to monetize the Mr.'s happy little collection of wrist-bound tick tocks.

Instead, Balz was passing through the collection rooms . . . back with the meteorites, the surgical instruments, the bats.

A new room now. Totally dark with no lights or windows.

As he entered, a ceiling fixture was motion-activated and a low-level, hushed illumination bled down from above.

Books. Everywhere. But not lined up on shelves, spine to spine. These were set in glass cases that ran up the walls, the tomes reclining on tilted stands like they were at a spa. In the glow of the soft light, gold lettering gleamed on covers as well as the edges of some of the pages. When Balz breathed in, he smelled dust—

And something else.

Tap. Tap. Tap—

His head slowly swiveled to the far corner. Set aside from all the others, in a floor display cabinet that was hip-high and spotlit, a tome separate from the rest had been given an exalted distinction from the others in the collection.

Tap.

Balz walked over, called by the sound. By the presence of the special book. By . . .

In the back of his mind, he recognized that he was powerless to turn away. But he was so captivated by what was before him that he neither took note of his thrall nor had any thought to change his destination. And as he came up to the encasement, he caught his breath.

"I'm here," he whispered as he put the watches aside on the glass top. "Are you okay?"

Like the thing was a child who'd been forgotten. Who needed rescuing. By him.

The priceless artifact was bound in some kind of dark, mottled leather that made his nape tingle in warning. Old. The single volume was very, very old. No title was embossed on the surface of the cover, and the pages seemed thick as parchment—

Something smelled bad.

Like death.

As a wave of nausea surged in his gut, Balz covered his mouth with his palm and bent forward to retch—

The sound of his cell phone ringing was an absolute electric shock, his body launching itself off the floor. What the fuck? He'd silenced the—

Weak and disorientated, he fumbled with the thing. "Hello? Hello . . . ?"

"Time to come home, Balz. Right now."

At first, he didn't recognize the voice. It certainly wasn't someone who hit him up very often.

"Lassiter?"

Why was the fallen angel calling him—

His eyes returned to the book on its stand and he jumped again. It had opened itself, the front cover thrown back, its pages flipping in a rush, the flurry of activity making no sense—

"Now," Lassiter barked over the connection. "Get your ass home right fucking *now*—"

Balz snapped to attention. Something in the angel's syllables broke whatever spell had overtaken him, and with a shot of clarity, he knew if he did not dematerialize away at this very instant, he was never going to be free.

Whatever that meant.

Just as he was closing his eyes, the book settled to an open folio, and he realized that it actually wasn't spotlit; in fact, it glowed all by itself. And he had to read what had been served up for him, and him alone—

All at once, his physical form aerosoled into an invisible cloud of himself, and he spirited away through the collection rooms to the lineup of windows that faced the Hudson River. Slipping in between the molecules of one of the glass panes, he traveled northward in a scatter, the cold, bracing air registering even though he wasn't corporeal.

Unless maybe that was just how he felt?

The call to return to downtown, to go back to the Commodore, to reenter the triplex and read what had been provided for him, and him alone, was nearly irresistible. Yet he knew, without a doubt, that there was an infection there, something that would enter him and eat away at his mind and marrow, a disease of the soul that might well be communicable.

Such that he could give it to those he loved most.

He had been narrowly saved just now.

And people didn't get that lucky twice, especially not in the same fucking night.

What the hell just happened? he thought.

Moments later, the Black Dagger Brotherhood's mountain loomed on his horizon, high-shouldered and dome-topped, its pine-covered contours establishing one flank of a valley. Protected by *mhis*, thanks to the Brother Vishous, the acreage was the kind of location that showed up on Google Maps, but, unless you knew what you were doing and where you were going on it, you couldn't find your way as soon as you set foot on the property.

Everything was blurry. Confusing. Disorientating.

You know, kind of like how he was feeling right now.

As he re-formed, nausea dogged him and he breathed through his nose to get his stomach to calm down—

"What the . . . fuck?"

Instead of being in front of the great gray mansion, he was around the back of the old stone manse, staring up at a set of second-floor windows.

This was not where he had sent himself. Why was he—

The mournful sound of an owl hooting broke through the silence of the night, and he had a sudden urge to get the fuck inside . . . as if there was someone—or, worse, some*thing*—coming after him—

From out of nowhere, memories barged into his brain. Between one blink and the next, it was no longer early spring, with the snow mostly gone from the gardens and the winterized pool. Abruptly, it was the dead of winter, everything blanketed in white, the frigid air slapping at his face and ruffling through his hair. He was not standing on the ground anymore. He was up on the side of the house, freestyle-glued to the mortar joints with his climbing shoes and his finger-grips, working on the second floor's daylight protection shutters. Several of the panels had failed in that blizzard, and he and some of the others had been doing what they could to get the steel safeguards down into place as the storm raged. Yeah, except he was no Tim the Tool Man Taylor with the Mr. Fix-It shit. The electrocution from the motorized gears had been a shock—literally and figuratively—and he'd had no memory of getting thrown off the sill into thin air.

He'd been dead as he'd fallen to the snowpack. Z and Blay had done CPR on him to save his life, and he'd been told it had been touch and go.

To thank them, he'd brought them back a message from the Other Side.

The demon is back.

Those were the words he'd spoken when he'd finally come around, though he had no memory of saying them—and no memory of dying, either. He only knew what had come out of his mouth because he'd overheard a couple of Brothers talking about it, and he was only aware of having briefly been a corpse because of what was in his medical record.

People didn't get like that if you had a paper cut—

The demon is back.

As he heard his own voice repeat the phrase in his head, sweat broke out under his clothes and he wiped his brow with a hand that trembled—

"You did the right thing."

As Lassiter's voice registered from a distance, he looked at the phone in his hand. Bringing the unit to his ear, he said, "I did?"

"I'm over here."

Balz looked to the right. The angel was way down at the corner of the house, standing in one of the French doors.

"Come here," Lassiter said as he held out his palm.

"Where did I go when I died?" Balz stared at the ground and tried to imagine what his body had looked like in the snow. Had he been on his back? Had to have been, if he'd been thrown off the house. "I know I didn't go to the Fade. I didn't see a door. You're supposed to see a door, right—"

"Don't worry about that. Come inside—"

He glanced down the mansion's flank at the angel. "How did you know to call me just now?"

Tap.

Lassiter wasn't looking at him anymore. He was focused on something up above and to the left, in the sky. "I need you to come inside. Right now."

Tap. Tap.

"Well, I need you to tell me what's going on—"

"Balthazar, trust me. You have to get inside—"

Tap, tap, tap, tap, taptap—

All at once, there was sound from everywhere overhead and Balz instinctively ducked and covered his head as he went into a crouch.

Birds. Taking flight in a rush.

Against the backdrop of stars, hundreds of not-nocturnal birds flushed from the forest, the desperate, fleeing wings of the sparrows, blue jays, and cardinals carrying them off in all kinds of directions, their delicate little bodies blocking the distant haze of galaxies in a discordant, flickering pattern.

For a split second, Balz thought of the bat skeletons.

And then all he knew was pure terror.

Giving in to the sudden burst of fear, he broke into a run—and somehow, he knew not to try any of the other doors of the house. Somehow, he knew that Lassiter was at the only portal he could use, the fallen angel his only hope, his salvation from a fate worse than death.

Although he knew not who or what his pursuer was.

Balz's lungs screamed for oxygen and his legs pumped faster than they ever had in his whole life. And as he closed in on where the angel was leaning out of the mansion, Lassiter started yelling at him to move, move, *move*—

The second Balz was in range, the angel reached out and dragged him inside, slamming the door and bracing his body against it as Balz tripped and yard-saled across the library's Persian rug.

Taptaptaptaptap—

As a barrage of that sound radiated through the room, through the whole mansion, Balz flipped over onto his back and crab-walked even farther away from the noise. The something that had wanted to claim him was hitting the glass of that French door, the noise a magnification of that which had called him to that room at the triplex, to the book.

Only louder. More demanding.

Petulant, as if it resented being denied.

"What the *fuck* is going on here," Balz demanded.

But the angel didn't seem to hear him. Lassiter had closed his oddly colored eyes and was straining against the closed door, his huge body braced and vibrating with power, his blond-and-black hair falling down over his flexed chest and arms.

Like he was the only thing keeping whatever it was out of the mansion.

"She's back," Balz heard himself whisper with defeat.

CHAPTER TWELVE

As the sun began to rise over Caldwell, the demon Devina turned off her Viking stove and moved the All-Clad frying pan aside to the counter. The plate she'd decided to use was square and white, and the two meat pieces she put on it with a pair of stainless steel tongs were cooked to perfection: Just a little salt and pepper. A splash of extra virgin olive oil to coat the pan and help with the crisping.

Simple stuff, prepared well. So much better than a gourmet meal that took a twelve-minute narration and a French dictionary to decipher.

Picking up her glass of wine, she took her food over to her table, and she chose the seat that faced out from the kitchen area so she could look at all the things she owned. Her private space, her lair, if you will, was a vast open area in the basement of one of downtown's older office buildings. Technically, it was one of a dozen or so storage facilities more typically used for—snooze—collections of corporate files and records, a perk for the businesses that took up whole floors of the upper levels.

Hers was different, and not just because she could camouflage it and its precious contents at will. Instead of stupid paperwork and useless hard drives or whatever the fuck was in those other ones, hers was filled with beauty.

Picking up her fork and knife—Christofle, sterling—she cut into the meat and put a piece in her mouth.

Crap. It was chewy. Proof positive that how good something looked was no true measure of its worth.

As she swallowed with a grimace, she picked up her sauvignon blanc and took a healthy draw on the razor lip of the crystal glass. Most other people would have gone with a red, but that was too heavy for her—and God, she hated what she was eating. It was like taking medicine, something that was nasty going down, but which had therapeutic benefits.

Or at least it had better have benefits. Otherwise, she was wasting her time.

To distract herself from the familiar, bitchy malaise setting up shop in her internal monologue, she looked with pride at all the haute couture she had collected over the decades. Some was original, from the seventies, eighties, and nineties. Some she'd snagged more recently from high-end vintage shops. And some was brand-new, from Fifth Avenue, Rodeo Drive, Worth Avenue.

Such masterpieces she owned: Gucci, Vuitton, Escada, Chanel, Armani, Lacroix, McQueen, McCartney. If she'd had a different aesthetic, she could have gone the Mainbocher and Givenchy route as well, but Audrey Hepburn had always given her heartburn.

And then there were the accessories. For fuck's sake, she'd had Manolos before Carrie-goddamn-Bradshaw, and the soles on her stillies had been red for years before the plebs had found Louboutin.

And not just from walking through the blood she'd spilled.

Back to her wardrobe's wonderfulness. Of course, part of the fun was the display, and all of the skirts and dresses and blouses and slacks were parceled out among countless hanging racks. There were sections for separates, and then outfit outposts organized by designer. A whole table for Birkins and a set of shelves full of Chanel. But the arrangements weren't static. On a regular basis, she switched things up.

Sometimes it was chronological order by era; sometimes it was chromatic. She'd tried once to do it by value, but that had been impossible to get right. The older stuff had price tags that were pennies on the dollar now, and rarity and history made some of what she had priceless.

Keep eating, she told herself. *You've got to keep eating.*

As she choked down the larger of the two pieces of meat, her eyes caressed the optical cacophony before her, the fine silks and sequins, the cashmere and fur, the handbags, shoes, and lingerie, all of it offering so many colors, so many textures, so many choices for individual expression. And the collection was such a source of satisfaction and happiness, each piece like a child adopted into a loving home. Whether she'd stolen it or paid the purchase price, taken it off a corpse or gotten it gift-wrapped to herself, her ownership was indisputable and immutable, and her beauty was always magnified a thousandfold by what she placed on her perfect body.

Her clothes were the halo that she, by her nature, would never possess metaphysically.

But fuck it, she could look good while she did evil.

And yet . . .

As her silverware clinked softly against her plate, there was such silence here, a reminder that what she adored might be grounding for her and an important source of hunt-and-peck, acquisitional excitement, yet in the end . . . these fashion masterpieces couldn't touch her. Hold her. Laugh and cry with her.

She was alone in a crowded room.

Shoving her plate away, she sat back with her wine, swirling the yellow wash around the inside of the clear glass.

Chianti and fava beans, huh? she thought as she regarded the golden color. *How common.*

Then again, human organs were hardly a delicacy, were they. And worse, the shit was not working.

She wasn't eating this for her health, for fuck's sake.

Not her physical health, at any rate.

There just had to be a way to capture the love that was out there, the love she saw between others who were coupled up, the love that everyone else on the planet but she had managed to find. Just because she was a demon didn't mean she had no emotions. No need to be cherished. No desire to be seen as valuable, distinctive . . . significant . . . by the one she found valuable, distinctive, and significant.

It was a natural instinct.

As well as one hell of a Dr. Phil show.

Devina, you know, I've been doing this close to forty years now, so I know what I'm talking about. How's your life working for you?

"Not great, Phil," she said aloud. "I just want what you and Robin have."

Her mental Dr. Phil leaned forward in his suit and tie, his big gold watch winking from under his cuff, his bald head covered with makeup so it didn't reflect the studio lights. *If you look back on your previous relationships, how would you say your behavior was? Were you a good partner?*

"Of course."

Devina, we can't change what we don't acknowledge.

She thought about her one true love, Jim Heron. "I only tried to kill his girlfriend once." As Phil gave her that look, she cursed. "Fine. A couple of times. But she was so fucking annoying, and I don't know how in the fuck he picked her over me."

Relationships are a two-way street. And it sounds like he was on a different road than yours.

"Well, then he needed to read his goddamn map right. Get back on course. Get with the program."

Look, I may just be a country boy—

"Oh, will you drop the Southern poverty bullshit. You have a net worth of over four hundred million dollars. It's time to give up the relatability-signaling of overalls you haven't had on your fat ass for half a century."

Imaginary Dr. Phil stared her straight in the eye. *If you were in a relationship right now, would you contribute or contaminate?*

"Fuck off, Phil."

With a lackadaisical fork, she poked at the heart muscle. How long had she been doing this? Hoping to find fate through her digestive tract?

She was running out of patience. And Gas-X.

On a wave of frustration, her eyes swept around her lair. And it was hard to pinpoint exactly when the thought occurred, but the next thing she knew, she was getting to her feet and going across to her display of Birkins.

The Hermès handbags were on display on a lovely partner's desk she had five-fingered from a French count with whom she'd had a lovely little dalliance that had satisfied her for a fortnight . . . and ended up with him disemboweled and hung on an iron fence.

But why focus on the unpleasant stuff.

Besides, her ending had been fine. She'd moved on to bigger and better things. Specifically a blacksmith who'd been hung like one of the war stallions he'd shod.

Now that had been fun. But again, not anything that had lasted. Lot of hair on the back—and she wasn't talking about the hooved mammals who were supposed to be sporting a saddle.

And this was her problem. In fact, *nothing* had lasted. Not even Jim Heron—because he'd never been hers to begin with.

For fuck's sake, she wasn't getting any younger.

Of course, she also wasn't getting any older.

Immortal, hello.

The most expensive of all her handbags was the iconic Himalaya Niloticus Crocodile Birkin 35 with the diamond hardware. The white-and-gray masterpiece was given pride of place on an inlaid antique bed stand that had two drawers—because come on, she had to put it on some kind of pedestal. And as she stood before the bag, she took a moment to appreciate the pattern of scales and the bilateral markings that meant the darker sections of the skin were on the outsides, the creamy white center a perfect contrast.

So beautiful.

And yet not her most valuable item—even though on the secondary market, because it was a 35 with the diamond hardware, it was worth a cool $400,000. Or more if she sold it with the matching diamond bangle. Which she had.

Below its white gold feet, she pulled open the antique stand's top drawer—and it was with piercing defeat that she reached forward. She supposed she was kind of like a guy in the way she never wanted to read the assembly instructions, ask for directions, or be told what to do at a crossroads. So for her to use an aid, even if Dr. Phil always referred his guests to experts for help, seemed like—

Devina frowned.

Leaned farther forward.

Patted her hand around the inside of the drawer. Which was totally fucking empty.

With an explosive curse, she ripped out the bed stand's top level. Nothing was in it. And even though her eyes were functioning just fine, like a fucking idiot, she turned the thing over and shook it.

As if what she'd expected to find in there was somehow stuck to the bottom.

The Book was gone.

In a frantic whirlwind, she opened the drawer underneath—in case she'd misremembered which one she'd put it in. Also empty. The drawers of the partner's desk were likewise Book-less, the silk thongs and bras bearing no resemblance to the human-flesh-covered tome she was looking for.

With shaking hands, she started to go through her other bureaus, the shelves by her bedding platform, the kitchen cabinets, the shit in the bathroom area. She even went to check under her bed before remembering that it was a fucking platform with nowhere to store anything underneath.

"Where the fuck is my Book!" she yelled into the silence.

And then she remembered . . .

Wheeling around to the far corner, she glared at the five-by-five metal pen with its water bowl and pallet. The goddamn thing was empty because the fucking virgin idiot she'd had in there had escaped.

"You sneaky sonofabitch," she breathed as she walked over.

It had been her fault, really. She'd obviously underestimated him— probably because she hadn't actually needed him. The abduction had been a compulsion rather than something demanded by her circumstances, a relic of past behavior that was no longer required. With her mirror destroyed, she didn't have to worry about protecting her privacy here as much.

She'd been lonely, though.

"You little shit," she said as she stared down at where she'd imprisoned him. "Did you take my fucking Book?"

He was the only one who'd been here since she'd seen it last.

The fucking bastard must have watched her flip through the pages that one morning.

Devina turned back around to the antique bed stand, now emptied of its drawers. There was, of course, another explanation, one that was utterly unthinkable. So she promptly discarded it.

The Book loved her. Of course it wanted to be with her.

No, *he* had taken her Book, the little shit, and even if she wasn't thinking of using one of its spells to bring her true love, she was still going to need the fucking thing back.

It was hers, after all. And she was nothing if not possessive.

"Mother*fucker*," she muttered.

Now she needed to find the goddamn thing.

CHAPTER THIRTEEN

The following evening, Mae was back at her garage door, car keys in hand, purse up on her shoulder. She hadn't slept at all during the day, and First Meal had been a single piece of dry toast that had gone down like sheet metal.

"I'll be back soon," she called out to Rhoger.

Why did she wait for a response? Like, did she actually think he was going to sit up in that tub of ice water, and put in an order for Jimmy John's?

In the back of her mind, a little warning bell went off. When you were talking to your dead brother and expecting him to answer, you were probably out of your mind.

Take out the "probably."

"I'll give your love to Tallah," she said before slipping through the door and relocking it.

As she drove off, she had to fumble in her bag for her sunglasses. The fact that the other cars on the road had their headlights on, and her neighbors were once again streaming home from work, didn't mean much to a vampire when it came to that barely-there glow on the western horizon. The fact that her eyes were stinging and her skin was prickling in warning under her clothes was a good reminder of exactly how nonnegotiable the whole no-sunlight thing was for the species.

But she couldn't have stayed in that house for a moment longer.

And yes, dematerializing out was an option. She needed fresh ice, though, and the driving also helped calm her down.

It was amazing how you could be trapped even when you were free to go where you pleased.

Tallah's cottage was on the far outskirts of Caldwell, a little stone jewel nestled in a glen of maple trees. The trip there took anywhere from fifteen to twenty minutes depending on traffic, and Mae put the radio on to distract herself from stuff she didn't want to think about. NPR didn't work, though. Her mind still chewed on things like the fact that vampire bodies sank, not floated, in water—something she hadn't known until she'd started taking care of Rhoger in his current state. She was also keenly aware that time was running out for her and her brother. And she worried that maybe that Book Tallah was talking about wasn't the answer to the problem.

Maybe all she had for an answer was a Fade Ceremony, a permanently empty house, and the crushing realization that she was the last of her bloodline, left alone on the planet.

If shared memories were the best kind . . . then memories you could no longer share with the collective that were in them were the worst. That kind of solitude turned you into a reference volume rather than part of a story, and she had a feeling the losses made every thought a platform for mourning.

To keep herself from tearing up, she cast a mental line back into a sea of undesirables, and guess what came up on her cognitive hook?

That fighter from the night before.

Great.

Still, as she followed the curving roads into the country, and the population density of humans drained away in favor of cornfields and small dairy farms, she chose him to focus on. It was the best of a bad lot, as her father would have said—and it wasn't like she had to work very hard at the preoccupation. She could picture Shawn clear as day, from his obsidian eyes, to the tattoos that covered his body, to his aggression . . . to his spilled blood on all that concrete.

How someone could go from nearly dying to just going about his business, she hadn't a clue. Then again, she had a feeling his little leak hadn't been the first one he'd sprung. God, if that had happened to her, she would have screamed until she lost consciousness even after she recovered.

Meanwhile, he'd seemed like he was merely stuck in the wrong lane at a supermarket.

And FFS, if she had told him to, he would have brought that male, the Reverend, back for her.

Maybe she should have taken that route. But then what? If the Reverend didn't know about the Book, how would dragging him back to that garage have helped? And maybe the offer had just been hyperbole on the fighter's part, a bluster courtesy of his chest-thumping complex.

Right?

As she pulled onto a dirt road that was choked with bushes and overgrowth, she was still debating the pros and cons of a decision that had been made the night before. But at least she was almost to Tallah's and then—yay!—she had other things to think about . . . like Books that may or may not exist, and may or may not be helpful when it came to her brother's situation.

In the meantime, she had the bad condition of this goat path to focus on. There were potholes to fight through, her headlights bouncing up and down as she tried to avoid the worst of them, and the brambles that grew up along the shoulder were so tight, the most aggressive of them scratched at the Civic's paint job.

But then the cottage made its appearance.

As she rounded a final turn, her car pinpointed her destination, the headlights blasting the old stone of the outer walls in an illumination that was kind of unkind. The place was in a genteel state of disrepair, the front door painted in a faded red that was partially chipped away, one shutter hanging cockeyed, the slate roof showing a missing tile here and there. The grounds were likewise a shaggy mess, the rose garden nothing but a tangled circle of thorns and weeds, the front path ragged and frayed by tree roots and mole tunnels. A fallen branch big as a car was in the side yard, and that old birch tree looked like spring's CPR of warmth and sunshine might not pull it through the winter's cold coma.

Putting her car in park, she canned the ignition and took a deep breath. She really needed to help more around the property, but between her full-time work online and taking care of her own house, the last year had gone by so fast. Previously, when her father had been alive, he had come here and done a lot of the handyman stuff, and her brother had helped out like that, too. It was amazing how fast things degenerated, though.

Three years without upkeep and things were nearly unrecognizable. And it was hard not to find a parallel in the collapse of Mae's own life, everything that had once stood strong and true now decaying and lost.

Her parents had seemed so permanent. Rhoger, too.

Youth and a lack of exposure to death had meant her family was immortal and the details of her life—where she lived, who she was related to, what she did—were written-in-stone facts, as immutable as the night sky, as gravity, as the color of her own eyes.

Such a fallacy, though.

Getting out, she almost didn't lock her car. But an echo of the fear she'd felt in that crowd of humans had her putting her key in the door and turning it.

As she walked over the flagstone path, Tallah opened things up, and the sight of the stooped older female standing in that familiar archway made Mae blink quick. Tallah was always the same, dressed in one of her loose housecoats, this time in a periwinkle blue, and she had on matching blue-and-yellow slippers. Her cane was likewise co-ordinated, a pale blue ribbon wound down the metal stalk of the support, and there was a corresponding bow at the end of her braid of white hair.

"Hi," Mae said as she came up to the front step.

"Hello, dearest one."

They embraced across the threshold, with Mae being careful not to squeeze too hard—even though all she wanted to do was pull Tallah close and never let the old female go.

"Come," Tallah said. "I have tea on."

"I've got the door," Mae murmured as she entered and closed things.

The kitchen was in the back, and as she followed Tallah through the tiny, familiar rooms, everything smelled the same. Fresh bread. Old leather armchairs. Faded fires in the hearth and fragrant loose tea leaves. The furniture was all too big for the small house, and it was of absurdly high quality, the tables marked with marble and gilt, the secretary set with fine inlaid woods, the chairs and sofas clad with faded and now-worn silks. Oil paintings in heavy gold-leafed frames hung on the walls, the landscapes and portraits executed by Matisse. Seurat. Monet. Manet.

There was a fortune under the roof of this tiny cottage, and Mae frequently worried about thieves coming out here. But so far, things had been okay. Tallah had been living here since the eighties and had never been bothered. It was a shame, though, that the female had refused to sell even one of those paintings off to better her living conditions. She had been steadfast in keeping her things with her, however, even if it meant that necessary improvements couldn't be afforded. The obstinance didn't make a lot of sense, but then it wasn't anybody else's call, was it.

Neither of them said anything as Mae took a seat at the kitchen table and Tallah busied herself at the counter with the plug-in kettle and two teacups. The urge to help the female with the tray was nearly irresistible, especially as Tallah hung her cane off her forearm and seemed to struggle with the load of creamer, sugar, and filled cups. But self-sufficiency was the pride of the elderly, and no one needed to take any more autonomy away from the female before it was absolutely necessary.

As Tallah set the things down, Mae nodded to the far corner of the table, where some kind of display of objects was covered with a threadbare monogrammed towel. "What's under there?"

Usually, the female kept everything neat as a pin, the minimal amount of stuff out on the counters, tables, shelves, mantels.

"Tell me again what happened last night?" Tallah said as she lowered herself down into her chair and passed a cup and saucer over.

The porcelain twosome rattled in her unsteady grip, and the sound reverberated through Mae's entire body. It was a relief to take the tea and end both the acoustics and the risk of a total spill, and she covered up her rush by giving a factual this-then-that of everything. Naturally, the report had redacted parts. She cut out the part where she roughed up that human woman in the wait line, and yeah, boy, there was a whole lot of gappage when it came to Shawn.

"The Reverend lied about the Book," Tallah said as she poured some milk into her tea. "He knows exactly what it is. But perhaps not where."

"Well, he's not going to be a resource. He was pretty clear on that."

As they fell into silence, Mae watched the curl of steam rising from her tea. With the cooling of the Earl Grey, the breadth of it was diminishing.

"Tallah . . ."

"What, dearest one?"

She pictured Rhoger in that cold water. "I don't know how much more time we have."

It wasn't that the body was decomposing—yet. But it would. And more than that, she wasn't sure how many more nights she could hit that Shell, and buy that ice, and go to that tub to drain the water and refill things . . .

Oh, who was she kidding. She would keep doing the job until there were only pieces of him left, nothing but a body-fluid soup in that bathroom—provided there was hope. And maybe that was what was dying for her at this moment.

She pushed the teacup away. "Tallah, this is hard for me to say."

"Please." The older female leaned forward and put her hand on Mae's arm. "You can tell me anything."

Mae focused on the flower print of the housecoat's sleeve, the little yellow and white flowers set off in the sea of blue.

"This Book, whatever it is." Mae looked into those watery eyes, and tried to keep the demand out of her voice, out of her expression. "I mean, what are we really doing here. I don't want to doubt you, but I can't . . . I'm finding it hard to keep going on this goose chase. You said the Reverend was our last hope, and we've come up dry. Again."

Well, and then there was the larger issue of what she'd been told the Book would do for her. She so needed to believe resurrection was possible, but she was beginning to worry that this was how urban legends set up shop and propagated: Someone in a vulnerable state, who needed to believe there was a metaphysical solution for their problems, got served up a hoax.

Desperation could mold truth out of any lie. And even if it was from a well-intended source, there was a cruelty to the false promise of help.

With a nod, Tallah took a sip from her cup. Then she sat back, holding the tea between her gnarled hands as if they were cold. "I thought that my losing my station would be the lowest ebb of my life. But watching all that you have endured these past few years . . . it surmounts even my saddest moments. How could I not help you?"

Mae had never asked for specifics, but at one point, Tallah had been at the highest level of the aristocracy, mated unto a member of the Council. Mae's *mahmen*, Lotty, had worked for her as a maid. Something had happened, though, and when Tallah had come here, Lotty had insisted on cleaning the house for free on the side—and soon enough, the whole family was involved in taking care of the older female.

How ironic that that fall from grace had ultimately saved the female's life. If she had still lived in that grand house? She would have been killed during the raids on the property, just as Mae's parents had been.

"The Reverend's real name is Rehvenge," Tallah said. "He is a member of the *glymera*—or was. I'm not exactly sure how many are even left the now. As I told you, I knew his *mahmen* very well. She used the Book herself once, and she told me of its power. That is how I first learned of it. It will provide you with what you need. I swear this on what little is left of mine own life."

Mae ducked her eyes. "Don't talk like that."

"It is the truth and we both know this. I shall die soon—but unlike your brother, my time to go is as it should be. I have lived my allotment of nights. His life was taken far too soon, however, and that is a wrong that must be righted."

Tallah reached across to the draping at the end of the table. As she pulled back the bath towel, what was revealed made no sense: White vinegar. A silver dish. Salt. A sharp knife. A lemon. A candle.

Okay, fine, if you were making salad dressing, the collection was handy, but why Houdini the stuff?

"What's all that for?" Mae asked.

"We're going to bring the Book to you." Tallah nodded at the ingredients. "If it will have you."

CHAPTER FOURTEEN

Up north, in the majestic foyer of the Black Dagger Brotherhood's mansion, Rehvenge strode over the mosaic depiction of an apple tree in full bloom. As he came to the grand staircase, he ascended at a good clip, his Bally loafers eating up the blood red runner, his mink flaring out in his wake. When he got to the top landing, the double doors of the Blind King's study were open, and at the far end of the pale blue, French-antique'd room, Wrath, son of Wrath, sire of Wrath, was in prime position—i.e., sitting behind a carved desk that was big as a grizzly bear on all fours, his ass planted in his father's throne. With all that jet black hair falling from a widow's peak, and his cruel face with those wraparounds, and his warrior's body, Wrath looked exactly like who should be running the vampire race.

And then there was the fact that even without his sight, he saw things very clearly, and he suffered no fools. Ever.

To Rehv, King of the *symphaths*, the pair of them were powerful allies. And for fuck's sake, they were going to need to be after tonight.

"His Excellency is early," Wrath murmured as those black wraparound sunglasses looked up from the golden retriever in his lap.

George, his guide dog, was in a glorious lounge on his back, his white belly hair all over everything, his head in a loll like he was at a spa. As he scented Rehv, his boxy head lifted briefly and he offered a wag. But then there was a prompt return to being adored.

"That dog's the real king around here," Rehv said as he entered and willed the doors closed.

As they clicked into place, one of the Blind King's brows lifted over the rims of those sunglasses.

"So you've come with good news," Wrath muttered. "How refreshing."

Rehv stalled things by going on a pace, his travels taking him on a little loop around the silk sofas and the collection of bergère chairs. When he finally lighted on the armchair opposite the carved desk, the retriever looked over again, this time with worried eyes.

And didn't that prove George had great instincts.

"Wow," Wrath said as he ran his fingers through blond chest fur that would have counted as shoulder-length hair on a biped. "Uncle Rehv's wound up. This is gonna be a good one."

"I would have come last evening." Rehv arranged the folds of his mink so they covered his legs. "But I had shit to deal with."

"More fun with your citizens?"

"Humans this time." All those refunds for that aborted fight. "It was a long night."

"Why do you fuck with them?"

"It's a character defect. But one of my less deadly ones, so I give in to it. Living a life of perpetual denial is like being in a coffin aboveground. And please don't tell me that I already have enough money. There is never enough."

As the King chuckled, Rehv glanced to the unlit fireplace and wondered if it was worth setting a flame to the preset logs. Even though it was a yeah-sure-fine seventy degrees in the room, he was perpetually cold, the dopamine he took to keep his evil side in check driving down his internal temperature.

Thus the full-length mink. Which he wore even in the summer.

And on that note, pause. Long pause.

Wrath turned in his throne and lifted up the golden like he intended to put George on the floor. The dog had other plans, however, shimmying around in his master's huge arms and wrapping his big front paws about Wrath's neck to hold on. Like he was about to be lowered into a lava pit.

Wrath chuckled as he eased back into place. "Guess that's a no, huh."

The King shuffled the dog around so that he was back to cradling George like a big baby. As he resumed the petting routine, Rehv focused on the inner-forearm tattoos that depicted Wrath's impeccable, purebred lineage.

"Start talking, *symphath*, you're fucking up my dog."

Rehv nodded even though his comrade in royal arms couldn't see it. "We've got problems, you and me."

"And here I thought you were coming to talk fashion. I was going to redirect you to Butch."

"Listen, there's only so much you can do with this black-muscle-shirt-and-leathers rut you've been in for a hundred years. I keep telling you this."

"Yeah, my goal's to get on the cover of fucking GQ. Now talk."

"Print is dead."

"That's a line from *Ghostbusters*. And a deflection."

Rehv settled his cane between his knees and batted it back and forth with his palms. "I had a female approach me tonight."

On a laugh, Wrath said, "Ehlena is totally secure in your relationship. And I know you better than to think you'd ever do something stupid."

"It wasn't like that."

"Good, 'cuz I ain't no Ann Landers."

"The female was looking for something neither of us wants her to find." He forced himself to lean back in the chair. "Have you ever heard of the Book?"

"I've heard of the humans' Good Book. You talking about the Bible?"

"The opposite. The one I'm referring to is a conduit to the dark side. It's bound in flesh and I have no idea what the pages are made out of— and I don't want to know the answer to that one. It's traveled through history, finding people and wreaking havoc."

"So it's a book of spells or some shit?"

"*The* Book of spells. Capital-*B* time."

Wrath frowned. And this time, when he went to set George onto the floor, he didn't take no for answer. As the dog collapsed in defeat at his feet, the King sat forward—and his expression as he looked across the desk at Rehv was so intense, you could forget he was blind.

"I've heard rumors about magic throughout the centuries." Wrath shrugged his powerful shoulders. "But I've been too fucking busy with the Omega and the Lessening Society to worry about hocus-pocus bullshit."

"It's not bullshit."

"So you've seen this thing? Or have you used it."

"Neither." Rehv dropped his eyes to the blotter. "But I had a . . . friend . . . who told me about the damn thing and what it could do."

"Friend" was not the right word for the *symphath* Princess who had blackmailed him into fucking her for decades. The fact that the sex had always nearly killed him had been only part of her fun; fuck knew there had been so many other amusements to the relationship for her. But he'd settled that score, and then some.

The sandman had come for her.

Still, he should have known she wouldn't be done with him, and this Book shit was the kind of blast from the past that made a male want to give himself a concussion.

You know, for the amnesia.

Wrath's eyebrow lifted again. "A 'friend' told you. This sounds like a confession on the Internet."

"Not even close. And before you ask, yes, she'd used it."

"To do what."

"Nothing good. I don't know specifics, but considering who she was? You can bet it was a rotten fucking idea."

"Okay, so a female came up to you and asked you for the Book. Do you know where it is?"

"Nope. It left my 'friend.'"

"Left her? Like, the goddamn thing called an Uber and headed out of Caldwell? Or wherever it was?"

"Something like that. From what she told me, it chooses its way in this world." Rehv rubbed his eyes. "Look, you can use the spells in it to do all kinds of shit you shouldn't. And the fact that this female knew to come to me? It's bad news, all the way around."

"So she knows your friend?"

"She was referred to me through an old acquaintance of my *mahmen's*. I followed the female so I could get her license plate number—not that it's going to help us much. Still, I gave it to V in case she's registered her human alias in a species database somewhere. And as for why she's looking for the Book? I saw her grid. She's desperate to the point of insanity. It's the worst combination—incredible dark power mixed with that kind of despair."

Wrath went silent.

"You know I'm not an alarmist," Rehv said. "This is *very* dangerous. I don't know what else to—"

"You don't have to tell me any more." Wrath lowered his head, and those blind eyes glowed behind the wraparounds. "The answer is easy. We get the Book before the female does and destroy it. End of."

Like it's going to be that simple, Rehv thought.

Still, at least Wrath was on board and taking shit seriously.

"We've got to find it first." Rehv stroked a palm over his Mohawk. "And as for part two of that plan? Something tells me it's not going to go without a fight."

"We'll use all the resources we have—and you know I hate losing."

Rehv cursed under his breath. "I feel like this is the part in the action movie when I say, 'This is unlike anything you've gone after before, Indy.'"

"Well, you've got that out of the way, then," Wrath muttered. "Good on ya."

"And as for the locating shit, there's only so much V can look up on the Internet, as smart as he is. And something tells me this ancient source of evil is not going to be Google-able."

"You leave the GPS'ing to me. I have an ace in the hole when it comes to finding things like that."

Rehv stared off at the cold fireplace and pictured the Princess, with her triple-jointed fingers and those scorpions in her ears. The memories of her perverted shit made his stomach churn, but he had to go there. He had to try to remember everything he could about the ancient tome.

"It's okay," Wrath murmured. "You've done enough coming forward."

"I'll check in with my people. See what else I can find out."

"That'll be good."

With a groan, Rehv got to his feet. "I was ready for a break, you know. The Lessening Society gone, the Omega outta here. It was supposed to be the start of a fresh chapter."

"Unfortunately, it's just the same ol' horror story, my friend. Life demands the battle for survival. That's just the way it is. And as for this Book, I'll call the Brotherhood in, tell them what you've said. You should be at the meeting."

"Fine. Let me know when?"

"How's now sound."

"I'll go get Tohr for you. He's in the billiards room."

"Perfect."

Rehv nodded and headed for the doors. As he went to step out of them, he paused in the archway. Wrath was back to focusing on his dog, the great Blind King crammed down underneath the desk and whispering to the animal, like he was explaining to George that everything was going to be okay, and he was a good boy, a very good boy, yes, yes, he was.

"Hey, Your Lordship."

Wrath's head popped up over the desk. "Yeah?"

"Can I ask you something?"

"Sure. But fair warning—if you want my opinion, you're going to get it, and it's rarely generous. Or so I've been told. Actually, the brothers made me a t-shirt."

Rehv lifted his brows. "Really?"

"The front says, 'Ask Me Anything.' The back says, 'Well, That's Fucking Stupid.' Apparently, I'm supposed to pivot around after they're finished speaking—it's so fucking stupid." Wrath looked off to the side and frowned to himself. "Damn it."

Pulling the halves of his mink together, Rehv cleared his throat and tugged at his cuff links. "Do you think I look like a cross between Liberace and Hannibal Lecter?"

Wrath shook his head as if he hadn't heard that right. "What?"

"You know. Like Liberace and Hannibal Lecter. Had a baby."

"Wow." There was a pause. "That's a lot of—first of all, why the hell would you ask a blind male what you look like?"

"Good point and never mind." Rehv turned away. "I'll get your boys ready."

"Tell them to leave the Chianti downstairs." Wrath raised his voice. "Unless you're feeling thirsty."

"Not funny," Rehv muttered as he walked to the head of the stairs.

"Come on, that's a little funny," Wrath called out of the study. Beat of silence. "Fine, bring a candelabra with you if you're feeling bitchy. Maybe it'll light a fire under your funny bone."

As booming laughter rippled free of the study and echoed around the entire fucking mansion, Rehv muttered his way down the steps. Note to self: Don't give the great Blind King that kind of ammunition.

He really should have known better.

CHAPTER FIFTEEN

T hat's right, put your wrist over the silver dish."

Mae frowned and leaned across Tallah's kitchen table for a closer look. Not that it changed the milky soup that had been made with the white vinegar, the lemon juice, the candle wax, and the salt.

Wrinkling her nose, she said, "You want me to cut myself?"

"Not deeply. But it has to be on your palm and across your lifeline."

"I thought palm reading was a human thing."

"It's a universe thing." Tallah extended the clean paring knife. "It has to cross your lifeline. And when you do it, imagine the Book coming to you. Finding you. Helping you as you need it to."

"I don't know what the Book looks like."

"If it hears you, you will see it." Tallah wiggled the knife. "Take this."

Mae almost shook her head and made an excuse to get up and go to the loo. But then she thought about how vampires sank in water when they were dead. And how she never would have known that if not for Rhoger being—

She carefully took the blade from the elder female. But she didn't put it to use. She thought of hoaxes. And Ouija boards. And crystal balls.

And how desperate she was not to be alone in this world.

"Tallah, you need to be honest with me. How are you so sure about all this?" When the female didn't immediately answer, Mae kept a curse to herself. "It wasn't just from what the Reverend's *mahmen* told you, was it."

Tallah's myopic stare dropped down to her tea, and there was a long silence. "I did use it once." Those watery eyes lifted. "But just so we are clear, I received the information about its power from Rehvenge's *mahmen*—and she told me how to ask for its presence. Which is how I know about this."

As the female indicated the silver dish, Mae sat up straight in her chair. "What did you use it for? Did it work? Did you . . ."

"It was not to bring someone back, no." Tallah worried the little blue bow on the end of her long, white braid. "In truth, I wanted to disappear somebody. I wanted the female who was taking my *hellren* from me to disappear."

"And what happened," Mae prompted in a whisper.

Tallah shook her head. Then shook it again. "You're different. Your intentions are nothing as mine were."

"What happened," Mae said more loudly.

"The outcome put me here." Tallah motioned around the simple kitchen. "And it hasn't been a bad life. A different life, but not bad. It turns out that what I liked most about my old station was what it sounded like as I detailed it to others. The actual living part of things was not quite so edifying."

"Did you kill someone?" And Mae feared the answer.

"I wanted her to disappear. That is all." Tallah swiped her hand through the air. "But none of that matters now. As I said, you are different. Your heart is pure. There is no evil shade to what you seek. You want to put matters right and return what was stolen unfairly—and intention matters. I was jealous. Possessive."

"He was your mate."

"The heart of another is never ours to demand if it is not freely given. That was the lesson I had to learn. Even after she was gone . . . he did not want me. Therefore, I received what I asked for, but not the result I desired. In fact, my *hellren* was so consumed by his grief, he could not be consoled, and the harder I tried, the more he resented me. He sent me away, banished me from his great bloodline, and all I could afford was this, given that no one would purchase any of my things. Disgraced females are not a provenance any collector wants. We can turn even masterpieces into junk—and I have no contacts in the human world."

So it wasn't that Tallah had been determined to retain her possessions after all, Mae thought.

"I am so sorry."

Tallah looked around as though she were taking in the cottage as a whole. "I have had a long time to consider my choices, their outcome, and my situation. You make peace with your circumstance, or you destroy yourself from the inside out." Refocusing, she reached over and squeezed Mae's arm. "That is why intention matters. I only imagined the female gone. I did not picture my mate and I happy and together. You get what you ask for, so make your intention clear when you seek to have the Book come to you."

Struck by a compulsion to know exactly what had happened to the other female, Mae nonetheless kept that line of questioning to herself. Besides, this wasn't about Tallah's past. This was about Mae's present—and from out of her most vivid, painful memories, she saw Rhoger collapsing as he came in through the front door, his strength spent, blood on his clothes, a desperate sound exploding out of him as he hit the floor and bounced as if he were already dead.

She had tried to keep him alive. She had failed. He died in her arms, her beloved brother . . . gone.

"It wasn't fair," she said. "What happened to Rhoger."

"I agree. You need to seek an audience with the King. You should tell the Black Dagger Brotherhood what was done unto your brother. They can help you find the assailant who attacked him, and ensure that justice is properly served."

"If only I knew what happened, though. Rhoger died before he could tell me."

"If you bring him back, he can tell them himself."

Mae blinked. Stupidly, she'd never considered that.

Focusing on the knife, she felt herself split into two halves. One that urged caution with this folly. The other that . . .

"What am I doing here again?" she demanded.

"Picture your good result, which would be your brother alive and healthy by your side, the two of you reunited. Imagine how you need help to get there. Have your mind full of this as you cut your palm across your lifeline. Then ask for the Book to come to you."

"And that's it."

"That's how I was told it worked, and that's how I used this spell. Although once you've asked, it does take time, it's not an immediate thing . . . but it has worked before and I believe it will work now."

Do not do this, a voice in the back of Mae's head said. *This is wrong. This is a door that should remain unopened—*

Squeezing her eyes shut, she pictured Rhoger in that ice water, the cubes floating above his haunted, vacant stare. As her pain washed over her, she opened up the vault in her heart and put her fearful hope out into . . . well, the universe because she wasn't sure she believed in the Scribe Virgin.

She tried to see Rhoger alive and by her side—

Mae closed a fist around the knife and gasped as she pulled the blade through. With her lids popping open, she got a clear image of red blood dropping through the knot of her hand and landing with a splash in the milky tincture in the bottom of the silver dish.

Drop. Drop. Drop—

She wasn't sure what she expected. But as moments turned into minutes, and all there was . . . was the dripping . . . a piercing dissatisfaction went through her. This *was* a folly, a fantasy born of her desperation and Tallah's desire to repay the service of Mae's *mahmen*. A dead end—

Tallah took something out of the big pocket of her housecoat, her bony hand extending over the table.

Held in her trembling fingers was a small triangular piece of what looked like parchment, two sides of it smooth as if cut, the long side uneven as if torn.

"That is from the Book," Mae breathed.

"I have saved it all these years. Saved it for . . . if I needed it. Thus I give this unto your quest."

At that, Tallah put the fragment into the silver dish—

The flash was bright and hot enough to have both of them shoving back from the table, Mae's hand and wrist humming with a sudden heat, a rhythmic pounding of pain in her palm having nothing to do with the knife cut.

All around the cottage, lights dimmed and flickered, and a gust of wind rattled the windows.

Everything went black.

Mae's chair fell over backward as she leaped to her feet. "Tallah, what's happening—"

There was a squeak on the other side of the table and then the sickening thud of the old female's body hitting the floor.

"Tallah!" Mae scrambled around the chairs, bumping into them, scattering them in a cacophony of noise. "Where are you—"

All at once, the lights came back on. No more flickering of electricity. No more sounds outside. Down on the floorboards, Tallah was sprawled unconscious, her eyes rolled back, the whites glowing as if she had been possessed by—

With a snort and a gasp, the elderly female came to, her wrinkled face registering shock. Then she lifted her head and looked around as if she had no idea where she was.

Mae knelt down and took careful hold of one of those wrinkled hands. "Are you okay? Let's take you to the healer's clinic. I have my car—"

Tallah coughed and shook her head. Then she batted Mae's worry away. "I'm fine. I'm fine . . ." Those eyes swept around. "I don't know what happened—can you help me up?"

Getting a hold on the female's thin arm, Mae dragged Tallah back into her chair. Then she went for her own purse.

"I'm going to call the clinic and tell them—"

"No, no . . ." Tallah stopped Mae's fumbling hands. "Don't be silly. You'd just be wasting their time—let them take care of people who need it. Honestly, I'm perfectly fine. The sudden darkness frightened me, that's all."

Mae stared down at the female, looking for signs of confusion or . . . God, she didn't know what. She wasn't a doctor. But as time went on, and Tallah stayed upright and seemed to make sense?

"You know, maybe I was wrong," the elderly female said with defeat.

"About what?"

"Everything." She put her head in her hands. "I'm tired."

"Would you like me to help you back into bed downstairs—"

The knocking on the front door was loud and persistent, and Mae twisted around to see the front of the house.

"Is that the . . ."

Tallah grabbed her arm. "Don't answer it."

The pounding went silent. Then resumed.

"Stay here." Mae pulled away and ducked a hand into her purse. "I'll be right back—"

"No! Don't open it!"

Mae marched through to the parlor, and just as she reached the door, she glanced back. Tallah had turned away to the table and was drinking the last of her tea, her head tilted as she seemed to down her cup for strength.

Refocusing, Mae brought up her canister of mace, her body shaking, her instincts screaming with warning.

But surely that summoning spell hadn't manifested some book that had the power to knock on doors?

Telling herself to get real, Mae ripped open the front door, put her mace out—

And jumped back in alarm.

"What the hell are you doing here?" she barked.

It was a moment before Shawn replied, as if maybe he couldn't believe where he was, either. But then the fighter from the night before, the one she had saved, the one she had been working so hard to never, ever think about ever frickin' again, shrugged.

Like they'd just happen to run into each other in the fruit section at Hannaford's.

"You mind lowering the bear spray," he said wryly.

She shook her head to clear it. "What?"

He nodded at the mace. "Unless you're planning on using it on an unarmed, defenseless male? I mean, I'm all for feminism, but that seems a little aggressive, don't you think."

"You? Defenseless. Really. Well, then I'm the tooth fairy."

"You don't look like a fairy." His eyes traveled down her body. "Unless you're hiding your wings somewhere that I probably shouldn't ask about?"

Mae closed her eyes and prayed for composure. And when it became clear she could wait until next month before anything close to leveling out landed on her proverbial front porch, she forced her lids back open and glared at the fighter. He was exactly as she remembered. Big, mean-looking, and with a set of black marbles that stared out of his harsh face with a combination of boredom and judgment.

Oh, and he was dressed like something out of a Deadpool movie, in all black, body-hugging combat gear.

"What the *hell* are you doing here," she repeated. Because really, what else was there to say?

"I was in the neighborhood. Thought I'd stop by." He leaned forward and sniffed the air. "Hey, you got any coffee in that kitchen of yours? I'm not much of a tea drinker."

✦   ✦   ✦

"Fuck me . . . oh, yeah . . . let me see you . . ."

Balz was on his back in his bed in his room at the Brotherhood's mansion. But he was not alone. Holy fucking hell, he was so completely and totally not fucking alone.

A dark-haired woman was straddling his naked hips and riding his erection, slow and steady. And like she read his mind, she arched back and planted her palms on the messy bedspread by his knees, spreading her thighs wide, letting him watch as his enormous, glistening cock slid in and out of her sweet, hot core.

"Oh . . . God, damn it . . . *fuck* . . ."

She was so beautiful, her breasts swaying with her movements, the tight tips pointing to the ceiling as she went even deeper into that arch of hers. Below their perfect weight, her abs undulated under her fine, smooth skin, and all of those luxurious brunette locks cascaded down onto his shins.

"That's right, fuck me," he groaned as he squeezed her knees and forced them even farther apart. "*Faster.*"

As if she had nothing better to do than cater to his every fantasy, she moved more urgently, her blood red lips parting, her pelvis working, the piercing hanging from her belly button winking in the low light. She was so flexible, it was as if she were made of water, her body flowing over him, covering him, even in the places her skin wasn't on his own.

In the back of his mind, he thought of the Mrs. at the triplex. He had done this kind of shit to that human woman, taken her, controlled her, given her the kind of pleasure that would recalibrate all the lovers she had ever had, and would ever have. That romp had been good fun. A fine way to blow an hour or two.

But this . . . *this* was game-changer sex—

Shifting her balance, the woman brought one of her hands forward. Her nails were long as talons and painted the same red color as her lips, and as she reached between her legs to her sex, they gleamed in the dimness.

On a rise of her hips, as his cock emerged from her slick hold, she raked them up his super-heated, super-sensitive shaft—

"I'm coming," he barked. "Fuck, I'm coming—"

Just as he was on the verge of ejaculating, as the pleasure sharpened to a point of anticipatory agony that he wanted to capture and hold inside of his balls forever, at the very moment when the orgasm was starting—she up and disappeared.

There was even a *poof!* and a little wisp of smoke—

Balz bolted upright.

Throwing his hands out in front of his bare chest and his stick-straight arousal, he waved through the air, searching for the warm flesh, the woman, the heat and the passion.

Nothing.

There was nothing there.

Rubbing his face, he looked around. Yes, this was his bedroom. Or at least he thought it—no, no, he was home. He could see the outlines of the familiar arrangement of antiques, and the pile of his thieving clothes on the floor, and the cracked door that opened into the marble enclave of his bathroom—

From outside in the hall, a series of low gongings started to go off. It was the grandfather clock in the second floor's sitting room announcing the hour.

He counted the callouts: One, two, three, four, five, six . . . seven.

Nothing else. So it was seven at night.

And it had to be at night, because he'd gone to bed at around eight in the morning. So yes, he was in the right place, at the right time. But as for the woman? Not a clue how she'd come to be in the Brotherhood's very carefully hidden mansion, in his room—except . . . it must have been a dream.

Jesus, he was stupid.

Of course it was a goddamn dream. A subconscious, existential pay-back for what he'd left the Mrs. with back at that triplex.

Balz's eyes went to his bureau. There, next to the lamp with the stained glass shade, still rocking back and forth as if they were babies in a crib who got fussy when they were trying to go to sleep, was the collec-tion of the Mr.'s watches. All six of them. Right where Balz had left them.

So yup, all that shit at the Commodore with the safe and the Mrs. and those Banksys in the stairwell had happened—

Unease rippled up his spine.

Something else had happened, though. Something that had delayed him. Something that had interrupted his departure—

The image of the mystery female's naked body, of her brunette hair and her dark eyes, of her incredible breasts, caused him to lock his molars—

Balz orgasmed hard, hot jets kicking out of his cock and landing on his thighs, his sheets, his lower abdomen, the streaks of come branding him. And as the release ripped through him, the woman was inside his room again, standing before him, her smile ancient, her body as nubile as one fresh out of the transition.

Except she was not a vampire. And she was not actually in front of him. His recollection of her was just that strong, though, every detail of her burned into his mind's eye.

It was as if they had been lovers for years. In fact, he had the sense that this was not the first time she had made him come, but rather that they had been fucking all day long.

He was only remembering this particular—

Bang, bang, bang. "Balz! Are you dead? What the hell."

Snapping to attention, he wrenched around to the door. Then he scrambled to pull the covers up and into his lap—where he held them in place like his erection was in danger of grabbing a top hat and a cane and tap-dancing off his pelvis.

Jesus, he was losing his fucking mind.

"Yeah, yeah." He cleared his throat. "I'm good."

Syphon, his cousin, and the best assassin anyone knew, poked his head in. "We've got a meeting in Wrath's study in five. And why weren't you at First Meal. And I brought you food."

The bastard tossed over a croissant wrapped in a dish towel and followed the carb bomb with a sealed travel mug. Balz caught one. Caught the other.

"Sugar and cream like you like it. Now get your ass out of bed. I'll meet you in there."

The door shut with a clap, the light that had streamed in from the corridor getting cut off, nothing but the glow from the loo seeping through the darkness once again.

Balz looked to where his shower was. Then shifted his eyes down to the dish towel and the travel mug.

Everything seemed exhausting, and he let himself fall back into the pillows. Closing his eyes, he took a deep breath and smelled his own arousal. Even though he was always good to go for a meeting with the Brothers, and in spite of the fact he'd pulled plenty of sleep over day, he really didn't want to go anywhere.

Maybe just a couple more minutes of shut-eye.

Yeah, just a second or two. Then he would grab a shower, and eat his First Meal on the way down to the study. Yup. Just a little more—

Oh, who the fuck was he kidding.

All he wanted was more of that woman. He needed her again like he needed oxygen to survive.

Even if she was only a figment of his imagination.

CHAPTER SIXTEEN

S tanding on the threshold of a stone cottage that belonged in a dollhouse catalogue, Sahvage waited to be invited inside for coffee. 'Cuz, you know, he was a gentlemale. A real stand-up guy with the manners of a fucking aristocrat.

Meanwhile, the female he was in front of was looking at him like he'd lost his damned mind. And maybe she was right.

Then again, maybe he'd lost his marbles a long time ago, and they'd only just met.

The female glanced over her shoulder into a dim interior. Then she stepped out of the little house and closed the door. Her hair was back in a ponytail again, wisps of blond floating around her face like a halo. No makeup, but it wasn't like she needed it, and she was wearing the same jeans she'd had on the night before—no, wait, probably not. He had a feeling, given her brittle self-control, that she was a clean freak and a little compulsive. No doubt she had three or four pairs of the same brand and size, and she rotated them through the washing.

Oh, but she had mixed things up tonight with a fleece on top instead of another sweatshirt—

God, she still smelled fucking amazing—and he couldn't help but stare at her lips. The fact that they'd been at his throat, sucking . . . licking . . .

Well, it made him resent like fuck that he'd been half dead when all that had been happening. And he better stop thinking of what she'd done at his neck, or he was going to have to rearrange himself—and not because his posture was bad.

"You are *not* here right now," she said in a hushed voice.

Sahvage cocked an eyebrow. "I'm not? Where am I, then? You better tell me, 'cuz otherwise I'm lost."

"That's not what I meant."

He leaned in and lowered his volume to match hers, like they were sharing secrets. "I'd suggest you pinch me to check and see whether I'm real, but I'm worried you'd deliberately misinterpret the invitation and throw a punch."

"Yeah, you definitely don't want to give me an opening like that. I'm not a violent person, but something about you—"

"Inspires you." He brushed a hand over his short hair. "Yes, I know, I have that effect on females—"

"You do *not* inspire me—"

"—who are looking for books. So have you found your little Beatrix Potter set yet? Or, wait, it's more like a Nancy Drew, right."

That shut her up for a second.

Actually, no, that wasn't accurate. Her eyes were talking to him pleeeeeenty.

"How did you find this house," she demanded.

"You fed me last night." Sahvage eased back. "Your blood is inside of me. Better than GPS."

And hey, at least he was successful in not licking his lips as he reminded her of what he couldn't stop thinking about. In his mind, though, he was all about the taste of her—and what do you know, that stroll down memory lane turned the cold night tropical. At least on his side of things.

For her? Antarctica had nothing on the chips of ice in her eyes as she crossed her arms over her chest. "No, I haven't found what I'm looking for."

"Pity it's just a book."

"I beg your pardon."

Sahvage shrugged. "I'm just saying."

"I am *not* looking for you. Just so we're clear."

"Oh, and now you're hurting my feelings." He put his hand on his heart and threw his head back on a recoil. "You're such a . . ."

"Such a what."

As Sahvage let his words drift off, he turned around and looked out over the tangled yard. The little stone house was set way back from the country road it was on, and the property had been let go for some time, so there were brambles growing everywhere. Likewise, the dirt drive into the acreage was marked by trees that were as graceful as arthritic hands and bushes that had overgrown their shapes.

"Go ahead," the female prompted. "Say it. You think I can't handle an insult—"

"Shh."

"No, I will not 'shh'—"

Sahvage threw his hand up and continued to scan the shaggy, shadow-infested landscape. "Stop talking."

The female snorted. "Okay, I realize this is going to come as a crushing surprise to you, but I do not have to listen—"

"Where's the sky."

There was a pause. "What?"

He pointed overhead. "Where are the stars. It was a clear night when I arrived here just now. Where are they."

"It's called cloud cover."

The hell it is, he thought.

And meanwhile, down on the ground, there was no wind to disturb anything and no moon to throw any light—and yet something had moved out there.

Even if his eyes were telling him nothing was wrong, his instincts knew better.

"Get in the house," he said in a low voice.

"I will. As soon as you leave—"

Sahvage pegged her with hard eyes. "I'm not bullshitting you. Something isn't right—"

Her stare shifted over his shoulder. And then she grabbed his arm and pointed into the messy brambles. "What the hell is that?"

He wrenched back around and moved so that his body was between her and whatever was out there—and it took him less than a split second to see what she was talking about. A shadow was swift'ing across the scruffy ground, traveling like a snake over the obstacle course of downed limbs and dead weeds. Yet there was no origin for it, nothing in the air above that would cast that kind of thing. No light source, either.

"Get inside—"

Sahvage didn't have a chance to finish the *and shut the fucking door* part. The slithering dark patch exploded up off the ground, becoming a three-dimensional figure that had arm- and leg-like extensions as well as a torso-core that was the size of a male.

Before Sahvage could marshal one of his weapons, the thing, whatever the fuck it was, rushed forward with a screeching sound that went into the ear and throughout the body. To protect the female behind him, Sahvage threw his arms wide—

The entity cast out one of its appendages and lashed across Sahvage's chest, the impact like the sting of a thousand bees, the pain ricocheting into his spine and rippling throughout his muscles. He stayed standing only through will alone, his determination to keep the female safe giving him a strength he otherwise wouldn't have had—especially as the second strike caught him in the face, blinding him.

As his brain clogged with agony and he staggered back and forth, for the first time in recorded memory he prayed like hell he wasn't going to die. He couldn't leave her defenseless in the face of whatever the fuck this was. So when his suck-ass vision told him the entity was coming at them again, he braced himself, baring his fangs and trying to marshal a defensive response—

Directly by the side of his head, extending forward from out of nowhere, an arm—a real one, not whatever the shadow was—appeared. Or at least it looked like that. His eyes were so fucking blurry—no, it really was an arm and it belonged to the female. And at the end of the thing, gripped in a tight hold, was a small canister-like object.

The female yelled as she pressed a discharge mechanism, the noise she made not from fear, but aggression. Yet the aerosol cloud that came out was instantly swept away, except like the shadowy thing had eyes? Still, it was good of her to give a shot—

There was a sudden yank at his waist.

From under his armpit, on the other side of him, the muzzle of his gun popped into sight. And as the female pulled the trigger, there was an explosion from the barrel, a bullet discharged toward the entity—but with only one hand, she couldn't control the forty's aim or recoil.

The mace wasn't going to have any effect, but those lead slugs sure as shit might.

Sahvage gripped her hand. "Aim! I'll stabilize it—aim, goddamn it! I can't see!"

With his huge palm locked over her grip, the female took charge, pointing and squeezing the trigger, his forearm muscles and biceps absorbing the kick, keeping the forty wherever she needed it to—

The shadow was struck square in the torso, the impact blowing it off the extensions of its lower body, the upper torso thrown off-balance, another terrible screech reverberating through the night.

Before Sahvage could tell her to shoot again, the female pumped that fucking trigger over and over and over. And even though he had no distance vision at all at this point, he could tell she was spot-on with where those big-ass lead slugs were going.

The whatever-the-fuck-it-was stumbled back and tottered.

"Keep hitting it!" Sahvage hollered over the sounds of the gun.

In preparation for her emptying the clip, he reached for the small of his back and got out one of his backups.

The second the last bullet in the magazine left the chamber, he barked, "Reloading now!"

He took the gun from her, kicked out the empty, slapped in the full, and re-angled the aim. This time, she gripped his forearm with both her hands and moved the gun around.

"Fire!" she said into his ear.

Sahvage followed her direction, and let her control his arm as if it were part of the weapon. And the bullets went where they had to go. As his pain levels improved, Sahvage could see a little better, and the shadow was pockmarking with holes—

And then it flew apart.

In a flurry of feathery shrapnel, the entity blew into component pieces, like a vulture hit by a cannonball.

"Get inside!" Sahvage shoved the female to the door. "Get in!"

God only knew whether that thing was going to put itself back together—

There was a creaking as the entry was thrown wide, and then Sahvage felt himself get pulled along. As he caught the toe of his boot on the weather stripping, he pitched forward and hit the floor. The good news? Before he could yell at her to shut the goddamn door, there was a resounding slam—

Immediately, the female was down with him. "Are you okay?"

As Sahvage tucked his gun away, his eyes were still not working well, but his nose was johnny-on-the-spot with its job—and oh, the scent of her.

He breathed in deep and couldn't stop from smiling. "I am now."

✦   ✦   ✦

Mae stared at the fighter. At Shawn.

His face was swollen in a ridge that ran across his mouth to up over one of his eyes, the skin unbroken, yet raised as if burned. And though the black jacket he had on was in one piece, she could smell fresh blood—so her trembling hands pulled his shirt out of the waistband of his combat pants.

Mae looked away as his tattoo made an appearance, the bony finger extending from its black background scaring her. But then she refocused. Oh . . . wow. His musculature was the kind of thing you couldn't help noticing again—and not with disapproval.

Except then she forgot about all the holy-cow stuff: His flesh looked like he'd been whipped, the welts crossing from his shoulder to his abs. And yet how had his clothes not been cut through?

"You're hurt," she breathed.

Unbidden, her hand reached out and touched the—

The fighter hissed and jerked up, and in doing so, his abs tightened like thick ropes under his skin, no fat obscuring the contours of his anatomy.

"He is indeed hurt!" Tallah exclaimed from the archway into the kitchen. And then the elderly female seemed confused. "Wait, who is he—and did I hear gunshots?"

"It's okay now," Mae said, even though she didn't believe that at all.

None of this was okay. Had she just shot a gun? And what the hell had that shadow thing been? And why—

"Are you hurt, too?" Tallah demanded. "Does he require a healer?"

"No, I'm all right." Mae put her arms out and looked herself over. "Nothing stings or hurts."

"And I'm perfectly fine," Shawn cut in.

With a groan, he got to his feet. And then, addressing Tallah, he said in the Old Language, "*It is my honor to make the acquaintance of a female of worth. I am Sahvage, and forgive me for my intrusion into your home.*"

As he spoke, he put his hand up to his sternum and bowed low. Like he was in a tux, and they were in a ballroom instead of the cottage's cramped front sitting area.

And what do you know. Tallah suddenly looked like a Disney Princess being presented with keys to a castle.

"*Sahvage, your presence is most welcome and appreciated in this manse,*" she replied with a brief curtsy in her housecoat.

What the hell, Mae thought. *Why didn't I get the fancy treatment?*

Then again, Tallah's inflection, whether it was in English or the Old Language, was totally aristocratic—there was only one set of vampires who sounded like she did. And clearly Shawn—Sahvage—had experience with them. Or was one of them.

Sahvage? she thought.

Then again . . . what else could his name be.

"So what happened outside?" Tallah asked as she clutched her hands to her housecoat's bodice.

"Nothing," Mae answered quickly as she stood up.

Tallah narrowed her eyes. "Well, that certainly explains the gunshots, doesn't it."

Shawn—no, Sahvage—looked toward the closed front door. "We need a barricade. Do you mind if I move that?"

Tallah and Mae both turned to the Jacobean cabinet that took up the entire side wall. The thing was made of old oak that was thick as the outside stone walls of the cottage—and maybe heavier.

"I guess I could help you?" Mae said.

"Nah, I got it."

He walked over to the eight-foot-tall, six-foot-wide piece of carved furniture—and stretched his arms from end to end. Then he sank down into his heavy thighs, took a deep breath, and—

Mae really expected the cabinet not to move.

Wrong. With a creak of protest and plenty of wood groaning, the hutch allowed itself to be carefully lifted off the ground. Then Sahvage eased it into a shallow tilt that meant all of its weight was on his chest . . . and walked the thing over to the front door of the cottage. His breathing deepened, inhales and exhales pumping in and out of his torso, but other than that? He was totally in control of the impossible load he was carrying.

And when he had it in place, he set the thing down like it was a feather, the feet reconnecting with the floorboards not on a slam but with a whisper, the old wood groaning again.

Sahvage straightened, clapped his hands as if his palms were a little numb, and pivoted around. After two breaths, he was back to normal. Like he hadn't just bench-pressed a car.

"Shutters for the windows," he said as he looked at Mae. "I need your help getting them all down. We have to secure the glass, and how many more doors to the outside are there?"

She was still so astonished by his feat of strength that she couldn't immediately respond. Her brain had gone to places that were sublimely unhelpful . . . like what else he might be able to do with that body of his.

And no, she wasn't talking about vacuuming or a little light housework.

"What exactly is going on here," Tallah said.

Mae shook her head to clear her thoughts. "We'll take care of everything. Don't worry." She glanced at Sahvage. "And yes, ah . . . there's a back entrance out in the kitchen. And there's also a storm door down in the basement, but that's steel and totally reinforced in the locked position."

He nodded sharply. "I'll take care of securing the kitchen. You start on the windows." He turned to Tallah and bowed. "*Forgive me for the disorder of your house, madam. But it is necessary to secure your safety and security.*"

Tallah blushed like she was sixteen and being asked to slow dance. "*But of course. Do as you wish.*"

"*My many thanks unto you.*"

Mae went across and hitched a hold on to the female's arm. "Sit down over here. I don't want you to pass out again."

As she settled Tallah into an armchair, Sahvage started pulling shutters into place on his way to the kitchen, locking the rolling panels into hooks mounted on the sills. The fact that dust flew from the drapes as he pushed them aside made Mae realize that the safety precautions for the sun hadn't been getting pulled and raised on a regular basis for a while.

So Tallah had been spending her days in the basement, alone, without being protected if she had to come upstairs. If there was a fire. If there was a problem.

"Stay here," Mae said as her heart broke.

Rushing into the kitchen, she tugged the sets of shutters down and clipped them securely—over the sink, by the table, even the little ones in the pantry and the loo off to the side.

When she came out of the bathroom, she stopped dead.

Sahvage was pulling another of his snatch-and-grabs, this time with the refrigerator. And he might as well have been moving a toaster oven across a counter for all the effort he seemed to be putting in.

"Wait! The plug!"

Just as the cord stretched tight, Mae lunged for the outlet and yanked things free so that the prongs weren't bent or worse, snapped off.

"Thanks," he said casually.

To avoid staring at the size of his back and shoulders, she focused on the footprint of dust and grime that had accumulated under the Frigidaire.

"My kingdom for an industrial-strength Roomba," she muttered.

"How about upstairs?"

Pivoting, she found him clapping his palms again, and as she measured that torso, and those legs and those arms, she resented how handy it could be to have a hunk of muscle like that in the house. Especially when, you know, something that was out of this world came at you on the front damn lawn.

Mae glanced to the table where the remnants of teatime were still on display—along with the ingredients of the summoning spell as well as the empty silver dish.

What had they called to the cottage? she wondered with fear.

"I'll do her resting room on this floor," she said. "And get us an exten-sion cord for the fridge."

"Any problems with me going upstairs?"

"No."

She meant to get moving as Sahvage headed to the front for the stair-case. Instead, she looked back at the table. The vinegar bottle, the salt basin, and the crushed lemon, along with that paring knife and the silver dish, were an all-wrong she wished she could undo.

In Tallah's ground floor quarters, Mae closed the shutters—and as she heard Sahvage moving around upstairs, the fact that sawdust fil-tered down from the floorboards overhead made her think she should move the elderly female in with her and Rhoger. For one, there was an obvious concern if Tallah didn't remember, or didn't have the energy, to maintain her safety shutters for the daylight hours. But for another, un-less there was some serious investment in the cottage, she was worried about its structural integrity—

Tallah appeared in the doorway, her cane bracing her weight, her face downcast. "I know what you're thinking. I meant to put the shut-ters down for the day last night. I really did. I just got tired."

"It's all right." Even though it wasn't. "I just, well, we'll talk about it later."

"I like him, by the way." The older female looked up at the ceiling as more of the heavy footfalls reverberated down. "He's very handsome. Where did he come from?"

The gates of Dhunhd, Mae thought. *To torture me.*

"Tinder," she muttered.

"You met him in a ring of fire?"

"Something like that." Mae rubbed her aching head and then focused on the elderly female. "You look tired—"

"I am sorry that the spell did not work." Tallah switched her cane to the other side. "And as for being tired, after a certain age, one gets exhausted with one's failures in life. It's not just about sleep, my dear."

"You haven't failed me."

"I thought the summoning spell would work."

"I know you did, and I'm grateful we tried."

As Tallah put her hand on the doorjamb to steady herself, Mae went over. "How about a proper nap downstairs. I'll keep an eye on things up here."

"You'll have that male stay with us, then? He's very strong. And so handsome, too."

Mae made a noise in the back of her throat. Which was what happened when you swallowed two f-bombs with a sonofabitch chaser.

"We're strong enough on our own, you and I," she said as she took the female's arm. "Come on, let's get you to your bed. You have a rest while I figure out everything."

Tallah refused to budge. "What was in my yard?"

"Just a coyote."

"It didn't sound like a coyote."

"Would you like me to bring you down some warm milk?" Mae asked in a pleasant way while steering Tallah toward the basement door.

"To be honest, I'm too tired to drink anything," Tallah said with defeat. "I am so glad you're here. I trust you to take care of things."

Well, at least that's one vote of confidence, Mae thought.

CHAPTER SEVENTEEN

About ten miles away in the 'burbs, in a nice little house that had been recently renovated, Nate was sitting at a round kitchen table alone.

Okay, he wasn't completely alone. He had a Thomas' plain bagel (toasted, lightly) with cream cheese spread on it (not too much) and a mug of Dunkin' Donuts coffee (homemade in the coffee machine, not the K-cups unit, with sugar). As he sipped his java and wolfed back his carbs, the heel of his right foot bounced under his chair like it was on a countdown to liftoff—and had lost all patience with how long the rocket boosters were taking to warm up.

The tip-tip-tip-tip drove him nuts, so he slapped his thigh. Then pushed down on it to hold his leg in place.

Checking the time on his phone, he looked to the sliding glass door on the far side of the table. The shutters were down still because Murhder and Sarah took no chances with sunlight. Even though it was now well past sunset, the house was still locked up tight—which was forcing him to do some mental gymnastics on the implications of him sneaking out through the garage. He knew the code to the alarm, but he wasn't sure if there was a secondary alert system on.

Wait, everything chimed down in the cellar, didn't it? Like, any time a window or a door was opened.

He glanced to the basement door. His parents were still down there, getting showered and dressed. So they might hear the sounds. Or get a notice on their phone. With the way the Black Dagger Brother Vishous set up these security systems, it would be stupid to think there weren't multiple redundancies when it came to tracking the breach of any contact.

He checked the time again. There wasn't any spelled-out rule prohibiting him from leaving before the shutters were up. Plus the sun had gone down about an hour and thirty-three minutes ago.

And twenty-seven seconds. Twenty-eight. Twenty-nine—

The sound of heavy footfalls coming up the stairs had Nate putting his phone away like he'd been caught looking at pictures of Emily Ratajkowski. And as the cellar door opened wide, he got back with the bagel program, chewing like he hadn't been planning anything stupid.

Just another normal night, in the middle of a string of normal nights, where he had a simple First Meal and went off to work at the construction site.

NBD.

"Look at you, up early," his dad said.

"Dad" was, at least on an eyeball level, a total misnomer. The Black Dagger Brother Murhder was the polar opposite of a doughy, bad-joking, Lee-jeans-wearing, reading-glasses-sporting Zeek Braverman type. Yeah, nope. Murhder was six feet, ten million inches tall, and, dressed in his black leathers and tight-fitting black fighting shirt, with his holsters of weapons dripping off one hand, and his black-and-red hair cut short, he looked like something that belonged in a video game.

On the wrong side of the good guys.

"So how'd you sleep?" Murhder put his holsters aside and then swung by the kitchen table, laying a huge hand on Nate's shoulder.

"Good." Chew. Chew. Sip. "I'mjustgoingtofinishthisandheadintowork."

"I'm glad that job's going well." His dad opened the cupboard over the K-cups machine and got out a mug with a snooty Englishman on it and the word "WANKER" underneath the etching. "And you're doing a service to the race. The young males and females who'll live there need the shelter."

Nate tried to plug into the conversation. "I don't get it, though. They're going to be by themselves?"

Images of human frat houses made him wonder whether all that new furniture they were moving in was going to last long.

"No, there'll be social workers on-site." Murhder put the mug in the machine and fired up things with a pod of Green Mountain Breakfast Blend. "Safe Place doesn't allow males past their transitions under its roof—which, considering it's a domestic violence resource for females and their young, makes total sense. But there are families that need to be kept together and kids just starting out on their own. So Luchas House is going to be good for the race."

"Mmm." Chew. Chew.

There was a wheezing sound as the coffee finished coming out. Then the tinking of a spoon as his dad stirred in his sugar. Finally . . .

"Ahhhhhhh."

Funny how this was now normal, this ritual of the pair of them with their coffee. Nate had gotten used to it all so fast. This was . . . home. And Murhder and Sarah were his family.

And sometimes he felt so lucky he cried alone in his room, holding a pillow to his face so no one could hear him.

Except that was not what was on his mind tonight.

"You okay, son?"

Nate looked up, all ready with an I'm-fine. But the way those eyes were staring at him? What he was selling was not going to be bought—and there was no way he was going to go into the truth. He was so busy denying it to himself, he couldn't imagine saying the words out loud.

But he did have something to talk about.

"Did you . . ." He cleared his throat. "Ah, did you ask Shuli to protect me?"

Murhder's brows crashed down over his eyes. "Protect you? Like an *ahstrux nohtrum?*"

"I'm not sure what that is."

"It's a bodyguard with a lifetime contract." Murhder put his palm out and waved it like he was erasing a bad idea on a whiteboard. "And no offense to your buddy—he's a perfectly fine young male—but he's not exactly tip-of-the-spear material, if you know what I mean. I'd pick a good Doberman pinscher over him any night if I was worried about your safety."

"Oh." Nate got up and went to the dishwasher with his plate and mug. "Okay."

"What's going on, son."

Not a question. And Nate trusted the male. How could he not? But . . .

"Nothing." He put his used stuff in with the other dirty dishes. "Shuli was just being weird—"

As Nate straightened and went to turn around, Murhder was right there.

"Talk to me," the Brother said.

"It was really nothing. We were out at the site, working on the garage—when that bright light thing happened."

"The meteorite that's on the news."

"Yeah. Well, we went to see the hole, and as we were, you know, closing in on the pit thingy, Shuli"—Nate edited out the gun part—"made this comment about how he was supposed to protect me."

"That shit did not come from us."

"Guess he was just being—"

"What kind of a weapon did he have on him." Murhder's stare was as direct as a baseball bat over the shoulder. "And don't lie. I can see it in your face."

"It was nothing." Three. Two. One . . . "It was a handgun, but he—"

"*Jesus Christ*," Murhder snapped. "What the hell is he doing with a piece? Is he properly trained? Of course not. So he's either going to shoot you in the head or castrate himself—"

"No, no, listen, it's not a big deal—"

"Any gun in the hands of someone who doesn't know what they're doing with it is a *very* big deal."

"I don't want him to get in trouble. Look, let's just forget it—"

"There's no forgetting this."

Nate raised his voice. "It's not your business!"

"When it has to do with your safety, you bet your ass it is!"

At that moment, the shutters started lifting from all the windows, and the cellar door opened wide. Sarah, Murhder's *shellan*, Nate's mom, stuck her head out. She was already in her white coat and scrubs to go work in her lab, her streaky brown hair pulled back, a set of clear plastic eye protectors hanging off a front pocket.

Her tentative expression suggested she was thinking about putting the safety equipment on right then and there. "Everything okay here, boys?"

"Fine."

"Yes."

When Nate realized he and his dad had both crossed their arms over their chests, he dropped his hands and headed for the sliding glass door.

"I'm late for work."

"No," Murhder muttered. "You're not. You still have half an hour."

Nate didn't dignify that with a response. He just pulled open the slider and slipped out into the night. Even though he was lit, he still managed to dematerialize off the property, and it was a relief to re-form at work, off to the side of the garage.

He didn't go inside, even though things had already been unlocked and people were moving big lumps of furniture out of a U-Haul truck that was parked right by the front door. Ducking off into the side yard, he hurried away until he was sure no one could see him.

Getting a jump start on the last bit of painting in the garage had never been the point of coming early. Instead, he headed for the fence line, pulling another over and under with its rails and striding off across the field. As he walked, he replayed the confrontation with his father.

And felt like an asshole.

After which he got frustrated with Shuli and all his shoot-'em-up bullshit.

As he approached the tree line of the forest, he breathed in, partially to calm himself and partially because he was a simp looking for a sign. Unlike the night before, there wasn't even a trace of that burned-metal smell. No steam, either. And no people. Vampires. Whatever.

Ducking under a branch, he pushed another out of the way—and walked into a third with a curse. Then there were ground obstacles to surmount, step over, go around. He felt like Godzilla wrecking a stage set with all the noise he was making.

The meteorite's landing pit appeared right where it had been the night before, and it looked exactly the same. But like the thing was a snowbank that was going to melt after hours of being in the sunlight?

At the lip of the impact site, he stared down into the three-foot-deep hole in the earth. Everything was scored from heat, the fallen pine needles and ground scruff burned away, the earth blackened inside the carve-out. Standing this close, he could catch a whiff of the burn-off still, though it was faint.

Where had the meteorite gone? Had it imploded on impact?

Looking up, he searched the sky overhead. So many stars . . . and he had a thought that maybe Earth was like a target at a county fair, celestial beings holding corn dogs aiming things at the glowing blue marble in hopes of winning a stuffed animal.

When that hypothetical made him worry about the mass-extinction event that knocked off the dinosaurs, he searched the trunks and branches of the forest. And the longer he tried to find what was not there, the more he was able to picture the female from the night before, that blond hair, the hooded coat, the darting eyes—

The snap of the stick behind him had him spinning around.

For a moment, he didn't think what he was seeing was real. He just figured his brain had coughed up a three-dimensional version of what he'd been dreaming of all day long. But then he caught the scent.

Her scent.

And as the complex interplay of absolutely-wonderful entered his nose, he felt transported even though his body never moved.

"It's you," he whispered with wonder.

CHAPTER EIGHTEEN

Upstairs, on the second floor of the little cottage, Sahvage went back to the guest room that faced out front. Lifting up the panels he'd just shut, he peered out at the overgrown yard. With the lights off behind him, he was able to see the night clearly through the old, bubbly glass panes.

Nothing was moving. Not around the maple tree. Down the lane. Through the brambles and the tangled veins.

Bending low, he tried to see if the stars—

They were back out. Like a storm had come through and passed by.

He thought of that shadow entity and knew in his bones what was going on—yet he wanted to deny it. After all these years, he had thought that that part of his life was over. Done with. Never to cross the path of his destiny again.

Sahvage rubbed his face. He didn't want to think about the past. Revisiting that shit in his mind was not the kind of stroll down memory lane he was looking to take—

"Are you okay?"

The words, softly spoken behind him, made him want to jump. But he caught himself and turned around smoothly to face the female who was like a bad penny to him.

Then again, he was the idiot who'd shown up on her front doorstep, so who was the evil one cent'er, here? And even though she no doubt would have been offended, he couldn't stop from checking to make sure she wasn't hurt. Again. But nothing appeared injured: She wasn't limping and he couldn't smell any blood.

And she sure as hell was staring up at him with totally clear, direct eyes.

That were actually . . . pretty damn attractive. He'd never thought about what color iris he preferred in a female. Attributes below the neck had been his sole focus when he'd been so inclined. But now?

He liked hazel eyes best. Unwavering, intelligent . . . hazel eyes that looked up at him like she was expecting him to justify the space he took up and the air he breathed by being a stand-up guy. Rather than a cold-blooded killer.

"Are you okay?" the female repeated as she waved her arms in front of him like she was in a crowd and trying to get his attention.

No worries there, sweetheart, he thought as he reclosed the shutter. *You could be standing in the back of a hundred thousand and I'd find you.*

"Everything's great." He nodded around the dusty room. "All locked into place."

The female hesitated in the doorway. Her blond-and-brown hair had frizzed up out of the ponytail she had it in, and her cheeks were flushed. Her hands were also shaking, and the instant he noticed, she crossed her arms and tucked them away.

And he wasn't surprised as she lifted her chin.

"Downstairs, too," she announced. "We're fine there as well."

Sahvage would have smiled. Under different circumstances. "Just curious. What exactly is your definition of 'not fine.'"

"None of your business—"

"I just realized something. I don't even know your name. Considering we've been all about the life and death for two nights in a row, don't you think it's time we make a formal acquaintance? Or are you going to tell me that's none of my business, either."

"Bingo."

"I didn't figure a strong, independent female such as yourself to be so petty."

"I'm not—"

"So prove you can rise above me," he drawled. "What's your name."

The female looked away. Looked back.

"Quite a quandary, isn't it," Sahvage murmured. "And you screw yourself either way, don't you—"

"Mae," she snapped. "My name is Mae."

Focusing on the female's mouth, he was tempted to ask her to say it again. Just so he could watch her lips purse.

"Now, now," he said softly. "Was that so bad, Mae?"

As she flushed and seemed to retreat into her head, no doubt to rustle up some truly creative uses of the words "fuck" and "off," he jumped into the tense quiet first.

"Is this where you tell me to go? Because I'm not leaving."

Man, he liked the way her eyes sparked. "This isn't your house."

"Yup. I know. It's why I knocked."

"This isn't your problem—"

"Oh, see, that's where you're wrong." He pointed to the window he'd just looked out of. "That thing nearly killed me, too. So you're crazy if you think I'm not involved now."

"It's gone. It's . . . dead."

"You think that entity was alive. Really." He leaned forward. "And how do you know so much about it? I sure as shit haven't seen a shadow like that before, and I've fought a lot of things—almost all of which were living, at least until I was done with them. Never faced off the likes of that. But you've, what, shaken its hand and introduced yourself? Traded phone numbers? Do tell."

"We're fine, okay. Tallah and I are fine here, together. Alone."

"You're willing to bet your life on that? And hers?"

The female tossed her hair over her shoulder, even though it was all pulled back. "You think you're the only one who can save us? Thanks, I'll pass."

Sahvage jabbed a thumb toward the windows that faced out front. "You couldn't hold that gun up without me—"

"You couldn't see to shoot—"

"So we make a perfect pair." As she huffed, he had to smile. "Now how 'bout that coffee? Great, thanks. I take mine black."

"Just like your soul, right."

Levity lost, Sahvage lowered his chin and stared out at her from under heavy brows. "Here's a little tip for you." As her hand went to the base of her throat, he thought of everything he had done in the past. "When your enemy is evil, you don't want your shield worrying about virtue. You and that old female are not going to survive this without the likes of me."

◆   ◆   ◆

Two hundred years in the past, and some indeterminate time following his demise from the penetrations of many arrows, Sahvage kindled back into consciousness, the gathering of his wits calling unto him an awareness that was gradual, yet irrevocable upon its arrival: The meadow was gone, replaced with a mist that was so thick, he felt as though he was floating, even as the weight of his body registered. The scent of his fresh blood was likewise no more, and the same was true of his righteous foes with their cries of judgment and vengeance.

The one thing he cared about, the only thing that mattered . . . Rahvyn . . . was as well nowhere to be seen, heard, or sensed—

Was this a dream? Had he lived? No, that could not be true.

With confusion, he regarded the front of himself. He was in a loose white garb that he neither owned nor had any memory of dressing himself in, yet did that truly matter? What was more germane was that no shafts pro-

truded from his chest, and, placing his hand over his heart, he breathed in
and felt no congestion, no struggle for draw. There was no pain, either.

Looking about, a shiver of awareness licked down his spine as he noted
the white landscape that was nothing earthly-bound. Mist . . . only mist as
far as he could see. Indeed, there was no division betwixt sky and ground, no
structures, no flora or fauna, and no one else around him. It was as if this
odd, troubling environ had been created for him and him alone.

Following a moment of collection, he turned to the left as if called to do so.

And when he saw what was before him, dread flowed throughout his
body, replacing the blood in his veins.

The door unto the Fade presented itself just as it had been described
unto him by a wahlker, and he recalled the male's words, spoken in a haunt-
ing voice: From out of the fog shall appear before you a door, and should
you desire to proceed unto the other side, then open it. If you wish to
stay among the living, do not lay your palm upon the latch. Once contact be made, your choice is ratified fore'ermore.

Sahvage wrapped his arms around himself, in the event his hand acted
on its own provocation, without his consent or prompting. Rahvyn was down
below, undefended, in the midst of a sea of males with cruelty in their hearts.
She needed him to keep her safe—

The latch depressed of its own volition, and there was the unmistakable
click of a lock disengaging. The portal unhinged from its jambs, opening with
an inexorable force and a manner that recalled the departure of his life force
down upon that meadow's soft bed of flowers, neither volunteered for nor de-
niable.

"No!" he called out to the milky sky. "I shall not proceed! I refuse—"

All at once, a swirling o'ertook him, the indistinct landscape casing 'round,
or mayhap it was he who was turning and churning within it. And then there
was a pulling, as if he had returned unto the birthing canal, his body sucked
through a narrow aperture that he could not see, but most certainly sensed, the
compression squeezing the air from his lungs and compressing his ribs such that
his heart could no longer beat.

Nausea roiled within his gut, and his head became fuzzy, thoughts refusing to form properly—and yet what could he know about what was done unto him the now? He was alive no longer, his body an abode which had been locked by death's key against his soul's reentry . . . unless all his prayers to be of service unto his first cousin had been honored? Mayhap—

A free fall followed a sudden release of the stifling compaction, his senses informing him that he was set upon a descent through air that offered no sufficient drag to slow him down. And as he strained to see where he was, his vision left him. Throwing out his arms, he clasped at nothing. Kicking his legs, he encountered nothing. Twisting and turning . . . he came up against nothing.

And in the midst of it all, there was no fear, only rage, as was his nature. Dhunhd.

Having rejected the gift of the Fade, having forsaken the eternity of love and life he had miraculously been given in spite of his earthly actions, he was now being punished for the temerity of attempting to determine his own destiny.

The Omega's den of suffering was to be his infinity—

Without preamble, a stunning impact registered throughout his limbs, his torso, his skull. It was as if he landed flat upon his back on the most unforgiving of stone, but without the bounce that would have characterized such a fall from such a height.

Blackness.

Utter blackness.

A claustrophobic strangulation claimed his windpipe, and he began to pant, his breath, heavy and urgent, echoing close unto his ears . . . what madness was this? He seemed to be in an enclosed space. A tight-quartered, clearly defined space.

Placing his hands up—

Sahvage could not bring them unto his chest. There wasnae room for him to bend his elbows, and his knuckles rapped against something hollow.

Wood. Directly above him.

Kicking his feet, he encountered the same down at the terminal of his body. And spreading his arms a-width, he learned the limits of his confines, so narrow and contouring of the shape of his corporeal form.

His conscious intellect informed him of his location.

And even as his mind rejected the conclusion, and his temper rose to unsustainable levels, it was as yet inescapable.

Could he be in a coffin?

CHAPTER NINETEEN

As Nate stared at the female he had spent all day thinking about, he felt suspended in thin air even though his feet were on the ground. She was just as he remembered, her pale hair streaming out from under the hood that covered her head, her hands hidden in the folds of her long, loose black coat. And as with before, she was off to the side, standing alone.

"Hi," he said, lifting his hand.

When she took a step back, he put both his palms out. "I won't hurt you, I promise."

She didn't move away any farther, but she looked behind herself as if to be reassured that the coast was clear for a dash. Or a dematerialize.

"I'm Nate." He pointed to his chest—and then felt lame. Like there was anyone else around making intros? "Are you . . . did you come back to see this again?"

She glanced at the divot in the earth.

"It was amazing, right? Who'd have thought—a meteor. Out here?"

Nate cleared his throat and wanted to get closer to her. But he stayed where he was, and like an idiot, even though they were only six or seven feet apart, he spoke more loudly. You know, just to make sure she heard him.

Over the din of the absolutely quiet, no-sound-anywhere forest.

God, he was an *idiot*.

"My buddy Shuli and I were working." He thumbed over his shoulder. "We're helping renovate a house over there, across the field. Anyway, we saw the flash of light in the sky. Did you see the flash? It was amazing. So . . . ah, where are you from?"

Great. Next thing you knew, he'd be asking if she came here often. What her major was, even though they were vampires, not human. Whether she'd like a drink, in spite of a total absence of bartenders, liquor, or glasses anywhere near them.

Such game. And he didn't even like alcohol.

"I live in town. With my parents." He tacked that second part on to make himself seem more approachable. "Do you live with yours?"

As opposed to a mate. Who was, like, big as Murhder and as possessive as a guard dog. Who would likely tear Nate limb from limb with his teeth and bury the pieces in his yard.

"My mom's a scientist. My dad's—" No, wait, he wasn't going to talk about the Black Dagger Brotherhood. "He's a fighter for the . . ." No, he shouldn't mention the King. "He takes care of people."

The female's head turned to the impact pit again, and he got a good look at her profile. It was . . . well, as perfect as the front view of her face was. Her features were fine and well-balanced, her eyes set a little on the deep side, her mouth a wisp of pink between her nose and her chin. There was a shriveled brown leaf in the ends of her hair, a leftover from what had fallen in the autumn, and he was so tempted to go over and pick it out of such delicate entrapment. Put it in his pocket. Keep it safe throughout his shift.

Hide it in his bedside table when he got home. Hide it forever.

Something told him he was going to want proof that he'd actually stood with her.

"Last night, I was going to talk to you." Jesus, he sounded pathetic. "I wanted to say hi. But I didn't think—well, there were a lot of people around."

She continued to stay silent, but as her eyes returned to him, they didn't leave—and he wasn't sure whether that was a good or a bad thing. She looked wary and weary.

And that was when he saw the dirt on the folds of her cape-like thing. And noticed how pale she was.

Nate narrowed his eyes. "Did you spend the day out here?"

She took another step back.

He shook his head. "I'm not judging. I just . . . it's not real safe. From the sun. From other things." He gave her a chance to say something. "Look, is there someone I can call for you?"

When he took out his phone, she put some more distance between them, the fallen pine needles rustling under her feet—which he could not see, and he hoped had shoes to cover their soles.

"Please," he said. "Just let me help you. I can call for help. Who can I call for you?"

"*I am lost.*"

"I'm sorry?"

"*I am lost.*"

He pointed to his ear. "I'm sorry, I, ah, I can't understand what language you're speaking. Can you—of course you don't speak English or you'd be speaking English." He talked slower—which was frickin' stupid. "I'm calling someone who can help."

With a hand that was kind of unsteady, he pulled a number out of his contacts and put things on speakerphone. "Just give me a minute. She's a good female, she can help—"

Two rings in, and from out of the tinny speaker, Mary, the *shellan* of the Black Dagger Brother Rhage, said, "Nate! How nice to hear from you. You all are doing such great work out at Luchas House. We're moving the rest of the furniture in tonight—"

"Mrs. Mary, I have a problem." He locked eyes with the hooded female and prayed—*prayed*—that she stayed where she was. "I'm here with a . . . friend . . . and she isn't speaking a language I can understand. She needs . . . a friend. Can you help me help her?"

There was only the slightest of pauses, proof positive that Mrs. Mary was the right person to call. "Okay, Nate. First of all, are you two in a safe place? Do you want me to send someone to you?"

He pictured the likes of the Brother Vishous showing up. Qhuinn. Shit—*Zsadist.* "No, no, we're perfectly safe. We're just in the forest by Luchas House. Where the meteor landed."

"Good. Can you put her on?"

"Here," he said, holding out the phone toward the female. When she just stared in confusion at what was in his palm, he felt like further assurances were necessary. "Don't worry. She's a professional. You can trust her."

Yeah, like any of that was going to help if she didn't speak English. *Shit.*

✦   ✦   ✦

"So you were telling me about this Book thing."

Over at Tallah's kitchen counter, Mae closed her eyes and swore to herself that the coffee she was pouring was going to stay in its ceramic delivery device. She was *not* going to toss it across the table at the male who'd put in his order like he was at a 24-hour diner.

How they'd managed to make it downstairs in one piece was a miracle of sorts. And not because they were being chased by anything.

Oil and water. They were oil and water together.

"Well?" Sahvage prompted as he put his leather jacket over the weapons he'd taken off his torso. Leaning back in his chair, he regarded her with a steady stare.

"I wasn't talking about the Book," she said as she carried the mug across to him.

"Thanks for this." He smiled as he palmed what she'd made for him. "It's perfect."

"You haven't tried it yet."

"You made it for me. That's all perfection requires."

With a frown, she sat on the other side of the table. "Don't do that."

"Do what."

"Try to be charming." She rubbed her aching eyes and wondered whether there was any Motrin in her purse. "It doesn't work."

"I've never been charming."

"Well, what do you know. We're going to put self-awareness on your short list of positive attributes."

"Someday, you're going to like me." There was a *siiiipp*ing sound. Then an *ahhhhhh*. "See? I told you this is perfect. Now talk to me about the Book. And yes, I'll stop being a smartass."

"Not possible."

"Give me a chance." Sahvage grew serious. "I want to know whatever you do about it."

As the fighter went silent and seemed prepared to wait, Mae felt herself recede into her mind—but it was not back to her brother, to that ice-cube-filled tub, to the terrible mission she'd set herself on. Instead, she was once again out on the front porch of this previously peaceful cottage, shooting a heavy gun that, Sahvage was right, she couldn't have held steady on her own.

"I didn't have two hands," she muttered. "With two hands, I could have done it."

"What?" he said. "Oh, you're thinking about my Glock. Yeah, it's a big one."

Mae narrowed her eyes. "You can stop with the double entendres. Anytime."

"You're going there, not me." He shifted to the side and put the gun on the table between them. "The name's right there on the weapon."

"What is it about males wanting to show off their guns."

"You can't give me an opening like that—"

"What did I say about the entendres—"

"You mean these guns?" he said as he curled up two huge biceps. "Oh, and now she shoots me the death glare. Like anyone wouldn't flex on that stage."

As Mae tried to not smile, she watched him tilt and reholster the weapon—and when she noticed how muscular his shoulders were under that skintight t-shirt of his, she couldn't stay sitting. Up on her feet again, she took the two teacups with her and Tallah's loads of cold Earl Grey to the sink. Then she came back for the sugar pot and the creamer pitcher. As well as the crushed lemon carcass.

"You take vinegar with your tea?" He picked up the bottle and inspected the label. "Strange palate."

"I'll take that."

When she went to grab the stuff from him, he didn't let go. "Talk to me, Mae. I know you don't like me and you sure as hell don't appreciate me barging in here. But that guy with the Mohawk is right. I owe you my life—and I may be a piece of shit, but I do have a code of honor. Besides, you've just seen how handy I am in a fight, haven't you."

Now he released his hold. He didn't stop staring up at her, though.

So as she turned away and put the vinegar back in the cupboard, she could feel his eyes on her.

"I promise to be good," he murmured. Then he chuckled. "Fine, I promise to be better. And make it last this time."

Leaning back against the countertop, Mae considered her options. Which didn't seem to include kicking him out of the house—and not just because she couldn't possibly have carried him to the door.

With a sense of defeat, she returned to the chair she'd been in. Putting her hands on the table, she linked her fingers and took a deep breath.

"Whatever it is," he said, "I'm going to believe you."

"What an odd thing to say."

She glanced at him. He was looming there in that seat, his huge body overflowing the chair, the table . . . the cottage. Yet he was still, and silent. Ready to hear her out.

"But this is all so crazy." Mae shook her head. "Really nuts."

"Life is crazy. The foolish thing is thinking it isn't."

"If you had to take a guess, what was that shadow thing outside?"

"Tell me about the Book. I have a feeling that's going to answer your question—and it's what you believe as well, don't you."

"Stop reading my mind."

"I'm not mind-reading." More with the sipping. "It's intuition."

"Isn't that for females?"

"Traditional sex roles are sexist."

Mae didn't want to laugh. So she covered her mouth with her hand to muffle the sound, hide the expression.

"You should do that more often," he said softly.

Flushing, Mae smoothed the flyaways from her face. Funny. Even though her clothes were on right and her hair still in a ponytail, she felt completely disheveled. Like someone had put her in a wind tunnel.

"I haven't had much cause to laugh lately," she heard herself say.

"Talk to me."

Mae's eyes went to the empty silver dish, nothing but the residue of her blood and the other ingredients of the spell left. "I've lost a lot of loved ones recently. And I'm not going to lose another."

"Who died. Or is dying." When she didn't reply, he shrugged. "Let me guess. Prayers haven't been working—or you don't feel like they go far enough. So you're taking things into your own hands."

"Do you believe in magic?"

When he didn't answer, she lifted her eyes to his. He was staring at her with a remote expression.

"As a matter of fact, I do," he said softly.

Mae had to look away—on account of a second warm flush that went up her throat and into her face. But surely she was reading . . . everything . . . wrong. A male like him? He was going to go for one of those fight-club women or females, the ones who belonged in the wait line with the others at the parking garage, the ones with the hips and the boobs and the outfits to show those kinds of assets off.

"What would you do to keep someone you loved alive?" she asked to get herself back on track.

No hesitation: "I'd kill anybody. Anything."

She eyed his jacket, and thought of what was underneath it. "I believe that. But I'm not talking about defending them. What if you could . . . make them live again? What if you had the ability to bring them back, change destiny, take fate into your own hands. Take control of a wrong result."

There was a long pause, and then his eyes left her. "You're talking about resurrection."

"See," she said. "I told you it's crazy."

"It's not crazy." His obsidian stare returned to hers. "Unbelievable, maybe, but not crazy."

"Aren't those the same thing?"

"What exactly are we talking about here, Mae."

It was a while before she could answer, before she could choose the right words. And then she lied. "Tallah is all I have left. She's coming to the end of her life. I can't let her die. I just . . . you have to understand. I have no one else in this world, and I'm not losing her, too."

Mae burst up from the chair again. Given that there was nothing left of the tea to tidy, no reason other than her anxiety to move around, she reached across to the silver dish. Picking it up, she went to the sink and rinsed the basin off.

"Sometimes you have to let people go," Sahvage said softly.

She glanced back at him. "Well, I don't want to."

"And you think this Book is your answer. She lives forever after you do what? Wave a wand over her forehead?"

"That's not funny."

"It wasn't intended to be. What's in the Book."

As Mae didn't have a solid answer for that, the flimsiness of her plan, or solution, seemed rickety to a house-of-cards degree.

"It's going to tell me what to do. To save her."

"Spells, huh." He took another drink from the mug. "God, I haven't heard of shit like this since the Old Country. And as for the immortality stuff, be careful what you wish for. Sometimes, you actually get it."

"Exactly. I don't want her to die and she'll be alive."

"People aren't supposed to live forever."

"I don't care."

He laughed in a short rush. "You know, I have a lot of respect for your kind of arrogant aggression. And on that note, how're you going to find this Book?"

Pulling a dish towel free of the stove handle, she dried the little silver basin. "We already did what you're supposed to do."

"Which is?" He held up his forefinger. "Wait, let me guess. Go to a bare-knuckle fight and try to get a guy killed by distracting him as a blood sacrifice. Great plan, and it's worked *so* well."

"You were going to murder that human."

"No, I wasn't." After a moment, he made a *meh* motion with his free hand. "Okay, fine, maybe I was. But it wasn't murder. He asked for it, and I've always said that other people's stupid decisions are not my problem. Now what did you do to get the Book. Search Amazon under *Hocus-Pocus for Dummies?*"

"It was a summoning spell. And I'm quite intelligent, thank you very much."

Although she felt like she hadn't been winning many IQ prizes lately.

His eyes narrowed. "So the Book is here."

"Not yet."

"When did you do the spell?"

"Right before . . ." She cleared her throat. "Right before you came."

There was a period of silence. Then he muttered, "And I'll say it again—you wonder why that shadow showed up?"

Actually, she didn't. "I think we should double-check your wounds. Just make sure you're okay."

"Changing the subject, are we."

"Not at all."

Sahvage put his mug to his lips and tilted his head back, finishing the coffee. When he set the empty down on the table, he smiled at her in that way he did—one side of his mouth lifting up, a knowing look in those glossy black eyes.

Like he had all the answers and every time he opened his piehole was an opportunity to man-splain things.

"FYI, I know what you're doing," he said.

Bingo. "What's that. And should I take notes, or is this going to be another statement of the obvious—"

"As you hear yourself talk, you realize how insane you're behaving, but your heart isn't going to let it rest, so you have to divert things. It's fine. We can look at my injuries again. But I don't think we should ignore what's actually happening here."

"You don't know a damn thing about me."

"You're right. I'm totally off base. So by all means, let's check me out because I'm the one who needs help."

With that happy little pronouncement, Sahvage took the ends of his shirt and did not look away as he slowly raised the damn thing . . . revealing that tattoo and all the musculature under his inked skin. As he tossed what had covered his torso aside, he resettled back in the chair like he was fully naked. Like he was absolutely confident in his body. Like he was very aware she couldn't not notice what he was showing her.

And respond to it.

FFS, with his chest now bare, he seemed to be even larger, and Mae swallowed through a tight throat. But not because she was afraid.

No, fear wasn't the problem. Not even close.

"Come tend to my wounds," he said in a low murmur. "And by the way, you can touch me anywhere. You know, for clinical purposes. Far be it from me to deny any assessments as to my health and overall well-being."

Mae blinked. Then recovered. "You are an ass."

"Yeah, I know." He leaned in and lowered his lids. "But you want me anyway."

CHAPTER TWENTY

Deep in the heart of downtown, Detective Erika Saunders pulled her unmarked over to the side of an alley that ran between two apartment buildings. Putting things in park, her headlights shed a whole lot of lookey-lookey on a boxy black SUV that was snuggled up close to a dumpster. Over to the left, there were a couple of uniformed officers milling around, and a patrol car was blocking the entrance off Trade. No news crews.

That was not going to last.

Getting out, she snapped on nitrile gloves and palmed her flashlight. The unis fell silent as she approached, and she gave them a nod as she zeroed in on the SUV's driver's-side door.

"When was this called in?" she said as she trained the beam inside the vehicle—or tried to. The windows were blacked out.

Leaning around to the hood, without touching the side of the vehicle, she pointed her flashlight in through the front windshield—

Fuck.

She didn't even hear what the reply to her question was from the officers. She was too caught up in the man and the woman who were sitting side by side in the front seats. The pair were prime-of-life candidates, although the whole "life" part of that descriptor was no longer applicable. And what do you know, the bodies had massive wounds in the centers of their chests, their clothes stained with blood, their laps soup bowls for all the congealing plasma.

Erika moved in closer to the safety glass, so she could see further into the vehicle. In between the seats, on the padded console, their hands were linked, the dead fingers intermingled. And up on the headrests, they were looking at other, their unseeing eyes focused on the space between their waxy, gray faces.

Erika swept the flashlight around. The young man was shirtless, a collection of tattoos randomly inked on his torso and down his arms, like someone had thrown a book of illustrations at his skin. He was muscular but thin, a wiry guy who was probably just around six feet. He reminded her of Pete Davidson. Next to him, the woman was voluptuous in her bustier, with some really good hair. Gold bamboo earrings. Nose piercing. Tattoos, but not as dense as the guy's and much more curvilinear.

They looked like they belonged together, sexy, into the club scene. Probably dabbled in drugs, but not too often given their otherwise state of good health.

"My killer's certainly got a type," Erika said as she went to open the car door. "Who called this in?"

"Jogger," one of the officers said from behind her.

The air that was released was dense, smelling like cologne, perfume, blood, and fecal matter.

Erika inspected the hole in the guy's sternum. Then she touched his cold neck with the fingertips of her gloved hand. No pulse. No shit. "And when was this called in again?"

"About twenty-five minutes ago. Maybe thirty."

"They've been here a while."

"Expensive ride. I'm surprised it didn't get stripped."

Easing back, Erika inspected the vehicle. "Mercedes. Blacked-out rims, blacked-out windows. I wouldn't have messed with it, either, for fear of which street dealer owned it—oh, and what do we have here."

A Louis Vuitton wallet had fallen out of the guy's pocket and was perched on the lip between the lower part of the doorjamb and the base of the driver's seat. Reaching in, she took the billfold out, and handled it carefully. Opening the front flap, she slid free a driver's license.

"Ralph Anthony DeMellio." Address was in the Italian part of Caldwell. "Twenty-two. So damned young."

She pictured the couple from the Commodore. And the two other pairs who had been killed similarly. All of the victims had been around this age, in their twenties. And all of them were part of the trendy, wealthy scene. And all of them had been loved up.

"He's finding them in clubs," she murmured as she slid the license back into its slot. "Maybe for sex. Or maybe that's where they cross his path and get ID'd as prey. Then he follows them home or somewhere quiet . . ."

She glanced around the alley. In this part of downtown, things were pretty well kept and crime was low. So there were going to be security cameras that were operational—and there were also a lot of apartment windows, although most of them had shades or blinds down.

While she was starting her mental follow-up list, a gray Crown Vic came on scene, and as the uniformed officers put their arms up to shield their eyes, its headlights were turned off. After the unmarked rolled to a stop, all kinds of stereotypical FBI got out: Gray suit and a black tie. Buzz cut. 1950s jawline.

Special Agent Deiondre Delorean was a zero-body-fat, straight-shouldered man with a degree from Howard and a military intelligence background that was still very much in his foreground.

He immediately took a look inside the SUV. "Another one."

"I'd say three couple's a charm, but we're up to four now."

"That you know about."

"Point taken." She showed him the driver's license. "I want to be the one who speaks with the parents. They've been waiting for him to come home all day long. You're welcome to ride with me, but I'm going to do the talking."

"And here I thought your reputation might be overexaggerated." Deiondre inspected the ID and then leveled a stare at her. "I've done family informing a few times myself, you know."

"And I've been on the receiving end of that horrible conversation with authorities. Have you?"

His eyes grew remote. "I'm sorry about your family."

"It was fourteen years ago. I'm over it. And guess you've done your homework."

"FBI, remember."

On the periphery, the two unis started looking at their shoes, like Mom and Dad were fighting. But if Erika worried about how people felt around her, her days would be eight hours longer and her temper two yards shorter.

"And how do you know his parents are waiting for him?" Deiondre asked.

"Address is in the Jersey Gardens neighborhood. That's not where young people live on their own. It's where older people live with their adult children in the basement. I'll bet his parents probably thought Ralph was at the girlfriend's house all day and that's why they haven't heard from him. But they're starting to worry now that it's been over twelve hours since they've talked to him."

Deiondre leaned into the car. "Same M.O. But maybe this pair are just a one-night stand and they were posed."

"The other three couples were serious about each other, and our investigation is going to show the same here. My killer goes for people in love."

Putting the wallet back where she'd found it on the floorboard, she went around the rear with her flashlight and then proceeded down the opposite side of the SUV, squeezing in between it and the sweaty wall of the taller of the apartment buildings. No scratches on the glossy paint job. No bumper stickers, parking lot passes, or even a dealer frame on the new-car temporary plate.

There wasn't enough room to open the passenger-side door, so she exited the narrow space and came out around the front grille.

Deiondre had his cell phone up to his ear, and she had a thought that he was bringing in federal crime scene people.

Back next to Ralph DeMellio's body, Erika stretched her arm under the steering wheel, making sure not to brush up against anything. The ignition button was on the far side of the steering column, and she had to poke around for it. When her fingers finally found the circular button, she pressed the thing.

A no-key warning flashed on the dash.

Carefully extricating herself, she shook her head. "They took the key."

"What was that?" Deiondre asked as he ended his call.

"They left the car unlocked and took the key." She opened the backseat door and trained her flashlight in. "Well, would you look at this."

"You got a weapon?"

Deiondre tilted in next to her—and joined her in checking out all the neat-as-a-pin: No litter in the foot wells, no errant clothing wads or running shoes. No gym bag.

Erika breathed in deep. "Smells like new car. Or at least new to him. He must have just bought this vehicle—real pride-and-joy stuff."

"We're going to his parents' house together."

Erika stepped back and stared at the SUV. "I'm going to catch this motherfucker. I'm going to nail him to the fucking wall before he does this again."

◆　　◆　　◆

Nate prayed like hell that Mrs. Mary drove to Luchas House fast and then flat-out ran across that field to the forest. As she couldn't dematerialize, it was going to be twenty minutes. Or more. Especially if she followed the speed limit, and he had a feeling she would.

"It could be twenty minutes," he said to the female. "Before she comes."

Please don't leave—

Without warning, the female jumped and stumbled back, putting her hands up to shield herself. On a surge of protection, Nate wrenched around—

Instead of panicking—or going on the attack, which was actually his first instinct—he got a good shot of relief. And the Black Dagger Brother who had materialized into the clearing was actually not much of a surprise, even if his imposing presence was a thing.

"Rhage," Nate said. And then he put his palms out to reassure the female. "Don't worry, he's with me. I'm with him. I mean—"

The Brother smiled at her and raised his hands. "*Worry not. I am a friend.*"

The female tilted her head. "*How do I know that? You are armed.*"

"*Not against you. And never against him.*"

As they threw out unfamiliar syllables, Nate went back and forth, playing a what-are-they-saying tennis match as they spoke in that language. And though he had no idea what they were talking about, he did notice that their accents were the same—and most importantly, the female wasn't leaving and she was less scared.

So hey, as far as he was concerned, the two could pull up some chairs and gab all night long.

Rhage switched to English. "My *shellan* is coming. I'm here to make sure you're safe—and he's safe."

"Is he your son—" The female clapped her mouth shut.

Nate frowned. "You could understand me all along?" As she looked away, he glanced at Rhage—as if the Brother could explain why she'd fronted. "The whole time?"

"I did not know . . . what to do," she whispered.

"It's okay. It's all right." Nate cleared his throat. "I'm just glad—well, you can trust Mrs. Mary. And the Brother Rhage."

Her eyes widened at the fighter. "You are a member of the Black Dagger Brotherhood?"

Rhage opened his leather jacket and flashed the pair of daggers that were strapped, handles down, to his huge chest. "I am."

The female exhaled. *Thanks be to the Scribe Virgin.*

"Listen," Rhage said, "if you're okay with it, I'd like to suggest we head over thataway. We have a house there. We've got some food and drink to offer you, and it's totally safe."

Nate frowned. "But there are a lot of workmen on-site—"

"Not when I tell them to go, there won't be. Can you walk her back to Luchas House?"

Nate blinked. And then flushed.

"Oh, yes, I can, yes, I will—" He locked his molars shut. "I mean, if it's all right with her? Or, you. I mean."

Shit.

The female looked back and forth between the two of them. "Yes, of course it is, but I do not want to cause trouble—"

"It's no trouble," Nate interjected.

"None at all." Rhage clapped his palms together. "I'm going to go clear the house. Nate, take care of her, will you?"

The urge to stand at attention and salute was nearly irresistible. And his backup to that ridiculousness was the idea of offering the female his arm, like he was somebody special. Like he could do anything to defend her.

As he settled for nodding at the Brother, Rhage gave them a wave and dematerialized—which meant . . . they were alone again.

"It's over there," Nate said as he pointed through the trees to the meadow and the distant lights of the house. As if there were another destination option?

The female nodded and came closer to him—and he was so stunned to see her move and scent her up close that he stood where he was like his boots had been nailed to the ground. Meanwhile, she passed him by—and then stopped and looked back.

"Sorry." He rubbed his hair. "I mean, here I come."

Together, they walked out of the trees and into the field. And that was when she stopped again. As she scanned the open area, she seemed so solitary. So sad.

If she had somewhere else to go, someone who she could trust, she wouldn't be here, he thought. Anybody would connect with a family member or a friend if they had one—

As she went to walk forward again, her foot caught on a tangle of dead weeds, and he reached out for her arm to make sure she didn't fall.

"Careful," he said as he caught her balance and promptly let her go.

With hands that shook, she pulled her hood up higher on her blond hair. "Forgive me."

"Oh, there's nothing to apologize for. Everyone trips. I—ah, what did you say your name was?"

She hadn't, actually. But he didn't want to come across as demanding.

And when the sounds of their feet *schmuck*ing through pockets of mud were the only thing that came back in reply, he felt like maybe he had been.

They were halfway to Luchas House when her voice, quiet and heavily accented, drifted across to him. "Elyn. Please call me Elyn."

"That's beautiful—" He cleared his throat. "I mean, wow."

He took a test glance at her in case she was staring at him like he was a creeper, but she wasn't. She was clearly deep in thought, her brows down over her eyes, even as she didn't appear to be focused on anything specific in front of her. And as they fell silent again, Nate's brain hot-fired to find conversation . . . except all he got were no-go's—and the fact that he couldn't come up with anything even remotely normal to say made him realize what a frickin' mutant he was.

But like he'd been socialized in that lab? By anything other than the white coats who'd been experimenting on him and that television they'd let him watch?

Lost in bad things, he came out of his trance as they arrived at the split-rail fence. He had a thought about lifting the top one off for her, but she slipped through the beams quick as a whistle and waited on the other side for him.

"This is a nice farmhouse, huh," he mumbled. Because he had to say something or he was going to explode. "I'm working on it—well, worked on it. We're basically done with the renovations."

As he led her around to the front walkway, he thought of her accent. It was really fancy, like his dad's. Like Rhage's. She probably wasn't going to be impressed with a blue-collar job like the one he'd been doing. And as all that he did not have to offer females in general, and her specifically, crashed against the shores of his self-esteem, he got as quiet as she was.

Yup, this was not how his fantasies had played things out. Which was proof positive you shouldn't let wishful thinking get in the way of reality. In his daydreams? He'd found her out by that pit and invited her for a meal at that 24-hour diner he and Shuli hit after work sometimes. Over hamburgers and slices of apple pie, they talked about everything and nothing at all until right before it became too dangerous to stay out—and just before the sun rose, he took her back to her parents' house, where she gave him her number and told him to call during the day.

It was all the start of a beautiful romance . . . that culminated in, one week to the hour of their first date, him kissing her. Softly. While they stood on her back doorstep.

And because it was all just a fantasy, that kiss happened to be, in spite of him having absolutely no idea what he was doing, totally perfect for the both of them—

"Hi, you guys!"

As Mrs. Mary greeted them from the front door of the farmhouse, she waved and stepped out into the pool of warm illumination thrown by an exterior coach light. The good news was that Rhage's female was exactly what anyone would want to see if they were looking for a safe haven: Her face was open and her smile sincere—which made her seem like somebody who'd be good at giving hugs.

No false advertising there.

Abruptly, people started talking. Mary. Rhage. And one of the social workers, Rhym, who also joined the group. Elyn stayed mostly silent, but she didn't seem frightened.

Nate took a step back. Through the open doorway, he saw that furniture had been arranged in the living room, and, off in the distance, the kitchen as well. Everything looked cozy. Safe.

The social worker went inside. Rhage went inside. Mary said something and indicated the way in.

Elyn nodded and started for the threshold.

As Nate watched her go, he knew he wasn't going to see her again. After he finished painting the inside of the garage? He'd be moved on to a different project by his supervisor, and any possible connection between them would disappear.

He wasn't going to have a chance to say goodbye. At least not in the way he wanted.

Not in the way where he got her phone number. Or she got his.

With a ringing pain in his chest, he thought it was weird to mourn the loss of someone he didn't even know—

Elyn hesitated and then looked over her shoulder at him. "Will you not come in?"

"Oh, you're in good hands now."

"Please. I'm scared."

Staring into her wide silver eyes, Nate felt a flush go through his entire body. After which he took a deep breath and puffed up his chest.

"I won't leave until you tell me to go," he said as he joined her.

CHAPTER TWENTY-ONE

S o are you going to examine my wounds? Or you can just stare at me like that. Both are fine."

As Sahvage eased back in the old wooden chair, there was a creaking under him, the spindly legs accommodating his weight with a lack of confidence. But if he ended up on the floor? Well, that was good with him. This female would offer him a hand up—because it was in her nature to help.

And maybe he could pull her on top of him.

"I am not staring at you like anything," she snapped. "I'm worried about your health."

"And I'm glad you are. My point is, worry about me anywhere you like with your hands."

"Oh, for heaven's sake," she muttered as she bent over his chest.

Sahvage focused on her face, with its frowning brows and laser-sharp eyes. He had a thought that if he just sat forward a little—not much at all—he could kiss her.

And finding out how her mouth tasted seemed like a very good use of his time.

"You know . . . these don't look right."

Or at least that's what he thought she said. His attention was elsewhere—and as shades of her at his throat came back to him, his hips rolled inside his combat pants and the urgency in between his thighs got thicker. Especially as he imagined her hair free and spilling over his naked chest—

Her fingertips traced a stripe of raised skin that ran from his collarbone all the way down to his abs.

When he hissed, she looked worried. "I'm sorry, I don't mean to hurt you."

Yeah, pain was not the reason I made that sound, Sahvage thought.

Although he was beginning to hurt from wanting her. Which was what happened when you noticed a female, then took your shirt off in front of her . . . and she touched your skin. Anywhere.

Backing off, she stared down at him. "Why in the world did you get that tattoo all over yourself." Before he could respond, she put her hand out. "I'm sorry—that's none of my business—"

"I want my enemies to know what's coming for them when they see me."

As he braced himself for another sanctimonious lecture on not killing things, he had to stop himself from grinning at her. And meanwhile, she was so focused on his chest, he was wondering if she would ever look away from him.

Fine with him if she didn't—and it was a letdown when she shook herself back to attention.

"So this is all about advertising?" she said dryly. "Couldn't you just pin a 'Hello, My Name Is Badass' on your shirt?"

"I never wear a shirt when I fight. And I would argue that name tags are antithetical to badassery."

"If you ask me, I'd think the stealth approach is better."

"Whatever you like."

"I don't like."

"My tattoo? Really? Then why do you keep staring at it?"

"I'm not looking at the ink—"

As she went to turn away, Sahvage caught her hand. "So what are you looking at?"

When their eyes met, there was a sizzling moment of stillness, and he was surprised that the pair of them didn't spontaneously combust. But she wasn't having it—and he let her pull out of his hold.

"Oh, wait, my injuries, right?" he drawled. "You were just staring at my owies. And you don't like that I got injured."

"Owies." She crossed her arms over her chest. "What are you, five years old? And you need a doctor."

"I want a nurse."

The female put her hands on her hips. "Stop it."

"Okay."

Cursing under her breath, she glanced around like she was searching for something, anything to do—and ended up reaching across to a paring knife that had been left out with that strange collection of salad dressing supplies and teacups.

At the rate she was going, she was going to clear the table sometime next week. Which was kind of adorable.

"You're normally not that agreeable," she muttered. "Are you feeling faint?"

"When you're looking at my body, yeah, I get light-headed. But do you really want me to talk about where the blood goes—"

"Ow!"

The knife fell from her hand, clattering to the floor as she made a fist and clutched her arm to her chest.

Sahvage bolted upright. "Let me see—"

"I'm fine—"

This time, he didn't let her go. And she didn't fight him as he opened her closed-tight hand.

She'd sliced her finger—and bright red blood was welling along the surgical-worthy cut.

Licking his lips—because how could he not?—Sahvage looked up into her eyes. She wasn't staring at the cut. Not at all.

Her attention was on his mouth.

"Let me take care of it," he whispered. "Return the favor. You know, just what you did for me last night—and no further."

She seemed caught, straddling the yes and the no, torn between what she wanted and what she knew was good for her. And all the while, the blood was forming a slow river that eased down her forefinger, circling 'round.

Sahvage ground his molars. "I'm going to wait until you tell me yes. I take lives against the will, but never females."

Time stretched out, lengthening like a cord with give in it, becoming longer and longer. And in the electric quiet between them, he became acutely aware of her breathing. It was getting deeper. And that pulse at her throat? It was getting faster.

"I won't hurt you," he vowed.

"Yes, you will."

She took her hand from him and turned away. Over at the sink, she ran water and put her finger under the rush with a gasp. Meanwhile, he stayed right where he was, a frown yanking his brows together.

When she cut the faucet and snapped a paper towel out of a roll, he said, "What the hell kind of male do you think I am?"

Pivoting back to him, she wrapped the wound up. "You're a killer. Right? You seem to have to prove that not only to me but to everybody you meet. And killers hurt people."

"You think you're in danger around me. Seriously."

"If life has taught me anything, it's that I am not due any special exceptions. So yes, I think you are dangerous to me."

He pointed to the front of the house. "I saved your fucking life out there."

"Well, then we're even, aren't we. And you can leave with a free conscience."

Sahvage looked at the shirt he'd taken off. Snatching the thing back, he pulled it over his head and got to his feet. As he loomed across the kitchen at the female, she met him right in the eye, not giving an inch.

"You're going to die," he said baldly. "Maybe with me around, but definitely without me. What's out there? You don't know where it went, and it's stupid to assume that any kind of grave was involved. But I can't make you save yourself or that old female downstairs."

"Thank you."

"Excuse me?"

"For the prognostication. Are you done, or do you want to try your hand at lottery numbers? Maybe who's going to win the Super Bowl next year?"

"Have fun picking out a matched set of coffins. God knows you always make the right decisions, don't you."

On that note, he picked up his jacket and his weapons, and walked to the front door. Moving the massive piece of oak furniture aside, he let himself out.

Pity there wasn't someone in the cottage strong enough to put the barricade back. But as that female had so often pointed out to him . . . not his problem.

◆   ◆   ◆

Mae watched Sahvage disappear through the front door. He didn't slam the thing shut. He didn't have to.

When she was sure that he was gone, she rushed across to the parlor and threw the copper lock into place. Then she put her back against the stout panels of the hutch and tried to shove it into the door. When all she got was a lot of slipping shoes and hard breathing, she clamped her mouth closed on the curses in her throat—

A groan from the floorboards overhead had her whipping her attention to the ceiling.

Heart pounding in her ears, she swallowed hard and wondered where she had left her mace. Then she remembered she'd emptied the canister trying to gas that . . . whatever it was.

Staring at the ceiling, she heard nothing further. No doubt the old cottage was just reacting to the night's drop in temperature—

Mae jumped and looked to the left. Was that something moving in between the legs of a side table?

Rubbing her eyes, she thought of Rhoger and melting ice.

And Tallah downstairs, all but passed out from exhaustion.

"We're fine. This is all fine."

Unable to stay still, she went into the kitchen—and stalled out. Not for long, though. Seized by an urgency utterly unrelated to the reality that she had all but kicked out her best shot at fighting anything that might show up at the cottage, she grabbed a bucket from under the sink and filled it full of hot soapy water. There was only a single sponge in the house, and it was going to have to take one for the team.

Getting down on her knees, she scrubbed the grimy square where the fridge had been. And scrubbed. And scrubbed.

Her arm went numb, her shoulder joint burned, her palms and fingers got raw.

But goddamn it, when she was finished? That floor sparkled.

Of course, the bright, sunshiny square made the rest of the old linoleum look like it had been laid back before the Punic Wars. And she was out of gas. Out of sponge, too.

Inspecting the thing's frayed corners and the nearly black bed, she decided it looked like she felt: all used up, worn down, shredded.

Glancing at the clock on the wall, she did some math. Then she measured the refrigerator that blocked the back door and all the shutters that were in place—

"Shoot. Extension cord."

It took some rifling around for her to find a three-pronged, mudbrown, ancient version of one, and as she plugged it in, she hoped it wasn't going to burn the cottage down.

Okay, fine, the kitchen. Whatever.

She was looking around at the counters and the stove, and the misplaced fridge, and the table and chairs—and imagining it all covered in bright orange and yellow flames . . . when something registered in the back of her mind.

Mae frowned and went over to the sink. The silver dish that she and Tallah had used for the summoning spell was all clean and dry, and she picked it up to look at the scalloped ridges that rode down into the belly of the basin.

"What is it?" she asked no one in particular.

Yet something was definitely catching somewhere deep in her consciousness, the tug persistent, but nonspecific. And the harder she tried to divine what it was, the more elusive the preoccupation became.

"Whatever," she muttered as she put the dish back down.

Given all the other things that were clamoring for mental attention and energy, she canceled the useless game of hide-and-seek.

"I have to go."

Okay, who exactly was she talking to, she wondered as she glanced to the basement door. After a moment of indecision, she got a notepad out of a drawer and used the stub of a pencil to write a quick message for Tallah. She left the pad in the center of the table, grabbed her bag—and doubled back to add her cell phone number just in case the elderly female forgot what it was.

As Mae went to leave through the front door, she made sure she had her car key ready, and she said a quick prayer before she—

Ripped open the heavy weight. Spun around and closed it. Relocked things and ran for her Honda.

At the driver's side, her car key refused to find home inside its lock, the metal slip-skipping around the hole. And the longer it took, the more she looked around frantically, all kinds of shadows pulling up from the ground, from the twisted vines, from the trunks of trees, everything coming to attack her—

The key finally went into the slot, and she nearly snapped it off as she cranked things free, fumbled with the handle, and threw herself into the driver's seat. Slamming things shut and locking everything back up, her heart was pounding in her ears as she played the same ring-around-the-rosie with the ignition.

Before anything landed on the hood, punched a hole in the sunroof, and dragged her out by her hair, she managed to start the engine and put the car in drive. Except then she had to throw things into reverse—because for once she hadn't followed her father's very wise advice about being prepared to leave in a hurry. Stomping on the gas, the tires spun up mud and got her nowhere.

"Damn it, damn it, damn it—"

The whole time, she searched the windows and braced for one of those . . . things . . . to come at her, cross the beams of the headlights, tear her door off, grab her, take her to her grave.

But there was nothing.

Nothing moving. Nothing coming for her. Nothing that was out of place.

Easing up on her lead foot, she panted. And then tried to coax the car backward, giving only a little gas—and as the tires finally grabbed, she resisted the urge to Danica Patrick. Inch by inch, or so it seemed, she moved down Tallah's little driveway so she could turn around, all the while keeping her hands locked on the wheel as her eyes bounced between the front windshield and the rearview mirror.

Mae hated the idea of leaving the elderly female alone in the cottage.

But she had no choice. Rhoger needed fresh ice.

And besides, it had been her blood that had gone into that silver dish. Whatever was out there, whatever they'd called out of *Dhunhd*?

It was after her, and no one else.

Tallah would be safe . . . even if Mae was not.

CHAPTER TWENTY-TWO

As a *symphath*, Rehv had never minded dropping drama bombs. When you took a person by surprise or better yet, a whole room full of them got a shot of WTF!?! from something you'd said, you ended up with all kinds of fun emotions roiling around, grids lighting up, people talking over each other.

Chaos. Dissention. Disagreement. All fueled by a delicious under-lying anxiety that proved mortals with hypo-deductive reasoning could get wound at the drop of a hat.

Symphaths fed off that shit. Ate it like cake.

That was not the case right now, however.

Well, okay, yes, the Brotherhood's current raft of buzzy aggression was all on him and his little news flash from that parking garage. But as he sat in one of the silk chairs in the King's study and listened to all his nearest-and-dearest bubble over with aggression, he was not happy about the angst he'd caused.

See? *Symphaths* weren't all bad.

Just mostly. And he was half vampire, thanks to his *mahmen*.

Of course, the first meeting they'd had about the Book thing and

that female had gone okay. Last night, people had kept their cool. Listened. Been content for more information. Now, though, they'd had
nearly twenty-four hours to think about the implications of it all, so this
"simple status update" had turned into Dramaggedon.

". . . all bullshit," someone was saying. "It was just rumors. Fucking
gossip—"

"My *grandmahmen* told me about the magic in the Old Country—
are you calling her a liar? Are you saying my *grandmahmen* is a fucking
liar—"

Oh, great. The only thing worse than someone calling a Brother's
mahmen out was if the offender went up a generation in the bloodline
and tossed his granny on the bonfire of disgrace.

Rehv checked his rose gold Royal Oak. Christ, they'd been in here
for an hour and a half. And with the way things were going? This bunch
of hotheads was going to be trading *rythes* for the rest of the night.

At least Fritz, the mansion's butler, would be happy. That *doggen*
loved to clean blood out of expensive carpets. If the male's gig running
this household full of killers ever went tits-up, he had a future at Stan-
ley Steemer—

Boom!

As Wrath's fist slammed into the great wooden desk, everybody
shut up, but no one jumped in surprise. Frankly, Rehv had been waiting
for the kibosh. He was willing to bet they all had.

"Enough of this bullshit," Wrath ground out while he stroked
George's chin to calm the golden's nerves. "We're done debating
whether magic exists or it doesn't. You want to jerk yourselves off on
that subject—or all over each other's fucking relatives—you can do it on
your own fucking time."

Ah, yes. Nothing like a leader with the interpersonal skills of a
chain saw.

Those black wraparounds swung to V, who was smoking a hand-
rolled by the fireplace. "You haven't found the female yet."

"No, I mean, I tracked the car registration and the address tied to that license plate, but that's just what she fronts to the human world. I checked out the house in question, but there were no vampires anywhere in it. I haven't found anything else on her, but if she and her bloodline haven't volunteered to be in a database, it's going to be needle-and-a-haystack time. But whatever, I'll go deeper, true?"

"That's what he said," someone muttered on reflex.

"When I saw her," Rehv murmured, "she seemed . . . really normal. Way too vanilla for where she came to find me. Hard to imagine what someone like that would want with the Book. Repaint her house? Find a missing Blockbuster videotape from back before the Internet existed?"

"You don't go after something like that unless you're crazy," Butch said.

Rehv nodded. "I read her grid. She's way fucking desperate. But her parents died, like, three years ago, and I don't think she's mated, given how she was with one of the fighters. I sensed a sibling, a brother . . . what's she missing? What does she need so badly that she's willing to roll dice with black magic."

"Most of the time"—V ashed on the hot side of the fender—"if I can see where someone's been, I can figure out where they're headed."

"It just doesn't add up."

"You'd be surprised how many people's insides don't match their outsides."

Somebody from the back piped in, "Does this mean you secretly like to cuddle, V?"

As V flipped off Rhage, conversation re-bubbled, although at a much more reasonable volume level—which wasn't going to last.

And as the Brothers started to get louder again, a voice cut in, "This is a *seriously* dangerous situation. No matter who the female is or what she's using the Book for."

Everyone looked to the study's doors. Another interested party had entered the chat, but with all the hot air in the room, nobody had noticed the arrival.

Lassiter, the fallen angel, was leaning back against the closed doors, arms crossed over a t-shirt that read "BOY MILK" on his pecs. With his zebra-print leggings, his blond-and-black hair spilling down, and all of his gold chains and piercings, he was what David Lee Roth going through a Mr. T phase would have looked like.

"The forces that can be unleashed courtesy of those pages?" Lassiter shrugged. "They're like nothing else on the planet. Real finger-of-God shit. And the problem is going to be, once you release those energies, it's a tiger out of the cage. Who hasn't eaten for a month. There's no reasoning with them, no stopping them."

"Why hasn't this come along before?" Tohr demanded. "I mean, we have stories and rumors from the Old Country. But nothing substantial."

"Balance." Lassiter fiddled with some of his bracelets, winding them around his thick wrist, the links offering up a soft chatter of metal on metal. "There has to be balance in the world, and the Omega was weighty enough on the bad-news side of the scale. He's gone now, though, and destiny has a *horror vacui*. That dark presence has to be replaced with something, and it has been."

"You know," Rhage muttered, "I have to say this again. I was really looking forward to a vacation. Not forever, but, like, twenty-five, maybe fifty years of coasting woulda been great. I mean, I've just started my online encyclopedia of ice cream favors."

"You're doing a virtual *Britannica* of that?" somebody prompted. "How long can it take? Even Baskin-Robbins only has thirty-one kinds."

Rhage shot a hard stare across the peanut gallery. "Baskin-Robbins has over thirteen hundred entries in their flavor profile, you provincial fuck-tart. And I'm talking all ice creams from all makers. I'm going to call it Wiki-licks."

V flicked his hand-rolled into the logs. "You better be careful that URL isn't taken up by someone with a different agenda on their tongue—"

"Focus!" Wrath barked. "Jesus Christ, you people are like Google without any direction. And meanwhile, we've got a problem we don't have any clue how to contain—"

"That's not correct," Lassiter said. "We can lock it down."

As all eyes returned to the angel, he was very fucking serious— and Rehv had a thought that as annoying as Lassiter could be when he was normal-nighting it, the flip side of the jokey-jokey was so much worse.

And frightening, even to a *symphath*: Lassiter had access to things no one else in the room did, and some of that shit made the Omega look like nothing worse than a two-year-old in a temper tantrum.

"You have what you need under this roof," the angel announced.

"We're going to get Rhage to eat the Book?" someone chimed in.

Hollywood raised his dagger hand. "I just need the right condiment and I'll choke it down somehow. I swear, I can do it."

"I vote we light the angel on fire and catapult him at the damn thing," V countered. "And I volunteer to toss that match."

"What weapon do we have that we're not seeing?" the King demanded.

"Follow me." Lassiter opened the study doors and walked out.

To his credit, V was the first one to get with the follow-the-leader shit. "I'm not saying I like him," he said as he marched for the stairs. "But I'll use any weapon we've got. Even if he's the asshole putting it in our hands."

Rehv stood up with the rest of the fighters and the King. And as they all filed out of the study and descended for the foyer, he felt like he was in school and going on a field trip.

Assuming school was a martial arts academy and the student body was made up of kids who could deadlift two Teslas with one hand.

Lassiter led the parade all the way through the dining room and out into the kitchen—where it was nearly impossible not to have a dessert tray, a traveler with coffee, or an entire leg of lamb pressed into your palm from the nervously helpful *doggen*.

Naturally, Rhage accepted a turkey sandwich like it was a football passed into the end zone. And a liter of Coke. And a bag of M&M'S.

Just as Rehv was wondering where the hell this was leading, Lassiter proceeded out into the garage—and that was when the math added up.

"Fuck," Rehv muttered as he stepped into the vast, unheated open space.

Rubbing his face, he glanced around at the gardening equipment and the bins of grass seed and fertilizer—and wondered whether he should be here at all. This was some private Brotherhood shit going down.

'Cuz ain't nobody here for the John Deere.

Sixteen coffins. Stacked two high and four deep.

The casings for the dead were made out of different kinds of wood, and they had aged in different ways—but what was inside them had something in common.

They were the remains of the damned.

Brothers who had not been granted proper Fade Ceremonies. Or could not be granted them.

Wrath had spilled the backstory one night when he and Rehv had been sharing-and-caring about how much "fun" it was to be King.

"Are we where I think we are," Wrath asked after a moment.

Lassiter strolled along the lineup of coffins—and then paused in front of the second to the last one on the top row. As he put his palm on the lid, he said, "Yes, you are."

Each of the coffins had inscriptions running down the sides and across the tops, and the Old Language symbols were not just names and dates. They were warnings.

Not to disturb the damned.

"There's no proof it wasn't just a coup for land and resources," Wrath murmured. "It could merely have been the *glymera* making another power move."

"Or that story was a ruse," Rehv said. "Because, hey, the aristocracy never lies or misrepresents historical events, do they."

"What the fuck are you two talking about?" V demanded.

Rehv held his breath as Wrath looked over his shoulder as if he could see the Brother. "A warlock."

Vishous's eyes narrowed, the tattoo at his temple distorting. "I didn't know we had one of them in here."

The King turned back in Lassiter's direction. "So I guess the rumor was true."

The angel spoke softly and patted the coffin. "We need what's in here. Even if it's not easily controlled."

"'Scuse me," Tohr said. "That brother is long dead. So aren't his personality defects kind of a moot point? Just like anything he could do to help us?"

"It's not him we're interested in," Lassiter countered. "It's what's in with him that we're after."

"We're not opening up that coffin here." Wrath shook his head. "There aren't a lot of protocols I give a shit about, but if we're exposing the body of a brother, that's only happening in one place. Even if he was damned in death."

Lassiter inclined his head. "I agree."

As the other Brothers nodded their heads and fell silent, Rehv looked around at their fierce faces, their strong bodies . . . their resolute wills—and felt a deep honor, as an outsider, to witness the living, breathing tradition of the Black Dagger Brotherhood.

All of these males, the King included, were part of the venerable history of service unto the race. And though the details and nature of that past were by definition untouchable and immutable, every once in a while, that which had gone before reached forward through the filaments of minutes and hours . . . to touch the present.

Something that had been killed a couple hundred years ago was going to be called into service now. And that was worthy of a moment of silence, of respect.

And there was another reason for the hush that permeated the garage's cold confines: These coffins were a reminder that those who were here now would sometime in the future be among those who had gone before.

To be mortal meant one had to die.

As a chill that had nothing to do with dopamine rippled through Rehv's mink-clad body, he thought of his beloved Ehlena—and had to look down at the concrete floor. Absently, he noticed that his Bally loafers, which were woven and black, were the perfect complement to his fine black slacks and the double-breasted jacket under his fur duster.

Normally, he would have been pleased to admire his wardrobe.

Now . . . all he could think of was dressing alone in that walk-in closet he shared with Ehlena. She had had to go into the clinic early. And she had forgotten to kiss him goodbye because she'd been in such a hurry—

A sudden, clawing need in the center of Rehv's chest drew him backward, away from the assembled. Away from the coffins. Away from the problem that he had brought to the Brotherhood's front door. Literally.

Slipping back into the house, he moved through both the mudroom and the kitchen, heading out into the foyer. As he came up to the grand staircase, he went around to the side and opened the hidden door.

The subterranean tunnel that connected the Pit, the mansion, and the training center was a straight shot of concrete through the earth, and he made as good time as he could given the way that dopamine he had to take created numbness in his legs and feet. Thank God for his cane.

He emerged through the supply closet into the office, then pushed through the glass door and strode forth into the training center proper.

Following his blood in the veins of his female, he went down to the clinical area and stopped in front of the closed door of an examination room.

Knocking softly, he wanted to break the panel apart with his bare hands—

"Is that my *hellren?*" came Ehlena's muffled voice.

Rehv pushed his way in. His beloved female was over at the desk, typing into the computer. Dressed in scrubs, she had a surgical net on her hair, surgical booties on her Crocs, and the tight brows of concentration with which he was well familiar.

For a moment, all he could do was stare at her. And think of that first time he had seen her, in Havers's old clinic. She had come into an examination room to check him into the system, and he had been . . . obsessed from the start—

Ehlena turned and smiled. "This is such a nice surprise!"

Wordlessly, he walked over and took her into his arms, gathering her up and out of the rolling chair. Closing his eyes, he held on to her.

"Are you okay?" she said as she stroked his back through the mink. "Rehv, what's wrong?"

"I just had to see you."

"Did something happen?"

How did he answer that, he wondered, without alarming her. And he wasn't thinking about the Book, or magic in the wrong hands, or what might be in any of those coffins. No, he was thinking about whether or not love actually survived even the cold hand of death. Ask any romantic and they'd say it was true—hell, if you believed in the Fade, it *was* true. You got your forever with your soul mate. But if you were a skeptic?

"No, nothing happened. I just wanted to see the female I love."

"You can talk to me," she murmured. "You know that, right. You can tell me what's going on."

"Like I said, it's nothing."

Well, nothing except for the fact that skeptics, generally speaking, didn't like to see coffins. They were a reminder that life ended, and he could not bear the thought of losing his *shellan.*

He literally did not know what he would do without—

Rehv jerked back as the image of that female at the parking garage—and her grid—shot into his mind.

"Oh, my God," he blurted. "She wants to bring someone back from the dead."

Ehlena shook her head. "I'm sorry, what—"

"A nice, normal civilian going after something evil? The only reason they'd do it is if someone they love is dead and they can't live with the pain. Her brother. It has to be her brother—it's the only person left in her family. I'll bet you something happened to him."

CHAPTER TWENTY-THREE

Sahvage rematerialized off to the side of the garage Mae had just parked her car in. As the panels started to drop back down, he glanced over his shoulder. Looked to the front of the one-story house. Checked what he could see in the back. He did not want her to get out of that fucking vehicle until things were safe—

And she didn't. She waited until everything was closed up.

"Good girl," he said softly. Even though she wouldn't have approved of being called a girl.

Sticking to the shadows, he got out of his pack what he had stolen from the cottage when she'd been taking Tallah to bed: Morton's un-iodized salt. Although he'd have taken it with the iodine. Didn't matter.

With a steady hand, he popped the top, and he was lucky on two parts: The container was almost full, and the seventies-era ranch wasn't big. Still, he was careful to ration the stuff. He only poured it on the ground in front of the doors and the windows. He'd have preferred to do the sealing all the way around, but he couldn't risk running out with any of the job left undone.

After he'd covered the ground floor, he materialized up onto the roof. No chimney, but there were two pipe vents, probably for the bathrooms, and he poured the salt on the shingles around them on a just-in-case.

Then he sat his ass on the mid-beam of the house and kicked his legs out in front of himself on the easy slope. He wondered what the female was doing beneath him, maybe grabbing something to eat, going through her mail. She would head back to the cottage for the day, though. She wasn't going to want that old female left alone.

Cursing himself, cursing Mae, he scanned the yard and the neighborhood with not just his eyes, but every sense and instinct he had.

He wasn't sure he believed in the salt. But it was something Rahvyn had always sworn by, and that was as good a recommendation as he was going to get in this nightmare.

God, he wished his cousin were here. She would know what to do.

Hell, maybe she could have talked Mae out of this madness—

The first thing he noticed was the stars disappearing overhead. But not because of clouds. It was as if a black shroud had been pulled across the sky directly above the ranch.

"Fuck."

Getting to his feet, he outed both of his guns, and eyed the neighborhood, which was suburban-tight and suburban-peopled: Both houses on either side, as well as the ones across the street, had humans in them, men and women winding down in bed, watching TV, having midnight snacks. The last thing he needed was a bunch of forefingers dialing 911 when he was trying to save that female's life.

"*Fuck.*"

With grim purpose, he walked down the roof incline to the gutter and jumped to the ground, landing with a boom. Turning to the front door, he was going to bang on it—except he stopped himself.

The garage. He hadn't sealed the garage door.

Shoving one of the guns into its holster, he ripped the Morton's back out, and ran for the tiny seam between those retractable panels and the concrete lip of the garage slab. The salt needed to be down on the ground before whatever had shown up at the cottage turned up again—

"You don't actually think that's going to work, do you."

The voice was female, and seemed to be coming from every direction. But as much of a shocker as it was, he refused to be diverted. He kept pouring, the lightness of the container freaking him out as he closed in on the far side of the broad entrance. Faster. Faster. Faster*fasterfaster*—

Sahvage all but threw the goddamn container at the corner formed by the house's edge and the concrete—on the theory that the salt was still in place, even if there was a cylindrical cardboard container wrapping around it.

It was as he looked up that he saw the leg.

The very shapely leg . . . that was plugged into a shiny black stiletto with a red sole.

His eyes followed the dainty ankle to its delicate calf—and went farther up to a very lady-like knee. After that, there were the thighs, the incredibly smooth thighs that were set on display by a black miniskirt that gave both "skintight" and "short" new meaning. And Jesus . . . the top half of the woman more than lived up to the bottom part. Between the black push-up bustier, and all that brunette hair, and that face . . .

"Hi," the woman drawled as she leaned up against the house, right over the salt container. "Fancy meeting you here."

Her eyes were jet black and gleaming like they were backlit, and her lips were blood red, and she was as beautiful a woman as he had ever seen.

And her malevolence made him want to get his other gun back out. So he fucking did.

"Now, now," she said, "is that really necessary. We haven't even been properly introduced. If you're going to shoot me, shouldn't we at least shake hands first?"

With a graceful bend, she picked up the Morton's. Meeting his eyes, she ran one blood red fingernail around the open metal spout.

"Just so you know, I'm totally resisting the urge to make some 'you so salty' jokes right now." That finger continued to play with the opening. "I'll say it again, do you *really* think you can keep me out of anywhere?"

In the pool of light thrown by an exterior fixture, she was an all-wrong trying to pull off perfectly-normal: The shadows under her body moved even when she didn't, and then there was her aura. A pitch-black shimmer tinted the air around her.

Because she radiated evil.

She tossed the Morton's over her shoulder, and the container bounced away like it was running from her. "You're going to need a lot more than shit for seasoning French fries to keep me out. But enough about entrances and exits, tell me something, does this skirt make my ass look big."

Pivoting around, she struck a pose and stared over her shoulder—as her hand took a stroll down the tuck of her waist to the perfectly proportioned swell of her hip.

"Hm?" she prompted in a throat purr. "What do you think of my ass."

Sahvage blocked his thoughts by picturing a closet, a closet that had shelves running up its walls from floor to ceiling. Inside his closet, the shelves were empty, the bald overhead light revealing all the absolutely-nothing in there. When he was sure he could see the details clearly, from the wood graining on those vertical boards to the little string hanging from the bulb, he shut the closet door. And locked it.

As the woman stroked her rear assets, he held that final image foremost in his mind: A stout door, a thick door, a reinforced door that was dead-bolted, protecting a closet with nothing in it.

The woman chuckled. "Look at you, with the parlor tricks."

Say nothing, he told himself. *You give nothing out loud.*

"So protective of the female under this roof, you are." The woman—"woman"—glanced at the house. "You must care deeply for her. Or are you just making sure she lives long enough so you can fuck her?"

Sahvage stared forward and barely blinked.

"I'm right, aren't I." The woman smiled as she turned back around to face him. "You haven't fucked her yet. But you want to, don't you. You want her naked under you and you're going to mark her as your own—like that means anything these days. Haven't you heard that monogamy is out of style?"

Her voice was low and seductive, backing up her body, her lips, her hair. She was such an enticing package, but once you got that ribbon off? Ripped free the wrapping paper?

"Or maybe there's more to you two." She extended an elegant hand and pointed her blood red forefinger at the center of his chest. "Does she have this? What beats in here . . . has she taken your heart?" There was a pause. "Already . . . wow. I'll have to take some pointers from her. She's not much to look at, but her game is evidently on fire."

I give nothing, Sahvage thought. *I give nothing, Igivenothing, IgivenothingIgivenothingIgive—*

Her eyes gleamed with menace. "You know, you make me want to get inside of you. I think it would be fun—for me, at least. And for you, for a short while. But hey, sometimes in life, all you get are short little funs, right? Itty-bitty funs. So what do you say, fighter. How about we fuck and I show you a really good time."

From out of the blue, a thought came to him, like a paper airplane sailing into his line of sight.

This woman, who was not a woman at all but something else . . . was his ticket off the planet.

After all these years, his death, which he had so often wished for, and too many times been denied, had finally crossed the threshold of his inner house and sat down in a chair.

To wait for the right moment.

The woman smiled, her blood red lips pulling into an expression of evil satisfaction. "You're going to be mine."

◆   ◆   ◆

The rush of the ice bouncing off Rhoger's immobile chest and falling into the sides of the tub was the kind of thing Mae was going to hear in her nightmares forever. And the tinkling sounds, so soft, so gentle, reminded her of how unhinged she had become. Even as she was able to dress herself properly and eat her meals and drive her car without disaster, she was chaos barely reined in, the undercarriage of all her seemingly a-okay really ten thousand volts of fucked-in-the-head.

"It's going to be fine," she told her brother as she crumpled up the dripping, empty bag.

Reaching for the next one, she tore through its plastic skin and then realized she'd forgotten to bang it on the floor first. It was a solid frozen chunk.

"Damn it."

Grabbing a towel off the rack, she wrapped the bag up and dropped the thing on the bath mat a couple of times, the shattering inside too close for comfort.

Now the chips poured out, though.

When she was finished refilling things, she sat back on her heels and propped her hands on the slick rim of the tub. Staring at her brother's face through the tesserae'd ice, she couldn't recognize his features. But she wasn't sure she would have anyway.

It had been a long time since she'd properly looked him in the eye, and not because he had passed.

"I'm so sorry," she croaked out. "I didn't mean . . . that night you left, I didn't mean to yell at you. I really didn't."

There was no answer coming back at her. Which hadn't been the way things were. Before Rhoger had taken off that night and not come home, they'd been fighting constantly.

Over such insignificant things—or so it seemed now.

God, she wished she had been more patient. Or maybe not have dug so deep with the criticism. Maybe if she hadn't been so hard on him, he would have stayed home that night.

Maybe . . .

She thought of the summoning spell. And everything Tallah had told her the Book would do for her.

Yes, she wanted to bring Rhoger back. But the truth was, it was *her* wrong that she wanted to rectify. She had started the downward spiral that had ended in his tragic death: After that particularly brutal argument, he had stormed out . . . and then crossed the path of his murderer at some point.

With a curse, she remembered those terrible days of waiting, sitting in the hard chair in the kitchen, praying for a call from him. And then the nights, trying to work at her desk, braced for the door to open when he came home.

The latter had happened, eventually . . . nearly two weeks after he had gone missing. She had smelled the fresh blood first, and then heard the stumbling feet. Rushing out of her room, she had come down the hall just as he had collapsed inside the front door, his loose limbs and out-of-joint torso the most terrifying thing she had ever seen.

"Rhoger," she whispered.

If he hadn't come home to die here? She never would have found him. She would have spent the rest of her life listening for the door, stuck with this house because it was where he would know to find her, wondering and imagining and torturing herself with a thousand different bad outcomes.

"I'm going to fix this," she told him. "I promise."

Getting to her feet, she groaned as every muscle in her body hurt—except that wasn't true. It was only her upper arms that ached, and for a moment, she couldn't figure out why.

Then she remembered being on the doorstep of the cottage. With Sahvage. Shooting at a shadow.

"I'll be back tomorrow night," she said to Rhoger. "I have to make sure Tallah is okay. It's . . . a long story."

The fact that she paused for his response made her feel really unhinged. So she went to her room and quickly packed an over-day bag. The truth was, she couldn't wait to leave the house—which made her feel guilty. But for godsakes, it wasn't like Rhoger was aware she was leaving him all alone. Besides, it was better for her not to be around the body. If another one of those shadows showed up?

If she didn't have him intact, she didn't know what the hell she was resurrecting.

Holy hell, what kind of life was she living.

Out in the garage, she took a deep breath—

The scent of spoiled meat put her paranoia back in the driver's seat: Was it a legion of the undead coming for her? Dear God, why had she told a weapon like Sahvage to leave? She was totally undefended—

Mae's head cranked around. To the rolling trash bin in the corner.

"It's Thursday," she muttered. "It's trash day."

As opposed to the Zombie-apocalypse.

Going to the Civic, she tossed her canvas over-day bag into the back along with her purse. Then she hit the garage door opener and marched over to the roller. As the panels trundled up, she tilted the weight and started to pull—

Directly outside the garage, there were two sets of legs.

That were standing toe to toe. Or boot to stiletto, as was the case.

She recognized the former. Those were Sahvage's cargo pants and footwear. But the female's?

As the door continued to ascend, Mae paid a whole lot of attention to what was revealed on the fairer-sex side of things: Lots of leg. Tiny skirt. Perfect hip-to-waist-to- . . . wow, that was a heck of a bust. Long brunette hair.

And a profile that was begging for a close-up.

Okay, so she'd been wrong. Sahvage didn't belong with one of those rave types from back at the parking garage. *This* was who he needed. The female was as stunning a specimen as he was, the extremely feminine balanced with the extremely masculine. And their bodies would fit perfectly together.

The fact that Mae was ever so slightly jealous was nuts.

And what the hell were the happy couple doing in her driveway?

Just as she was about to bring up the trespassing laws of New York State, Sahvage's head snapped in her direction.

He didn't say a word. But his eyes were communicating a clear warning.

And then the woman looked her way.

"Hello," the brunette said in a voice that was part Sophia Loren, part Judge Judy. "It's soooooo nice to meet you."

As she spoke, Sahvage didn't move. It wasn't even clear whether he was breathing. But those eyes of his. So intense, they did not even blink.

Meanwhile, the woman's glittering stare drifted down Mae's body. "You know, I'm sure you're all well and good—and that your mother loves you. But I'm really surprised he's risking his own life to save the likes of you." She put her palms forward as if to be reassuring. "No offense, I mean, I just think honesty is the best policy, don't you? And you're not exactly what I'd expect."

Sahvage looked down. But not because he was being called out. He was focusing on something.

Sending a message.

Mae let the woman continue to talk while she tried to figure out what he was directing her to—wait, was that a salt container on the side lawn?

The woman sauntered up to the edge of the garage's concrete slab. "Anyway, enough with the chitchat. I'm thinking about buying a place in this neighborhood." She indicated her fabulousness, sweeping a hand down her curves. "You can thank me for improving your property values later. But right now, how about you give me a tour of this incredibly quaint little abode of yours? I'm just *dying* to see what you did with the kitchen. Harvest gold, right? With macramé plant holders and a throw rug the color of an avocado. I mean, you look like someone who peaked in the late seventies, early eighties. Assuming second grade teacher is, like, a style or an era."

The smile was a study in condescension.

And as Mae looked back at Sahvage's face, the woman threw her hands up. "Oh, will you stop worrying about him? Fine, yes, I'm going to fuck him, but I assure you, it'll mean nothing on my side, so it won't threaten your relationship—well, until he kills himself. That's not going to be my fault, however. Besides, take my word for it, he's a bad bet for anything long-term. You should never trust what you cannot control. Something tells me you already know that, though, don't you."

Mae focused properly on the woman.

And in a slow, clear voice, she said, "You are not welcome here. I do not welcome you into my home. Now and forevermore."

The woman's black stare narrowed. "I think you're mistaken."

Sahvage took three steps forward and crossed over onto the concrete slab. Facing the female, he stayed silent and went still again.

The expression on the rare beauty's face shifted, her lashes lowering over eyes that now glittered with rage.

"Oh, you fuckers," she said in a low voice. "You're not that smart, either one of you. And parlor tricks aren't going to keep me away. I am everywhere."

Backing up, Sahvage extended his arm and punched the button to close the garage door.

As the panels began to trundle shut, the woman growled deep in her throat, like a predator.

"You'll be seeing me again soon," she said. "That's a promise."

CHAPTER TWENTY-FOUR

Knocking.

Lots of knocking on Balz's bedroom door.

As his heavy lids lifted, he couldn't figure out why in the *hell* someone was waking him up in the middle of the day. He was fucking sleeping.

"*What,*" he snapped.

At his kind invitation, the door opened and airmailed him a shaft of light from the hallway that was like getting rusty-spiked in the iris. With a hiss, he went classic Dracula, putting his forearm over his face and rearing back.

"How are you still in bed?"

Syphon, back again. Of course. The Mother Hen motherfucker was an alarm clock that ran on gluten-free organic smoothies, almond shakes, and organic porridge.

On that note, if only there was a bag of Doritos to throw at the guy.

Or anything that had Red Dye 40 or GMO shit on the ingredients list.

"Yes, I'm still in goddamn bed," he shot back. "It's almost one in the afternoon. The question is why you aren't in—"

"It's midnight." When Balz didn't respond, the bastard went *hello*. "Twelve a.m. Like, one dozen bongs from the grandfather clock out in the—"

"I can count."

"Can you?"

Balz threw out a hand to his bedside table. Grabbing his Galaxy S21, he checked the time, ready to throw the hour back in his cousin's face—

12:07 a.m.

Sitting up, he pushed his hair out of his face, even though he'd recently gotten it cut and there was nothing in his eyes. Sure enough, next to where his phone had been, there was that travel mug and the croissant that was still wrapped in a dish towel.

Jesus. He'd slept like he'd been punched in the head.

And no dreams of his female.

The lights overhead came on as Syphon flipped the switch, and then the fighter said the words every Brother and bastard dreaded like the second coming of the Omega.

"I've called Doc Jane."

"What?" Balz tried not to scream. "Why? I'm perfectly fine—"

"You were electrocuted."

Balz frowned because he couldn't have heard that right. When his cuz merely stared back at him expectantly, like the bastard had just proved for a fact that pigs could fly, it was apparent that true logic was going to have to be spelled out.

Where were a whiteboard and a marker when you needed them?

"Back in December." Balz indicated himself. "And in case you haven't noticed, I don't glow in the dark."

"And you think that means you're fine."

"I think it disqualifies me as a night-light. And being a patient of Doc Jane's four months ago—"

"Did someone say my name?" The good doctor, and V's *shellan*, poked her head around the doorjamb. "How we doing?"

Balz groaned and flopped back against his pillows. "Can someone explain to me why doctors use the royal 'we' when they're talking at people they think are sick? Who is this 'we'?"

The blond female walked by Syphon and gave the bastard a pat on the shoulder—which was the universal sign for *We're good, thanks.*

"I agree," Balz muttered. "You can go, Cousin."

"Both of you are *so* cute." Syphon marched over and parked it in the chair by the bureau. "Really. It's cute."

Having clearly lost that fight, Balz focused on Doc Jane and shook his mental hat full of excuses, not really caring what came out. And as she patiently stared back at him, it was hard to be frustrated at her. With her short blond hair and level green stare, she looked like the kind of person who could treat anything from a hangnail to a ruptured aorta with competence, compassion, and calmness.

And she really needed to take all that expertise somewhere else, to someone who actually required it.

"So I understand you're fatigued," she said as she sat down the edge of his bed.

"Of this visit? Yes, and we haven't gotten started yet, have we." He cursed. "Sorry, I don't mean any offense."

"None taken." She leaned in. "You wouldn't believe what patients have said to me over the years."

"Just don't tell your *hellren*. I like my arms and legs right where they are."

"Your secret is safe with me." She smiled at him. "Now tell me what's going on."

"Nothing." He glared at Syphon. "I swear—no, wait. I am suffering from cousin-itis. Can you remove that noisy, malignant growth for me? I've been finding it really irritating lately—"

"He missed a meeting of the Brotherhood." Syphon stared across at the doc. "He never does that."

"I slept in!"

Syphon rolled his eyes. "Until midnight? And actually, you missed two meetings, haven't you—"

"Okay, okay." Doc Jane made cool-it-boys motions with her hands. "How about I do a quick exam? If the vitals are good and there's no fever or anything, we'll call this case closed."

"Great." Balz glared at his cousin as he took off his t-shirt. "And listen, Doc, after you're done certifying all my perfectly-fine, I'll drop and do three hundred for this asshole, just so he's sure I'm tight."

Syphon nodded. "I'll count 'em so you don't have to."

Doc Jane grabbed her stethoscope from her dreaded black bag. "This won't take long—"

"Unless you find something," Syphon cut in.

Balz wadded up his shirt and pegged the bastard in the head with it. "You're like GE, you bring good things to life. When you shut up."

"He was electrocuted, you know." Syphon peeled the [adult swim] logo off his face. "I mean, he was dead—"

"She treated me! And that was *months* ago—"

"Boys. Please."

As Syphon tossed the t-shirt away and Balz tried to look like he wasn't sulking, Doc Jane plugged the stethoscope into her ears and went in with the disk.

"Take a deep breath for me," she said. "Good. And another?"

She moved the receiver around his pecs. Then she put it in the center. "Just breathe normally now."

After a moment, Doc Jane straightened from him. "Sounds good—I'm just going to listen around back, too."

Balz leaned forward so she could do whatever she needed to—and resisted the urge to stick his tongue out at Syphon. Because that was totally immature.

So he flipped the fucker off with both middle fingers—

Doc Jane did a double take and yanked the plugs out of her ears. "How did this happen?"

As Syphon sat forward sharply, like he was ready to be called in to help with a code, Balz glanced over. "How'd what happen?"

"These scratches. They're all over your back, like someone gripped you while you were—oh."

As the doc flushed, a sense of foreboding had Balz tossing the covers aside and stalking into his bathroom. There was no reason to flip more lights on. That overhead fixture out in the bedroom cast plenty of—

What. The. Fuck.

As he flashed his spine at the mirror over the sinks, he got a load of the long stripes that had been torn into his skin on both sides of his shoulders, his rib cage . . . and right above his ass.

Well, at least he knew why Doc Jane, the unflappable physician, had given him an "oh." There was only one reason why marks like these would be on a male—and it had nothing to do with him having a medical problem.

Quite the opposite.

When he came out of the bathroom, Doc Jane was closing up her black bag and getting to her feet. "I think we're okay here, aren't we."

Balz crossed his arms over his chest. "Like I said, I'm fine. I was just tired."

He looked pointedly at Syphon.

"But call me if you need me, okay?" Doc Jane opened the door into the hall. "Promise?"

"I promise." Balz smiled at her. "And thank you. I'm sorry that Mr. Panic Button over here jumped the gun."

"No worries." Doc Jane waved at them both. "I'm always here, and I'd rather you hit me up for nothing than not call me at all."

As the door closed, Balz stared across at his cousin. "Now do you understand why I might need a little lie-in?"

Syphon put both palms up like someone had a loaded gun between his shoulder blades. "Clearly, I was wrong. I apologize."

"You're forgiven."

"Soooooooooooooooooo, tell me who the female is. And can you share?"

No, he was never sharing his brunette. With anybody. Ever.

"She's not one of us." He gave a *pshaw* with his dagger hand. "It was just the wife of this guy I visited last night. She was all alone when she shouldn't have been, and I took care of her."

"A pity fuck? Not your style."

"Oh, it was no chore, trust me." Balz shrugged. "She just needed somebody to make her feel beautiful again."

"And you very obviously obliged. Several times. I'm jealous." Syphon clapped his thighs and stood up. "Which clearly is why a guy would need some extra zzZZzz's and miss a couple—"

"So what was the Brotherhood meeting about?" Balz asked.

As the question was answered, his ears went on the fritz, and it was a relief for so many reasons when his cousin left.

The second he was alone again, he went back into the bathroom. Staring at himself in the mirror, he thought about the time he'd spent with the Mrs. at the Commodore. He'd treated her like the queen she was, worshipping her with his hands, his mouth, his tongue. A lot of the sex hadn't registered with any specificity, but he knew one thing for damn sure.

Twisting his back to the mirror again, he stared at the scratches.

The Mrs. hadn't had long nails.

But dreams didn't leave love marks . . .

Right?

◆   ◆   ◆

As her garage door bumped to a close, Mae turned to Sahvage, aware that her legs were shaking and she couldn't seem to breathe right. And when his eyes swung over to her, she moved before she had a conscious thought.

She ran across and threw her arms around him. "I'm so glad you're here—"

"Thank God you didn't invite her in," he said roughly as he held her tight. "You did the right thing. She can't get at you now because I've salted the entrances."

The fact that he shuddered was a shock—but then his broad palm cradled the back of her head, and all she could think of was the warmth and protection he offered.

Squeezing her eyes shut, she whispered, "Who was that?"

"I don't know."

Mae pulled back. "Was she even . . . she wasn't a vampire. And I don't think she's human, is she?"

"She's not of this world. That's all I know."

Okay, was it crazy to feel relief that that . . . thing . . . wasn't a girl-friend of his?

As Mae struggled with some seriously stupid emotions, given the situation, Sahvage's jaw went hard. "And before you get on me for fol-lowing you, I just couldn't leave you unprotected. The only reason I came here was to seal the house. That's it. I swear."

Mae broke away and ended up wandering over to the trash bin. But there was no way in hell she was taking it out now.

"I should never have done that summoning spell." She looked back at him. "It was a huge mistake. But I didn't know what else to do. I still don't."

Sahvage shook his head. "Let Tallah go. That's what you have to do. Love her while you have her . . . and then release her to travel unto the Fade when it's her time."

"I can't do that." She put her face in her hands. "You don't under-stand. I'll be . . . I'll never forgive myself."

"Death is not something you control unless you're a killer. Trust me. And loss . . . Mae, loss is something that happens to all of us. You can't run from it, you can't duck it . . . and you sure as hell can't stop it."

Mae lowered her palms. "You don't understand."

"I do. I promise you, I do."

His eyes were grave. And more than that, they were full of pain.

"Who did you lose?" she whispered.

When he didn't immediately answer, she figured he wasn't going to. But then his voice, rough and low, crossed the space between them.

"Myself. And say what you will about mourning other people, it's nothing compared to grieving the loss of your own damned self."

God, she knew all about that. She'd been missing herself as well . . . the old Mae, who came home to a family at dawn, who worried about things like what she was going to have for First Meal and whether she was going to get a promotion at work, who actually slept during the day.

"I'm so sorry," she said. "What happened?"

"It's not important. All that matters right now is that you stop with this Book thing. Nothing good is coming out of it already."

Turning to the door into the back hall, she pictured Rhoger. In that tub. With the ice.

"No, I need the Book." Her voice drifted out into the silence. "The Book is the answer."

And yet even as she said the words, she was losing her conviction. In fact, the only thing keeping her locked into the path she'd been on for the last two weeks . . . was that she had no other solutions.

Except for the one she couldn't stomach.

"I'll find the Book, and everything will be fine. I'll make it okay."

When Sahvage didn't comment, she glanced over her shoulder. He looked exhausted, positively overwhelmed with fatigue.

Mae rushed back over to him. "And as for that woman, or whatever she was—she had a shadow around her, like . . . a halo of darkness. Just like what that shadow entity was made out of. So if we can shoot that, we can shoot her."

Oh, God, what was she saying?

Sahvage seemed to need a moment to regroup. Then he rubbed his short hair on the top of his head. "Do you have a gun that you know how to use?"

"No, but I can get one." Mae started talking faster and faster. "And I need to go to Tallah's right now and put salt across her doorways—"

"I sealed the cottage, too. Before I left. She's safe."

"Thank God." Mae grew dizzy with relief. "But how did you know what to do? With the salt?"

"I wasn't sure whether it would work. Back in the Old Country, my cousin used to do it to our house, to keep evil out. I thought she was nuts, but I don't know . . . after that shadow showed up? It seemed like a good goddamn idea." He stared at the closed garage doors. "I don't fucking know. My head's a fucking mess—"

"Thank you for coming back."

Sahvage's eyes returned to her own—and the surprise on his face suggested gratitude was the last thing he'd ever expected to come out of her mouth.

"I am so grateful." She thought of Rhoger. "I don't know what would have happened if you hadn't come to help me."

"It's okay. It's nothing—"

"Help me find the Book."

Sahvage opened his mouth. Shut it.

"Please," she said. "I know I haven't been easy to get along with, and I apologize. I'll do better with that, I promise. But the reality is . . . I do need your help. You're right. I was wrong."

When he looked away, and then stayed silent, she shook her head. "You came to that cottage tonight to help me, and now you won't? After you followed me here, too?"

He crossed his arms over his chest. "You accused me of being a danger to you, remember? And you think I'm in a big hurry to play Good Samaritan just 'cuz you've had a come-to-Jesus revelation."

"For what it's worth," she said dryly, "I do *not* think you're Jesus."

"And I may be in over my head as well. I'm not some magic solution to this." He nodded to the closed door of the garage. "We're facing shit even I haven't seen before."

"But you knew about the salt. And you know about other things, don't you." She took a deep breath. "Because you're a member of the Black Dagger Brotherhood, aren't you."

Sahvage's face froze into an absolute mask. "No. I'm not."

"I saw the star-shaped scar on your pec. After you took your shirt off. I didn't put it together right away, but that's what the marking is, isn't it." She wasn't surprised when he didn't comment. "My brother used to study the Brotherhood. He told me about the scarification that every Brother has. I thought it was part of your injuries, but it's not. And your name fits, too—"

"I'm not a member of the Brotherhood."

"I don't see why you can't admit it."

"Easy. Because it's not true." He shrugged. "I'm not lying to you, and besides, after that shadow attack, don't you think I would have called in backup if I had it?"

Mae flattened her mouth. Then said, "Are you in or out with me."

He stayed silent for a very long time, and though his eyes were on her, she had a feeling he wasn't seeing her.

Just as she was deflating, as she had the sense that she had made too many mistakes with him, he said gruffly, "I'm in."

"Thank God—"

"With one caveat."

Mae narrowed her eyes and wondered how far he was going to go. "And what exactly is that."

CHAPTER TWENTY-FIVE

"A re you sure we can't pick up anything for you from where you stay?"

As Rhage made the offer to the female in the hooded robe, Nate was ready to volunteer for that trip, wherever it took him. Cross the state? Yeahsurefine. Cross the country? Yupsurething. The only trouble? He had a feeling that Elyn had no things to pick up. Or no place safe to get them from.

"No, thank you," she said softly with that beautiful accent.

Elyn was sitting on a sofa that was so brand-new, the pillows were still in plastic—and she was as self-contained as those still-packed cushions. With her perfectly straight back, and her legs crossed at the ankles, and her hands linked in her lap, she was as proper a female as any in the *glymera*, her posture transforming that rough cloak into a ball gown.

Oh, and her hair wasn't blond. In the true light, it was snow white, without any pigment at all, the long ends curling naturally as they drifted out of the hood's confines.

"I'm really glad you'll come stay with us at Safe Place today." Mrs. Mary glanced at the social worker and looked back at Elyn. "And then I think Luchas House will fit your needs. We just need another twenty-four hours to get things set up and we'll be ready for you."

"Thank you," Elyn said. "You have been most generous to a stranger."

"You're not a stranger." Mrs. Mary shook her head. "We take care of people in the race who need help."

"I do not know how I will pay you back."

"You don't have to worry about that."

Well, Nate sure as hell would have volunteered to give his wages over. And he'd decided that one good bene about being on the sidelines of this conversation was that he had an excuse to stare at Elyn without being a creeper. The not-so-hot thing? He'd studied her expressions over the last half hour, and he knew that she was not buying into this housing plan as much as Mrs. Mary thought.

They might get one night out of her at Safe Place. Here, though? She wasn't comfortable with that, even though she'd been assured there would be social workers and staff always around: He could tell by the way she did not meet Mrs. Mary's eyes whenever Luchas House came up. At the moment—and tragically—Elyn was exhausted and hungry and cold. But she was going to run at nightfall tomorrow, and none of them were going to see her again.

"So let's get going, shall we?" Mrs. Mary said as she stood up. "I'll drive you to Safe Place—and hey, it's cookie night."

Rhage smiled at Elyn. "It's always cookie night at Safe Place. Just so you know."

The Brother escorted his mate and the social worker to the door—and as the three went out and clustered together to talk quietly on the front stoop, Nate had a feeling they were doing it on purpose, to give him and Elyn a chance to say goodbye.

"You're going to be okay with them," he said as he looked over at her. "I promise you."

As Elyn's hands twisted in her lap, he wanted to hold them. Hold her.

"I am sorry I lied to you." Her silver eyes lifted to his. "About knowing English. But I do not know who to trust."

"Totally forgiven." He swept the air with his hand. "Forgotten."

Her head turned toward the front door. "I think perhaps I must go the now."

God, he could listen to that accent for hours. "Maybe I'll see you again—"

"Yes, please," she said. Before quickly adding, "But I do not want to be a burden—"

"Never!" He cleared his throat. "I mean, you know, don't worry about that. Ever. Let me give you my cell phone number."

He all but jumped over the sofa to get to the kitchen. And when he started to frantically pull open drawers, Rhage came back in and took a Sharpie out of the pocket of his leather jacket.

"Here," the Brother murmured with a knowing look. "And use this to write on, it's not perfect, but it'll do."

Nate took the Tootsie Pop wrapper he was offered like it was a sheet of gold and hastily scribbled his digits. On the way back to the couch, he flapped the purple waxed paper back and forth to make sure the ink dried.

Elyn got to her feet as he came over to her, and he really wanted to put his digits deep into a pocket of hers, just to make sure nothing was lost. Instead, as she took the wrapper, he removed that leaf that was still nestled in the lengths of her hair.

When she seemed startled, he flushed. "Sorry, I just . . . would you like it back?"

Dumbass. *Dumbass*—

Except she wasn't looking at him.

Instead, she was focused on a mirror that had been mounted on the opposite wall, and as she stared at her reflection, she seemed haunted. Almost afraid.

Like she was in a trance, she went over and stood before the glass. With a shaking hand, she touched the hair that curled out of the hood.

"Are you all right?" he said softly.

Her eyes met his in the mirror. "No, I do not believe I am."

Abruptly, tears trembled on her lashes. But she wiped them away and squared her shoulders.

Clearing her throat, she said, "I am very sorry I lied to you. I do not know who to trust."

Nate nodded—and had a thought that she had no idea what she was saying, no clue that she was repeating things.

Abruptly, she turned away from herself and looked at what he'd written. As her brows pulled together, he worried that the numbers had been smudged. They hadn't been—so he worried whether she was rethinking taking them.

At least she put the wrapper away in her robing.

As wind whistled outside, he wanted to give her his coat. But of course, he hadn't put one on as he'd bolted out of his house.

"Good eve, Nate," she said as she lowered herself in a brief curtsy.

Nate bowed even though he had no clue what he was doing. "Just call me. Anytime."

Today, he thought. *Maybe as soon as you get to Safe Place.*

Before he could say anything else—although, really, what else was there that wouldn't make him seem like more of a jackass—she was gone, that long, loose cape-thingy she was wearing trailing behind her as she stepped out of the house. As the door closed behind her, the smudges of mud on its hem stuck with him, and it took him a minute to figure out why: She knew what it was like to be alone and afraid.

Guess that made them soul mates.

"You okay, son?" Rhage asked.

Nate did a double take. "Oh, I thought you'd left."

"I am now." The Brother went over to where he'd been on an armchair. "I forgot my jacket and had to come back for it."

There was a pause, and it was clear the older male wanted to say something. And not about the weather.

"Please don't tell my dad . . ." Nate mumbled.

"What, that you gave a female your number for the first time?" As

Nate blushed, Rhage nodded. "Not to worry. That's your story to share, not mine. Take care of yourself, son."

Ten minutes later, Nate was still standing in the newly kitted-out living room when the front door opened again and the guys started coming in with their overalls and their tools. As he nodded at the crew, and tried to play it cool, he had a thought that there wasn't much else to do at the site—and what a pity that was. Considering this was an extension of Safe Place, he felt like as long as Elyn was there and he was here, a connection between them still existed.

Yeah, unlike that cell phone number, which seemed way too tenuous, and not because it was on a lollipop wrapper. She had to choose to use those numbers, and time was running out before she took off—

"What the hell is wrong with you?"

With a start, he turned to Shuli—and felt like he didn't recognize his friend. Which was nuts because the guy was wearing the same Izod polo, cashmere sweater, and khaki shorts kind of thing that he always did. He even had a pair of Ray-Bans tucked into the V-neck—like James Spader in that old movie. *Pretty in Purple?* What was the title?

"Hello?" Shuli waved a hand. "Anybody in there?"

Absently, Nate's eyes tracked the glint of the fancy watch on his buddy's wrist. And because he didn't want to think about anything else, and because he certainly didn't want to talk about all the things he didn't want to think about, he blurted out, "Why do you work here?"

"Huh—oh, why am I on the crew? My sire thinks minimum wage builds character."

"I don't think it's working."

"Ouch—but you're probably right. I can be a prick sometimes. And on that note, why are you looking like someone punched you in the nuts?"

"I'm not. I don't. I mean—let's go finish the painting in the garage."

As Nate started hoofing it, Shuli chuckled and followed along. "So that's why you're not rubbing one out on a regular basis. It explains a lot."

"What the hell are you talking about?"

"No nuts, no erection. Problem solved."

"Not even close," Nate muttered.

"No, really, it's how it works—"

"Please, for the love of God, stop talking."

"Like, about nuts? Or anything at all?"

The glare Nate sent over his shoulder answered that one. And as they filed out into the garage, he prayed Shuli gave him two minutes to recalibrate. When the guy blessedly started opening the cans and organizing the paint brushes in silence, Nate tried to pull it together, and looked down at the leaf he'd taken out of Elyn's hair—

Frowning, he turned it over to check the back. And then turned the thing faceup again.

When he'd first seen the maple leaf in her hair, out by where the meteor had landed, it had been dried up, brown, past its life cycle.

What he was holding now was pliable and yellow with red tips, as if it had just fallen from its autumnal branch.

"What the hell you looking at?" Shuli said. "And for what it's worth, if it's your love line, I'm worried about where that's headed."

"It's nothing," Nate muttered as he put the leaf into his pocket. "You ready to paint?"

◆   ◆   ◆

Collective wisdom was wrong. You could, in fact, be in two places at once.

As Sahvage stood in front of Mae inside her garage, another part of him was out in the dark with that other woman. Female. Thing-that-shall-not-be-named.

With the specificity of a newscaster, he was replaying everything the brunette had said to him, what she'd looked like, how she'd behaved. It was like searching for underground mines in a field, lifting rocks to see if he'd found all the danger.

"So?" Mae prompted tersely. "What do I have to agree to."

"I'm sorry, what?"

"Let's have your caveat."

Shaking himself back into focus, he said, "If I tell you to leave me, you have to promise you will. When I go down, you need to leave me where I fall and save yourself."

As her eyes widened, he couldn't help her. Something inside of him was once again looking into the misty future . . . and seeing a moment in time for them both where only one walked away.

He stared into her eyes. "You have to leave me when it counts. Promise me."

Mae's brows went down hard. "What if I refuse?"

"Then I leave you now."

"That makes no sense."

"Well, that's the way it's going to be."

She opened and closed her a mouth a couple of times, but he just waited for her to come to whatever conclusion she did. This was a non-negotiable, and even though she'd pissed him off, he was glad they'd had to renegotiate their—well, whatever this was between them.

"Okay. Fine."

Sahvage put his dagger hand out. "On your honor. Swear to it."

She hesitated for a moment. Then she shoved her palm forward and clasped what he offered her with a serious squeeze—as if, in her head, she was ripping his arm off and beating some sense into him with it.

"Say the words," he demanded.

"I promise."

He nodded once, as if they'd made a blood pact. And then he glanced at her car. "Leave that here and let's dematerialize back to the cottage. I cracked the shutter on the front left on the second floor. We can get in that way."

"Did you seal the second-story windows, too? With salt?"

"Evil can only enter a place on the ground floor or with an invitation."

"And if a house isn't protected?"

"She can walk in any way she pleases." He rubbed his aching head.

"Come down the chimney like Santa Claus if she wants. I don't fucking know."

"I'll say it again, thank God you did what you did." Mae went over and got her bag and purse out of her car. "And you're sure this house is safe."

"You saw for yourself. She couldn't get in."

"I can't believe this is happening."

Sahvage went across to a rear window. The daytime shutters were down, and he released the locking hooks to pop the seal—but made sure things stayed mostly in place.

"I'll get you back to the cottage," he said, "then I'm going to my place to pick up some more weapons."

"I can help. I'll go with you—"

"You need to stay with Tallah. You two should be safe together and I'm not going to be gone long—"

"Can I ask you something?"

He glanced over. Mae had her purse up on her shoulder, and a two-handled bag in her left grip. She looked frazzled, her hair fuzzing out of that ponytail, her eyes too bright, her cheeks too pale. But it was clear she wasn't going to quit.

Fucking hell. He was going to miss her when he left.

"Depends on what you want to know," he said softly.

"Where do you live? Who is . . . do you have anyone in your life?"

"Don't worry. Nobody is going to wonder where I am or what I'm doing and get nosy. Your privacy, and Tallah's, is locked tight."

Mae cleared her throat. "I'm sorry."

"For what?"

"That you're alone."

"It's by design, I assure you—"

"So that's why you're telling me to leave you before we even start, huh. Even if you're hurt. Even if you're . . . dying."

All Sahvage could do was shake his head at her. "Don't play the hypothetical game."

"Excuse me?"

"I'm not changing my one demand just because you're restating it to me, sweetheart. Now let's head out, I need some fucking air—and yes, I did just sweetheart you again. You want to yell at me for it, hold your breath for when we get back to the cottage."

Mae walked over to him. Tilted her chin up. And—

"Not now," he all but groaned. "Please. Just go and I'll meet you at that old female's. She's the one you care about, remember?"

"You don't need to remind me where my priorities are."

With that, Mae left—and for a split second, as he glanced around the garage, he entertained a brief, insane fantasy where he came home at the end of the night, and she was back from whatever work she did, and they sat across from each other at a dinner table and talked over the hours they'd been apart.

Never going to happen, he thought as he ghosted away. *For so many reasons.*

As he traveled out of suburbia in a scatter, he followed the echo of his blood in her out into farm country—and re-formed inside the bedroom at the front of the cottage. She was already there and going for the stairs, her purse clapping against her side, that bag swinging in her hand.

"Checking on Tallah?" he asked.

"What do you think," she muttered.

Or at least he assumed that's what she said.

As he listened to her descend the old, rickety staircase, he came to two conclusions, neither of which gave him any comfort: They were going to need weapons she could use, too. And shit, he wished he believed in the Scribe Virgin.

He could have used someone to pray to.

"I'll be right back," he called out.

No response. But he hadn't expected one.

Listening to her move around down on the first level, he gave her a chance to walk off some stress. Then he heard her go into the cellar, the sound of her footfalls growing dim.

Closing his eyes, he sent his instincts out, just to make sure that there were no sounds, scents, or strange disturbances of any kind in the cottage. When nothing came back to him, he figured things were as safe as they were going to get.

Needless to say, the trip back to his place was going to be a real fucking quick one. And shit, he didn't think he had enough firepower.

Then again, he could have had a missile launcher in the side yard and still felt like he was light-packing.

CHAPTER TWENTY-SIX

As Lassiter walked through the forest of the Brotherhood's mountain, it was not with a swagger, like he owned the joint. Instead, he carefully picked the places in the leaves and craggy underbrush where he could safely put his booted feet. And he constantly brushed off his shoulders, convinced things were dropping on him from overhead. And that sweet, natural pine smell? Irritated the fuck out of his sinuses.

For all the dominion he had over earthly matters, and vampires in particular, he fucking hated nature. Something was always sneaking under your collar and fifteen-feeting it down your spine. Or pooping on your head. Or poking you in the eye. Or giving you rabies.

Plus rain. Snow. Sleet. Hail. Which led to the fun and games of faucet-running noses, frostbitten toes, and oh, yeah, black ice that sent your car face-first into a tree trunk.

And then, because June through August didn't want to miss out on the opportunity to harass people, you got the too-hot summer. So in addition to bees, wasps, and yellowjackets, you had armpit sweat. Chafing. Flip-flops.

He couldn't fucking stand flip-flops. Nobody *ever* needed to see anybody else's piggies-go-to-market.

And there was another part to it all. To make his climate intolerance and allergy to nature's so-called wonders worse? He lived with Vishous. Who was only too happy to call a person out as a "pussy" if they happened to bring up the fact that maybe staying indoors was a great idea when the temperature was higher, or lower, than seventy degrees.

Whatever. Put that snarky SOB in a world full of Hallmark cards, MLM hun-bots, and "Save Britney" hashtags, and see how *he* did—

As the wind changed direction and half of the angel's pec-length hair spidered into his face, he batted the stuff away and glared to the northeast.

"I swear to fucking God, I will put a muzzle on you."

Aware that he had just told a force of nature to quit it or he'd give it something to cry about, he decided maybe he was just spoiled. His office was on the Other Side, up in the Sanctuary. Where it was always seventy degrees with no breeze—and no ticks, hornets, or mosquitos. Brown recluses. Asps.

Vishouses.

Talk about muzzles. Technically, there were options for dealing with that brother. In the hierarchy of things, the real flowchart of authority? Lassiter was the apex asshole, above even Wrath. And no matter how annoyed that made V, it was what it was: Gravity. The rise and fall of the sun. The supremacy of Eddie Van Halen's guitar licks, Bea Arthur's sense of style, the New York Yankees' batting average . . . and Lassiter's buck-stops-here.

Actually, he didn't really give a fuck about baseball. He just *really* enjoyed messing with V's Red Sox obsession.

"Like shooting fish in a barrel," he said to himself.

As he considered fresh approaches to winding up tall, dark, and judgy, the cave he was looking for came forth to greet him. The craggy hole in the side of the mountain was utterly unremarkable, nothing but a split in a vein of granite that was camo'd by trees and brush. Unless you knew it was there, you'd never see it—and that was the point.

Slipping inside, he got a prickly whiff of earth and mold—another grand recommendation for camping—and in the darkness, he orientated himself by throwing a golden glow around the low-ceiling'd—

Directly in front of him, on just an any-closer-and-it-woulda-bit-ya foot away, was a mound of pottery shards that was hip height and wide as a dance floor.

The remnants of the Black Dagger Brotherhood's collection of *lesser* jars.

Picking up an irregularly shaped piece that had a blue glaze, he thought of the Omega. The Lessening Society. The end of that era.

How many trips had it taken to clear the mess out? he wondered as he tossed the shard back and stepped around the pile.

Heading into a subtle curve in the fissure, he came up to a set of iron gates that were covered with a shiny-bright mesh. The bars were thick as a male's wrist, and the fine weave of steel, which prevented vampires from dematerializing inside, had been soldered on. The lock was copper.

With a sweep of his hand, he cast the venerable barrier aside and stepped into a hall set with torches that hissed and spit on their mountings. The sounds of brooms a-whisking escorted him forward, and soon enough, the ruination presented itself. From floor to ceiling, shelving made from hand-hewn planks was hanging in disarray, the lengths broken or mostly missing, the ragged ends like something had bitten at them. As he went along, he pictured things as they had been before, the horizontal levels set with jars of an incalculable number of different shapes and sizes and colors. There must have been . . . shit, a thousand of them? No, maybe more. And inside of those jars? The hearts of the *lessers* that the Brotherhood had killed.

The containers had been from every century, from ancient pottery ones that had been handmade all the way up to cheapo, mass-produced stuff from Target.

The collection had existed for so long, and been added to for so many years, that it had, in the manner of all things frequently seen, been taken to be permanent. The Omega had fixed that. Like a late-summer wasp on its last throes, the evil had come in to sting one final time, reclaiming the hearts he had removed during inductions to bolster his lagging strength.

The evil had ultimately been defeated, however.

And now? A new enemy had come to Caldwell.

Lassiter could only pray to himself that what they needed to fight the Book was still in that coffin.

Down about forty yards, Butch and Vishous were doing the brooming thing, the pair of them dressed in long black robes, some kind of conversation back-and-forthing between them.

No doubt the cop was trying to chill his roommate out about something.

How that former human managed to live with a Molotov cocktail like V was a shining example of forbearance.

"Speak of the devil," Lassiter said to Vishous. "And how're ya, Butch?"

"Don't you ever knock?" V bent over to corral a wedge of debris into a handheld dustpan with a *Joe Rogan Experience* sticker on it.

"Nice to see you, too." Lassiter sauntered by. "And jeez, you boys are handy with the tidy-up. If I had a car, I'd ask you to detail it."

"Why are you here again?" V said as he sloughed the dust off Rogan's face and into a Rubbermaid trash roller.

"Oh, same ol', same ol'." Lassiter shrugged. "I haven't seen you for almost twenty-two minutes and I just wanted to be in your presence. You know, to recharge myself with all the warmth you put out into the world."

As V straightened and glared across the narrow corridor, Butch clapped his roommate on the shoulder. "No, you can't hit him with your broom. Don't even think about it."

"I'm going to start calling him your zookeeper, V." Lassiter winked and kept going. Then, over his shoulder, he added, "See you at the altar, boys."

"I wouldn't cross the road to piss a fire out on your dead body," Vishous announced.

Lassiter pointed to the top of his head without turning around. "Immortal, remember?"

The *sanctum sanctorum* of the Black Dagger Brotherhood was deep inside the mountain, the vast subterranean cavern having once served as the reservoir for an underground river. And down at the terminal point of the gradual descent was the focus of it all: A raised dais, lit by black candles on stanchions, on which a stone altar had been set so that the ancient skull of the first brother could be properly displayed. Behind that precious artifact? An enormous wall of marble that was inscribed with the name of every member of the Brotherhood, from the first . . . to the most recent, John Matthew.

There would be others. Not that he could share that.

Fate was, after all, a need-to-know kind of jam.

Lassiter stopped before the skull, meeting the black voids of the eye sockets as if he were trading gazes with a living thing.

"I wish I could reassure them," he murmured.

It turned out, when you were in charge, there were things that the rank and file were not permitted to know. And of all the surprises that had come since he'd accepted this job from the Scribe Virgin, the biggest shocker was the amount of information he was not able to share with the people who would be most affected by it.

Evidently, knowing the outcome sometimes changed the "free" part of the will thing.

So as much as he hated it, he had to zip it a lot of the time—

Voices, deep and far off, percolated down to him, and before the Brotherhood arrived, he took a final look around at the stalactites, the black candles, the torches . . . the altar, the wall.

Stepping away from the skull, he went off to stand at the side. Moments later, the voices dried up and were replaced by the approaching sounds of heavy boots and the shifting of heavy fabric.

The first of the black robes entered alone. And even though the ceremonial garb's hood was up and shielding most of the facial features, it was obvious that it was Wrath—and not because of the white cane sweeping side to side, either. He was just bigger than the others, in ways that had nothing to do with physical size.

The next in line was Tohr, a spot of honor earned by virtue of him being the first lieutenant of the Brotherhood. And as the fighter's presence registered, Lassiter had a memory of finding the male in the forest and bringing him some McDonald's. The grief-stricken widower had been surviving off the blood of deer, waiting impatiently to die so he could join his *shellan* and unborn son in the Fade.

Destiny had had other plans for him, however.

Behind Tohr, the rest of them filed in, and the four in the middle were not empty-handed. Or empty-shouldered, as was the case. Rhage, Vishous, Phury, and Zsadist had the old coffin up on their shoulders, and they bore the responsibility with solemn honor.

The Black Dagger Brother Sahvage was back in the house, so to speak.

The coffin's wood had darkened nearly to black, the paneling run with age-created cracks and spotted with wormholes. But the carvings were still evident. Symbols in the Old Language detailed warnings on all sides, and woven among the dire missives was the brother's name.

At the altar, Tohr bowed before the skull. Then he picked it up and gave the relic to Wrath, the King's black diamond flashing as he accepted the sacred symbol of all that had gone before.

The coffin was placed upon the slab, taking up all of the flat surface.

The brothers tightened their circle around it, standing shoulder to shoulder, and as Wrath held the skull over his head, a low chanting started up, the voices of the males blending together to become one tone, one sound, that was amplified by the acoustics of the cave.

Tohr stepped forward, taking out of the folds of his black robe a silver wedge and an old hammer with a wooden handle. Finding the seam of the coffin lid, he drove the tool's sharp cleave in with a series of bam-bam-bams, and then repeated the process all around, teasing loose the single plane of wood that sealed the mortality box. The air that was released hissed out, and the sense that something imminent was closing in on the group made Lassiter's nape prickle in warning.

If he'd been Catholic, he'd have made the sign of the cross. Fortunately, Butch O'Neal did that for them all.

Hey, it never hurt to belt-and-suspenders with the God thing.

The coffin nails were long and rectangular, having been forged by hand centuries before, and there seemed to be a hundred of them. With every turn of the wedge, they protested against the separation they had been called into duty to prevent, the squeaks a reminder that not only were they good at their job, they had been doing it for a very, very long time.

Putting the tools back into his robe, Tohr nodded at the lineup of brothers, and Rhage and Vishous joined him, one at the head, one at the foot.

The chanting got louder as the three brothers squeezed their fingers in between the lid and the body of the coffin—and Lassiter had a thought that he was glad this wasn't a John Carpenter movie.

The nails came free in a series of pops and then the interior was revealed.

With a synchronized tilt, the Brotherhood leaned in as if they had linked arms, and Lassiter did the same off to the side. As his heart started to pound, he told himself that he had given them the right advice.

The solution to all of this was in there—

Everyone froze, including the three who were holding the lid.

"What the *fuck*," V breathed.

CHAPTER TWENTY-SEVEN

While Sahvage was up on the cottage's second floor listening for the boogeyman, Mae was down in the basement, staring into the darkness of Tallah's bedroom. The light from the cellar stairs was enough to let her see the old female lying on the chaise lounge by her antique writing desk. She'd cast her fragile body out on the silk cushions, one arm over her head, the other across her midriff. Her feet in those slippers were extended into arched points, like she was a ballerina about to come down for landing.

If she had been back in her youth, her recline would have been sensual. In her dotage, her pose seemed as sad as all her fancy furniture stuffed into this run-down little house: Evidence that the best of her life had come before, and what was left was only remnants of glory and youth, both faded to the point of no return.

"I lied to him," she whispered. "I couldn't tell him about—"

A creak up above in the kitchen made her shoulders tighten with anxiety.

Turning away, she tugged the hem of her fleece down and went over to the base of the wooden steps. Looking up at Sahvage as he stood at the top, he was nothing but a looming mass, faceless yet not shapeless, his muscles carving his presence out of the illumination streaming from behind him.

"Did you leave already?" she asked quietly.

"Yes. I'm back now."

Wow, that was fast. "She's sound asleep."

"Everything's secure up here. And I have . . . what we need."

Mae was careful on the ascension, making sure to sidestep the creakers in the planks. As she closed in on where he was, Sahvage backed up to give her some room.

Closing the basement door behind herself, she glanced around. "So . . . yeah."

"No, there still aren't any errant books. Anywhere."

"That wasn't what I was thinking."

"Yes, it was."

Mae crossed her arms over her chest. "I refuse to argue about what's going through my head with a disinterested third party."

Sahvage's lids lowered. "Oh, I'm hardly disinterested."

Mae leaned back against the cellar door. There was the temptation—nearly irresistible—to go back and forth with him, but instead she rotated her sore shoulder and stayed quiet.

"What are we going to do now?" she said.

"Sit and wait."

"For what."

"What's up with that shoulder of yours?"

"Huh? Oh." She rubbed the knot in the muscle with her opposite hand. "I was in a car accident a couple of years ago. The seat belt saved my life, but it caught me right across here—and ever since, it gets to talking to me."

"Sit down," he said as he spun one of the seats at the table around. "I'll take care of it."

"I'm not looking for help."

"No, really?" He clasped his hands to his chest. "What a reversal. I'm *reeling* over here. *You,* turning down aid?"

Mae smiled a little. "You're crazy."

"Maybe, but I know what I'm doing with shoulder injuries." He patted the chair. "Come on, what are you worried about? That I'm going to kiss you?"

Mae blinked. And thought, *No, I'm worried that if you do, I'm going to ask you to do it again. And again. And again—*

"No." To prove the point, she went over and planted her butt in front of him. "Do whatever you like."

Just as she was about to qualify that with a "shoulder only" chaser, she felt his broad, warm hand slide over the spot in question. Bracing herself, she got ready for him to pull some chiropractic move and snap her in half—

"Ohhhhhh . . ." she groaned as he massaged the top of her arm.

"Am I hurting you?"

"No, that's amazing."

He was gentle but firm as he worked the tension-filled cords that ran across the side of her neck . . . and God, the way the warmth from his palms translated into her skin, her muscles, her bones. And that weave of heat wasn't contained to just where he was touching. The connection between him and her body flowed everywhere, from her head to her feet.

The next thing she knew, she wasn't just sitting in the chair, she was relaxing into it. And after that, she noticed that her breathing was slowing and the persistent ache she'd had behind her right eye was also getting up and leaving—its presence registering because of its sudden absence.

So much stress over the last couple of weeks, winding her tighter and tighter. But with every subtle squeeze and rotating touch, Sahvage was taking it away from her, giving her a temporary peace that she knew was going to last only as long as he was massaging her.

But damn it, she was going to take the respite were she found it.

"Here, I'll come around and do the clavicle," he said.

She barely noticed Sahvage moving, but then he was in front of her and his thumb was pushing into the hollows above and below the bone that had been broken and healed wrong.

The second she winced, he stopped. "Too much?"

"No, it's wonderful," she murmured. "Please keep going."

There were a pair of cracks from his knees as he knelt down, and he was so big that his face was in front of hers even though the rest of him was on the floor. And as he fell into a rhythm of pressure and release, her torso moved back and forth, becoming a wave, as opposed to an intractable I-beam of stress.

It was hard to say when relaxation turned to awareness.

When she started to focus on how close he was to her.

When her eyes, which she hadn't been aware of closing, slowly reopened.

Sahvage was staring at her face instead of where he was rubbing, and his harsh features were a mask, showing nothing. His stare, though . . . it was full of heat.

I take lives against the will, but never females.

"I think you're good," he said as he dropped his magical hands.

In the silence, he didn't rise to his full height. He didn't move in to get closer. He just stayed where he was, showing her nothing and telling her everything with his obsidian eyes.

And that was when she realized . . .

"Not black, but blue," she whispered.

"What?"

"Your eyes." Her voice got huskier. "I've been thinking they were black. They're a very dark blue."

"I wouldn't know."

"How can you not know what color eyes you have?"

"Because I don't care."

Their voices were low and soft in the silent cottage, but not because either of them was worried about waking up Tallah. At least that wasn't on Mae's mind. No, to her, they had created a separate space from the entire world, and there was no reason to speak any louder than it took to cross the infinitesimal distance between them.

"How can you not care?" she said.

"I don't like to look at myself." He reached up and brushed a strand of her hair back. "Mirrors are not my friend."

"Why?"

He shrugged. "I can't stand my reflection."

Her hand lifted of its own volition to his face. The second she made contact with his cheek, his breath seemed to catch—which seemed strange given how powerful his body was.

With careful fingers, she traced his jaw . . . and lingered at his chin. "You have a five o'clock shadow."

"Do I."

"Do you shave without a mirror?"

"Yes."

She shook her head. "How?"

"I do it in the shower."

Sure as if he had implanted the image in her mind, she pictured him under a cascade of water, his head tilted back, his hair slick from the moisture . . . his naked body the peaks and valleys the spray traveled over. Glistening. Glossy.

As it rushed down his torso toward his—

"Do you ever cut yourself?" she breathed.

"No. I've been doing it that way for years."

She stopped with her hand cupping the side of his face. And as she fell quiet again, he turned to her palm . . . and pressed his lips to her life-line, to the place she had scored herself with the knife so she could bleed into the silver basin and call the Book that had yet to come.

"I'm sorry," she said roughly.

"For what."

"I don't know."

Sahvage took her hand down and ran his thumb over the already-closed cut. "I thought you hurt your finger, not here."

"No, this was from before."

"You're not very good with knives, huh."

"Guess not."

Lowering his head, she closed her lids as he brushed his lips over the healed slice.

She stayed exactly where she was for what felt like an eternity.

When she opened her eyes, he was staring right at her—and she spoke one and only one word:

"Yes."

CHAPTER TWENTY-EIGHT

S ometimes you had to go in for a second look.

Or twelve.

Deep in the Black Dagger Brotherhood's sacred Tomb, Lassiter elbowed his way through big male bodies to get to the coffin's edge. But it wasn't like proximity changed what he was seeing.

Which was absolutely fucking nothing . . . except half a dozen old bags of—

"What is that?" someone said.

V outed one of his black daggers and stabbed at the discolored burlap sack. As a white powder was exposed, he speared some onto the blade.

"I'd think twice before throwing that in your nose," somebody else remarked.

"Oat flour," Vishous announced as he scented it. "Really fucking old oat flour."

What the fuck, Lassiter thought.

No skeleton surrounded by spiderwebs. No mummy. No zombie with perpetually rotting flesh and a hankering for fresh meat. Not even a generic set of remains where there was a collapsed death shroud and some dust over a bunch of discombobulated bones.

But no, they had something Fritz could make a bread loaf out of.

And not the weapon Lassiter had brought them here for.

"Someone better tell me what the fuck is happening," Wrath growled as he yanked the hood of his robe down.

"Nothing is happening." Lassiter looked over at the King as the other brothers likewise lost the coverings over their heads. "There's a couple bags of flour in there. Otherwise, the coffin is empty."

The happy little announcement made the great Blind King register surprise behind his wraparounds. "Sahvage. Is gone."

"If he was ever in there." Lassiter backed away and ended up looking at the wall of names. "Maybe we have the wrong coffin."

Tohr picked up the lid. "His name is carved into the damn thing. Along with all the warnings."

"So they didn't kill him," Wrath said with a shrug. "Those guards must have not killed him, after all."

"Warlocks aren't immortal, if that's what you mean," Lassiter said absently. "Just because you practice magic doesn't mean you live forever. It doesn't work like that."

"And just because you say you killed someone and nailed 'em into a coffin doesn't meant that's what you did," Wrath shot back. "The *glymera* lying. Imagine that. That *never* fucking happens."

"He must have used the supposed death to his advantage," Tohr said. "He disappeared and stayed that way because he knew nothing good was going to come from what happened with that aristocrat, at that castle. He would have wanted to spare the Brotherhood the problems—"

Phury spoke up. "For those of us who don't know the story, can anyone please explain?"

As Lassiter went over and checked out the names that had been inscribed into the marble wall, he listened to Wrath lay out the fact pattern: Sahvage with the hocus-pocus in the Old Country. Local *glymera* leader gets spooked. A hunt-down that supposedly ended in the slaughter of an aristocrat and his guards, and Sahvage's own death. The brother put in this coffin along with the Gift of Light.

Except not so much, as it turned out.

"And what is the Gift of Light?" Phury said.

"It's a source of energy," Lassiter replied as he found Sahvage's name in the lineup of inscriptions. "But more than that. It's incredibly powerful, and if you want to fight evil, it's really fucking handy."

"So you weren't going to try and resurrect Sahvage? I thought bringing him back was the point of all this."

"No." Lassiter shook his head. "Sahvage was never the thing. He was supposedly buried with the Gift of Light, and that's what I want you to have."

"What is that exactly? A sword? Another book—"

"Yeah, like we need a second hardcover in all this," V muttered.

There's something wrong here, Lassiter thought. *This is not the way it's supposed to be.*

Turning away from Sahvage's inscription, he cleared his throat. "The Gift of Light is a prism, a sacred relic of an ancient time that goes all the way back to when the Scribe Virgin was creating the vampire race. It reflects whatever goes into it. So if you leverage it against great evil—"

"Then that's what you get back out of it," V finished.

"So you could turn evil on itself?" Phury said.

"Only certain kinds of evil." Lassiter pushed a hand through his hair. "It wouldn't have worked against the Omega. He was the other half of the Scribe Virgin, so it was too close to him—I have to go now."

"You're kidding me, right." V glared across the empty coffin. "If you're leaving us because *Golden Girls* is on—"

"No, it's not that."

"Then what the hell's wrong with you?"

Shaking his head again, Lassiter repeated some combination of the I'm-out-of-here album blaring through his skull—and dematerialized directly out from the Tomb.

Good job the Other Side was never far away for him. All he had to do was pierce the veil that separated the earthbound from all that was eternal and *poof!* he was in a glorious field of grass that did not require mowing, turning his face to a milky white sky that never stormed, taking a deep breath of temperate air that was perfumed with the delicate scent of tulips.

But there was no peace for him right now.

As he strode off toward his destination, he went past the bathing temple, with its beautiful, shimmering basin of water, and then continued on by the columned villas where the Chosen had stayed when they'd lived here. There was also the Treasury, with its baskets of loose gems and special artifacts, and even more important . . . the Scribing Temple.

He stopped outside of the sacred confines where, for millennia, the most cloistered of all the Chosen had spent the forever-hours of their existence staring into crystal seeing bowls and recording the lives and events unfolding down below on earth.

Opening one of the solid doors, he viewed the scribing stations set in rows, the desks still sporting the ink pots and feathers as well as the bowls and the folios of fresh, unused parchment. Everything was as it should be, the chairs aligned perfectly, the plumes of the quills all gracefully extending up at the same angle, no dust on anything, no cobwebs, the space as it had been at the moment it was established for its purpose.

Even though it had been abandoned.

Stepping inside, his boots echoed around the high ceiling, and he had a thought that with the Scribe Virgin retiring and him taking over, all these functions that had once been so vital were gone.

Talk about relics.

On that note, he went past the scribing stations and proceeded to the library—and even for an angel like him, who was pretty damned impervious to being impressed, it was daunting to take a gander at all the stacks and stacks of the recorded history of the vampire race.

Inside the countless volumes, which were arranged chronologically, every major and minor incident of every soul housed inside every body with vampire blood had been faithfully recorded. By hand. In ink.

It was all the knowledge that existed of all the lives that had gone before—and he was going to go through the pages and find every mention of the Gift of Light and Sahvage and that goddamn Book.

The brothers and the other fighters in the mansion often gave him a hard time for not taking his job seriously enough.

And for the first time, he worried that maybe they were right.

Because something wasn't adding up here; he just didn't know what.

◆   ◆   ◆

Devina walked through the club, high heels clickin'—not that anyone could hear her Louboutins cross the grimy floor. Overhead, SoundCloud rap was thumping, the auto-tuned, distorted voice of a guy mumbling about drugs and sex punctuated with a lot of high-fiving synthesized beats. In her opinion, the track had as much in common with actual music as a Twinkie did with a homemade Victoria sponge, but what the fuck did she care.

It was chum into the sea, pulling out of houses and apartments all manner of humans, creating a buffet for her base instincts.

As she visually interviewed the various couples and throuples—assessing all manner of body type and wardrobe choice, but mostly the eye contact between and among the connected—she had a thought that she was feeling just a liiiiiiiiiiiiiiiiiiiiiiiittle aggressive.

And didn't that self-awareness show personal growth?

Sure as fuck did, she thought as she focused on a pair of men who were nose to nose, eye to eye, their bodies moving in sync. Behind them was a man and a woman. Next to them, all around them, were more of the same, combinations of sexes and heights and hair colors coming together.

So they could come together.

The fact that she was surrounded by so much one-night-standing was the only thing that kept her from exploding the place, just running the people through with her wrath so they blew apart in chunks. Which would be so fucking satisfying . . .

Okay, fine, it would be so satisfying for maybe as long as it took for the pieces of arms, legs, and torsos to stop bouncing up from their landings on the floor.

But that was something, right?

Yeah, and then where was she going to be.

Right back where she was.

Stopping in the center of all the groping, directly under the light fixture that shot laser beams into the writhing masses, she turned and turned and turned . . . until she was like the after-school-special transition into flashback that wound faster and faster until everything blurred up and funneled away . . .

To Something That Brought Meaning or Revelation to Present Events.

Of course that was not what was actually happening at the moment. In spite of the Instagram revolution of narcissism, which she fully supported, people's lives, even if you were immortal, were not actually film productions with jump cuts, off-camera narration, and soundtracks. There were no scripts, no stage markers for where you were supposed to stand, no let's-try-that-take-again-with-a-little-more-emotion.

Which fucking sucked.

She wanted a do-over. And some better lighting. And a leading fucking man, thank you very much.

As her frustration sharpened even further, she surveyed the landscape of lovers and knew two things were true: One, not all of these one-night stands were going to stay that way. Some of these couples were going to develop their connection, and forge relationships, and someday in the future, laugh between themselves, or maybe with friends, at how they'd found true love at a club.

Can you believe it? We were so fucked up on Molly when we met, but now here we're picking out china patterns and a sofa. We're just so lucky, Todd.

You're right, Elaine, so lucky!

Yeah, fuck off, Todd and Elaine. Oh, and the other thing she knew for sure? She was no part of this and not because she wasn't human. While all of these useless tools were coupling up, she was locked out of a happily ever after, sure as she'd been blocked from entering that stupid fucking ugly-ass, fucking piece of shit, motherfucking ranch.

By salt. Damn it.

Not that there was going to be anything in there she'd want. For fuck's sake, the place was no doubt home to fifteen-year-old couches, carpets she wouldn't touch with a ten-foot pole, and faded flocked wallpaper that had been bought at Sears back when Jimmy Carter had been the president and *Taxi* had been on prime time.

But sometimes you just wanted to get into a place you weren't allowed to go.

You just wanted the things you weren't given.

You just wanted to fuck shit up and walk away with the mushroom cloud behind you, feeling like you owned the world because you were able to destroy it.

Devina stopped turning.

Enough with this bullshit. Time to pick her fun for the rest of the night—because if she didn't get a shot of enjoyment soon? She was going to lose her motherfucking mind.

Oh, and that vampire? With the salt?

It was going to be good to eat his heart. Because whether he knew it or not—whether he wanted to admit it to himself or not—he was totally in love with that female and her dumbass ponytail. And just as pathetic? She was in love with him. It was obvious in the way they'd communicated with each other, no words necessary to make meaning clear, their bodies turned to each other's, their connection tangible.

Fine. Whatever. Those two lovebirds might be able to keep a demon out of that house.

But they weren't going to stop her from kicking down their goddamn sandcastle.

CHAPTER TWENTY-NINE

As Sahvage heard the word that Mae spoke, the three-lettered door opener went into his ears and throughout his whole body. *Yes.*

Yet she stopped him as he moved in toward her lips. "I don't know . . . how far this is going to go."

"I do." He brushed her cheek. "It's going as far as you want it to. And no further."

The tension left her body and she eased toward him. "I shouldn't be doing this."

"I'd ask you why, but I don't have to."

There were too many reasons, for both of them, not to complicate things even more. But clearly, neither of them was going to stop the inevitable . . . so those were the last syllables they spoke before their mouths met—and what a kiss it was. He'd thought he was prepared for the sensation of her softness and warmth, but just because you wanted something didn't mean you could handle it.

Mae melted him.

And he only wanted more. Keeping his touch gentle, he moved his hand up to the side of her neck to draw her even closer—and when she came willingly, he groaned and tilted his head. Deeper, the kiss now. Even deeper still. Until his tongue entered her.

He wished they had a big bed, with plenty of privacy.

But he needed her so badly, he would have done this in the middle of a war zone.

The chair she was on creaked softly, and the next thing he knew, he was in between her knees, cradling her face, learning about what she liked as he took it slow, took it easy, everything drifting away for him—

Well, not everything. His threat instincts remained on alert—but at the moment, there was nothing wrong inside or outside the cottage.

And his guns were on him.

God, he shouldn't be doing this. She was a civilian; he was a bloodthirsty rogue fighter with no home, no bloodline, and no identity anymore. And yet he needed this like he was suffocating and she was his air.

They kept kissing, and even though his lust began to choke him, he wasn't going to rush her—and wasn't that a serious change of pace for him. For all his post-transition life, when the mood struck him and the female or woman was willing, he took care of business and then headed out.

With Mae? He wasn't interested in this being over anytime soon—and even if he could have left the cottage, he was so very content to stay with her.

When she eased back, he hid his disappointment.

Except then she took things in a direction that was very appointment'ing.

If that was even a word.

With her soft, small hand, she took his palm from the side of her neck . . . and placed it on her breast.

✦   ✦   ✦

Sahvage was the best kisser Mae had ever known. Which, considering she hadn't kissed more than two males in her fifty years of life, probably didn't sound like much. But holy . . . well, shit, honestly . . .

Was there really anything better than this?

The problem? For all his obvious arousal, he seemed to be stuck in a delicious neutral.

As their lips met and clung, and his tongue was a stunning penetration, as her body roared with heat, and so did his own, she sensed his powerful restraint . . . and waited for him to get exploring. Waited to do some exploring herself. And yet he stayed with the kissing.

So, yup, in a surge of uncharacteristic self-determination, she solved the issue of how far things were going to go by taking his palm and putting it where there was an ache she needed him to caress away. Kiss away. Suck away.

Mae gasped as the warmth of his hand transmitted through her fleece, her shirt, her bra. Sure as if she were naked.

"Is this okay?" he asked as he pulled back.

When she went to answer, he swept his thumb over her nipple—and didn't that make her brain stop working right. In lieu of answering verbally, she arched forward and retook his lips as she pushed herself into his palm—and he got the point. He treated her to a stroking that made her pant into his mouth, and then he was slipping under things and finding her skin. As he went upward and stroked her ribs, she grabbed on to his shoulders.

Which were so big, she felt like she was trying to grip an oak trunk.

"Please," she begged.

"What do you want?"

"Touch me . . ."

"Where." He kissed up the side of her throat. "I want to hear you say it."

"My . . . nipple . . . again . . ."

Now he was groaning, and with a surge, he pushed both of her bra cups up, her layers of clothing wedging under her arms. When one of his thumbs went exactly where she'd told him to go, she gasped again and needed to know what his mouth would be like there, his dark head down at her breasts, tasting her, marking her—

Sahvage pulled back so fast, her hands fell off of his shoulders and slapped into her lap. Confused, she looked down at her messed-up tops, the erect pink tips of her breasts peeking out from under the rolls of cotton and fleece.

Just as she was going to ask him what she'd done wrong, how she'd turned him off, he yanked her tops back into place and leaped away from her. Like maybe she'd become radioactive.

"What did I do?" she said in a voice that cracked.

The cellar door opened wide, and Tallah's wrinkled face peered around the jamb. "I'm not interrupting anything, am I?"

Mae blinked. The old female had changed out of her housecoat, trading the blue and yellow flowers for a long red dress made of a lustrous material that was likely pure silk, given her background. She had also put on makeup, a subtle pink blush tinting her cheeks, her eyes emphasized with tasteful shadow, a red outline and gloss on her lips.

And her hair was down, the waves of white and gray flowing around her shoulders like a cape of sterling silver.

"No," Sahvage said smoothly. "Not at all. Mae was just telling me how long you've been here and how often she's come out to keep you company."

Mae glanced in his direction. Somehow, in the nanosecond between when he'd yanked her fleece down and Tallah had made her presence known, he'd managed to pick up a teacup and the hand towel. With steady, lazy hands, he was pretending to dry that which was not wet.

And what do you know, he was doing all that right in front of his hips.

On that note, Mae pivoted toward the table, bringing the chair with her—just so she had an excuse to turn away and make sure her clothes were where they needed to be.

Thank God. Shirt and fleece were looking pretty good on the re-arrange. Not great, but okay enough. And at least her bra, which was still up and over its charges, so to speak, wasn't showing its disorder. Then again, she didn't wear any padding or underwires.

"Would you like something to eat?" Mae asked as she couldn't meet Tallah in the eye.

The truth was, she had no clue how to handle this situation.

Virgins were not known for their game—and she did her best not to dwell on how business-as-usual it all seemed for Sahvage.

Clearly, he'd had experience . . . in a lot of things.

"I am hungry, thank you," Tallah said as she came forward. "But I feel like cooking."

"Listen, I need to run out for second." Sahvage put the teacup down on its saucer, and went over to the flak jacket he'd tossed over the arm of the sofa. "I'll be right back. Just a quick errand."

As Mae looked across at him, he shook his head like he was reading her mind and seeing the *Again?* that was all over it. "It's not going to take long. I promise."

"Oh, okay."

He nodded, and then he was gone, dematerializing right in front of them. Which meant he was using that second-floor window again.

In his absence, Tallah smiled and patted her hair. "A male like that makes you feel young, doesn't he?"

Where was he going? Mae thought.

She hid her flush and her worry by getting up from the table. "How can I help you with food?"

"Sit, sit, sit." Tallah waved the offer away as she went to the stove. "I brought some meat up from the refrigerator downstairs. Let me make you and him a meal. It's the least I can do for you."

"Speaking of which, do you mind if we stay here today?"

Tallah's eyes twinkled in a way Mae hadn't seen for . . . years. "I would just love the company. How delightful!"

CHAPTER THIRTY

O kay, so here's a moral quandary.

Nah, not really.

As Sahvage re-formed outside of a trailer with bullet holes in its cheap aluminum siding, he looked around at the crap-ass yard: Two pickup trucks off to the side, rusted parts of cars strewn around like the biopsies from junkers, a BBQ grill without a lid or a propane tank listing by a busted picnic table. The acreage was crowded with trees and vines, and as he thought of the cottage, he wished he were sticking around in Mae's life. He liked the idea of getting a mower and clippers, tidying the place up, taking care of—

Jesus. One kiss and she'd turned him into a suburban househusband. Next up, beer cozies, football in the fall, and a dad bod.

Never gonna happen, he thought as he palmed one of his guns.

But what he could do for her? Was make sure she was safer.

There were three loose wooden steps that led up to a door that was probably the only solid thing on the property. Raising his fist to knock—

The scream of pain from inside was muffled. But it was clearly a woman's, high-pitched and desperate.

And then, much, much louder: "You fucking whore! Where's my fucking money—"

"I gave it to you! It's right there—"

The slap was so loud, it rang in Sahvage's ears. Annnnnnnnd he'd had enough of this.

Grabbing onto the knob, he ripped the door from its frame and led with the muzzle of his forty.

Over on a worn-out plaid couch, a hollow-eyed woman in faded blue jeans and a blood speckled t-shirt was trapped under the lanky body of a greasy meth-head Sahvage had known for all of two and a half weeks. Crumpled bills littered the threadbare cushions around them, and a three-foot-tall bong that was charred like a tailpipe had been kicked over to drool on the filthy, matted carpet.

As they both looked over at him in surprise, Sahvage leveled his gun at the man. "Let her go."

To his absolute insanity, the misogynistic fucker recovered quickly. "Fuck off! What the fuck are you doing—"

"Dave," Sahvage said in a reasonable tone, "let her go or I'm going to shoot you in the head."

"This is not your fucking business." Dave twisted the woman's hand back until she whimpered. "And we did not have an appointment."

"Like this is a dentist office?" Sahvage narrowed his eyes. "On three. You let her go, or I shoot you in the head. One."

Dave wrenched around with a glare—while using his grip on the front of the woman's throat to keep his balance. "You're making a fucking mistake here—"

"Two."

"You're not going to shoot me."

With a coordinated move—like he'd had to do it before—Dave lunged into the couch cushions for a gun.

"Three," Sahvage said as he pulled his trigger first.

The discharge was a loud clap in the grungy confines, and then Dave's rather limited IQ exploded out the back of his skull, speckling

the wall behind him with blood and gray matter. The gun he'd gone for
went off as the hand holding it contracted on an autonomic squeeze, but
its muzzle had been on the swing around instead of in position—so the
bullet just hit the cheap cabinets over the sink and rattled whatever
dishes were in there.

The woman screamed again and pushed herself away from the collapsed body.

"Sorry about that," Sahvage said grimly.

He didn't have a chance to offer help. She swiped up the loose
money, hooked a black pack on her arm, and dodged around the trash
and debris to tear out of the trailer. A split second later, a muffler-less
truck roared to life and threw up the loose gravel of the drive.

Sahvage exhaled and kept his gun out as he went over to the sofa
and took the gun from the now-dead hand of his arms dealer. Then he
went down to the bedroom. Kicking the door out of its hinges with his
boot, he leveled his weapon at the six-by-nine-foot steel cabinet across
the shallow space.

Two shots. Both of which ricocheted into the bed's bald, stained
mattress.

As the panels of the armory safe lolled open, he made quick work
of stealing the guns that Dave had stolen from God only knew who.
Which was the nah-not-really to the quandary of whether it was
thievery to take things from a person who had lifted the shit themselves.

And oh, look. There was a duffle bag right over by a collection of
pristine Nikes. Handy for transport.

Taking the bag and leaving the shoes, Sahvage filled his new piece of
soft luggage with rifles, shotguns, and a nine millimeter for Mae. The
ammo was in the bottom of the weapon wardrobe, and he took boxes of
bullets.

He would have paid Dave for it eventually. He had $2,800 in cash
back at the shithole he was camping out in, and one more fight with the
Reverend would have covered the rest of the $5,000 or so he'd have been

charged: He hadn't come here intending to steal, more like borrow on layaway.

Shoot-away was more like it.

But good ol' Dave didn't have to worry about his black market business's balance sheet anymore, so Sahvage was considering the debt discharged.

As he came back out, he stared at Dave—and took a minute to think about the nature of dead bodies. The next thing he knew, memories he had been trying to mentally outrun overtook him on a tackle that landed him smack back into the past.

◆   ◆   ◆

Within the confined space of his coffin, Sahvage gathered his wits, marshaled his strength. There was the temptation to thrash and batter, yet he could sense naught of where he was. He smelled no dirt, and he took that to mean he had not been buried. Beyond that? He was sure of nothing.

No sounds gave him cues. No particular smells, either.

Other than the fresh cut of the wood planks that surrounded him.

There was no calming himself to dematerialize. No sufficient measure of self-control to be mustered as his heart thundered for all that had to be occurring for Rahvyn. Thus he fashioned his palms upon the lid's underside, and with ever-increasing force, pushed, pushed, pushed—

The nails sang and squeaked, but yielded before the pressure, the lid lifting a crack, air entering, even as no light did. One deep breath suggested a location that made little sense, though as he could have been under six feet of earth, he would take the scents of flour and oats o'er raw dirt. And just as the lid popped free of its many moorings, he grabbed its edge so as to not make a clatter—

With a hiss, he bit his tongue to quell calling out as his hand was scored by the teeth of the nails. The smell of fresh blood sprang into his nose as his flesh wept, and he prayed that this food-storage area was free of drafts that would carry his scent unto the noses of others.

As he lifted his torso from its recline, he was of care with the lid, setting it aside silently—

Something fell from his chest. Beads? It sounded like marbles.

Feeling about, he encountered a wad that was damp and disturbing. His blood? Someone else's?

He couldnae worry about that right the now.

Across whatever space he was in, there was a door . . . he could see the glowing outline created by its loose fit, and though the illumination did not carry far, it was a sufficient grounding whilst he stood up slowly.

Now Sahvage breathed more deeply, more evenly, and his sense of smell confirmed certain gastronomic basics: Again, the flour. Spices of some kind. Further grains.

A dry storage room. And there was such evident abundance that it could only be within Zxysis's castle.

An unlikely venue for any coffin, but that gentlemale would need Sahvage's to be kept hidden. As a member of the Black Dagger Brotherhood, his remains would be considered sacred by his brothers, something to be reclaimed and promptly ahvenged. *But herein, secreted amongst stores for the use of the aristocrat's servants, of whom all were dependent upon the lord for his beneficence? The* doggen *would say not a thing and would ask no questions. Nor would anyone searching for aught of a coffin description think to look here.*

As he went to step out of the casket, he discovered two further details: He had nothing on his feet, and a loose robing upon his body. A quick inspection of his form yielded no remarkable points of pain, the arrows having been removed at some point, whate'er damage done by them already healed. Pausing for a moment, he lifted his head and offered a quick prayer of gratitude unto the purebred Chosen from whom he had fed a mere three nights before.

Without her strength? He would surely have expired.

Turning unto the door frame, he resolved to find his cousin. And worried about how long he had been sleeping. Through the day? Through a day and a night?

There were crates and burlap bags in his way unto the exit, and he listed and lurched around them, attempting to keep both his balance and his silence in the darkness, in the unknown course of obstacles. When he came upon the hearty oak planks in their vertical alignment, he pressed an ear unto them and ceased his own breathing.

Naught upon the other side, that he could hear or scent.

As he cast a hand to the jamb, in search of latching, he prayed there was one on the interior—

When he found the metal pin and rod, he lifted the bolt with care and cracked the portal. Pale stone walls suggesting a hall, alit by torches. No sounds. No scents. Or at least none of either that alarmed his instincts.

Leaning out, he regarded the hallway in both directions. Then he glanced at the robing that covered him. Black feathers, matted with some kind of dampness, fell to his feet in a clump, along with some pebbles of some sort, and he had a whiff of something he could not place. Touching the front of the robing, he then brought forth his fingers. They were stained with something red. His blood. But what else—

As a whiff of astringent tingled his sinuses, he realized what had been done.

Zxysis and his guards had marked his body with magic, to keep that which was not *a warlock—and was* not *in fact deceased—dead. No doubt so that they could prepare a hidden grave for him.*

Their misguided determination of his status, on both of those levels, would have been laughable had they not had Rahvyn in their clutches.

Stepping out, Sahvage retrieved a torch from its iron seat upon the stone and went unto the right, following a faint trail of fresh air. As he padded along in his bare feet, he attempted to remember the castle's layout. He had been within Zxysis's seat of power for festivals from time to time, back before Rahvyn's special nature had begun to assert itself. But he had never been down herein. What did it matter, however. He would find a weapon, even if he had to makeshift one, and he would locate his dearest cousin.

And then he would force her to leave this hamlet with him, even if he had to tie her to the saddle of his warhorse.

After that? When he was assured of her safety?

He would return and slaughter them all.

As his destiny became not only clear but inevitable, he was not unaware that it would split him from the Black Dagger Brotherhood. But he could not involve them. This was his right, and his duty unto his cousin. He would accept no aid, and when the Council balked at his actions? They would go to his brothers and seek retribution of their own.

And 'round and 'round it would go. Yet he would not be dissuaded nor would he seek any permission for his actions. So from now on, he was rogue.

Mayhap it would be best if all believed he was deceased.

It was as this thought occurred . . . that he slowed to a halt. Looking back at where he had come from, he found that he had gone some distance without encountering any member of the vast household. Moreover, the resonant silence all around sank properly into his consciousness. He cursed. Indeed, it must be the day, in which case a rescue of his cousin was going to be complicated by sunlight's ever-present threat—

A portal opened and closed farther down the corridor, and the blast of fresh air must have been a doggen *coming in or departing, for that subspecies of the race was not affected by the rays of the day. As footsteps approached him, he whispered unto a door and was relieved when he opened it and discovered another storage room. Ducking in, he waited, and as the servant passed, he stayed still and silent.*

When things were clear, he leaned out once again and frowned.

That was not the scent of a doggen. *That was a male vampire.*

Thus it had to still be night?

Picking up his pace, he continued on, following the corridor to its terminus before ascending one set of steps and then another. And still the silence persisted, up above, all around. Where were the castle's inhabitants?

A broad staircase, capable of accommodating many males shoulder to shoulder, presented itself, and that was when he smelled something that made him pick up his pace rather than worry about remaining undetected.

His cousin! She was near!

Upon the head of the steps, the great hall unfurled—and he gasped. "Rahvyn!"

Rushing forth, he crossed the stone flooring unto the hearth where the fe-

male had been chained to steel loops mounted in the thick, mortared wall, her head hanging loose, her robing marked with dirt and blood, more blood matting her dark hair.

"Rahvyn, dearest Virgin Scribe, Rahvyn . . ." He was gentle with his trembling hands as he brushed her locks back. "Look at me—"

As she lifted her face, he felt a rage that went to his bones.

Both of her eyes had been blackened, her lip was split, and there was a bruise around her neck.

Her stare, however, glittered with a power he could not immediately comprehend.

"Rahvyn, I shall get you free—" Heedlessly dropping the torch, he went for the pinnings struck into the wall. "I shall—"

"No," she hissed. "They cannae hurt me—"

Sahvage froze. Then redoubled his efforts.

"Whate'er you say?" He yanked at the steel chains and formulated a way to carry her out. "Just a moment—"

"I am back now. They cannae hurt me."

Sahvage frowned. Something in her tone of voice, her words . . . "What?"

"I was gone, but I have returned. And I shall not be hurt again."

"How did they hurt you," he said baldly.

"You are likewise released. You are free the now. Go forth and worry not for me—"

"What do you mean, I am free?"

"I have freed you, and now you may go—"

"I shall not leave you—"

In a voice that warped with an authority he did not understand, Rahvyn pronounced, "I shall take care of myself. And you shall leave, for the only power any shall e'er have over either of us is me."

He shook his head. "What say you."

"We shall be separate from now on."

Sahvage resumed his yanking. "No more of this talk. I shall remove you away from here and take well care of you—"

Heavy, pounding footfalls the now. Many of them, some number of *males of great weight and armament coming forth from elsewhere within the castle.*

Sahvage pulled so hard against the steel chains, he felt a pop in his shoulder joint, but the ring came out, the chains rattling. He went to the other side.

"Stop," Rahvyn ordered. "Unhand the chains. I am unafraid."

"After what they did to you—"

"I have been unlocked through Zyxsis's violence. I have no regrets—"

The second pinning came loose, and then he tried to scoop her up in his arms.

His beloved cousin shoved him back. "No! I am not going with you—"

"Are you mad?"

"If you do not separate us, I shall, Sahvage. We must needs be apart, and you are free now—"

And that was when a stand of guards came unto the archway. They were a full flank's worth, uniformed in the ribbon colors of Zxysis's bloodline, armed with weapons of sword and gun.

As Sahvage placed his body between his charge and his now-sworn enemy, he took up the torch once more as the only defense he had outside of his physical form. Bracing himself, he orientated his position unto the exits, which were the stairs he had come up and the—

The guards stayed where they were, weapons poised, bodies prepared for attack, yet the violence remaining on the brink rather than called unto realization.

Fear marked their eyes.

As none moved, a strange sense of foreboding had Sahvage looking back at his cousin. She was staring at the guards with a concentration that seemed like something he could reach out and feel, like a rope or a set of chains such as those that fell from her wrists.

"I told your lord to leave me," she said unto the males. "And he did not listen. I shall not give you such a choice of retreat."

All at once, the scabbards and flint rifles lowered and then dropped unto the stone with a clattering. And then came the trembling. Those male bodies, so stout and strong in their protective leathers, began to shake. Every one of them. And then hands reached for throats, reached for temples, reached for chests. Panic flared eyes even wider—

Moans echoed about the great hall as mouths stretched to grab at air, and cheeks became florid from straining, and sweat coursed down faces and dripped upon chest coverings—

The head of the guard on the farthest right exploded first, a pumpkin kicked, fragments of skull and fluffy white pieces of brain flying off in a spray of bright red blood.

As the headless body flopped to the floor, landing upon the weapons once held by vital, fighting hands, the others screamed and flailed, but they were trees a-rooted, going nowhere. One by one, they followed the fate of the first, the bloody chaos overwhelming and inexplicable, for there were no hands upon them, no bludgeoning tools o'er their shoulders or afore their faces, no contact brought to bear upon them.

And yet it was real, for their airborne blood speckled Sahvage's black robing, and the scent of their raw, meaty flesh was within his nose.

Turning around to Rahvyn, he took a step back from the female he'd thought he knew as he knew his own reflection.

"Who art thou," he said roughly.

◆   ◆   ◆

With a jerk, Sahvage came back to the present—and discovered that he had walked up close to the couch and was staring at the burst of blood and brains on the wall behind where Dave was sprawled in his perma-repose. Even now, even after all these years, and all the person-to-person fighting Sahvage had done . . . he had never gotten over what he had seen that night when Rahvyn had come 'round from a stupor and literally blown the heads off a stand of guards.

"Sleep well, asshole," Sahvage muttered as he hitched the duffle bag full of guns up on his shoulder and hit the exit.

Out by the remaining truck, he was tempted to take it as well, but not for long. He'd never needed a car, and like he could fence the damn thing without someone tracking him back to this now-murder scene? Whatever. Best to keep things clean, even though he wasn't going to be in Caldwell for much longer.

Although now? Given his persistent premonition of dying, he had a feeling he was leaving feetfirst. Death was going to be a relief, and if he could steer Mae away from making a mistake with that old female's inevitable fate? Well, then he'd have done one thing right in this world.

Just before he dematerialized back to the cottage, he looked to the sky and thought of Rahvyn. It had been a while since he'd done that. A couple of decades.

And he felt no better now than he had before. She was his ultimate failure.

Shaking his head, he ghosted out. With any luck, he wouldn't have to think of her ever again soon. He'd be in that black void that came after your last heartbeat, no more worries, no more cares, no more anything.

Although he had learned the hard way that magic existed in the world, he no longer believed in the Fade. Death was a full stop.

Nothing but lights-out.

Thank fuck.

CHAPTER THIRTY-ONE

o, no, no, no . . .

N
As Erika elbowed her way through a moving forest of
half-dressed, fully drunken clubgoers, she was pissed off and
on edge. Ahead of her, the bouncer who was leading the way parted
most of the sea, but there were stragglers who got in her way—and she
had to resist shoving them off. And then there were the lasers. And the
buzzy music. It was like being in a hurricane, everything blasting her in
the face, too much between her and where she needed to be.

Fortunately, the trek didn't last forever. Even if it felt like a year and
a half.

In the far corner of the club, outside a hallway that was the only
thing properly lit anywhere, two plainclothes officers were arguing with a
guy who had slicked his hair back with what had to be shellac and was
wearing black jeans that had been surgically mounted onto his skinny
legs. A minor kibitzing circle of partiers were playing peanut gallery, but
most of the clientele were doing their thing at the bar, on the dance floor.

". . . you can't make me," Mr. Smooth was saying to the officer. "You
can't tell me I have to shut down—"

Erika pushed past the argument and went to where a uni was standing outside the women's bathroom.

"Ma'am," he said as he opened the door for her. Then he flushed. "Sorry—I mean, Detective."

Whatever, she had other things to worry about.

Jesus. The smell of the fresh blood was so thick that it overrode the vape stain in the air, and as she slipped on a pair of booties, the copper tang blooming in the back of her throat made her think about throwing up.

Stepping into the women's facilities, she snapped on her nitrile gloves and looked around. Everything was either stainless steel or tile and she was willing to bet that the place got hosed down with a bleach wash at the end of every night. There weren't even proper mirrors, but panels of polished metal, like the bathroom was in a public park. Blowers, not paper towels. No trash cans, which explained the condom wrappers, wads of tissue, and questionable flecks and specks all over the floor.

The stalls were on the right, four of them. On the other side of things, two sinks and more than enough counter space to have sex on.

The pool of blood was coming out from under where the last toilet was.

As she approached the stainless steel door, she watched from a distance as her hand went forward and pushed the panel wide—

"Shit," she breathed.

Another heterosexual couple: The man was seated on the toilet with his pants around his knees, his shirtless torso sprawling back into the corner created by the tiled wall. The woman was straddling him face-to-face, short skirt up around her hips, the line of a thong that had no doubt been pushed aside barely visible between her buttocks area. Her remains were listing to the opposite side, her forehead on the partition that separated the stall from its next-door neighbor.

The blood loss for both was extensive, the red wash traveling down all sides of the toilet base, the pools joining and rivering toward the drain out in the center of the bathroom's floor.

In the center of the man's chest . . . a ragged wound that flashed white ribs in the midst of the red muscle and the now-graying skin.

Given the blood puddle under the woman's torso? She'd been done like that, too.

Erika shook her head as she turned away and strode back out into the hallway. Marching up to the club's manager and the plainclothes cops, she looked at Mr. Smooth.

"Close the music down right now, and no one leaves the premises."

The guy threw his hands up. "We have another set of bathrooms! We'll block this off—"

"This whole club is now a crime scene. You're no longer in charge."

He pointed over her shoulder. "There's a fire exit right down there. If you need to take the bodies out, you can just—"

"Two people were murdered in that bathroom," she snapped. "So the whole club and everyone in it has to be processed. Turn the lights on, and let us get to work."

"Wait, you're taking the staff's names?"

"I'm taking everyone's name."

Mr. Smooth crossed his arms over his chest and shook his head. "You are going to put us out of business, lady—"

"I also need your security feeds—inside and out. And don't tell me you don't have them."

"I'm not giving you shit!"

Erika got up in the guy's face and lowered her voice. "Two people just died in your business or your boss's business, whichever this is. Two human beings. And someone in here did it. So you're no longer calling the shots. We can do this nicely, or we can put you in handcuffs and you can enjoy paying a lawyer to defend you against the obstruction of justice charge that's heading your way."

Mr. Smooth deflated faster than she anticipated. "He's going to fire me. I'm going to get fucking fired for this."

"I can't help you with that, but you can help us. By doing the right thing, right now."

There was a pause, and then the guy glanced over his shoulder. "Tibby, shut it down."

Erika turned around—and ran right into Deiondre Delorean's big chest.

"Nicely handled, Detective," the special agent murmured.

"Those charm school lessons haven't completely worn off."

The lights came on all at once, some kind of breaker thrown, and as the music was cut off as well, it was as if the illumination had chased the beats away. Naturally, the response from the crowd was immediate and drunkenly disgruntled.

Disdrunkled, Erika thought absently.

Corralling this bunch of intoxicated potential witnesses into any semblance of order was going to be fun, and like he read her mind, Delorean got on the phone to call in more agents. With the crime scene unit already dialed, Erika went back into the bathroom—and stared at the closed door of the stall. The congealing blood on the tile. The smudge of the man's heel edge as he'd swept his leg from side to side, likely from pain, fear.

She also stared at everything that was not there.

No bloody footsteps on the flooring outside the stall. Or on the way to the exit.

No blood drops anywhere except inside the stall.

Erika pushed the metal panel open again. Plenty of blood underneath the bodies, but except for some flailing of the victims' hands, nothing on the walls.

How in the hell did someone take out two hearts from two people in a public place and then leave without a trail or anybody noticing?

Maybe the club's patrons could answer some of that, but she worried she was going to get more dead ends than leads.

As her phone went off, she answered it on a reflex, snapping the thing out of her jacket pocket to her ear. "Saunders—"

"Check your email."

She rolled her eyes. "You could have just put your head in here, Delorean."

"I'm on my way out of the club. HQ's called me in, but I've got another four agents coming in to back you up. Check your email."

The connection got cut, and she muttered as she called up her work account. She was still talking to herself as she opened what the special agent had sent. Talk about short and sweet. The email had an attachment . . . a video file . . . and Delorean had typed out three words without punctuation: "taken last night."

Triggering the footage, she—

Dim lighting. Crowd of noisy people in a circle. Someone in the center—

Ralph DeMellio. Shirtless.

The camera was bouncing all around, like the cell phone's owner was being knocked into, but she knew what Ralph was doing: Underground fight club. Erika was well aware they went down in town, and for the last couple of months, she'd been expecting to get called into the aftermath of one when someone died from a bare-knuckle punch—

"Holy shit," she breathed.

The camera panned around to Ralph's opponent, and Erika recoiled as she got a look at the guy. The muscularity of the man's chest was that of a professional athlete, and the tattoo that covered every inch of the skin was gang-member-worthy, the black field setting off the bony hand of a skeleton reaching forward.

"Jesus, Ralph, what were you thinking," she muttered.

DeMellio had clearly been a hobbyist fighter, based on his build and what she'd learned after speaking with his parents. But this opponent? She didn't need his rap sheet to know he was a killer: He was staring forward with the cold, dead eyes of a predator who had no conscience.

For a split second, Erika felt a chill go through her. Then her professional grit came back online and she watched what happened as the fight started, the pair circling each other, Ralph's hands up while his opponent's arms hung in a relaxed way.

When the action finally got underway—Ralph doing an approach with fists that looked like a child's in comparison to what he was going to try to hit—she put herself in his shoes, heart in her throat, knowing what was coming next and not just with whatever happened in this bare knuckle contest. These were among the last couple of hours of the kid's life, and she couldn't help but think of what it had been like to sit across from his mother and father and break the terrible news of his death to two perfectly nice people.

The father had cried more than the mom had.

Erika, meanwhile, had lost it later, when she'd been home alone—

It happened so fast that a replay was necessary: The opponent dominated Ralph quickly, but something caused the man to look up into the crowd—and Ralph outed a knife and sliced that thick throat clean through.

The file ended abruptly with a wild jostling, like whoever was filming had taken off in a run along with the rest of the audience. Lot of concrete underfoot. Then a jammed-up stairwell.

It could be a lot of places downtown, she thought. But maybe a parking garage? Or the arena?

Erika played the footage again and turned up the volume on her speaker. On the second trip through, she noted that Ralph was wearing the same jeans he'd been killed in; she recognized the designer-made rips and frays. And as for the girl he'd been found beside? It was difficult to see much in the crowd, but it wasn't going to be hard to freeze-frame images and double-check for her presence.

They needed to know more about the source for this footage.

As the moment came for the opponent to look up and go still, Erika stopped the play and closed in on that harsh, cold face. Then she did the same just as the knife finished its arc.

Hard to believe that the man lived through that, and under normal circumstances, she might think that Ralph's death was caused by one of the guy's crew, as payback. But not with the track record of so many others with their lovers and no hearts in their chest.

But what happened to the opponent? she wondered.

There had to be a body associated with that arterial bleed, and it was going to show up, sooner or later.

Just another part of the mystery.

CHAPTER THIRTY-TWO

The following evening, after the sun had sunk below the horizon, the outside lights came on around Nate's neighborhood, but not all of the humans were staying home. Friday night. Time for dinner and a movie. Topgolf. Comedy clubs, the theater, a poetry slam.

Nate was leaving, too. The moment First Meal was over.

He had his excuse to go to Luchas House all thought out: He was going to call the farmhouse and tell them that he was looking for a jacket that he might have left in the garage, and could he come take a look.

As he replayed his casual, no-big-deal request in his head—for like, the hundredth time—he was vaguely aware that his parents weren't talking. Murhder and Sarah were in their regular spots at the table, and the eggs and bacon, bagels and fruit, were standard issue for this meal, but neither of them were saying a thing.

Whatever. Nate had to get his segue right. After he hit whoever answered the Luchas House's landline with the jacket story, he needed to be prepared to walk into the farmhouse, check the garage for what he knew was not there—and casually bring up Elyn. Where she might be. Whether she was expected to turn up . . . anywhere. He was going to have to keep his tone light and his eyeballs neutral. Nothing nervous or shady.

Even though his true intent was not casual. In the slightest.

He'd gotten no phone calls during the day.

No, that wasn't true. Shuli had called. Twice. And there had been work texts, assigning him to a job starting on Monday. Which meant he had the night and the weekend off with nothing to do but wait, and wonder, and jump every time Shuli called to ask him to go out.

What the hell was he going to do—

"Fine, I was the one who asked Shuli to watch over you."

Nate froze in mid-chew as Murhder did the same with a forkful of scrambled egg on the way to his mouth.

"What?"

"What?"

As they both spoke at the same time, Sarah shoved her plate away and crossed her arms over her lab coat. Her honey-colored eyes were so upset as she smoothed her shoulder-length hair back.

"I just . . . I'm sorry, Nate. You were starting your first job. You were going out into the dangerous world. I was scared. I did the wrong thing, fine, but I won't apologize for trying to keep you safe. You have had . . . well, trauma, you know? And I wasn't sure how to help you, and sometimes parents do dumb stuff. But I certainly *never* intended for a gun to be involved."

At that point, she burst into tears, grabbing a napkin and pressing it into her eyes. With sniffles rising up and her shoulders shaking, Nate looked to Murhder in a panic—but the Brother was already on it, scraping back his chair and going over to kneel by his *shellan*.

"I'm fine." She batted at her mate. "I just hate that you two aren't speaking! I can't stand being in the same house with all this tension, and it's my fault and, oh, shit, can I have your napkin, too."

Nate slowly sat back as two of the syllables she spoke sank in. *Same. House.*

"Do you think I can move into Luchas House?" he blurted.

They both looked at him. And then Sarah started to cry even harder.

"I didn't know you were so unhappy here—"

"What's gotten into you?" Murhder rose to his feet. "I don't get it—"

"Are you on drugs?"

"You're doing drugs?!"

Shaking himself back to attention, Nate felt like he was in an episode of *Who's the Boss?* as both his parents talked over each other in full our-son-is-an-addict panic.

Putting his napkin next to his plate, he went to get up. "I've got to make a phone call—"

At that moment, Murhder's cell started to ring. "Goddamn it." As he shoved a hand into his back pocket and then checked the screen, he cursed again and pointed to Nate. "You sit your ass back down right now." Then he barked into the phone, "*What.*"

Nate glanced over to where he'd left his backpack on the counter. Maybe instead of going the lost-jacket route, he could call Mrs. Mary and ask if there was a room in Luchas House for a caretaker person type thing. It was his only shot at being there on a regular basis, and for setting up a cross-paths with Elyn: Obviously, he couldn't work at Safe Place because males were not allowed in there—well, and he had no counseling degree or experience. And he couldn't be at Luchas House as a social worker for the same reason. But maybe if he lived there as lower-level staff?

Because maybe he'd been wrong about Elyn leaving?

Although who was he kidding. She hadn't called him and like that wasn't a tea leaf he should read?

"—he's right here." Murhder frowned and looked across the table. "Uh-huh. Okay—well, lemme talk to him and Sarah. Sure. Yeah. Later."

As the Brother hung up, he frowned. "That was Rhage. He said that Mary's looking for a little help at Luchas House tonight. Guess there's a young female moving in there and they need the furniture in her bedroom set up—"

Nate jumped out of his chair. "Yes! Did you tell him I'll do it, yes? Yes!" He wheeled around for his backpack and fumbled to get his phone out. "I'll text him—"

"You can sit the fuck down," Murhder snapped, "and tell us what the hell is going on here first."

"Nothing?" Nate lowered his butt back into his chair and put his hands in the air like it was a stickup. "I just want to help. Over at Luchas House. You know, they're doing really special things—you know, the helping of people. Over there."

Murhder looked at Sarah. She looked back at him. And then they both eyeballed Nate.

"I am not doing drugs." He put his backpack onto the table and opened every zipper the thing had, flashing pockets and pouches that showed a whole lot of nothing-illegal. "And you can go through my room. Each drawer, under the bed, in the closet . . . all the jackets and pants I have. I'm not into that stuff and I'm never going to be."

"So it's really about the Shuli thing?" Sarah said. "I am honestly sorry—"

"No, it's not. I mean, I thought the Shuli move was weird, but I don't really care."

There was a long pause while his parents x-rayed him with all kinds of what-are-we-going-to-do.

"You can always come and talk to us," Sarah said as she sniffled and patted under one eye. "Anytime, about anything. And again, I do apologize for getting Shuli involved. I had no idea he would take it as far as he did, and I should have come to you with my concerns first."

"Well, I've fixed that 'too far' thing," Murhder muttered. "Trust me."

"Can you text Rhage?" Nate asked in a hurry as he rezipped everything. "Call him? I'll call him. I'll go over there right now—"

"What the hell is over at Luchas House that's so important—"

As Murhder went on another roll, Sarah got a strange look on her face. And then put her hand on her mate's forearm, some kind of aha draining the anxiety out of her and replacing it with a soft surprise.

"We'll text Rhage," she said. "And of course, why don't you head over there right now."

"Great! SeeyouforLastMealokaythanksbye!"

Nate bolted for the sliding door behind the table, yanking back the glass and all but falling out onto the terrace. Slam-closing his eyes to dematerialize, he shut things back up and had to slow his breathing and—

Nothing close to dematerializing happened.

He stayed where he was, his beating heart skipping in his chest.

Taking a deep breath, he ruffled his arms. Refocused.

When that didn't work, he double-checked on the 'rents. Murhder had his phone in his palm, but he was focused on Sarah and looking a little poleaxed. And as the Brother glanced out through the slider, Nate reshut his lids—

This time, he managed to ghost out.

Traveling in a scatter of molecules, he couldn't get to Luchas House fast enough, and when he re-formed, he bolted across the lawn to the front door. He was all but choking on the excitement and the hope and the—

Well, the all kinds of everything.

Except he had to remind himself to chill. It could be another female—but then why would Rhage call? The Brother knew what was up, and come on, they had other hands on deck to help assemble furniture.

Unless they really did need help.

"Shut up," he told his brain.

As Nate rang the doorbell once—and then wanted to push the button a hundred thousand times—he had the dampening thought again: What if it was someone else, what if they really did just need another—

The panel cracked, and half a face entered the seam.

As Nate recognized the features, he started to smile. "Hi," he said.

✦   ✦   ✦

Tallah was not a good cook.

As Mae started to run some water over the mound of dirty pots and pans in the cottage's kitchen sink, she thought it had been so sweet of the elderly female to insist on making a meal the night before, but . . . yeah. In addition to her being incredibly inefficient with the utensils and anything with a handle, Gordon Ramsay would not have let that stew out of service, and probably would have thrown a couple of plates on the floor to make that point. But like Tallah had ever had to cook anything in her old life? Her previous household had been filled with *doggen*, and not only had there never been a reason for her to learn how to prepare food, it would have been considered way beneath her station to do so.

And since then? Well, she reheated Stouffer's frozen dinners like a pro.

Sahvage hadn't seemed to mind the stew, however, and afterward, when Tallah had insisted on playing Monopoly, he had humored her on that, too—and so had Mae, until she'd fallen asleep on the sofa halfway through the game. At some point, someone had thrown a blanket over her, and when she'd woken up a few moments ago, it had been to find Sahvage asleep sitting in the armchair across from her. Tallah had no doubt retired down below, and the Monopoly board, like the pots and pans, had been left in a state of post-use disorder, green houses and red hotels dotting the properties, fake money in scattered stacks cluttering up the coffee table, the shoe and the dog still on Park Place and Pennsylvania Avenue, respectfully.

The second Mae had stood up from the couch, Sahvage's right eye had cracked open, but it didn't stay that way. As if she had passed some kind of review—perhaps an unconscious one—he resettled and seemed to fall back to sleep.

Mae wasn't hungry, her stomach still churning over Tallah's home-cooked splendor however many hours later, but she couldn't sit around.

Besides, every single thing you could put on the stovetop had been used for that stew. If somebody wanted eggs for First Meal, they had nothing to cook them in, and this exposed another truism about females of worth from the *glymera*.

Not only couldn't they cook, they didn't know how to clean up, either.

Hitting the pool of warm water with a squeeze of Ivory dish soap, she glanced back to make sure she wasn't making too much noise. Fortunately, Sahvage's heavy-treaded boots were in the same position, crossed at the ankle, so he remained where she'd left him.

Mae tried to stay as quiet as she could as she used a wad of paper towels as a sponge—given that she'd destroyed Tallah's only scrubber on the kitchen floor the night before. Looked like she was developing a track record for nervous cleaning—

At the sound of a creak, she froze and looked over at the refrigerator that barricaded the back door. When the sound didn't repeat, she took a deep breath, and told herself that even though she couldn't do anything about whatever was outside the cottage, goddamn it, she could wash and dry the mess in front of her.

When the rack got too full, she paused with the soaping-and-rinsing and reached for a dish towel—

"Oh!" she gasped. "You're up."

Sahvage was leaning against the open door into the full bath, his arms crossed, his lids low as he studied her. He seemed bigger than ever before, but she was beginning to expect that knee-jerk impression. It seemed like anytime she saw him, she had to get used to his size all over again.

And that wasn't the only thing that kept making a fresh impression. His eyes. His lips. His . . . hips.

"I didn't mean to wake you." She started drying the pile she'd created. "I, well, cleanup is required if anyone wants to cook ever again."

"I wasn't sleeping. Just resting my eyes. Tallah up?"

"She usually doesn't rise until midnight." Mae smiled a little. "She believes in beauty sleep. It used to drive my *mahmen* nuts—well, anyway."

"No, continue."

Mae circled the towel around the inside of a sauté pan. "Tallah loved my *mahmen*. And it was very mutual. They were as different as could be, but they had a wonderful friendship that crossed the barriers of servant and mistress."

"So Tallah must miss her."

"I think she does, yes."

There was a long silence. Then he said, "Listen, we need to talk about the elephant in the room."

Mae had no intention for her eyes to travel down his body. But they did. And she didn't mean for her face to flush. But it did. And she prayed he didn't notice either of those.

But he did.

As Sahvage straightened from his lean, she swallowed hard and got real determined not to drop the pan in her hands. So she put it down.

Throughout the daylight hours, she'd had vivid dreams of him approaching her. Taking her into his arms. Lowering his lips to hers—

And every time, just before the kiss happened, the image disappeared. Over and over again. It was like a loop that wouldn't stop, a tantalizing promise that never came to fruition.

A mirage that was ever on the brink, never on the actual.

Although with the way his hooded eyes were focused on her now, and how his body was moving toward her, and—

Sahvage walked past her and went back out into the parlor. Over next to the armchair he'd been in, he picked up the black duffle bag he'd always kept by him—and by the sounds of metal on metal, she knew what was inside.

Yet it was still a shock as he put things on the table and got to the unzipping.

"So many . . ." she whispered.

Weapons, she finished in her head.

Mae watched as his big hands went through the tangles of muzzles and stocks or whatever the hell you called them. There was ammunition in there, too, loose bullets that were long and pointy, and then boxes as well.

The gun he brought out was a small, handheld God-only-knew-what.

"This is a nine millimeter autoloader with a full magazine," he said. "It has a laser sight. Point and shoot, literally. Using both hands. And make sure there's nothing you care about behind whatever you're aiming at. The safety is here. Off. On. You try."

Under any other circumstances, she wouldn't have gone anywhere near the thing. But Sahvage couldn't possibly stay with them forever, and . . . well, that brunette, for one thing. That shadow, for another.

Mae's hands were surprisingly steady as she accepted the weight from him. Then again, she wasn't trying to do anything with the gun.

"Off. On," she said as she mimicked his flicking of the safety.

"Here, let me take the magazine out." After he removed a slide full of bullets, he gave the weapon back to her. "Do you see the button there on the grip. Squeeze it—that's right, that's your laser sight."

Mae moved the red dot around the kitchen, steadying it on the GE logo of the refrigerator—and then the bathroom's doorknob. After that, she picked out a pan in the drying rack and trained the beam on a chair.

"Keep the safety on at all times until you're ready to shoot," Sahvage said. "No holster, but you can tuck it into your pocket."

"Even when I'm just in the house."

"Yes. I would have given it to you before, but I didn't want to alarm Tallah." He nodded toward the bath. "I'm going in there to shower. Here, take the magazine, and put it back properly so you know what it's like."

She took the slide and reinserted it. "I've never shot a gun before. Well . . . alone, that is."

"Hopefully, it won't become a habit."

Mae nodded and then cleared her throat. "Listen, I have to go back home—you know, to pick up some work stuff?"

"I can go with you—"

"No, no. I'm more worried about Tallah than myself."

"That's a bad assessment of reality."

She cleared her throat and tried to be casual. "Look, can you just stay here? The ranch is protected, you said so yourself. Plus, if Tallah wakes up, I don't want her to think we've abandoned her—or, worse, that something's happened to me."

"You have a cell phone. She can call you—"

"She's not good with phones. Please, I won't be gone long."

Sahvage shook his head. But then shrugged. "I can't stop you. But you're going to take that with you."

As he pointed at the weapon, she nodded. "Yes. I will."

"Gimme a minute to have a shower. Then leave?"

"Absolutely." She put her hands out to reassure him—and realized there was a gun in one of them. So she dropped her arms. "I mean, take your time."

"I won't be long," he said as he disappeared into the little room and closed the door.

Left by herself, Mae sagged and wondered how she was going to get through the night. Then she thought about what Sahvage was doing and where he was doing it.

When Tallah had moved into the cottage, Mae's father had retrofitted that first-floor bath with a modern shower—because she had insisted she might have guests. The guests had never materialized, so Mae wasn't sure when the last time that showerhead had been called into service.

It seemed so strange to think this stranger was going to be the one to turn that faucet on.

In a way, it connected him with her father.

"I'm just going to do the dishes," she murmured for no good reason to the closed door.

Which hadn't closed. Not completely.

Mae opened her mouth to point out the six-inch gap to him—

Oh. Okay . . . ah, yeah. He was ditching his clothes really damned quick, the shirt doing an up-and-over, that skull with the fangs on his back making a shocking reappearance. With no tattoos on his arms, it was easy to forget all the ink he had.

And then she wasn't thinking about any of that.

She was watching the muscles move under his smooth skin . . . and wondering what it would be like to run her hands over his shoulders. His spine. His hip . . .

Sahvage twisted around and looked back at her, the light from the sink fixture casting shadows under his pecs, the ridges of his abs, the cuts of his arms.

Mae flushed and tried to make like she hadn't been gawking at him. "Sorry, sorry—I, ah, I was going to tell you about the door—"

"Don't apologize."

When she glanced back at him, he lowered his chin and stared out at her from under heavy brows. "I like when you watch me."

Parting her lips, Mae found it hard to breathe.

"What else do you want to see?" Sahvage said in a low, guttural voice.

CHAPTER THIRTY-THREE

Balz liked to be on time.

Particularly when it came to monetizing a night's work.

As he re-formed on the edge of a human's out-in-the-sticks acreage, he had to move fast, but he was ready for what came after he got his cash. He was all set in his fighter clothes, his leathers and weapons in place—not that he would have come out here to this shithole in a tuxedo.

Or without all kinds of metal.

Twenty minutes and he had to be in the field with Syphon.

The trailer was hidden away on enough land so that you wouldn't come looking for the property unless you were fencing property. The guy who crashed here was a real fucking gem, but he dealt in everything there was, and his cash was real.

So honestly, what other qualifications were required.

Hopping up the steps, he rapped on the door, which was hanging rather loose. When there was no answer, he knuckled louder and glanced at the truck. Fucker was in, and they'd made this appointment yesterday. Besides, Dave wasn't the sort who double-booked. In his line of work, anonymity was everything. You didn't want your suppliers to cross with your buyers or you found yourself out of your middleman job.

"Come on, Dave," he called out. "Open the fuck—"

He pulled on the busted door as a way to rush Dave off whatever phone call he was on—

The scent that wafted out was of blood that had aged a little.

Balz already had his gun discreetly palmed, and with his vampire vision, he could see some of the dim interior. Breathing in deep, he made sure there was no one else in there.

Looked like good ol' Dave had played his hand a little too hot.

Stepping inside, he found the man in a recline on the ratty sofa with most of his brains blown out the back of his skull, abstract art without a frame.

"Damn it," Balz muttered as he glanced around. "I got these watches, my guy."

The bedroom was on the other end, and he strode down to the bare-mattress-on-the-floor decor just to see—well, lookey-lookey. Somebody had busted open Dave's Glock-in closet and cleaned it out.

Back in the trailer proper, Balz stared down at where the sitting area had had its gray-matter, blood-splatter renovation. Fucking wonderful. Now he had to find another fence.

It was like Starbucks discontinuing the Verismo. He'd been hoarding pods for months, and when that goddamn machine broke or he finally ran out of them, he was going to have to reinvent his perfect coffee.

Fucking inconvenience over nothing.

Just as he was turning away, he caught sight of something on the floor, half-concealed under the filthy fringe of the death sofa. It was a Hannaford plastic bag, and the thing was partially open . . .

. . . and flashing a whole lot of B. Franklin faces.

Going over, he pulled the bag free of the dust bunnies and the grab of something nasty on the carpet. As he fought the resistance, he heard Flula's voice from "Beer Pong, You Are Terrible."

Cranberry juices. Sticksy, sticksy. Lick, lick, lick, lick—

The bag came free, and as he opened the thing wide, he whistled at all the bundles of hundies.

"Well, this is just about right, isn't it, Dave." Determined to be a team player, he smiled over at the pasty face with its sightless eyes and the little red hole off center on the forehead. "Gotta be about twenty grand in here. Fair trade."

Retail, the watches from Mr. Commodore's collection would be over a hundred grand. But you were lucky to get twenty percent when you were on Balz's side of commerce.

"I'll just leave these right here." He winked at his cold, immobile business associate as he put the watch case on the coffee table. "I'd hate to steal from you. It'd just *ruin* my reputation on LinkedIn."

He would have rolled the bag around the cash and just shoved it inside his jacket, but licky, licky, don't you know. So he took the bills and let the nasty bag drift down to the matted carpet.

"Take care, big guy."

Just as Balz was about to step out of the trailer, a pair of headlights washed the front side with all kinds of hi-how're-ya. The blinds were down, so he went over and parted the dusty slats. It was a shitty sedan with a lot of rust lace behind its tires. An older man in a set of overalls got out, his scruffy beard and chopped hair gray, his face lined and loose. He lit a cigarette and looked at the trailer with an expression of exhaustion.

Dave's dad. Had to be. They had the same bone structure, but more than that, the way the guy stared forward? It was like he had been waiting for what he was going to find inside.

An unexpected sadness wrapped around Balz's heart.

Thieves should still be mourned, he thought as he dematerialized. *Even if their lives aren't worth shit.*

✦   ✦   ✦

Over at Luchas House, Nate walked into a bedroom on the southwestern corner of the farmhouse. There were large cardboard boxes tilted against the wall, a rolled-up carpet, and two mattresses stacked in the middle—so not exactly cozy and inviting. But as he went over to the window, he got a good view of the big maple in the front lawn.

"If you put your bed against this wall"—he pointed to the longest stretch in the room—"you'll be able to look at it lying down."

When there was no response, he glanced over his shoulder. Elyn was in the en suite bath, leaning into the mirror, staring at herself like she didn't recognize the reflection—or maybe like she wasn't sure where she was and was trying to ground herself in her own features.

Nate went across to her. Downstairs, there were sounds of people moving around, voices, laughter. And the scent of freshly baking Toll House cookies. He wished he could bring that life up here, up to Elyn.

Her silver eyes met his in the glass. She didn't say anything, but she didn't have to. He knew exactly what she was thinking.

He cleared his throat. "You know, the hardest thing for me when I got out was trusting I was going to *stay* out. That I actually was where I was standing. It was like at any moment I was going to get pulled back. I didn't trust reality."

Elyn turned to him, her eyes wide. "Wherever were you held?"

"Somewhere I didn't want be." He had to look away. "It's not important where. I just know how hard it is for you right now. And it gets better, I promise."

When he could manage to meet her eyes, he hoped she would open up and talk about her story, even though he feared the details.

"Are you safe now?" she whispered.

He nodded. "Yes. And so are you."

She turned back to the mirror. "I am lost. I thought . . . I would be free, but I am lost."

"I know and I'm so sorry. I've been where you are and it sucks."

"Tell me."

"I, ah, I . . . can't." He was *not* going to lose it in front of her. And somehow, talking about the lab was going to make him feel more naked than if he actually were naked. "I wish I could, but I can't."

Elyn drew in a deep breath. Then she reached across the space between them and took his hand. As she closed her eyes, he couldn't believe she was touching him—

The bolt of electricity flashed through his body, and in the aftermath, he was immobile and totally numb, yet still standing. Then came the fluttering. At first, he thought it was something physical, but then he realized what was happening was in his brain. It was as if his thoughts were being shuffled, a deck of cards.

And then Elyn gasped.

In the midst of his strange fugue state, Nate focused on her eyes as they widened and the color drained out of her face. Tears formed and fell onto her cheeks, flowing down and dropping off the sides of her jaw. The shaking came after that, her mouth parting with the lower lip starting to tremble. With her free hand, she covered her—

Elyn dropped her hold on him and took a stumbling step back, her hip banging into the sink.

As the numb feeling drained out of Nate's feet, sure as if it were a tangible level of some kind of liquid, he was aware of a great shame flooding into his void.

It turned out that however painful the lab had been, having Elyn horrified by him was a worse agony.

Clearing his throat, he focused on the boxes out in her room. "Well, I'll just get started on these."

Turning away from her, he—

Elyn jumped in front and embraced him so hard, he had no breath in his lungs.

"Oh . . . Nate," she said in a voice that cracked. "Oh, dearest Virgin Scribe. What they did to you. To your *mahmen*. They hurt you."

Nate was so shocked by the contact, by her scent, by her . . . everything . . . that the content of her words didn't register. But then he caught up with everything.

Her hands were smoothing over his back. "I am *so* sorry."

Nate wanted to hold her back. So he did—but things went further than he intended. He dropped his head onto her shoulder, opened up the internal lockbox he kept his horrible memories in . . . and went into his pain.

It had been a while since he had done that, the rhythm of his nights and days, the normalcy of life with Sarah and Murhder, obscuring his past—and thank fuck for it. Yet Elyn called that which he staunchly ignored to the forefront.

And somehow, though it was agony, her sympathy eased him in ways no amount of therapy with Mrs. Mary had.

Down on the first floor, people kept talking, and laughing, and making cookies.

Up in Elyn's bathroom, the world stopped as two broken people became whole again. Through the magic of not being alone.

CHAPTER THIRTY-FOUR

Sahvage put his shirt on the sink counter and focused on Mae. She was standing on the far side of the kitchen table, one hand gripping the gun he'd gotten for her, the other floating in the breeze like it was looking for something to do.

And what do you know, he had some suggestions for that—and she was clearly open to them: Her delicious scent gave her away. Her eyes, as they traveled down his bare chest, gave her away. The way she breathed . . . gave her away.

"Tell me, what do you want to see, Mae?"

Please God, let Tallah sleep for another hour, he thought. Two. Eight. Because the way Mae was staring at him? They had things to do together that did not need an audience or any kind of interruption.

"What do you want, Mae." No question this time. "Do you want me to close this door?"

She answered that one without touching anything or moving. The wooden panel that separated them, the one that offered only a seam of sight for her, moved so that it opened more. So that she could see him properly.

All of him.

Sahvage certainly hadn't willed the change of its position, and there sure as shit weren't any drafts that could have done that.

So she had. Because what he wanted to show her was what she wanted to lay her eyes on.

And far be it for him to disappoint a female of worth.

His hands went to his belt, and he pulled the leather strap free of its buckle and tongue. Then he popped the button and waited with the zipper.

Mae's chest was rising faster and faster, and her eyes were locked on what he was doing. And the scent of her arousal was getting thicker.

Which made him want to go slow as molasses—so this on-the-verge, which was both torture and pleasure, would last forever.

"Is this what you want?" he asked in a growl.

"Yes," she breathed.

Well, wasn't that the right answer.

Sahvage lowered the zipper—and his erection took it from there, bursting free of the lock-and-key it had been straining against, the thick arousal jutting straight out from his hips. As he let his pants go, they dropped to his feet.

She bit her lower lip and moaned. But she didn't come over.

And that was hot.

"Do you want me to touch it?" he said in a low voice.

When she nodded, he took his hand and wrapped his palm around his shaft. He groaned—he couldn't help it. He wanted it to be her doing the grip, and he wanted to be kissing her while she stroked him—and that was why this got to him so much. As he rode himself up and down, while watching her watch him, his mind spun with what it was going to be like when it was her. When Mae's hand was on him. When she was making him come—

Fucking hot as fuck.

And she must have felt the same way because she tucked the gun away and came forward. With every step she took, he stroked. Stroked. Stroked. As she arrived at the door, he prayed she entered.

She did.

Over the threshold. Door closing behind her.

Except she leaned back against it, wrapping her arms around herself and staring at him. "Now is not the time."

Her voice was incredibly disappointed, and what do you know. That shit speared through him like a sword.

Sahvage halted his hand, but did not release his hold. "I find myself wanting to argue the point. But as you can see, I'm a little self-interested at the moment."

Mae's pink tongue, her delicious, erotic, pink tongue, traveled across her lower lip. Then she nipped that soft flesh with her fangs, biting down like she was swallowing a moan.

"What if Tallah wakes up?" she whispered.

"I stop."

There was a pause. And then, thank the frickin' Scribe Virgin, Mae nodded. "I just want to see . . . what you look like."

Bracing his free hand on the wall, he had a feeling he was going to need the help with his balance. "When I come?"

"Yes," she sighed.

"Tell me what you want. You know, just so I'm sure I get it right."

"I want you . . . to make yourself . . ."

"What," he demanded.

"Come."

That word leaving her lips made the world tilt and spin. And he wasn't losing his chance. Even though he wanted his hands on her body, and he wanted to pleasure her, if this was as far as they were going? Fine. He was totally fucking into it.

Kicking his pants free, he went base to head with his palm, finding a slow rhythm that juiced his erection up more than some of the best sex he'd actually had—and that was not because of his handling technique.

It was all because of Mae. Her mere presence, even without any physical contact between them, was hotter than the other females he'd physically been with.

He didn't know why. And he wasn't inclined to waste time on that one.

He had a feeling the answer would scare the shit out of him—

As Mae lifted her fingers to her mouth, she brushed her lower lip back and forth like she was imagining him kissing her—

Sahvage hissed and squeezed his eyes shut. He was so on the verge already and he didn't want it to end so soon. This sacred space, just for the two of them, was like a vault locking out the world, and fuck, he wanted that right now. Had wanted this kind of amnesia for a long time.

Except then he had to pop his lids again. And get back to work.

As the heat rose, and his cock became hypersensitive, he tightened his grip and moved faster.

"Say my name," he commanded. "I want to hear it."

"Sahvage . . ."

"Do you want this?"

"God . . . yes." She closed her eyes. But only for a split second. "I want you."

"How much." Faster. Faster. "Tell me how much."

"So bad. Sahvage . . ."

As she moaned his name, he let go of the wall and grabbed a towel, but he didn't cover the head of his arousal. He put the soft folds out in front as the ejaculations started so she could watch, so she could imagine him filling her up, his rhythm unchanging as he milked himself into her. And fuck, he wanted to keep looking at her, but the pleasure was so intense, his lids squeezed shut on their own.

Fine. He would just picture him on top of her, her breasts against his pecs, her legs spread wide, her body arching to receive what he was pumping off into her—

He started to come again. Before he'd even finished.

God, the only thing that could have made this hotter? Was if she were orgasming along with him.

✦   ✦   ✦

Mae had to hold herself in place against the bathroom door. Sahvage's body was magnificent, so powerful, so virile, the contracting muscles of his massive pecs and arms in stark contrast to her own body, that tattoo of his bringing an edge of danger, the scent of him too delicious to describe. And his broad hand on that thick erection? She was going to be seeing that on the backs of her lids for pretty much the rest of her sleeping days. Maybe during the waking nights, too.

God, she hoped Tallah didn't wake up. For like a year.

Meanwhile, Sahvage just kept orgasming, and it was . . . beautiful. It was raw, and a little scary because he was so big. But he seemed to understand that opening the door—literally and proverbially—to her doing that to him was going to have to be on her time.

She couldn't imagine pleasuring him like that. But she was willing to bet he'd show her what she needed to do—

Why not, she thought. *What was she waiting for?*

Mae stepped forward toward him, and as she did, she was nervous. Especially as his eyes flared like she'd surprised him. She was not turning back, though. When was she going to get another chance like this?

Especially because she knew he was temporary in her life.

"What do I do?" she said softly.

There was a pause, as if he wasn't sure what she was asking.

"Anything you like." He let go of himself and leaned back against the wall by the shower. "You can touch me anywhere you goddamn like, and any way you want."

"But what . . ." As he looked at her in confusion, she flushed. "I, ah— tell me what pleases you."

"Your hands on me. Wherever. Your mouth. All over me. That's what I want." Abruptly, Sahvage stiffened. "Mae . . . have you ever touched a male before?"

Well, crap. She wanted to lie. She wanted to front like she was sophisticated, like she was that brunette, all sexually confident. Like she was anything other than what she really was. But this was not something to hide, even if it made her cringe.

And besides, what did she have to be ashamed about?

Mae shook her head. "No."

He blinked. Twice. And then he covered his sex with the towel.

Swallowing a curse, Mae stepped back. Until the closed door caught her shoulder blades with a bump.

"Changes things, huh." She brushed her hair out of her face. "Sorry."

"You have nothing to apologize for."

"I know." Clearing her throat, she shrugged and rubbed her upper arms for warmth. "My parents were super conservative so both my brother and I . . . well, that's not important now. Such a mood killer, though. Looks like I'll be leaving now."

As she fumbled her way out of the bathroom, her heart was pounding and a chill followed her, although she had a feeling that was because the cold spot was inside her body and unrelated to any drafts.

The thing was, waiting until she was mated to have sex was how she'd been raised, and it hadn't been something she'd thought a lot about. All her feedings had been supervised, and the couple of times she'd had her needing, she'd gone to the race's healer for sedation. Finding a male and settling down had always been a sometime-in-the-future kind of fantasy. And after her parents' deaths in the raids, romance had been the last thing on her mind. She'd needed to make sure she had enough money, and that the house was taken care of, and that everything didn't fall apart, especially when it came to Rhoger.

Yeah, and look how well that had turned out.

But what the hell did all that matter now.

What she had to do was re-ice her dead brother. Because as gruesome as her nightly job was, it was a better option than being here with all her virgin status out in the open while a smoking-hot male took a lucky, lucky bar of soap for a test drive on his proverbial racetrack. And yeah, sure, she was supposed to be all self-actualized and stuff, all female-hear-her-roar, unapologetic of the choice she'd made about sex—which hadn't felt like any choice at all, P.S.—but when you were attracted to a male and you were past the age when most females had had a couple of lovers? You felt like something was wrong with you.

And God, the way he'd covered himself? It was like he thought he was a dirty pervert or something. But come on, consenting adults and all that.

The bathroom door opened. And Sahvage came out, fully clothed.

Mae put her hand up. "Please. Don't say it."

"How do you know what I was going to say?"

"I can guess. You're sorry, it won't happen again, you didn't know, couldn't guess, didn't mean to offend me." She cursed under her breath. "You didn't do anything wrong."

He nodded at something in her hand. "Are you leaving now?"

Mae glanced down and discovered she'd gotten her jacket and her purse. Huh. Go figure. "Ah, yes. I am. But I'll be right back."

"Mae."

She closed her eyes at his tone. There was so much compassion in it, pity, too. And if that didn't just suck the sexy right out of the air between them. Not that there was anything left of that heat.

Mae shook her head. "I can't talk about this now." Try, ever. "Besides, there are more important things to worry about. See you in a little bit."

As she rushed toward the front door—because she was going to have to way chill herself out before she could dematerialize—everything was a blur and she fumbled with the dead bolt, her hands sweaty, her fingers sloppy. When she finally got things open, she all but jumped out onto the front step—and it took some self-control not to slam the door, not because she was mad, but because she was totally uncoordinated.

The night air was cool against her hot face and she took some deep breaths. She had to in order to ghost out, but her lungs were also burning and she felt as though there was a hand around her throat. Walking forward, she was vaguely aware of the moon overhead. Just a sliver, though, so it didn't cast much light—

A shaft of illumination blared out of the cottage from behind her, her shadow going long over the winter-dead grass, the shape of her body distorted.

As she turned around, Sahvage came at her, and when he stopped in front of her, she gasped as he took her hand and put it between his legs. The ridge that was contained by his fly was still very large and very hard—

"You didn't turn me off," he said in a guttural voice. "I just was surprised, and I wasn't sure how to handle it."

He rubbed her palm back and forth against his arousal, and as she felt him through his cargo pants, he hissed and shut his eyes.

"Nothing has changed for me." His voice was so rough, she almost couldn't understand him. "At all. I still want you all over me."

Mae tilted her head up to look at him, and at that moment, he looked down at her. There was a white-hot moment of anticipation—and then the kiss was immediate and intense, her arms shooting around him and holding on to him hard. His arms did the same. He was so big, and that was what she wanted him to be. She wanted him massive and hungry and heavy on top of her, capable of canceling out everything.

Even Rhoger and the Book and that brunette.

When they finally paused to take a breath, she stared into his stark, starving face. It was impossible not to imagine them lying down and looking into each other's eyes while they—

As a shadow passed through the shaft of light, she glanced back into the house. Tallah was emerging from the basement, the cellar door opening.

"I'll be right back," Mae vowed as she stepped away from his body.

"I'll be waiting."

It took a moment to calm herself enough to dematerialize, and as she disappeared from him, she caught a glimpse of him pivoting back to the little stone house—

When Mae re-formed behind the garage of her parents' ranch, she was smiling. And it almost didn't matter whether they actually hooked up again. Just the fact that he accepted her as she was? That was enough.

Getting out her car key, she thought about what that kiss had felt like.

And decided . . . well, maybe the whole acceptance thing wasn't *quite* enough.

CHAPTER THIRTY-FIVE

Out in the field downtown, Balz walked side by side with Syphon through a bottom-feeder retail neighborhood, the storefronts locked with retractable grates and marked with *70% Off!* sale signs that suggested cash flow was a perpetual issue for the grungy establishments. Lot of graffiti. Lot of random trash clustered by the wind, the urban equivalent of sand dunes in the desert. And the uneven concrete under their shitkickers was the kind of thing you had to keep checking— no matter how tight your swagger or how many weapons you strapped or how much leather was zippered onto your body, catching a steel toe on a crack could bring you back down to earth on so many different levels.

"Yeah, and then what happened?" Balz asked as he scanned from left to right.

"Nothing was in the coffin."

Balz frowned and glanced at his cousin. Syphon was in his typical saunter, his dark hair freshly tinted with stripes of dark green. Given his orthorexic diet, one might assume he was actually turning into a smoothie. But no, he and Zypher had gone ham with the hair color over day.

Zypher had gone with some positively fetching dark purple under-tones.

"What do you mean, nothing?" Balz prompted.

"Well, no body. But we've got some two-hundred-year-old oats if we want to play Russian roulette with gastroenteritis. And the Gift of Light or whatever it was? Nowhere, either. Rhage told me that they stood around the open coffin all what-the-hell. Tic Tac?"

Balz put his palm out, a shake-shake preceding a two-drop that went right into his mouth. "So now what?"

Idly, he glanced behind them. Ever since the Omega had bit it, these nightly patrols were nothing but strolls, and he missed the fighting.

"I don't know. Wrath says we gotta find the Book another way—"

Balz stopped dead. "What?"

Syphon went a couple strides farther, halted, and looked back. "The Book. The one I told you about. The one Rehvenge came to the Brotherhood about—why are you looking at me like that?"

As a feeling of light-headedness made Balz think the cement under his feet was undulating, he turned blindly to the stores so he could pretend like something had caught his eye. You know, in a normal way.

"What about this Book," he said evenly.

"I told you."

"Tell me again."

Syphon shrugged his big shoulders. "It's some kind of book of spells. A female came up to Rehv looking for it, and he was all bad-news on that idea."

"Just curious, what does the Book look like?"

"I don't know. Rehv didn't say. Got the feeling that you know it when you see it."

Putting an unsteady hand to his eyes, Balz was vaguely aware that his cousin was continuing to talk, but he couldn't hear the guy. And as he tried to pull himself together, he—

Purple palm print.

Frowning, he blinked a couple of times—and nothing changed

about what he was staring at: He was apparently standing in front of a purple palm print the size of his chest. Over it, in blinking, neon cursive, was a flashing sign that read "PSYCHIC."

Syphon stepped in between him and the window. "Where'd you go, Cousin?"

"I'm right here," he muttered as he stepped around and tried the purple door.

When it opened, he wasn't surprised, and not just because it was after dark and PSYCHICs probably didn't quit at five, even in this kind of zip code: It was as if some kind of doorbell had been rung in reverse, not him seeking someone inside, but rather someone in there seeking him.

"What are you doing, Cousin," Syphon demanded.

The staircase that was revealed was narrow and steep and painted purple, and Balz surmounted the steps urgently, like his name was being called up on the second floor. Like he had been here before, even though he hadn't. Like this was the whole point of . . . everything.

Behind him, Syphon was having a lot to say.

Balz heard none of it.

There was a door on the top landing, marked with another laminated purple-palm symbol. And he was not surprised that before he had a thought about trying the knob, the portal swung open for him.

Fuck, it was dark in there. In fact, the pitch-black interior was so dense, so pervasive, it was like a tear in the fabric of time and space—

Syphon grabbed his arm and yanked. "No!"

"Let me go—"

"Don't go in there—"

Everything happened so fast. One moment, the two of them were playing tug-o'-war with his arm, the next?

The lights flickered in the stairwell, and then something grabbed Syphon around the chest and peeled him back. But he did not fall. He became suspended in the air over the steep steps.

A shadow, that somehow had strength and substance, was clutching him like he was prey, claiming his fighter's body. And Syphon was arching back and screaming in agony, his face running pale, his eyes peeling wide.

Save him, Balz told himself. *Save—*

And yet he glanced back at the door that had opened for him. The pull to proceed inside, to enter and be lost in the darkness, was like a tangible stroke over all of his skin, a beckoning that was food to a starving male, cash to the poor, recovery to the terminal. Something was in there for him that would save him, save him from—

Syphon screamed again, and the sound of the bloody agony snapped Balz out of the thrall. With a gasp, he wrenched around and grabbed for his forty.

That was when the perfume came.

The smell was grape-ish and deep, an old fragrance that he had scented back in the eighties, on females in the species who were above him socially, on women outside of the species who lived in cities and walked the night streets on the arms of men in tuxedos.

Poison by Dior. He'd looked up the name because he'd loved it so much—

Even before he turned his head back to the void, he knew what he was going to see in the darkness.

He was not wrong.

From out of a black hole, the brunette of his dreams appeared, and she was magically beautiful, unreal yet solid.

"It's you . . ." he breathed.

As she smiled at him, Syphon screamed again, but it was as if her presence turned down the volume on everything else on the planet— including his cousin.

What was happening over the staircase suddenly seemed like the dream instead of her.

"Miss me?" Her voice was heaven, absolute heaven, in his ears . . . a symphony mixed with a marching band, seasoned with hip-hop and some jazz. "I missed you. It feels like forever since we were together. Why don't you come inside, I have a bed we could use—"

Syphon screamed even louder.

"Don't worry about him." She licked her red lips like she was anticipating what Balz's cock would taste like. "He's got nothing to do with us."

His woman stepped back into the darkness and beckoned him with her blood red fingernail. "Come with me, Balthazar, and I will show you pleasure you have never known and riches that will make even you stop stealing. No more hollow places to fill with the objects of others, no more itch that cannot be scratched. You will finally be sated. You will finally find the peace that has eluded you. With me, you can rest, Balthazar."

Tears speared into his eyes. "How do you know me," he whispered.

"Silly male, I've been inside you. Did you think I wasn't walking your halls and trying out your furniture while I was there? Lonely place, your soul, and I've seen a lot of them. But you don't have to worry about that anymore. I'll be with you every step of the way from now on. All you have to do is come to me now."

The decision was made before he was aware of arriving at a conclusion: His body took a step forward. And another.

Balz didn't look back at his cousin.

He was powerless to deny this female.

Anything.

✦   ✦   ✦

As Mae dematerialized, Sahvage rearranged his erection in his pants and went back into the cottage.

Shutting things up, he looked around the heavy hutch through to the back and saw that the cellar door was open. But Tallah wasn't in the kitchen or moving around upstairs.

Clearly, she was back in the cellar, something forgotten or required in her underground quarters, and he was guessing it had to do with her outfit. The old female certainly stayed true to her *glymera* roots. Even though she wasn't living in a mansion, she dressed the part. She'd come out for Monopoly looking like she was going to a formal event—and it was kind of sweet the way she blushed whenever she looked at him.

A little sad, too.

And it was obvious how much she meant to Mae, and vice versa. No wonder that Book was such a topic of discussion. If there were any lives worth preserving with dark magic? Tallah would be on the list.

He glanced over at the dirty dishes that were left.

But God, that stew had been awful.

Determined to be useful and not just decorative, he took over where Mae had left off, picking up her soggy, soapy paper towel wad and going to work on the remaining stuff in the sink. How Tallah had managed to use seven hundred thousand pots and pans was a mystery. There had been all of two root vegetables and a couple handfuls of meat in that liquid-cement broth.

As he washed and rinsed, he thought about Mae standing against that bathroom door, her eyes on his hand job like it was the most amazing thing she had ever seen. Fucking hell, he'd felt like he'd had a palm full of gold as she'd watched him, but when he'd learned that she was . . .

Of course he still wanted the female. He just didn't want to take something permanent from her when he was less than temporary in her life.

It wasn't fair.

With that thought in mind, he got through the mess in the sink. Dried everything off. Put things away in the places Tallah had gotten them out of.

And just as he checked the clock over on the wall, something registered, his inner bell getting rung, even though he wasn't sure by what.

Although the fact that Mae had been gone almost an hour was not great news.

Palming up the gun he'd tucked, he glanced to the refrigerator barricading the back door. Looked out toward the front door. Checked the cellar stairs. What the hell was it—

As his eyes surfed across the table, they double-backed to what had caught his subconscious attention.

"Shit."

Shoving the forty back into his waistband, he picked up the nine millimeter he'd gotten for Mae. She'd left it behind in her frazzled rush to leave.

"I'll be right back," he called down at the basement.

Dematerializing, he traveled up to the second floor and out of the shutter he'd left cracked since the night before. There was no trouble finding Mae's ranch, and as he re-formed by the garage, the lights were on inside of it.

The shutter around back was still as they'd left it, so he was able to get in by her car with no problem—and he frowned. The scent of fresh exhaust was obvious, so she'd clearly gone out for some supplies—and the door into the rear of the house was propped open with a stop.

He wished he could have helped bring whatever it was in for her.

Stepping into a short hallway, he saw Mae's purse and car keys on the washer-dryer. Her jacket, too.

There was a damp trail on the tile that led into a modest kitchen, and as he followed it, he heard a strange rushing sound deeper inside the house. As he went along, he found the single-story ranch small, with furniture that wasn't new, but everything was clean and he felt comfortable with the lack of fussiness.

Another round of that *whoosh* sound escorted him even farther into the house, to a hall that he assumed took him to the layout of upper bedrooms. A bathroom door was open halfway down, and he started to smile as Mae's scent got louder in his nose.

"Can I help you—"

As he came around into the doorway, he—

Stopped short. Because he had no idea what he was looking at.

Mae was on her knees in front of a bathtub, empty ice bags scattered around her, one held up so its load of chips could join the others'. All of that was odd, but not what halted his boots as well as the breath in his lungs.

Inside the tub . . . there appeared to be a corpse. The head was down by the faucet, the feet up at the other end, the white and waxy toes peeking out of the ice.

With an expression of horror, Mae wrenched around and stretched her arms wide, as if she were protecting that which she was keeping cold. Or maybe trying to hide it.

"What are you doing here!"

"You forgot the gun," he said slowly as he showed the weapon from the side. "I brought it to you so you'd be safe—what is that."

Or *who*, was more the question. Although he had a feeling he knew. That dark blond hair was just like hers.

"Mae . . ." Sahvage dragged a hand down his face. "No."

"Get out," she said in a trembling voice. "Leave us alone—"

"You want to bring him back using the Book. Oh, God . . . Mae . . . *no*."

CHAPTER THIRTY-SIX

There were precipices more dire than life and death. And Balz was on one.

As he trembled on the lip of acquiescence, as every part of him wanted to follow the command of the woman of his dreams, he knew an inevitability that was like a second birth: A choice made for him by someone else that caused him to exist in a world. And so, yes, he would enter the psychic's domain, and he would follow the beckoning of the brunette before him, and he would live out what had been his destiny all along.

"That's right," she said with a smile of those blood red lips. "Come to me—"

From out of nowhere, an image slapped him sure as if it were a dagger palm across his face: He saw his cousin back in the Old Country, in a forest hovel where they were sheltering from the sun. Syphon was smiling while draped in weaponry and the rugged leather of war, a healing slice on his temple the result of a *lesser's* blade that had been quicker and more nimble than its target.

A comrade. A friend. A protector.

Family.

His eyes were so blue, his grin so wide, his goodwill inexhaustible even though they had no warm food in their bellies and only raw dirt in a cave for their bed—

Here, take it.

His cousin's invitation, spoken in the Old Language, was as clear as if it had been spoken to Balz right now, and he could see the fighter leaning forward, his hand outstretched.

And in the palm, the last heel of bread he had.

Are you no hungry, then? Balz had asked.

Nay, it shall be for you, Cousin. Take and feed yourself. I shall find something else.

Syphon had spoken the simple words over the growl of his own stomach and in spite of the reality that there had been no food anywhere in the cave—

Balz's eyes flashed open, though he had not been aware they'd closed. And the smile that was in front of him, the smile of seduction, the smile of evil knowing that it had captured another soul . . . was nothing like his cousin's had been.

Nothing like his cousin's was.

"You know what you want to do," the woman said. "You know you're going to come with me—"

With a battle cry, Balz spun around and lunged off the top landing of the stairs, reaching for his cousin's dangling legs as the shadow lifted the helpless male higher and higher, as if it was going to break out through the window mounted high above the entrance and take Syphon away.

"You fucking idiot!" the brunette yelled from the abyss. "You fucking asshole!"

Just before the shadow entity busted the glass and disappeared with its prey, Balz caught his cousin's left shitkicker with a grasping claw—and he backed up that insufficient hold with a rock-hard grab at the ankle.

The shadow let out an unholy screech as the added weight dragged it down, and then something gave way, the entity dropping its load.

Balz's back broke the fall, his body landing with a crack on the wooden steps and starting on a descent that was sure to put him in traction—and his cousin's body was a horrible chaser, all that weight banging him even harder into the unforgiving, uncarpeted stairs. As his brain was overcome with pain, there was a moment of stunned paralysis, but the shadow entity's quick counterattack meant there was no time to whine about the pain—or even check if Syphon was still alive.

Throwing a foot out to stop their jangling, tooth-loosening descent, Balz shoved a hand down to his hip holster and palmed one of his forties. Just as he brought up the muzzle, the shadow shot forward, snakelike tentacles lashing out, striking at his cousin, striking at him. When his forearm was hit, he cursed in pain, but he hit his trigger.

The autoloader did its thing, kicking out bullet after bullet—and thank fuck they worked. The shadow let out another one of those ear-killing screeches, recoiling as if it had been burned. Yet it came back.

So Balz outed a silver dagger. As one of the tentacles got too close, he stabbed it—and was rewarded by that high-pitched holler. But then Syphon, who'd lost consciousness, started slipping down the stairs again, and as Balz tried to grab him, they both ended up bouncing head over heels toward the bottom.

As his body blendered, he did what he could to stab and shoot at the shadow, making sure that neither any of him nor any of his cousin was in the way—

Boom!

They landed in a tangled heap at the base of the steps, their big bodies crammed up against the closed door. With a shove, Balz shifted his cousin to the side so he could keep shooting, but as the last bullet left his weapon, that was a moot point. And he couldn't reach his backup clip or his other forty—

Syphon's hand appeared in front of his face with a full magazine.

"Thank God," Balz muttered. "Can you get me another gun?"

As he got a grunt for a reply, he swapped the clips and kept shooting—and like magic, another Sig Sauer appeared in his face.

Ditching the dagger—where it hopefully wouldn't Swiss cheese them or be used by this entity—he went Deadpool, kicking out lead slugs from both autoloaders, driving the shadow back, holes appearing in its translucent body—or maybe it was more like the structure that held it together was beginning to fail. Now it was like a school of fish, the whole devolving into coordinated parts and undulating in a pattern that became increasingly erratic.

Another clip appeared by the side of his head, Syphon's shaking hand punching through their heap of bad-angled limbs. And a third. All Balz could do was aim and shoot and reload—

"I'm out," Syphon said in a hoarse voice.

At that very moment, as the last bullet left the second forty, the shadow exploded, the airborne shrapnel like the feathers of a raven, blowing apart and floating down on lazy currents.

Meanwhile, up at the top of the stairs, the brunette was leaning around the doorjamb, her furious eyes boring down at Balz.

"You're a *fucking* fool," she bit out.

And then, justlikethat, she was gone.

Balz sagged, his breath tearing up and down his throat, some kind of weird nausea curdling his stomach, a feverish shimmy prickling his skin. As he twisted over and retched, he felt all kinds of pain bloom in all kinds of places.

Now that the immediate threat was gone, he remembered the stories of shadows in Caldwell. And shit, he should have grabbed some of V's special bullets. But he hadn't taken those reports seriously enough.

And he needed to call for help before more of these fucking shadows showed up.

Pushing himself up, he tried to stand—but lost his balance and slammed his hip into the banister.

"You 'live?" he mumbled as he barely noticed the new injury.

From at his feet, there was a groan. Then Syphon lifted a face that was lashed with red welts, the features so distorted that he was barely recognizable.

"I'm calling us in," Balz said as he triggered the emergency locator on his communicator. "And I gotta clear up there."

"I have a dagger. I'll be okay."

Balz didn't have the heart to point out that his cousin could barely see. "Good, hold the fort."

As Balz limped up the steps, the going was uneven. Bullets littered the staircase, balls of lead that had free-fallen when they'd hit the shadow.

At the top landing, he back-flatted by the open door—and then fired up his flashlight and pointed the beam into the dark interior.

The space was mostly empty: Couple of tables below the bank of windows that faced out front, a clutter of candles, pots, and herb bundles crowding the tops. In the center of the room, there was the proverbial crystal ball on a round reading station with two chairs and a lot of draping. Elsewhere, there were futons with cushions and a sitting area of threadbare armchairs. Swathes of brightly colored fabrics shot with cheap gold thread were nailed to the walls, rainbows trapped and captured.

Absolutely no brunette.

She was gone.

Balz breathed in deep. He couldn't catch the scent of anything other than the acrid, metal-backed burn of gunpowder and an unpleasant, fleshy tang of fresh meat.

Had she even been there?

He told himself that he had made the right decision. He had done the right thing. He had chosen family over . . . whatever she was.

And yet he mourned. Like a lover left behind—

As a beeping went off on his communicator, he angled his head to his shoulder. "I need medical help. STAT." He looked down the stairs. Then jogged down them. "One wounded, extent of injuries . . . hold on."

Back with his cousin, he took the lax hand of the fighter he was probably closest to. Syphon had passed out again, but he was breathing through those bee-stung lips.

Oddly, his clothes were all intact. Which made no sense.

"Extent of injuries is severe," Balz choked out as he lost the strength in his own body and collapsed on his side. "Do you have my location . . . ? Good. Fucking hurry."

❖   ❖   ❖

Back at her parents' ranch, in the bathroom where she had never intended anyone to see what she was keeping cold, Mae tried to block Sahvage's perfectly good view of the tub . . . of Rhoger. But it wasn't like a dead body in ice was the kind of thing eyes ignored, even if only parts of the remains were showing.

"Close the door," she barked, because it was all she could think of saying. "Don't look at him like that."

Except Sahvage wasn't focused on Rhoger. He was staring at her.

"Mae—"

"No!" She covered her ears with her palms. "I'm not listening."

Instead of continuing to speak or doing what she'd demanded with the door, Sahvage backed up until he was against the hall wall. Then he slid down until his butt landed on the floor and they were on the same level.

Now he didn't look at her or Rhoger. He put his head in his hands.

As he stayed quiet, Mae collapsed against the side of the tub. Looked through the ice at her brother.

"You don't understand," she whispered. "It's all my fault."

Sahvage made an exhausted sound. "Unless you killed him with your own two hands, I'm very sure it's not."

"Our parents were really strict," she heard herself say. "Very old school. After they were killed in the raids, Rhoger started to change. He stayed out all day, sometimes for a week at a time. He was hanging around with a different crowd. He just . . . spiraled. Meanwhile, I was here taking care of the house, paying the bills, trying to hold what was left of our family together. I got resentful."

She reached into the tub and shuffled the ice around more evenly.

As her hand got cold, the difference in temperature between her palm and the chips was a stark reminder of everything that separated her and her brother.

Mae choked back tears. "The last night he left . . . we had a terrible fight. I lost it. I told him he had to get a job or move out. He yelled back. It got so ugly." She shook her head, even though she wasn't sure Sahvage was looking at her. "He didn't come back. For two weeks . . . maybe it was almost three. I can't keep it all straight. I tried to find him. I called his phone constantly. I went to his friends' houses. No one knew where he'd gone. Then one night, I was working here and—he came through the front door. He was all . . . he was bleeding from so many places and he looked like he hadn't eaten since he'd left. I rushed to him and he died in my arms." Mae rubbed her stinging eyes. "I didn't have any idea what happened to him or what to do. I called Tallah. I don't have anyone else in my life and I couldn't think straight. After I told her everything and I managed to calm down a little, she got so silent on that phone . . . I thought she'd hung up on me. And then she said the words . . ."

"The Book," Sahvage gritted.

Mae glanced out of the bathroom to him. "The Book."

"You can't do this. Mae, you have no idea what you're opening up here."

"But it was okay to prolong Tallah's life," she muttered bitterly.

"I never said that."

Mae threw up a hand. "Rhoger is all I have left."

"That's what you said about Tallah."

"We're *really* going to argue about how few people I have in my life right now? Really?" Mae gathered the empty bags of ice around her. And then didn't do anything with them. "I can't get off this path. You don't understand. It's . . . it's all my fault. I drove him out of this house and into the hands of someone who tortured him so badly, he died of the injuries."

Sahvage cursed. "He left because he left, Mae. It could have been any other night—"

"Don't pretend you know us."

"And don't you pretend what you're doing is right."

"That's my brother in all that ice," she choked out.

"That's a dead male," Sahvage countered. "He might have been your brother when he was alive, but not anymore."

Mae exhaled sharply. "How can you say that."

"Because it's the truth."

"Stop it." She closed her eyes. "Just stop it."

When she opened her lids, Sahvage was right in front of her, and as she reared back, he took one of her hands.

"Please," he said. "Don't do this to him. If you love him, you will not do this—"

"What, bring him back to me? How is that wrong!"

Sahvage swallowed hard, and his voice was barely audible. "Leave him in the Fade. I beg you. The consequences are not worth it."

Those midnight blue eyes were boring into her, and his expression was so intense, she knew this was not just a case of someone looking out for her best interests.

"What aren't you telling me?" she demanded.

"It's just what I've heard to be true—"

"Bullshit. What do you know. And do not lie to me."

Sahvage broke the contact between them and sat back onto his ass. As his eyes went to Rhoger and the ice, he grew very still.

When he finally spoke, his voice, like his expression, was haunted. "I only know that people are not meant to live forever . . ."

"I don't want him to be immortal, goddamn it. I just want to bring—"

"And you think you're setting the terms? You honestly think you're going to set the rules here. You're toying with the very foundation of mortality."

"Fuck mortality! Rhoger got robbed. And I'm going to fix it if it's the last thing I do!"

CHAPTER THIRTY-SEVEN

Sahvage had only had one other moment in all his earthly years that revealed a blindness this great, a blindness that changed everything about where he was. And it wasn't that Mae had lied to him. It was that he had failed to anticipate her ulterior motive. He had taken at face value what she had said, and moved on to other things.

Like the sexual attraction he had for her.

Funny, how that shit had a way of wiping the slate clean.

"I have no other choice," Mae announced.

"You are wrong about that." He shook his head. "Death is not something that is bad."

"How can you say that? Rhoger is barely seventy years old. He was cheated."

"But if you believe in the Fade—"

"You mean to tell me that my father and *mahmen*, who didn't get along all that well when they were under this roof here, are enjoying a perfect relationship on a cloud somewhere in the sky? Please. I was fine with the theory of the Fade until I did the math on the people who are supposedly up there. An eternity with our so-called loved ones is just a fairy tale fed to us so we don't lose our minds in the very situation I'm in right now—and yes, I'm aware I'm crazy. But you don't know what this is like—"

"I lost my only family member, too. So I know *exactly* how you feel."

That shut his female up.

Not that she was his.

"What happened?" Mae asked in a softer tone.

"It was back in the Old Country." Sahvage rubbed his face. "She was my charge, my first cousin. I was responsible for her. I was her only family, her protector . . ."

When he didn't go on, Mae sat forward. "And you . . . lost her."

"I failed her completely. She was taken from me by an aristocrat. And then she was . . . brutalized." Sahvage pegged Mae with a hard eye. "So yes, I know what that is like, too—and it was all my fault as well."

Mae's eyes glowed with tears, her face flushing with compassion. "That's why you don't like to look at yourself."

"No," he said grimly. "That's why I *hate* to look at myself."

Shit, this was getting way too real, he thought.

"How can you say you don't understand where I'm coming from, then?" she prompted.

"I never told you that. I said what you're trying to do is wrong. With the Book. Forever on earth is not meant for mortals, Mae, and not for the ones we love, either. Let him go. Give him a proper Fade Ceremony . . . and let him go."

Mae was quiet for a time. "I'm sorry . . . I just don't think I can live with myself. I need to see this through. If I find the Book, I'm going to proceed."

"Is there anything I can say to make you change your mind?"

"No."

His eyes left hers and went to the empty bags of ice she'd crumpled up and put next to her hip. One of the bags had unfurled and was displaying a cartoon penguin with a red scarf. The fucker looked quite cheerful. Inappropriately so, given the circumstances.

"I'm sorry I lied to you," she said remotely. "About Rhoger."

"That hardly matters now."

"It's a difficult thing to talk about."

Sahvage stared across at her, wishing she were human and he could manipulate her mind. "Of course it is. Because you know this is wrong, and if you say it out loud to someone or have someone see this, you run the risk of realizing how bad an idea this is for yourself."

Mae blinked. A couple of times. Then she leaned forward, her eyes narrowing.

"Are you even kidding me." She shook her head. "You're a stranger. I've known you for forty-eight hours—and I met you when you were bleeding out at an underground, bare-knuckle fight with a human—"

Sahvage put up his forefinger. "I wouldn't have been bleeding if you hadn't distracted me—"

"Will you quit it!" Mae threw up her hands. "God*damn* it. My point is, you're not exactly someone who's properly in my life. And this"—she jabbed a finger at her brother—"is killing me, okay? It's *killing* me. So, no, I wasn't in a big hurry to share it with you."

Her voice cracked and her eyes watered with tears again. But it was clear she wanted no kind of sympathy, at least not from him: She angrily slashed her palms across her cheeks and then wiped them on her jeans.

"I can't just sit here and do nothing," she said roughly. "So the only thing you and I have to talk about is what you're going to do now. Are you in or are you out. And before you find some way of pissing me off again with one of your sweetheart comments, yes, we are here at this crossroads. Again."

Sahvage closed his eyes. After a period of tense silence, he intended to give her an answer. But instead, the present drifted away, and was replaced by the past that he had resolutely ignored for so long . . .

◆   ◆   ◆

In the great hall of Zxysis the Elder's castle, Sahvage felt as though a veil had fallen from his eyes, his sight now clear, though he had been unaware that it had been obstructed, the world around him no longer beset by fogged haze, though he had assumed all was as he believed it to be.

And what he saw revealed before him was terrifying.

"Who art thou?" he whispered again as he stared down at Rahvyn, his cousin, his charge, his only family.

Behind him, the headless bodies of the stand of guards jerked in their pools of blood as the last of their animation deferred unto death's cold call of im-motion. And afore him, Rahvyn was unbowed, even in the face of the beating she had been given, of the violation that had occurred unto her virtue.

But she had good reason to fear nothing, did she not.

Lifting her arms, she looked at first one, and then the other, of the steel cuffs that had bitten into her fragile wrists. They dropped off as if commanded to do so, clanging to the stone floor.

"I am who I have e'er been," she said in that voice of power. "Only unleashed, the now."

Zxysis had somehow known of this power within her, Sahvage thought.

It was clear that the aristocrat had cobbled together the stories from the village and seen the trailheads for what they were. Meanwhile Sahvage, who had supposedly been the closest to the female, had missed the trajectory.

She needed not his protection.

She needed no one's.

"We shall go our separate ways, Cousin." Now her voice changed, returning closer to that which he had known. "You have discharged your service unto me, the vow unto my sire, your uncle, fully met. And as I know you shall not leave me, I shall leave you—"

"Rahvyn, where is Zxysis. What did you do to him?"

The smile that pulled at the corners of the female's mouth terrified him. "What he did unto me. No more, no less. I repaid his attentions by getting inside of him." Rahvyn limped over to where a black cloak had been thrown over one of the banquet seats. Pulling it around herself, she faced him. "You shall not find me. Do not even try."

On a reflex, he protested. "My duty unto you is sacrosanct—"

"And I hereby release you of the burden." Abruptly, her eyes softened.

"Sahvage, you are free. Of it all. No more worries concerning me that distract you from your true calling. You shall be the most powerful fighter that e'er have served the Black Dagger Brotherhood. Glory shall be yours, for the race shall ne'er have seen such a protector as you."

"No! My defense of you is more important than—"

"Not anymore." She blinked away tears and lifted her chin. "Be well, Cousin. I have so much faith in your future. I urge you to join me in this optimism, even as I depart from your life. This era is over."

"Rahvyn!" he yelled as he rushed forward.

But she dematerialized from the great hall, leaving naught except her scent . . . and the bloody carnage she had caused.

"No!" he yelled. Even as he knew not what he was denying.

Dragging his hands into his hair, he paced around. And around. And around in a tight circle. But naught changed. Not what his charge had done, not what he had seen with his own eyes. With a curse, he released the hold upon his head and went to stand over the dead. The tangle of bodies and unhanded weapons were layered in a mess, blood glistening on leather togs, on flesh, on stone . . . on bright steel scabbards and gunmetal-gray rifles.

"Rahvyn," he whispered, "what else have you done?"

Except there was no Rahvyn anymore, was there.

As the realization struck, an urgency called unto him with the clarity of a brass bell, and he took care to arm himself with the weapons of the dead before he hastened down the broad thoroughfare that marked the way unto the drawbridge. As he jogged in silence and with speed, there was much to surmount. A field of debris marked the stone pavers: clothing fragments, foodstuffs in their nettings and pouches, pages from diaries and books littering the way unto the exit.

A flurry of people, fleet of foot and panicked of mind, had of recent rushed forth upon this very route, their objects of secondary import to their very lives.

What had scared them so? 'Twas a question he feared the answer to.

When the fortification's grand entrance presented itself, Sahvage slowed. Then he stopped.

The view through the vast opening provided a ready vista of the cleared field surrounding the castle. Trampled rivulets through the grasses illustrated the scatter of the inhabitants who had fled, and the drawbridge, which had remained lowered, was likewise covered with the same detritus trail.

"Whate'er did they know," Sahvage whispered as he stepped through the great iron-and-steel gates. "Whate'er did they see whilst they abandoned this entirety."

Drop. Drop . . . drop.

At the soft sound, Sahvage glanced down beside the fall of his robing. There, on the old, worn surface of the drawbridge's wood, a puddle glistened in the moonlight.

Red. Brilliant red.

Sahvage turned and looked up—"Dearest Virgin Scribe."

Up above the grand and formal entry, speared upon the iron stanchion that carried the silks of seat's the bloodline, was . . .

Zxysis the Elder.

And it went without any question that he was deceased.

As if the impaling wasnae a clue.

Verily, his skin had been stripped from his bones and muscles: Everything that had once bound his corporeal form was gone, his intestines drooling out of his pelvis, organs seeping free from under his rib cage. His face had been preserved, however. Those features that defined his identity within the glymera and this household and village had been left untouched, his expression one of utter horror, his lips stretched wide over his bared teeth, his blind eyes staring in terror out over his landed estate.

"Rahvyn—"

A brilliant light exploded into the sky, so bright that it readily outshone the moon, so painful that he groaned and lifted his arms to shield his eyes. Stumbling back, Sahvage sought the protection of the stone walls of the castle, and when he was under their cover, he attempted to sight what he could withstand of the celestial being.

Whate'er it was traveled across the velvet heavens, eclipsing the twinkle of the stars, seeming to suck up all illumination from overhead. And as it

reached the horizon to the north, there was another brief intensification—
and then it burned out to nothing.

In its departure, all was as it had been before.

Except no, that was not true upon the earth. None of what was around
him was as it should be.

And Rahvyn was wrong.

She had not freed him with her departure. She had framed him for the
killings she had wrought against her abductors.

None would believe that he had not dispatched Zxysis and his guards as
they had been: His reputation within the Brotherhood not only justified the
nomenclature he had been given upon his birth; it preceded him where'er he
went.

The bodies in the great hall. Zxysis's o'erhead, skinned as an animal,
pierced as a carcass. And whate'er else had been done to whome'er else had
hurt Rahvyn. All would be accorded unto Sahvage, and thus the glymera
would come looking for him, demanding explanations he would not be able
to provide. And the Brotherhood would be put in an untenable situation, for
they knew what he was like in the field—and they knew what his charge had
meant to him.

They would also know the whispers of the village around the castle, the
old females and young who spoke of magic in the forests and inexplicable
happenings in the town.

To protect his charge, Sahvage had been content to accept the curse of
being called warlock when he was as far from being one as any mortal. And
besides, Rahvyn's magic had been harmless . . . or at any rate, naught to be
afraid of.

He closed his eyes and pictured Zxysis.

No more for the harmlessness.

Thus, nay, Sahvage was not free, no matter what his cousin maintained.
Her actions had condemned him to death—

With an abrupt pivot, he turned to the way he had come.

And then he set off at a run.

As he came up to decapitated guards, he leapt over the bodies and the blood. Onward, still, he went, unto the steps he had at first ascended . . . and past them farther into the castle's lower levels.

When he came upon the storage room he had awoken in, he took a torch inside and placed it in a mount just within the door. Going over to his coffin, he put his weapons down and replaced the lid as it had been—and it was then, courtesy of the torch's frothing light, that he noted the warnings that had been carved into the wood. A cursed dead was herein, the symbols announcing it on all sides.

Sahvage looked around. Then promptly removed the lid once more—and picked up bags of flour that were close by, three of them, four of them, more of them still, laying their weight where his body should have been. Finally, he lowered the lid and used the stone from a grinder, wrapped in a sack, to hammer home that which he had disrupted. Finally, he retrieved the scabbard he had purloined. Utilizing its stout point, he carved his name in the lid and on the vertical panels, for that had not been among what had been inscribed.

Reshouldering the rifle, he took the torch and returned unto the corridor. Checking both ways, he confirmed that the resonant quiet persisted—although that would not last. Superstition would keep vampires away, and humans likewise, but only for a time. The greed of thieves would soon enough overwhelm their senses of self-protection, and there was much to be pilfered from within. And this would serve his purposes. In the course of such trespassing, his coffin would be found, and of all the things within the castle walls, it was the one that would not be touched. No soul would want to assume dominion over such an artifact. Yet word would get out.

Eventually, the Brotherhood would find his final resting place, but whether they accepted the remains—or whether they would discover his duplicity? Who could say.

Sahvage, however, would not be around to ascertain the outcome of his purported dead body. Instead, he was going to search for his cousin until he found her, and then, when she was thinking with proper logic, he would ensure that the pair of them stayed hidden. And his supposed death would ensure that was possible—

Tap.

Just as he was about to run off, Sahvage turned to the sound.

Tap. Tap.

In the unnatural quiet of the castle, the soft noise stood out far more than its soft volume would have permitted under any other circumstances.

Tap. Tap. Tap. Tap—

Leave it be, he told himself. His mandate with regard to a prompt exodus was clear—

Taptaptaptaptap—

As a cold premonition brushed the back of his neck, his will directed him unto the exit. His body, however, proceeded in another direction.

Such that he followed that strange, soft sound.

CHAPTER THIRTY-EIGHT

As Sahvage went silent and seemed to retreat into his own mind, Mae put her hand on the edge of the tub.

"I can't let you go," she whispered to Rhoger. "And I promise I won't. I know how to fix this."

She meant the words, especially the last ones, but the refrain was weak, as if she had used the syllables too often and was wearing out their strength. Or maybe they had never had any power to begin with, just the panic-fuel of her desperation—and how far did that ever take anybody in real life?

"No changing your mind," Sahvage murmured.

She looked back at him. "Never."

The word had more vigor than she did. But it was like if she stood up to him, she was standing up to Fate, and that had to be her mindset . . . in spite of the fact that she didn't have the Book yet. And she was taking what Tallah had told her on faith.

"All right," he said finally.

"Are you leaving?"

"No." He shook his head. "I'm not going anywhere."

Mae closed her eyes and sagged with relief. "I promise, it's going to be okay. Everything is going to be fine. We're going to be fine."

Yes, and then what, she wondered. Even though she knew the answer to that when it came to the two of them.

Sahvage would go on about his life. She would go on about hers. And it was in the nature of nothing-in-common that the pair of them would diverge. As they had no intersections to begin with, nothing was going to keep them together.

Getting to her feet, she gathered up the ice bags. "Let's go back to the cottage."

Funny how normal it felt to say that. Then again, a person could get used to anything—and unused to it, too.

As she stepped out of the bathroom, he moved his legs to the side and then stood up, too. And when she shut the door, it was firmly— except did that change anything? Like she could lock out the awkwardness? The lie of hers?

Nope.

"I'm going back to my place," he said.

"Okay, you don't have to stay. I mean, at the cottage, or with—"

"Yeah, I do. Now more than ever. But I need clothes."

He didn't look at her as he walked out toward the garage, and she rushed after him, grabbing her purse and her keys from the washer. As she locked the house up, he nodded at her and dematerialized through the gap in the shutter. Left alone, she glanced at the trash that had still not been taken out—and remembered the reason why.

On impulse, she got in her car and started the engine. Maybe they'd need a vehicle. Or maybe she just needed to drive around.

As she was backing out—because she'd been so distracted coming back from the Shell station that she'd broken her father's parking rule again—she thought about how the Book was taking its own damn time . . . and tried not to see the lag for what it was:

A sign this was all a big folly. And she was a desperate fool.

K-turning in the street, she thought of Tallah, home alone at the cottage. With a curse, Mae hit the gas and headed out of her neighborhood, consumed by obsessions about shadows and brunettes and huge males naked in bathrooms—

Unable to stand the chaos in her head, she turned on the radio. She'd left the station on NPR, and some dulcet-voiced woman was droning on about public funding for libraries, so she switched to FM.

"—serial killer here in Caldwell. The CPD reported that another man and woman were found dead last night. The bodies were discovered at club Eight-Seven-Five, and both of their hearts had been removed—"

Mae's eyes went to the radio, and she cranked up the volume.

"—just as the others' had been. The identities of the newest victims are being withheld at this time, pending the notification of families. The count is now up to five couples, including the most recently identified pair, Ralph DeMellio and Michelle Caspari. Allegedly, DeMellio was involved in an underground fighting ring, and authorities believe that he was killed shortly after one such fight. Footage found on Instagram suggests he had faced an opponent with a distinctive tattoo covering his chest—"

Mae's left foot stomped on the brake—

The blare of a horn behind her drowned out the rest of the report—and then the world exploded, the strike of the rear-end collision blowing Mae's head against the rest as the airbag broke out from the steering wheel and her car careened off her lane with a scream of locked tires.

All momentum stopped with a furious impact, the Civic's front grille striking something that had no give in it.

As the airbag deflated with a hiss, Mae drooped forward, her consciousness fuzzing out . . . and then returning in a fog. In her car's headlights, through some kind of steam rising out of the busted hood, she read a sign mounted on a brick wall: *Poplar Woods.*

She'd run into the marker for the development next to her own.

Fumbling with her seat belt, she released the latch on her door and popped things open. On a loose list to the side, her body fell out, her arms and legs not listening to the commands she gave them, and with all the grace of dead weight, she spilled onto the ground, dirt going into her mouth, her nose. She flopped onto her back and took some deep breaths.

A frantic face entered her field of vision. It was a human man with rimless glasses, a receding hairline, and a cell phone up to his ear.

"I couldn't stop in time!" he said. "You threw your brakes on so quick—I'm calling nine-one-one—"

"No, no—don't call—" Mae put her hand up, like she could somehow take that phone from him. "No, no—"

"Hi? Yes, my name is Richard Karouk. I need to report a—"

With an abrupt gasp, Richard Karouk stopped talking, his eyes flaring wider behind those glasses. Then there was a clicking sound, and his mouth dropped open.

Blood flooded out onto his business shirt and his nice jacket, a bright red flush.

As he slumped to the ground in a heap, a figure in a bustier and a set of skintight black leather pants was revealed. The brunette.

And she had a long steel knife in her hand that was stained red . . . red as her lips, her nails.

"Hi, honey." She smiled. "Looks like you hit your noggin and totaled your car. Thank *God* I'm here when you need a friend."

◆   ◆   ◆

Sahvage did not go back to the shitty place he was crashing at. Instead he re-formed on the top of a rise in a public park, and as he stared across at a wide, sluggish river, he decided the lights of the houses at the opposite shore were like a galaxy fallen to ground. Twinkling, distant . . . untouchable.

Is there anything I can say to make you change your mind?

No.

That exchange with Mae replayed in his head a couple of hundred times, and of course, the repeat thing did not change her reply—even though he had some delusion that maybe the discourse would improve over time, the needle in the proverbial LP record finding a different groove, a better one.

With a curse, he took out his phone. And as he made a call, he knew that he was setting himself to as immutable a course as Mae was on. Then again, her intentions drove his. And it was what it was.

After a terse conversation, he ended the connection and put his phone away.

He was still standing where he'd planted his boots when a male materialized in front of him.

The Reverend was who he had been at the fight, an imposing figure in a full-length fur, his cropped Mohawk and amethyst eyes not the kind of thing you saw every night. Given the elegant bulk of that mink, it was not immediately apparent whether there were weapons under the duster, but a strange sense told Sahvage that the conventional stuff you could buy at your local click-click, bang-bang shop wasn't going to be necessary for the guy's protection.

There was something off about him.

And the fact that he was involved with the Book seemed right.

"Fancy hearing from you," the Reverend drawled. Then he frowned. "This isn't about the fight money, is it."

"No."

"How's your female?"

"She's not mine." Sahvage ignored the chuckle. "But I need to find that Book she's looking for."

"Valentine's Day isn't for another ten months, and as romantic intentions go, you might have just as good a result with chocolates, only without the fucking hassle—"

"Where can I find it. And don't tell me you didn't lie to her. You know a helluva lot more than you're saying."

Abruptly, the jokey-jokey shit left the chat.

"I am under *no* obligation to humor your drama." The Reverend smiled coldly, flashing long fangs. "And you're not trying to get it for her, are you. No, no, you've got other plans for the Book."

"Of course it's for her."

A dark eyebrow lifted. "You're either lying to me or lying to yourself."

On his side of the conversation, Sahvage was busy blocking every thought he had—and it was clearly not working. Which he took to mean he was definitely talking to the right male.

With a shrug, he said, "I'm just helping for a friend."

"Yeah, 'cuz you're the kind of male who does shit like that." The Reverend put his hand in his pocket. Then grew still. "You're not going to tell me to keep my palms in full view?"

"No."

"So trusting. Another surprise. We keep this up and you're going to tell me you're turning into a pacifist next."

"I don't trust you at all. But you can't hurt me."

Those amethyst eyes narrowed. "That, my friend, is where you're wrong."

"No one can hurt me," Sahvage countered grimly.

"You know"—the Reverend took his hand back out—"I've heard of toxic narcissism before, but you're taking the cake. Here's your money."

"Keep it and tell me what you know about the Book."

"No offense, this is couch change to me. So you're not doing me any favors."

"Keep it anyway. And tell me what you know."

The Reverend disappeared the cash again. Then he just stared at Sahvage. "Where's your lost family, fighter."

"What?"

"I have this cute little knack for knowing what people hide." He tapped the side of his head. "Such a handy thing out in the world, really. And you lost your people, your family, a long time ago, didn't you."

"I didn't lose anybody, and I just want the Book."

There was a long period of silence. Then the Reverend switched his cane from one hand to another. "As it turns out, I have someone you're going to want to speak to. I don't know where the fucking thing is, but a friend of mine does. You'll want to ask him. He's an absolute angel."

"Fine. Tell me when and where."

"I'll be in touch."

"Make it quick."

"You are hardly in a position to make demands."

Sahvage slowly shook his head. "You don't know who you're dealing with."

The Reverend open his mouth like he was going to make a snide comment. But the male didn't follow through on the impulse.

As a calculating look came into those eyes, he smiled a little. "Fascinating." Then he nodded with respect. "And I do believe you are right. I don't know who I'm dealing with—but neither do you, fighter. You'll be hearing from me."

The Reverend bowed. And then he was off, disappearing into the night.

Left on his little lonesome, Sahvage went back to staring over the slow-moving water. The fact that he didn't know the river's name was a testament to how many places he had been over the last couple of centuries. From wandering the Old Country's various nation-states to coming to the New World fifty years ago and traveling all around the South and the Midwest, the globe was a blur to him. Then again, he'd never used maps. Maps were for people with destinations. The sole direction he took was no daylight and veins only when he absolutely needed them.

Otherwise, he roamed in search of a moving target.

No, that was actually no longer true. He had come to this side of the big pond because he had finally given up on finding his cousin. Just as he had predicted the night he resealed his coffin full of oat flour, his "death" had freed him of any ties, and he had gone to ground, following up on leads, gossip, and tenuous stories of magic in hopes of finding Rahvyn.

Not one single trace. She must have died somewhere along the line—and now he was here, an ocean away. But no longer purposeless.

The Reverend was right. He wasn't going after the Book for Mae.

He was going to find it and destroy the goddamn thing before she could ruin her brother's life.

And her own.

CHAPTER THIRTY-NINE

B alz limped around in circles outside one of the training center's operating rooms. There were a lot of people with him: Xcor and the rest of the Band of Bastards, the Brotherhood, the other fighters in the house. On the far side of the closed door, Syphon was being treated for God only knew what.

On that note, Balz pulled up the sleeve of the flannel shirt he'd changed into after his own medical exam. The welt on his forearm was calming down, the raised flesh less angry, less swollen. There were a lot of the damn things, mostly on his chest and arms. Maybe twenty percent of his entire body.

Syphon was at more like eighty percent.

If the male died, it was all Balz's fault.

Back at that psychic's, Manny had arrived with his mobile surgical unit a mere eight minutes after the call-in for help, and Xcor and several of the Brothers had loaded Syphon into the treatment bay. Balz had refused any medical attention at that point, and insisted on riding in to offer protection.

Not that he had been much use. He'd been in killer pain.

But self-blame was a better analgesic than morphine, go figure.

In recounting the attack, he'd done what he could to fill the docs and the other fighters in on what had happened. But he'd given them all an edited version—although he'd been totally up front about the shadow. Again, it had been a goddamn shame that he hadn't had water from the Scribe Virgin's fountain in those bullets—

"There's a new evil in town," Butch muttered. "Maybe the shadows are something of hers."

As a cold rush of awareness fell on Balz's head, he pivoted around and faced the Brother. Butch O'Neal was a sharp dresser when he was off the clock, a great fighter when he was on it, and wicked handy—as he would have said—with a potato launcher. He'd also been up close and in person with—

"Hers?" Balz heard himself say.

"You remember what happened with the Omega. The woman—or yeah, whatever the fuck she is."

"Oh, right." Balz cleared his throat. Twice. "Right. Right, sure."

His brain, his awareness, was like a Victorian stereoscope, where two flat photographs of the same thing were merged and became a three-dimensional image.

He felt like he couldn't breathe. "Just curious. What did she look like?"

Butch shook his head as he glanced at his roommate, V, and then looked back over. "You mean, did I see her driver's license?" Then he frowned. "Wait, you're serious. What she looked like?"

"Yeah." Balz shrugged and tried to appear casual. "I mean, if she's out there on the streets of Caldwell, with some kind of shadow army, shouldn't all of us have an idea of what she looks like?"

Butch shrugged and then nodded. "Good point. Ah, well . . . she's pretty much the most beautiful brunette you've ever seen. Until you look her in the eye. And then . . . she's horror and destruction and disease . . ." Butch made the sign of the cross over his heavy chest. "She is as enticing as poison in a rosebud."

Conversation bubbled up at that point, the Brothers who had seen her chiming in. But it wasn't like Balz needed any more descriptors— the truth was . . . he'd known the answer before he'd asked the question.

To make it like there was nothing wrong, he hung out for a little longer, and then he broke away, making sure he told Xcor he'd be right back. The locker room for males was next door, and as he stumbled inside, he went past the lineup of lockers to the row of sinks by the shower stalls. Running some water in one of the basins, he splashed his face and scrubbed the moisture off with some buff-colored paper towels from a dispenser.

Dropping his hands, he stared at himself in the mirror—

Don't worry, I forgive you, lover boy.

As the female voice echoed through his head, he wheeled around. "I'm not yours for the taking," he said to the shower stalls.

How 'bout we bet on that?

The locker room door opened, and he went for the gun he'd loaded—

Butch walked in, and the Brother's stride was as casual as Balz had tried to make his own when he had left. That face, though, was not relaxed in the slightest, and those hazel eyes were knowing. You could tell the guy had been a cop in his earlier life as a human.

"Tell me where you've seen her."

Good thing that as a thief, Balz was an accomplished liar. The truth, after all, was only one more safe to break into and steal from. You just did it with words instead of grabby hands.

"I don't know what you're talking about—"

"Don't bullshit me." Butch crossed his arms over his chest, his leather fighting jacket creaking. "It's not going to help either one of us. When did you see her and what did she do to you."

With a curse, Balz thought about that pause, that moment, when he'd been stuck in between saving his cousin and . . . whatever she was.

There shouldn't have been any hesitation at all. And that's what was terrifying him now.

"Tonight." He took a deep breath. "Tonight at that psychic's. And before that, during the day in my bedroom. She came to visit me and I thought I was dreaming, but she somehow scratched my back."

Butch took a deep breath, as if he were relieved. "Good."

"I'm sorry?" Balz said with a frown.

"I just, look, I know you're a big boy and you can take care of yourself. I also know you would never lie about something like that."

"Of course I wouldn't."

"I was just worried that you'd seen her. I'm glad you didn't."

"What?" Balz shook his head because clearly his ears weren't working. "I just told you I did. That she was with me—"

"We can't be too careful, you know. I feel like she's kind of like an infection. Once she gets in you, she takes over until you die." Butch clapped Balz on the shoulder. "Sorry that I was paranoid—and really glad she hasn't crossed your path."

Balz stared after the Brother in total confusion. When Butch got to the door, the fighter glanced over his shoulder and smiled.

"But hey, we get our hands on that Book and we've got all kinds of demon-icillin."

"What?" Balz asked.

"Word has it that Book can be used for lots of fun things. Including getting rid of pesky trespassers—and I ain't talking about your uncle Norman over the Christmas holiday."

As the Brother ducked out of the locker room, Balz mumbled, "I don't have an uncle Norman."

He sure as shit had a trespasser, however, and he had a feeling she was working through him in ways he wasn't aware of.

This realization would have flat-out terrified him.

If he hadn't already been shitting bricks.

◆   ◆   ◆

Back at the cottage, Sahvage entered through the second-story bedroom window, and as he came to the head of the stairs, he called down for Tallah.

He did the same on the first floor.

At the cellar door, he leaned in. Then went down. The old female's room was open, and the light from the hall shone inside. There was a lot of pink silk with flowers, and furniture that he had seen in what the humans called France, back when he'd been traveling the Old Country. Over on a chaise lounge, Tallah was fast asleep. She had dressed formally once again, her gown a faded teal, her silver fall of hair loose and tangling in the seed pearls that had been stitched on the bodice.

Beside her was a tray with a cup of tea, some half-eaten toast, and a pot of jam.

The life span of vampires was very different from that of humans, and not just from a longevity point of view. Unlike that other species, vampires looked pretty damn good for their entire lives, up until their last decade or so. At that point, the aging process slammed into the body and the mind, and the degeneration of everything occurred on a fast-rate escalation that led right into the grave.

Tallah was not far from a headstone—

"Sahvage?" the female mumbled as she lifted her head. "Is that you?"

"I'm sorry I woke you. I was just checking on you."

"Oh, that is so kind. Where's Mae?"

"She's on her way back." He took a deep breath. "You haven't eaten much."

"I was not very hungry. That stew last night was so filling."

"You just rest. You look tired."

"I am."

As he went to turn away, Tallah said, "She's lucky to have you."

With a noncommittal sound, he headed back upstairs and took a seat at the kitchen table. Checking his phone, he frowned at the time and texted Mae. And then he waited for a response. Which would be coming at any second. He was quite sure. She'd probably taken her car.

He glanced at the clock on the wall. Yeah, that was it. Mae was driving back with her car and it would take her—he glanced at the time on his home screen again—probably another ten minutes. Fifteen at the most.

As the quiet in the cottage seeped into him, he found the past coming back one last time. Good thing. He'd lost his patience with his memories . . . then again, that had been true at the very moment they had been made.

✦   ✦   ✦

Tap. Tap. Tap . . .

The plaintive sound led him unto the broad staircase that ascended to the highest level of the castle. As he followed, a dog upon a scent, he was aware that the volume did not change. Though he instinctively knew he was closing in on the destination, the tapping did not become louder. It was as if the sound was in the very walls of stone, in the floor, in the ceiling.

Or perhaps no.

It might well be inside of him.

His journey ended in front of a stout door, the heavy planks reinforced with iron bars. And on either side, silk flags with golden trim were mounted upon proud poles.

He pictured Zxysis, impaled in the rectum—

Tap. Tap. Tap . . . tap.

As if its purpose had been served, the sound evaporated. And the door opened with a creaking, though he neither willed it so nor placed his hand upon its latch.

The master's bedchamber was revealed, a blast of fresh air rushing forth as if it were anxious to depart the luxurious confines. Then again, all was not well.

In the flickering light of agitated candle flames, a scene of violence had even Sahvage closing his eyes.

Rahvyn's simple underdress, the one that she had worn many times before, was torn to shreds and stained with blood, parts of it here . . . there . . . on the bedding platform. And beneath a canopy marked with the silks of the bloodline, the smell of blood and sex was at its strongest, even with the open window.

There she had been taken in violence.

"*Dearest Virgin Scribe.*"

But that was not all. There . . . in the corner . . . there was a bundle of leather, pale, unfinished leather . . .

Zxysis's skin.

Sahvage drew his dagger palm down his face. Though he had never been a spiritual male, one caught up in prayers or the promised consolation of the Fade, he could not help but utter the mahmen *of the race's name o'er and o'er again—*

Tap. Tap. Tap.

Wheeling around, he frowned. The sound was coming from a trestle table by the hearth, and as he approached, he saw that a book lay open beside a black candle, an earthen dish, a dagger, and some herbs. As he breathed in, he caught a scent that was familiar.

His robing.

Lifting the front of the black fall that covered him, he sniffed. Yes, that was what had been pressed onto him—and within the bouquet . . . Rahvyn's blood.

He looked at the ancient tome. There were lines of ink upon its parchment, the rusty brown color suggesting that blood had been in the quill that had stroked o'er the pages. The letters and symbols, however . . . were unlike any he had e'er seen before. However, he had a guess as to the content.

A spell, for surely these ingredients were inexplicable for any other purpose.

And Rahvyn's vein had been opened.

He thought of the warnings carved on the outside of his coffin. It was not a difficult conclusion that some kind of containing spell had been wrought upon him, although obviously Zxysis hadnae been successful in the attempt.

Turning the cover over to close, Sahvage grimaced. He did not care for the feel of handling any part of the book. And as for what it was bound in? The ugly leather was riddled with cracks and fissures, as if it were aged beyond centuries. There was also a smell, like curdled milk or decaying flesh.

He dropped his hold and rubbed his palm upon his hip. Even after a vigorous scrub, he felt as though something was retained on his fingers, his palm—

The cover flipped back open of its own volition, the pages ruffling in a rush, sure as if ghosted hands were skimming through them. Sahvage backed away, but stopped as the book came to a rest in a different place than had been exposed previously.

Tap. Tap. Tap.

Narrowing his eyes, he recognized the symbols of the language he had learned as a young. Indeed, he could now read what was upon the parchment, and he had the sense that it was a message for him. Or perhaps a calling . . . or a command—

Sahvage covered his eyes. "No."

He knew not what he was saying, nor to whom. But the denial had to stand true, stand strong. He somehow had the conviction that if he set his gaze upon the pages, if he absorbed the symbols and translated them into words, he would embark upon a path from which he could not depart.

With a wrench, he turned away. The slatted shutters of the windows were, as the drawbridge had been, open and offering a ready exit.

Tap. Tap. Taptaptaptaptaptap—

As the summoning sound started up once more, and became so loud it was the now a pounding like heavy boots upon a wooden floor, Sahvage closed his eyes and breathed deeply of the fresh night air. He had to block out the scents that made him violent, the blood and the sex of an innocent taken by force, rendering it impossible for him to calm himself.

So he needed must put them aside.

As he focused on dematerializing, he was as the others of the household had been, compelled by a sense of survival to depart, depart, depart—

◆　　◆　　◆

Sahvage jumped back to present awareness with a full-body jerk and a suck of air. For a moment, the now-familiar details of Tallah's kitchen were utterly foreign. But then he saw the pots and pans he had washed drying in the rack, the refrigerator against the door, the duffle of guns and ammo on the table in front of him.

"Shit," he breathed.

Rubbing his head, he could still picture that trestle table in the bloodied bedchamber, and what had been with the Book made him think back to what Mae and Tallah had laid out here, the salad dressing ingredients that were not for any lettuce leaves ever—

He looked around sharply. "Mae?"

His hand shot out and grabbed his phone. As he checked his texts . . . nothing from her. No calls, either. And it was over an hour and twenty minutes since he'd left her house.

Where the fuck was she?

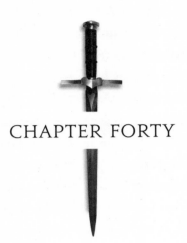

CHAPTER FORTY

Mae came back to consciousness slowly, and the markers that her brain was back online were mainly the physical information that she began processing: Her head hurt. She was lying on something that had thin ridges. One whole arm was numb.

And what was that smell?

She focused on the fragrance for no particular reason, and as a mental connection was made, the image that her memories coughed up was one that didn't make a whole lot of sense.

The Galleria Mall. Christmas time.

The perfume counter in Macy's. An aggressive saleslady double-fisting spray bottles that had had hair triggers. Mae getting hit in the face with something that had made her eyes sting and her nose tickle like she had a single strand of fine cat hair up each nostril.

Her eyes flipped open.

Right in front of her face . . . there was a pattern of wires. But that couldn't be right . . . ?

It took some deep breaths before things focused properly and she discovered that what she thought she was seeing was correct—and also wrong. The thin ridges pressing into her were a weave of black coated wires.

She was in a cage. Like a dog cage.

"You're reminding me of someone."

At the sound of the familiar voice, Mae moved her eyes, not her head. Through the pattern of crosshatches, she looked across an open space . . .

Wait . . . was this a department store? There were racks and racks of clothes . . . a display of designer purses and shoes . . . a makeup table. But there was also an exposed kitchen that ran down one wall and a bathroom without walls or a door. A king-sized bed.

"I'm over here, dummy."

Mae tracked the sound to the center of the whatever-it-was. Sitting on a white leather sofa, with her legs crossed like a lady, the brunette had changed her clothes and done her hair over. Now she was in a white skirt suit, the top formfitting to her tiny waist, the bottom with a slit that went to mid-thigh. The stilettos were black and white, and there were pearls, lots of pearls.

But that wasn't all.

She had a spectacular white hat on, a derby hat, with a brim that carouseled around her beautiful face and her graceful neck, lower in some places, higher in others.

"Do you like it?" the brunette murmured as her blood-red-tipped fingers hovered around the delicate black piping on the bill.

Mae pushed herself up and banged her head on the top of the cage.

"Oh, sorry. It's for dogs." The brunette smiled. "Big dogs are not as big as grown females, though, are they."

Shuffling her feet around, Mae sat up as much as she could, her head at an awkward angle. With a better look at the area they were in, she saw four thousand square feet with a low ceiling held up by thick, featureless supports. No windows. And a single door.

So that was where she needed to get to.

"Alexis Carrington Colby." The brunette swept a hand down her smooth legs. "This is her outfit. From the season-two first episode. And not a copy, this is the actual suit. I bought it off the wardrobe guy. Or, rather, I let him fuck me for it. He was small, by the way, and size does matter. But this suit—with the hat? So worth it. Besides, I was so much hotter than the shit he usually got that he lasted a minute and a half."

Mae blinked.

"Okay, fine. It was two minutes, tops." The brunette frowned. "Hold up, did you not watch it? How could anyone not watch *Dynasty*? Although, considering your sartorial choices . . ."

The dog cage had a latch right in front, and also one on the short side. Both were locked with a padlock. The wire was steel. Not exactly mesh, and if she had been calm, she would have been able to exit the cage safely. But she was in pain and terrified.

The brunette seemed piqued by a lack of fawning. "You know, I dressed up for you. You could show some appreciation." When Mae didn't respond, there was an elegant shrug. "Fine, you've been out for a while now. How's your head? Hm?"

The cage was made up of panels that were collapsible, the hard corners of right angles held in place by virtue of the two short sides having been pushed up to hold the top.

"You don't say much." The brunette flashed her hand. "Do you see this diamond? Twenty-five carats. Do you like it?"

Mae knew her only hope was to kick at the sides and bend the metal hooks until the structural integrity of the panels failed.

"It's glass." The brunette put her hand out to herself and moved the huge stone from side to side. "You know, some would say that pear shapes are not classic, not like rounds or emeralds are. They're supposedly like marquise cuts—or that fucking princess-cut shit. But see, this is the ring that Joan Collins wore. I got it at an auction like three years ago. I would have paid more—"

Mae shifted around and planted her boots on the cage's short side. Cramming herself against the other end, she started to put her strength into it—

"What are you doing." The brunette lifted a stenciled brow. "Honestly, you think that is going to work?"

Straining, Mae felt the wires bite into her shoulders and the back of her neck, her head. The injuries from the car accident—her bad shoulder from where the seat belt had tightened on it, her face from landing on the dirt, her temple from God only knew what—began to hum louder and throb. Especially as she started to kick.

The brunette laughed and rose to her feet. "Getting a good workout? And one, and two, and one, and two—tell me, are you feeling the burn?"

Bang, bang, bang, rattle, rattle, rattle—

Mae grunted. Sweat broke out across her face. Her eyesight swam as her body protested at the demands she was putting on it.

"After this"—the brunette smiled—"can we work the core? Core is *so* important."

Things were loosening up in the cage, the top sinking as she punched out, popping back when she retracted her knees.

"I swear . . . you remind me of someone." The brunette came over to stand by the commotion. "But that's not important—"

With one last, powerful extension, Mae busted the end out, the lattice of heavy wires bouncing on the floor. Half of the top came down on her, and she shoved it off as she shuffled out of the escape route she'd created.

The second she was free, she scrambled to stand up—

Her balance was for shit, her body totally uncoordinated, and she was aware of the brunette laughing as Mae hit the hard floor and tried to stand again. And again.

She collapsed in a sprawl, panting, her head spinning, all kinds of pain pretty much everywhere.

"And where do you think you're going now?"

The pair of black-and-white stilettos appeared right next to Mae's face—which was the only reason she figured out she had ended up on her side with her ear and cheek on some cool, cool marble.

"You know," the brunette murmured, "you ruined a perfectly good cage. I'm going to have to make you pay for it, one way or the other. And I'll be choosing something other than cash, of course—"

"You won't hurt me."

"I beg your pardon."

Mae lifted her head. Lifted her torso. Tried to lift her whole body, but settled for sitting up against the wall where the cage had been.

Even though her eyes were still focusing intermittently, she trained them in the direction of the brunette.

Taking a deep breath, she said, "You. Aren't. Going. To. Hurt. Me."

Those glossy red lips flattened and that voice got nasty. "You keep thinking that, then. We'll see how long the bullshit lasts."

With a sudden rush, an invisible force levitated Mae up off the floor and pinned her against the wall. Bone-crushing pressure covered her entire body, a blanket that weighed as much as a car, and as she struggled to draw breath, she tried to fight the squeeze, but there was nothing to fight against.

The brunette walked up and struck a pose, one hip curving out, the opposite hand poised on her waist. Yet her face was drawn in harsh, ugly lines.

"I'm going to do anything I want to you." Her eyes raked down Mae—and then surprise registered. "Well, well, well. Looks like that big male hasn't gotten into you yet. A virgin? Really? What a prize you are." Now she smiled again. "Just what every guy wants, fumbling hands and awkward winces of pain. How sexy—"

"You can't hurt me," Mae grunted, "because you need the Book."

The brunette went silent and closed her mouth. Then she turned on one stiletto and walked over to the display of boxy, two-handled purses with little locks on them. There were easily a dozen of them, in a rainbow's worth of colors and with just as many different textures.

"You know," the brunette said, "I've used a lot of male virgins over the years. And tsk, tsk, tsk, not like you're thinking. They were necessary for a private, non-sexual purpose—which sadly is no longer applicable—"

"You need me alive." Mae coughed. "Because I summoned the Book. You need me to get the Book."

The brunette looked over her shoulder, her eyes narrowing. "I wouldn't be so cocky, honey. I have other sources for that."

"Then kill me. Right here and now—"

Mae let out a scream as the pressure became unbearable, the bones in her face threatening to collapse flat, her ribs squeezing her heart and lungs, her pelvis nearly cracking. And just as she began to black out, at the moment she felt herself slipping away, she was able to drag some air down her throat.

As her eyes started to clear a little, the brunette was right in front her again. No longer angry, but pensive.

"Tell me how you did it," she said.

"Hmm?" Mae wheezed.

"Look at you. You're not bad-looking, but you're hardly worth crossing the street for. You have no style, no personality, nothing to recommend you, and no experience in bed. And yet . . . that male. He's so fucking into you. I don't get it."

As the brunette went silent, Mae put some strength in her voice. "That's what you want the Book for. Isn't it."

"No."

"You're lying."

The brunette's glare was a promise of misery. Infinite misery. "And you can kiss my fucking ass."

All at once, the pain and suffocation returned, and Mae knew she'd overplayed her hand.

It was the last conscious thought she had.

CHAPTER FORTY-ONE

Out on a rural property that had a lot of junk on its grounds, Erika ducked her head as she entered a dilapidated trailer. Inside, there was mess everywhere on everything, pizza boxes, crumpled cigarette packs, and empty booze bottles choking out the details of the galley kitchen, the floor underfoot, the ragged furniture. Unsurprisingly, there was also a collection of bongs, syringes, plastic baggies, and bricks wrapped in supermarket bags.

The body was over on a couch that was so stained it looked like it had started its life a muck brown. Victim was a male, somewhere in his twenties, and he was sprawled back against the worn cushions, his face frozen in a stare-ahead, the single execution-style bullet wound nearly dead center in his forehead.

As her eyes went down to the front of his chest, as opposed to the red wash on the wall behind his skull, she heard her sergeant from back late in the afternoon.

You need a night off, Saunders. You've been going too hard for too long—

We're short-staffed after Pam went on maternity leave and Sharanya moved. What else can we do—

—and that's how mistakes are made.

I haven't made any. And I won't—

This is not a request, Erika. I can't remember when your last break was, and neither can you.

"The father called it in," one of the uniforms—the younger of the two—reported. Because the older one was on the phone. "Poor man. Nobody wants to see their son like this."

Erika leaned down and checked out the bullet wound in the forehead. No gunpowder residue, so it hadn't been a point-blank kind of thing. The shooter had been back some distance.

"Professional shot," she murmured.

The uniform continued, "The victim's name is David Eckler and he's got a record. Mostly selling stolen property, but he has a number of drug charges, two of which were just dropped on technicalities. Detective de la Cruz took the father down to the station to talk."

Outing her penlight, she looked around at the mess on the floor. "Here's a shell."

She bent down to put a marker on it, and before she straightened back up, she found herself going eye level with an off-kilter coffee table that had had one of its legs replaced by a milk carton. In the midst of its clutter? A leather box about a foot long and five inches wide. Unlike everything else in the trailer, the thing was of fine construction and without dust or scratches.

"Surprise, surprise," she murmured as she peered through its glass top.

The lineup of watches inside were big names even someone middle class like her would know: Rolex. Piaget. Okay, fine, she'd never heard of Hublot.

"How'd you even say that," she said. "'Whoo-blot'?"

"Huh?"

And that was when she saw it. A little wink in the far corner off to the side of the couch: A lens that had caught her flashlight beam.

"We have security," she announced.

"You mean a dog chained in the yard? I didn't see one—"

"No, as in a camera."

She leaned in and carefully inspected the recording unit. Then she followed the wires around the back of the sofa—avoiding the victim—to a cupboard. Inside? A laptop that was shiny new and plugged into a surge protector. The thing was running.

"Thank you, baby Jesus," she muttered.

"Aren't you supposed to be off?"

Erika straightened and looked at the uniform properly for the first time. "Dick?"

"Rick." The fresh-faced guy pointed to his badge. "Donaldson. I'm still on the beat, but I hope to transfer to homicide soon."

"I'm Detective—"

"Oh, I know who you are. And I thought you were supposed to be off tonight—"

"How do you know my schedule?"

The guy looked around like he was hoping someone else would answer that. Unfortunately for him, the older officer was still on the phone.

"Ah . . . everyone knows your schedule, Detective."

As headlights washed the front of the trailer, slices of illumination speared into the interior.

"Well, you're in luck." Erika clicked off her flashlight. "I'll see you in the morning. I'm going home to get some sleep."

While Dick-Rick-whoever Donaldson looked relieved, like someone had spared him a trip to Target on Black Friday, Erika hit the broken door. It took every ounce of self-control to step out of the trailer, but the reality was, the crime scene folks were going to need four to six hours to clear everything, and it was now, what—? She checked her watch. Three a.m. Perfect. She could be in her bed at home in forty-five minutes, with her teeth brushed, her feet in fresh socks, and her head wrapped in a blanket to cut the noise of the early-risers who lived in the apartment above her.

Totally living the high life, she thought as she started her unmarked and waved at the crime scene investigators.

She would be back in the proverbial saddle no later than eight in the morning. And then the sergeant couldn't have a good goddamn thing to say about her shift work. Nailed it.

Besides, as long as there was a heart still in that victim's chest? She was okay turning the case over to someone else.

◆   ◆   ◆

When Syphon was finally resting quietly, and the folks in blue scrubs with the ticker-listening necklaces were satisfied he was going to be okay, Balz was the first to beat feet out of the training center. And he once again looked casual—or tried to appear that way.

Inside his skin, he was screaming.

At the far end of the underground tunnel, he stepped out from under the mansion's grand staircase and then dematerialized up to the second-floor sitting room. As he went down to his own bedroom, he moved silently, like the thief he was, and prayed he ran into no one. In his suite, it took him under a minute to change into his all-blacks, and not much longer than that to cinch a double holster around his waist.

Whispering back out into the hall, he looked left and right. Voices bubbled down from the second-story sitting room, so he went the back way, taking the servants' stairwell on a fast descent. At the bottom, he made all kinds of deflections to the *doggen* who were getting Last Meal ready in the kitchen. Then it was out through the garage and back-dooring it into the battened-down-for-winter gardens behind the mansion.

Closing his eyes, he dematerialized without a struggle, which surprised him given the scrambled eggs he had for brains, and as he traveled in a scatter away from the mountain, he headed for downtown.

Balz re-formed on the Commodore's rooftop.

No more gentlemale's rules of engagement for this infiltration. He opened the steel door by the HVAC venting systems with his mind because its dead bolt had no copper in it, and he would have ghosted down the concrete steps, but he couldn't be completely sure whether there would be debris or any fire doors in the way.

Three floors down, he made no sound as he entered the carpeted hall. Skirting past the doors of five or six condominiums, he came up to the elevators just as one set of doors was opening.

The two women inside were standing together, their chic clothes and good haircuts suggesting that they had both disposable cash and the taste to know what to do with the shit properly. Just to be safe, he froze them, scrubbed their memories . . . and sent them back down to the lobby.

Tap . . .

Balz stopped and looked over his shoulder. But he knew there was no one behind him.

No, it was where he was going that he needed to be wary of.

The entrance to the triplex gave way on his approach, and as he went inside, he disarmed the security system with a whacker programmed with the code he'd lifted from the alarm's database.

Tap. Tap . . .

A quick inhale revealed no scents. Guess the happy couple were once again not at home.

It wouldn't have mattered if they were.

Nothing mattered.

Well . . . one thing did.

Tap. Tap. Tap . . .

As his chest got tight with emotion, he proceeded through the viewing spaces, revisiting the bat skeletons, the Victorian surgical instruments—as well as one full of taxidermied animals that he'd missed during his first trip through.

Tap. Tap. Tap. Tap . . .—

All at once, the room with the shelves and the books presented itself in front of him, sure as if it had been doing the walking, not Balz.

Staring down at his shitkickers, he halted just inside of it, and for a brief moment, his heart pounded with terror that he was wrong. Then it skipped beats because it was terrified he was right.

Finally, he looked across the beautiful parquet floor.

"Shit," he whispered. Because there was no question.

This was the Book.

And it had called to him. It *was* calling to him.

Tap . . .

As the final *tap* traveled over to his ears, it was so soft, like a sigh. And even though he didn't want to, Balz went forward—not with reverence, though. Not with the thrall he'd been stuck in back at the psychic's, either. There was resignation to his stride—a sense of inevitability.

Everything had been leading up to this.

When he stopped in front of the display box, the ancient volume of God only knew what vibrated on its stand, a puppy wiggling with happiness. And then, as if its joy could not be contained, it jumped and flipped itself open. Pages flew in a rush, too fast to track—yet when they stopped, it was with a decisive halt, as if the particular passages exposed had barged through the movement and taken over.

Balz leaned down.

At first, he couldn't decipher the lines of writing. But then he rubbed his eyes, and as he dropped his hands, everything was in English. Plain, casual English, the kind you'd find on a flyer for a garage sale. With modern slang.

Given the age of the parchment and the wear-and-tear on the cover, he couldn't reconcile how "NSFW" would appear at the top of any page in the binding. But he was not going to argue with all the whatever. He wasn't arguing with anything.

Reaching out, he lifted the Lucite cover off the display case, and though he anticipated resistance, there was none. The protective cube came up like the thing was levitating, and as he went to set the thing aside, it felt light as a feather—

"*Fuck*," he muttered on a recoil.

The smell was god-awful. Like a *lesser*, but without the sweet overtones.

And then he didn't worry about his nose's problems.

"No," he said as he started to read the words. "That's not what I want. I need something else."

The Book fluttered, like it was disagreeing with him.

"I'm not looking for . . ." He shook his head. "I'm not looking for love. You're nuts. I'm actually looking to get rid of a . . . woman."

He couldn't say the d-word—

"Don't move! I have a gun!"

At the sound of the booming male voice, Balz rolled his eyes and turned around, putting his body between his Book and the triplex's Mr.—who was standing in the archway of the room of shelves, a shiny little poodle-shooter in his doubled-up palms.

Like he'd seen a lot of Roger Moore-era 007 films.

Goddamn it, Balz was so fucking distracted, he'd missed the scent—

"I'm calling the police!"

The Mr. had had a lot of Botox, so his eyebrows were locked in the down position, even though he was panting from shock and super flushed. Guess only the bottom half of his puss was capable of exhibiting surprise. Oh, and those plaid pajamas? Not exactly a vibe if you were trying to be taken seriously as a protector of your happy home.

Rolling his eyes, Balz froze the human where he stood—and then had to wonder if the Mrs. was in res as well. Not that it really mattered.

"Put that thing away, for fuck's sake," Balz muttered.

On command, the Mr. lowered the gun and then blinked like he was waiting for further suggestions as to what he needed to be doing.

Glancing back at the Book, Balz frowned. "Lemme ask you something. Where'd you find this thing?"

"It's a new acquisition." The Mr. looked around Balz's body, and the instant his eyes rested on the Book, love poured out of his stare. "I just knew I had to have it. It was like . . . it was destined to be mine."

As Balz's dagger hand snuck to his own gun, he told himself to fucking relax. Was he really prepared to shoot this motherfucker over a book—

The Book, he amended.

The Mr. continued: "There's a rare book dealer here in town. He knows that I buy the unusual, particularly if it has—shall we say, an edge?" The man smiled in an I'm-a-naughty-boy kind of way, those brows moving not in the slightest. Then he dropped his voice and tilted forward. "My seller told me it's bound in human flesh."

So much about this sonofabitch made Balz want to kick him in the nuts. On principle.

"So where the hell did it come from?" he demanded of the guy.

"It's very old."

"No shit."

"And it's written in Hungarian."

Balz glanced behind himself at the "NSFW." And all the English words underneath that heading. "No, it's not."

The Mr. puffed up his chest. "Are you saying I do not know the first language I learned."

Pointing at the Book, Balz said, "No, I'm saying that's English."

"You, sir, are wrong." If not for the Botox, there clearly would have been a serious arch over one of those eyeballs. "But as it is my book, I'm not going to argue about it with a stranger."

"What do you use it for?"

"Use it . . . ?" That stare went hard upper right. Which was what liars did when you got inside their little games. "You don't use a book like this. It's for display only."

"You're full of shit, but I don't care about your answer." At least not to that. "I need to know when you bought it?"

"About two weeks ago. It's my newest acquisition."

"Yeah, you already said that. Did the dealer tell you where he or she got it from?"

The Mr. smiled and nodded. "Such a crazy story. Some lowlife brought it into the bookshop and dropped it off. Said he found it in some back alley downtown. He refused to take any money for it—he said, and I'm not sure whether this is true, but he said it told him to bring it to the shop. Can you imagine?"

"How much did you pay for it?"

The Mr. inflated his chest again, like he was used to telling people how much he paid for his shit. 'Cuz he liked making those kinds of reports. "It was in the six figures."

"Well, you better get ready to put a claim in on your insurance."

"Why?"

Balz reached out for the Book. "Because it's coming with me—"

Just before his hands made contact with the ancient tome, the lights flickered—

And then everything went black.

CHAPTER FORTY-TWO

Mae came back to consciousness because she dropped to the floor—and the sudden impact hurt. But it was also a case of her being able to breathe again.

Gone. The crushing, invisible pressure was gone.

As she started to cough and gag, she rolled onto her back and shoved her hair out of her face with a loose, flappy hand. Staring up at a bald white ceiling, she was confused about where she was, but then her brain began tossing context into the boat of her consciousness, the images and sounds and smells of her short-term memories like dry-dock fish flipping around, spastic and overlapping.

The brunette—

With a shot of adrenaline, Mae shoved herself into a sit-up and put her hand to her head. Even though everything went around in a circle, she managed to track enough so that the racks of clothes registered and so did the purses and the shoes . . . the kitchen area. The bed.

She was alone.

The brunette woman—or whatever she was—was nowhere to be seen.

Mae's legs were loose as she stood up, and she needed to brace a hand on the wall to keep vertical. Looking around, she expected the evil woman to jump out from behind the partition over by the bathroom area . . . or re-form right in front of her.

When neither of those happened, Mae stopped thinking about immediate self-defense and possible weapons—and started worrying about survival and getting the hell out of wherever she was.

With a lurch, she headed off to the door on the other side of the— what was this, anyway? An apartment in a converted warehouse? It had to be underground given the no-windows, and she tried to scent things to get some clues, but whether it was all the perfume or that her nose was broken, she couldn't smell anything except that Macy's-counter stuff.

The only exit she could see was solid steel. With reinforced bars riveted in place.

It didn't budge as she pushed at the handle, but like that was a surprise? And there was going to be no dematerializing for her. She had no clue where she was or what was on the other side of any of these walls or that door. Plus, with how much pain she was in? No way she could calm herself—

Phone!

Mae shoved her hand into her pocket—her phone. She still had her phone! Yanking the thing out, her hands trembled.

No service.

"Shit."

But at least it was three in the morning. She had been gone for hours. Surely Sahvage had noticed her absence? Surely he was looking for her? And even though she had been unconscious for a while, there was still enough time before sunrise to get home.

Holding the cell phone out straight, she walked around and hoped to pick up a bar. When that didn't happen, she circled the perimeter of the space, looking for any viable option to get out.

There was nothing. No other feasible way to leave except for that one bank-vault-worthy door. Yes, there were a couple of vents over the stove, and in the bathroom area, and two heat exchangers in the corners that pumped in warm, dry air. But that was too suicidal. You dematerialized and tried to travel through a venting system you weren't familiar with?

All it took was one steel-based air filter and you were Swiss cheese.

For a split second, her brain fritzed out with panic, and the go-nowhere buzz got worse as she glanced at the dog cage she'd broken free of.

But losing focus was not going to help.

She reminded herself that Sahvage would know she should have been long home by now. He would look for her. He might even find her car at the side of the road—

Oh, God, that poor human man who had rear-ended her. He was dead because he had tried to help her.

She had to get out of here—

A low rumble emanated from somewhere above—no, not above. All around. Terrified, Mae covered her head and ducked down, her injuries screaming at the awkward position as whatever it was came to a culmination of volume, with a vibration that emanated up through her legs.

And then . . . it faded.

As Mae straightened and dropped her arms, she looked around.

The subway, she thought.

She was definitely somewhere underground.

◆   ◆   ◆

"No, no, I'm happy to . . ." Nate glanced at Elyn and decided not to finish that thought out loud.

I'm happy to go anywhere with you seemed a little intense.

"It's a nice idea to walk outside," he concluded as he made a point to look up at the starry sky. "And get some air."

The two of them had spent most of the night setting up all the furniture in her bedroom. They'd been a good team, following the directions, using tools, figuring out where everything needed to be arranged for best effect. The fact that Elyn had nothing to put in the drawers of the bureau or hang in the closet hadn't been lost on him.

"You know what we could do sometime?" he said as they ducked under the top rail of the fence in the side yard. "There's a place to go shopping. A mall? It's like a bunch of shops that are under the same roof. People say they're dying out, but the Caldwell one is still going strong."

One thing he'd learned about Elyn was that she wasn't familiar with so many things he took for granted. Apparently, she hadn't called him because she wasn't sure how to work a phone. He'd thought it was a joking excuse, but as she'd stared into his eyes, he realized she was dead serious. And then, when they'd taken a break at midnight for a snack, she'd had no idea how to use a microwave and the juicer had scared her as it buzzed. Oh, and the TV had captivated her.

To the point where she'd gone around and looked behind the flat screen, as if she couldn't figure out where the images were coming from.

When she'd asked him to take a breather from the house just now, he'd totally gotten it—

Abruptly, Elyn stopped and looked up. The moon was bright overhead, stripes of clouds drifting over its face.

"When I got out of the lab," he heard himself say, "everything was too much. Too loud. Too many. My adoptive parents helped a lot and I did get used to it. But for a good month or two, I had to decompress every once in a while. I'd go lie down in my bedroom with the lights down low and some classical music playing. It helped."

As she focused on the night sky, he studied her profile, and the sadness on her face was something he knew all about. Mourning looked the same on everyone's features, no matter whether they were old or young, male or female.

"Who did you lose," he said in a low voice.

"I cannot . . ."

Her words drifted, and he was not surprised that she didn't finish the thought. Or, more likely, couldn't.

"I won't say anything to anyone," he vowed. "I promise."

The assurance seemed like the only thing he could do to help her with wherever her mind was at.

With a shake of the head, she started walking again, her eyes down, her hands tucked into the pale gray parka she'd been given at Safe Place. She'd been provided with the whole outfit she had on, too, the jeans, turtleneck, and cozy sweater fitting for the weather. And out of that draping black robe thingy she'd been wearing, she was a lot smaller than she'd seemed—and that just made him feel worse about whatever had been done to her.

She needed protection.

As she lead the way across the meadow, he wasn't surprised that she took them into the forest, back to the meteor impact. And when they emerged from the trees into the clearing, she didn't stop until she was right at the edge of the pit—and she was quiet and still for so long, he had to walk around because one of his legs started cramping.

"I had to leave him," she said abruptly. "I had no choice."

Nate's gut clenched . . . and yet he wasn't surprised. Abusive males were the reason Safe Place and Luchas House existed. And thank God she'd gotten out alive.

"You have to save yourself." With his eyes, he traced her beautiful features and the way the moonlight turned her white hair into spun silver. "Thank God you're safe."

As she fell silent once again, he knew she was reliving her nightmare and he wanted to hug her.

"I had to save both of us." She brushed a hand over her face. "He was not going to leave me, and it was too dangerous for him to be around me. I am dangerous."

Nate recoiled. "What?" He reached out and took her arm. "You are not. Don't let anyone make you think that."

After a moment, she lifted her eyes to his. "You do not know me, Nate."

The grave expression on her face gave him a moment of pause. But then he shook that off.

"I absolutely know you. And whatever your abuser told you is a lie. You need to never see him again—"

"Abuser?" Elyn frowned and then shook her head. "Oh, no. He was good to me. He was too good to me. He was going to lose his life for me, his calling for me. I had to separate us. He deserved so much better than the vow he undertook as my father died, and he was such a male of worth, that regardless of circumstance, he was never going to diverge our fates."

She refocused on the pit. "He was one of the best males e'er I have met. Honor and strength were but the start of his many virtues."

"Oh." Nate dropped his hold. Took a step back. "I thought . . . well. Maybe you should have stayed with him, then."

"I was his responsibility, and he protected me better than anyone could have. It made a target out of him and my enemies resolved to kill him. They wanted me, but they knew they had to take him first, as he would have died before he let anything happen unto me." She closed her eyes and moaned. "And in the end, I was taken just the same . . ."

Something about the way she said it made Nate's mind go into very bad places.

"Do you know if the male you lost lived?" he asked hoarsely.

Elyn was quiet for a time. "There has been . . . a vast distance between us. So vast."

"When was the last time you saw him?"

"Centuries ago."

Nate blinked, dumbfounded. "Um . . . do you want to try to find him?"

Elyn took a deep breath. "I believe I do. But I do not want him e'er to be hurt again on my account. I barely survived the burden of that

once, verily I could not live through it again. And yet . . . well, he is all
that I have."

Nate rubbed his hair to make sure none of the profound heartbreak
showed on his face. "How can I help? Do you know if he's here in Caldwell?"

"He is here. That is why I arrived thus."

"Okay, so we've got a variety of ways to find people." He thought of
all the things she was confounded by. "There are databases to search.
Places we can go to—or, like, you can go. I mean, I don't want to get in
the way—"

"You cannot help me, Nate."

Oh, you're wrong about that, he thought. *I'm totally pumped to help
you reunite with the male you love. Sign me up.*

"Of course I can."

"It shall be . . . dangerous."

Nate frowned. "Who is after you?"

"He is dead, the now."

"So you're worried about his kin?" When she didn't answer, Nate
felt a warning ripple down his spine. "So his kin lives?"

"He was of fine bloodline."

"*Glymera?*" As she nodded, Nate exhaled in relief, even though there
was no verified reason to. Yet. "You may not know this, but many of
them are dead now."

"In truth?"

"From the raids a couple of years ago." He was not surprised when
she stared at him blankly. "The *lessers* infiltrated their homes here in
Caldwell. So many were killed. Can you tell me your enemy's name?
We can check and see if his bloodline was affected? We can ask Mrs.
Mary's *hellren* and he will know—or know how to find that out . . ."

When she once again stared into the impact pit and didn't answer
him, Nate tapped her on the shoulder—and waited until her silver eyes
rose to his own.

"I'm not afraid," he said.

Her response was grim: "You should be."

Instead of waffling at the warning, Nate felt a certainty in his chest that he had never known before, a surety that was so rock-solid, it was as if the end point of wherever they were going to go had already occurred.

"I am not and I won't be," he said in a low voice. "No matter what happens."

"Nate—"

"You think I haven't lived through pain? I've had surgeries with no anesthesia. Viruses and bacteria forced into my veins. I've been examined for the sole purpose of degrading me—and I was a young when all this happened. There are no miseries I haven't endured, and if I lived through it once, I can do it again."

Especially for her, and even though there was clearly no future for them. She was in love with her male, and given the hero-material the guy obviously was? Who could compete with that.

After a long moment, Elyn reached up and put her hand on the side of Nate's face. "You are so brave."

As the contact of her flesh on his own registered, he froze where he stood . . . and realized, as he stared down into her silver eyes, that he was as the male she loved had been.

Willing to lay his life down for her.

"Your *hellren* is a very, very lucky male," Nate said roughly.

Elyn frowned and tilted her head to one side. "*Hellren?* I am not mated."

"The male you love, then."

"No, 'tis not as that. I do love him, but he is my first cousin. He is my family, not my mate."

As her words sank in, Nate's soul smiled. He couldn't describe the feeling in any other way. But he pulled his shit together quick, as Elyn was still looking very serious.

"Then let's find him," he said. "Together."

As she looked into his eyes, he wanted to be even taller than he was.

Bigger. Stronger. He was through his transition, sure, but compared to his dad, Murhder? He was a pip-squeak.

"You have been so good to me," she murmured. "You have been a friend when I need one, a shelter when I had none, a well of compassion in this darkness in which I am trapped. Thus I cannot, and will not, do anything to endanger you. This has always been my quest, and it must needs remain thus."

They stared at each other for the longest time.

Kiss her, Nate thought. *Now is the moment—*

Off over Elyn's shoulder, a tiny flare of light appeared and began to move. And another. And a third.

She turned and glanced at the little galaxy that had inexplicably formed behind her. "Oh, they are back."

Elyn extended her palm, and the flickers came to her, coalescing above her outstretched hand.

"Fireflies," Nate murmured. "Wow."

The glow was such that it illuminated her face, making her positively resplendent—no, it was more than that. Her silver hair and her silver eyes seemed to pull the golden illumination in and reflect it back out, so that a halo formed all around her.

Without warning, she pegged him with a hard stare. "I shall not allow anything or anybody to hurt you, Nate."

Touched as he was by the sentiment, he didn't have the heart to state the realness. Out of the two of them? She was hardly in a position to do any protecting.

That was his job.

CHAPTER FORTY-THREE

B alz smelled the brunette first.

In the midst of the dense darkness inside the triplex's book collection room, that perfume, that grape-undertoned, darkly sensual Dior scent, pervaded the still air.

"Devina?" the Mr. said through the void. "What are you doing here?"

The lights came back on, and as Balz blinked the retina sting away, he didn't shift from the position he was in, his arms and hands still outstretched toward the Book. But he did turn his head. Between him and the Mr., the brunette—Devina, evidently—was posed like a cover girl, wearing a formal white skirt and jacket and a hat that looked like something you'd wear to a royal wedding.

"You're supposed to stay at corporate headquarters," the Mr. said. Then he glanced behind himself and lowered his voice. "I thought we agreed you'd never show up here unannounced. Idaho is where you have to—"

"Oh, shut up, Herb," the brunette snapped. "And I've never even been to Idaho, you fucking idiot."

"B-b-but . . ."

Devina focused on Balz and rolled her eyes. "Humans. Really. They're all in remote control cars they think they're driving. So fucking ridiculous—"

"Herb" marched over and took the brunette's arm. "This is not a game you're going to win. I want you out of here, and if you're going to keep seeing me, you're never doing this again. Do we understand each other. My wife lives here."

The brunette looked down at where Herb's hand was. And in the beat or two of silence that followed, Balz was tempted to tell the guy to let the fuck go of her—but there was no saving stupid.

"Are you touching me right now," the brunette said in a soft voice.

Herb rose up on his tiptoes a little so he could glare down at her given her heels. "I will touch you anywhere the hell I want, and you're leaving *now*."

As Balz straightened from the Book, he had a thought that Herbie-boy was going to choke on those words.

"This behavior is really not becoming on you," Herb felt the need to tack on.

Devina's perfectly arched brow lifted over her perfectly made-up right eye. "You don't say. Well, wait'll you get a load of this."

Herb's body flew back against a set of the display shelves, sure as if invisible hands had picked him up and thrown him across the room. And as books were dislodged from their props, and all kinds of things landed on the floor, Balz frowned. There was no noise. Nothing made a goddamn sound, not the flopping of the first editions as they hit the parquet wood, not the clattering of the Lucite stands as they fell, not the banging of the varnished planks.

Likewise, as Herb was pinned against the wall, and his mouth cranked wide to start screaming, there was no sting in the ears from the high-pitched agony, no banging as those heels kicked at the Sheetrock, no tearing as his clothes—

Oh, shit. The loose PJs poor Herb was wearing were ripping at the crotch.

But that was hardly the worst of it.

Like someone had spread-eagle'd him and was dragging his legs apart like the wishbone of a turkey, the Mr. started to rip at the center-piece, a fault line initiating at his hey-nannies and proceeding up his pelvis, his abdomen—

All kinds of internal organ-ish stuff fell out and landed like over-boiled lasagna noodles, glossy, mushy, and disturbingly pink and brown.

"Oh, man," Balz muttered, "that's gonna get whiffy."

The tearing-apart along with the pulling-asunder kept up, cracking Herb's sternum, halving his set of lungs, stopping at the base of his throat. And then all his nearly-there was dropped to the floor.

Herb, the former hedge fund manager, now hedge mound fertilizer, twitched a couple of times . . . and then didn't move at all.

Well, that wasn't exactly true.

His blood was still leaking out of his major veins and arteries.

"You know," Balz commented dryly, "I bet you don't worry about get-ting mugged much, do you."

Devina wiped her hands off on her hip even though she hadn't di-rectly touched the guy. "No, I'm good out on the streets alone. And speaking of mugging, it's time that you and I stop fucking around. Give me my Book."

Balz, who'd straightened from his stretch-forward during the laughy-taffy interlude, glanced back at the ancient volume. It had closed itself up, and the spotlight that was mounted on the ceiling hadn't come back on. Or maybe it hadn't been on in the first place, and the halo around the Book was just dimmed.

"Give me what's mine," Devina demanded as she put her hand out.

Like maybe Balz owed her a fiver and was just going to slap a bill right on there.

"If you don't give it to me," she said as she sex-walked her way over, "then *that* is going to happen to you."

Ridiculously, she pointed to the mess on the floor—like anyone might have missed the example of all her Ginsu knife skills.

Balz narrowed his eyes. Then he took a pointed step to the side. "You want it, you take it. Just pick the thing up and leave. There's nothing stopping you."

Or is there, he wondered.

The pout on her face was poetic. "After everything we've meant to each other . . . surely you can help a lady out."

"No offense, but can you really call yourself a lady when you just field-dressed that motherfucker?"

"Now he's part of the exhibit."

"As a human anatomy illustration?"

"Exactly."

They both laughed a little. Then it was enough of the jokey-jokey on both sides.

"So Balthazar, here's how this is going to happen." The brunette smiled again, but her eyes were chips of obsidian, cold, bright, and hard. "You're going to pick that up and give it to me. And then I'll decide whether or not—"

"'To blow your ship from the water.'" As she blinked in confusion, he shook his head. "Come on, *Raiders of the Lost Ark*. Dietrich to Katanga. You remember, they were on the deck of the ship and—"

"Shut up!" She jabbed her red-tipped forefinger at the Book. "Give it to me."

"No." He put his hands up. "I'm not going to. Now what?"

"Give it to me!"

There was a pause, and he waited for her to throw him back against the wall. Or maybe castrate him with thin air and make him eat his own nutsack. When nothing like that happened, he was interested in just how far he could push her.

"You know, if you stamp one foot, it's going to really persuade me. Even better, tap-dance. I'll whistle a tune—"

The roar that hit him in the face was like getting sandblasted with a hurricane, his hair streaking back, his skin flapping like he was in a wind tunnel, his chest getting compressed—and yet the sound seemed to be only between his ears, the effect only on his body.

"I own you," Devina snarled over the din, "and you're going to give me what I want."

◆   ◆   ◆

Sahvage found Mae's car after four hours of searching for her. There had been nothing back at Tallah's cottage. Nothing at her own home. Nothing that he could sense anywhere.

It was as if she had disappeared off the face of the planet.

Or, even more untenable, was no longer on it . . . because she had gone unto the Fade even though she did not believe in it.

Just as he'd been about to lose his ever-fucking mind, as he was making yet another circuit back from the suburbs and out to the cottage, with no Mae at her house and no Mae on his phone and no Mae—

Blue lights. Flashing blue lights.

He'd first seen them on the previous trip into town from the rural farmlands, but because he hadn't sensed her anywhere near the scene, he'd ignored them. Besides, the truth was, about two hours into looking for Mae, he'd stopped expecting to find her—and started bracing himself to be found.

By a brunette with demands.

Or, Scribe Virgin forfend, body parts.

Except with nothing else to go on, he decided to check out the accident scene. Materializing in the darkness thrown by a stone wall, he surveyed the front-end car accident—

"Mae!"

Sahvage shouted her name as he recognized her Civic—and as the cops looked up from what turned out to be a body on the ground, his blood ran cold. He knew it wasn't Mae, but as he was downwind from the scent, he prayed it wasn't Tallah.

"Sir, unless you're a witness or can identify—"

As a female officer came over to him, he didn't give her the chance to get any further with the bug-offs. He busted into her mind and got the details he needed: Male victim on that grass had been stabbed and was dead. Car that was off the road was registered to a Christopher Wooden who had died in 1982 and lived ten miles away. Passerby who had a house in the neighborhood had called the scene in.

No other material anything—at least not that mattered to Sahvage. But that was definitely Mae's car, the name on the registration an identity shield to keep things legal on the human roadways.

So where the hell was she?

And yet even as he asked the question, he knew. He was willing to bet that somehow, the brunette had come here and abducted Mae—

As his phone went off, he fumbled the thing out of his jacket to check the screen. When he saw who it was, for, like, the hundredth time, he flat out lost it.

"Oh, for fuck's sake—*what*," he snapped as he answered the call. "Can you *fucking* leave me alone—"

"You're the one who called me, asshole," the Reverend shot back over the connection. "And given what you're looking for, I'd have assumed you'd have picked up your *fucking* phone one of the last four goddamn *fucking* times I called. Now do you want to find the Book or not."

Sahvage looked at the dead guy and dragged a hand over the top of his head. "Unless you've got it in your lap, I have other priorities right now—"

"Meet me out at the city park where we were before. Fifteen minutes. If you want the Book, you'll be there. This is your one and only chance. After this, you'll never hear from me again and you'll never find me."

As the line went dead, Sahvage nearly threw his fucking phone at Mae's totaled Honda. But he held on to the thing because he was still hoping, by some completely impossible miracle, that she would call him.

He was cursing as he glanced around—

And realized all of the cops on the scene were frozen and staring at him like they were ready to get a list of jobs. Or maybe a clue as to what their first names were.

He went over to Mae's car. The driver's-side door was open and he leaned in. Both airbags had blown, but the keys were still in the ignition. Snatching them out of their slot, he didn't see where her phone or purse were. They might well be in the hands of the cops already, but he wasn't worried about the CPD showing up at her house—and God forbid, finding her brother in that tub. Like the registration, all her IDs would be in the name of someone else with an address other than where she actually stayed. It was standard procedure for vampires living in heavily populated human areas.

"Shit," he muttered. "Shit, shit—"

"Can I help you?" the female cop said. "Anything you need?"

"What I need is . . ."

As he let his thought trail off, a word came to him from out nowhere, like it had been implanted in his head: *Leverage.*

That's right, he thought. He needed some motherfucking leverage.

The kind of thing that when that brunette showed up again—and she was going to—he would have something she wanted. Something she needed. So he could get what he had to have in return.

Which was Mae. Safe.

"Leverage," he said out loud as he looked at his phone.

As he dematerialized, he freed the cops out of their neutral, but only after he wiped any memory of his presence from their minds. For all they'd remember, he'd be nothing but ether.

Him as a ghost made so much sense.

But he was a ghost with a fucking mission. Having already let one female down in the course of his life, he was *not* doing that shit again. Even if it killed him.

And he was hoping it would.

CHAPTER FORTY-FOUR

ere's the thing," Balz said to Devina. "I'm not a gentlemale, not by a long shot. And sorry to break it to you, but you're no lady. So I'm just going to leave you to do what you will with this Book you seem to want so badly."

As fury turned that beautiful face into something that was rank ugly, he knew she wasn't walking away with shit tonight. He wasn't exactly sure what the rules were, except she wasn't going to be able to touch that fucking thing.

He had no idea why, but that did not matter at the moment.

"Take care of yourself," he said.

"I'm going to kill you."

"Not tonight and not here. Your bluff's been called."

With a little wave, he closed his eyes and dematerialized the fuck out of there—and he wasted absolutely no fucking time getting back to the mountain and the Brotherhood mansion. He was willing to bet that the brunette was going to have a second or two of dumb shock—because really, when was the last time a man didn't do what she told him to? And then she was going to try to negotiate with the Book itself.

She was going to lose at that bargaining table.

But she would give it a try.

And that personality defect of arrogant narcissism was going to be the only reason he was able to get inside the *mhis* alive. What happened after that? Who the hell knew, but he had a feeling she could only work through him if he was asleep.

Otherwise, she would have appeared to him in person when he was awake.

As Balz re-formed on the front steps of the mansion, he went to run up to the enormous door—but then he thought about the scratches that had been on his back and stopped.

"Fuck," he muttered as he looked down at himself.

And wondered just exactly what was inside of his skin.

Taking one step back . . . and another . . . and another . . . he kept going until the courtyard's fountain bumped into his shoulder blades.

Staring up at the mansion's great gray stone walls, and the gargoyles at the corners up high, and the slants of the slate roof, he thought about who was behind all those glowing leaded glass windows—but he kept the images in his mind vague. He had the sense that he needed to make sure his thoughts were as indistinct as possible.

With a feeling of dread, he took his phone out. The first number he called didn't pick up. The second? No answer. The third? Voice mail.

As his heart started to pound, he had a sick fear that things had taken a very bad turn.

The fourth number was answered before the initial ring had even started to fade. "Sire! How fare thee? May I please be of your service—"

"Fritz," he said grimly. "Drop the shutters. All around the house. Drop them right now—I don't have time to explain."

Any other butler, in any other royal household, might have taken a breath to ask why. Maybe gotten a little flustered or thought that he needed to talk to one of his true masters.

Not Fritz Perlmutter.

"Right away, Sire."

And by "right away," the *doggen* meant exactly this second: All over the mansion, on every floor, on each side, the shutters began to lower.

"What else, Sire."

"Where is everyone," Balz asked. "No one's answering their phone."

✦   ✦   ✦

As Sahvage re-formed at the park, he was partially obscured by a mist that had started to come off the river, the result of a strange imbalance in the weather that had most certainly not been going on when he'd been down here earlier. In between the spooky banks of fog, the ring of trees at the edge of the clearing appeared and disappeared, and overhead, the moon and the stars were likewise masked and revealed by turns as clouds drifted by.

With no streetlights or lanterns around, it was very dark, the sky-scrapers off in the distance offering only glowing spears rather than anything that could help you see.

"You are not afraid."

At the sound of the Reverend's voice, Sahvage turned around. "Where's your guy."

The other male stared at him silently, as if he were making some kind of assessment. "And still you're not arming up."

"If it'll light a fire under your ass, I'm more than happy to point a gun at your head. Now show me your guy or I'm fucking leaving."

The Reverend nodded with a little bow. "As you wish."

And then the male disappeared.

"Fuck this," Sahvage muttered as he looked around.

Nothing but that fog. With a curse, he took out his phone. You know, just in case he'd missed the call he'd been waiting for from Mae. In the 3.2 nanoseconds he'd been out of commission as he'd come over here—

Sahvage lowered his phone. Put it away. Palmed up a gun.

There was nothing coming to his nose, but his instincts told him he was no longer alone. In a major way.

"Well, get on with it," he called out to the tree line. "I'm not going to wait all fucking night."

With the next ebbing of the fog, a figure emerged from all the trunks and bare branches. And when he recognized the male, his heart skipped a beat.

You lost your people, your family.

Tohrment, son of Hharm, was as he had been centuries before, a tall, broad, uncompromising soldier with a level stare and calm presence. There was a white patch at the front of his dark hair now, and his leathers were modern. But the black daggers that were crossed, handles down, on his chest, were just as they had always been.

"How many are with you," Sahvage said roughly as the Brother came forward.

"All of them."

At that, more figures stepped forward . . . Vishous, who now had a goatee. Murhder, who was still red-and-black-haired. And then there were others whose faces he didn't recognize.

And there were others who he expected to see and did not.

But it had been a very, very long time.

Things changed.

On that note, the wind shifted directions and carried their scents to him—and as he breathed in, his eyes watered. He told himself that it was because of the cold breeze in his face. Yup. That was it.

And motherfucker, he should have known this was going to be a setup. More than that, he should have known not to swing through Caldwell after hearing the King was based here and had finally decided to rule. Too close, given that where Wrath was, the Brotherhood would never be far behind.

He never should have fucking set foot in the zip code.

Sahvage cleared his throat. "So is this where you try to kill me for bringing disgrace on the Brotherhood?"

"What happened to you?" Tohr asked without rancor. Which was, after all, his way—and no doubt the reason that he had stepped forward first. Still the levelheaded one. "We thought you were dead."

"So you found my coffin, huh?" Sahvage checked his phone even though it hadn't rung. "Look, I don't have time for a reunion and I'm not interested in catching up. We've been our separate ways"—What the fuck was he saying?—"for all this time, and we're going to keep it that way—unless you want to fight it out. In which case, let's get down to it. I've got somewhere I need to be."

Where exactly that was, he didn't know.

"What happened to you?" Tohr asked again.

"I got some tattoos. That's pretty much it."

For a split second, he went back to how it had been with the males: His training with them in the Bloodletter's War Camp. The fighting. His induction. He had been a part of the Brotherhood for a little while, but then his uncle had been killed by *lessers* . . . and Rahvyn had been left with no one.

After which . . . came meadows and fireflies and arrows. Headless guards. And an aristocrat on a flagpole.

As all kinds of images played through his mind, he was aware of holding back his emotions inside his chest. Then again, mourning had never been his thing, had it.

He thought of Mae and her brother.

Then just thought of Mae.

"I was a bad pick from the jump," he said roughly. "And I'm sorry I snowed you with my coffin shit. But that's the only apology you're going to get—"

"We're not here to catch up, either." Tohr's eyes did an up-and-down. "And we don't need an apology or an explanation. We need your help."

Sahvage laughed in a short burst and stamped a boot. "You're in a sorry fucking state if you're looking for help from me."

"Exactly," Tohr said in a grim voice.

CHAPTER FORTY-FIVE

S till stuck in the brunette's . . . lair, or whatever the hell it was . . .
Mae walked another circle around the wardrobe area again—even
though it wasn't going to make any goddamn difference. And as
she went past what she had come to think of as sparkle alley, she heard
the rumble of the subway again.

"Think, think, thinkthinkthink . . ."

She'd already done as much as she could with the door—which was
absolutely fucking nothing. That thing was solid like it had been soldered
in place. And still no windows or viable vents. And time was passing.

Which increased the likelihood of the brunette returning.

In frustration, Mae closed her eyes and let her head fall back. If she
didn't figure this out, she wasn't going to be able to help Rhoger. Tallah
would be alone and scared. And Sahvage—

As her eyes opened, she almost kept walking . . . but just as she went
to take a step forward, the fixture on the ceiling, which she had just happened to stop under, registered.

A sprinkler head.

Suddenly alert, she looked for others. There were six in total, mounted at equidistant intervals around the space. And not only were they bright and shiny, they had blinking red lights—so they were part of a working system.

Mae turned to the kitchen area. The Viking stove was an eight-burner, and sparkling clean as well. With her heart pounding, she went over and cranked one of the knobs. There was a clicking sound . . .

Poomph!

A blue flame popped up, all accommodating. All hot. All . . . ready to get busy with anything that came into its vicinity.

Blindly stumbling back to the clothes, she considered her options—and decided to go for the purses. For one, they could carry a flame and not just burn quickly like kindling. And two, she could use the handles to hold the heat close to the sprinkler head. But which one?

"You're not pulling together a frickin' outfit," she muttered.

In the center of the display, there was a boxy bag of some kind of exotic leather, the pattern of scales shades of gray on the edges that faded to a creamy white center. As she grabbed it because it was the closest, the little lock in front sparkled with diamonds.

Over at the stove, she held one of the corners to the open flame. The smell was like BBQ—but the insta-burn she had imagined did not happen.

As seconds turned into a minute or more, she glanced back at the main door. Just as she was getting desperate, a burst of yellow and orange caught purchase on the leather. Mae waited until she was certain the transfer was complete . . . and then she started walking. Fortunately, the nearest sprinkler was not far.

"Come on . . ." she groaned as she stretched up onto her tiptoes and lifted the purse as high as she could.

No alarm went off. No water rained down. No anything.

The ceiling was nine or ten feet tall. Maybe she wasn't close enough? But crap, her arms were getting tired because the purse was so heavy.

With a curse, she lowered them . . . and then went over and pulled a chair away from the table. Under the sprinkler again, she stepped up and put the flames right on the steel fixture.

The smell of burning leather got stronger. Smoke began to waft in her face. She coughed and had to turn her head away.

Still nothing happened.

Glancing over her shoulder, she checked out the other sprinklers. "Damn it . . ."

She didn't need to see a clock to know that she was seriously out of time. And had no other options.

◆   ◆   ◆

In spite of Sahvage's minor surge of emotion, he didn't let Tohrment, son of Hharm, go any further with whatever problems the Brotherhood had.

"You guys need to deal with your own shit." He waved a hand toward all the strong male bodies standing in the mist and then refocused on his phone. Which—goddamn it—had not rung. "You've got resources, and you've been dealing with the Omega and the Lessening Society for centuries. You don't need me—"

"The Omega is gone."

Sahvage looked up from his cell. Surely he'd heard that wrong. "What."

"The Omega no longer exists. The Lessening Society is no more."

As he properly focused on the Brother, he had a thought that those two statements were pretty much the only thing that could have diverted him, even for a split second, from worrying about Mae. Even though it had been so long since he had reflected on the war, to hear that it was over and the species was safe was a shock—and he found himself searching out the faces that he recognized in the Brotherhood.

There was no running to greet them, however. And none of them were making any moves to embrace him, either. But it had been a long, long time.

"We won?" he said because he still couldn't believe it. Then he shook his head. "I mean, you won? You did it?"

"We did. But there's a new evil."

Sahvage glanced down at his phone. Looked back up at the Brotherhood. "Like I said, you need to deal with—"

"We need you—"

"I'm no different than—"

"It's a demon."

Sahvage's body stilled of its own volition. "A demon? What kind of . . . demon."

"We're trying to figure that out. And we know you have special skills—"

Putting his hand into the Brother's face, he stopped the talk. "It's a female, right? A brunette. And she comes with shadows—"

One of the Brothers he didn't recognize, who had dark hair and was shorter and wider than the others, stepped forward. "That's right. She can be a brunette. But she can also be a lot of other things."

The accent was strong, but not in an Old Country kind of way—in an American one, though Sahvage didn't have enough knowledge about New World dialectics to pinpoint any orgin in particular.

"You've seen her?" Sahvage asked the male.

"Yes."

"Where. Do you know where to find her?"

Tohrment leaned in and put his face in the way. "You know her?"

As Sahvage contemplated his answer to that, the Brotherhood closed in on him, but not in an aggressive manner, in spite of all their weapons.

"I don't have time to explain." He put his phone away. "Listen, I just need to know where she is. I think she has someone . . . she's taken someone. Tonight. And if I don't find that demon, I think somebody I care about is going to be killed."

"I know of one place she's gone before," the stocky fighter with the accent said. "I can take you there."

"Let's go!"

Tohrment put his whole body in the way. "Not until we have your word."

"Fine! Take it! You have it." Sahvage threw up his arms. "Whatever you need, I don't give a fuck—"

"You're going to help us after we help you. You're going to do what only you can do when we need you to."

Sahvage stared into his brother's—former Brother's—eyes. "You don't actually buy that bullshit, do you. About the warnings on my coffin? I can assure you, I got no special powers."

"You're lying."

"Look, that bitch took the female I lo—a female I care about. If I were so fucking powerful, you think I wouldn't be strangling her right now?"

"But back in the Old Country—"

"You shouldn't believe everything you hear."

Tohrment glanced at the Brotherhood. "So you didn't slaughter Zxysis. Or his guards? You didn't do all that. You're not a warlock."

Protecting Rahvyn was a reflex, but there was no reason to keep up the lie anymore. He hadn't seen her or heard anything about her in two hundred years.

"No, I'm not a warlock. And that wasn't me."

"I don't believe you."

Sahvage shrugged. "I don't give a fuck whether you believe me or not. Look, I gotta go, I have to find—"

"I'll take you to where I found the evil," the Brother with the accent said. "No strings."

Sahvage crossed his arms over his chest. "I don't know you. So why would you do that."

"Damsel in distress aside?" The Brother narrowed hazel eyes. "I'm a good goddamn Irish Catholic. So demons gotta go."

"Are you sure Catholics can talk like that?"

"If you're from Southie, fuck yeah."

"In return," Tohr cut in, "you're going to help us find what we're looking for. You're going to owe us, and you've always been a male of your word."

"Keep telling yourself that—"

"We find the Book, and you're off the hook."

Sahvage leaned in sharply. "I'm sorry, what did you say you're looking for?"

CHAPTER FORTY-SIX

Vernon Reilly wasn't having it. As he looked at the other security guard on duty, he was *so* sick of this shit.

"You gotta stop, okay? I'm over it."

Buddy Halles seemed surprised that someone, anyone, would take exception to his bitching. "I don't see why you're taking her side of this."

The security office was a box with a single door, two swivel chairs, and a bank of monitors and equipment—and they were lucky to have the space they did. The building they were responsible for was an oldie but goodie, with what had been a big stack of floors for when it had been built a century ago. Now, of course, it was an antiquated stone stub compared to the graceful, mirrored sky-spears that marked the rest of downtown.

In this respect, it was kind of like Vernon. Old school, but still useful.

At least for another two months, three weeks, and four days, in his case.

Buddy sat forward in his swivel chair and pointed to his shiny shield. "I'm busy. I got a job, I got responsibilities. She have to understand where I am. This affects me, man."

Buddy was a twenty-seven-year-old Caldie born-and-bred who was growing out his hair anywhere there was a follicle, and who seemed to think, in the ways of the younger generation, that absolutely everything revolved around how he was feeling.

Vernon had had to listen to the trials of the kid's internal sense of self for every eight-hour shift since Buddy had been hired back in October.

"And my mother knows how I feel."

Who doesn't. "Mm-hm."

"I have a right to feel safe in my own home—"

"It's your mama's house. And you're not paying rent."

"I'm allergic to cats, though. She knows I'm allergic—"

Like a gift from God, one of the sensors started blinking on the console. As Vernon sat up to enter the diagnostic coding request into his computer, he hoped—for the only time in his professional career as a security guard—that there was an actual fire.

"Maybe your mama sending you a message," Vernon remarked while he waited for the IT response.

"You mean . . . you think she's doing it on purpose? To get me out of the house—"

As the assessment reading came back, Vernon got out of his chair. "It's another malfunction. There's no heat registering. I've canceled the alarm, but I'm going to go check anyway."

"I'll come with—"

"No." Vernon pulled on his jacket. "You stay here. Someone has to monitor."

Buddy was protesting the seniority factor as Vernon stepped out into the hall. As the door shut behind him, he closed his eyes and listened for the click.

Ah . . . heaven.

If he played this right, he could stretch the investigation out for an hour or more. The security office was on the first floor right next to the freight elevator, but he was no fool. He was taking the stairs. Slowly.

Down on the basement level, he whistled a tune that had no name, the same one he always fell into when the pressure was off. It was like a combination of Earth, Wind & Fire's "September" and Smokey Robinson's original version of "My Girl." And chances were good he was going to be a-whistlin' for as long as he was inclined to. Unlike the rest of the floors above, the basement didn't have any office spaces in it, only storage areas, but more to the point, it was so damn late, all the suits were gone for the night, even the ones who liked to work the long hours on weekends.

And that was another reason he was sure the alarm was a malfunction. Down here, there were no coffeepots left on. No one sneaking cigarettes and ashing into a combustible bin in a men's room. No gooseneck desk lamps angled too close to an out-box of memos or computer equipment sparking . . . or any of the thousand bizarre things that he'd heard about or seen personally in the building.

Being security for a property like this for thirty-seven years? You learned about all the different ways human beings screwed up. He'd busted people out of elevators they'd stopped on purpose after hours to have sex in. He'd rescued people off the roof, people who'd had it with their lives. He'd turned the other way when some arguments got loud in the stairwells—and interceded in others so no one got hurt. He'd tolerated everybody, no matter what their status, stats, or proverbial serial number.

The fact that Buddy was driving him nuts was probably the best indicator, other than that he turned sixty-five next month, that it was time to hang up the ol' uniform and find a hobby. He'd never had a hobby. Maybe shipbuilding. He liked things with little parts, and God knew he was a natural when it came to making order out of messes.

Which was why he'd always liked this job—

The burning smell got his attention, even though he didn't get understand the shadings inside the nasty aroma. It was like . . . leather burning?

Vernon picked up his pace. Like the rest of the building, he knew the basement by heart, and he hustled down to the storage space that was having what appeared to be a very non-malfunction.

Getting out his old-fashioned ring of keys, he also had his passcard ready. Each of the storage units was privately leased, and if he entered, he had to swipe to record his ID along with the date and time for security purposes. And in this case, the particular space was rented to one of the insurance companies, so there was a lot of sensitive information inside.

When he came up to the door, he put his palm on it—and frowned when the steel wasn't hot. He put his key in the lock anyway, and as the dead bolt gave way, he pushed the heavy weight with his shoulder.

Immediately, he got a whiff of what had grabbed his attention. The smell was definitely coming from inside, but as the motion-activated light came on—

"What the hell?" Vernon muttered.

Stepping into the storage area, he swiped his ID card to quiet the beeping of the door alarm, and then he just walked around . . .

All the completely empty space.

The walls were as expected, painted dark gray, with the ceiling and the floor done in black. This made sense. Every time one of the units was leased, the maintenance crew slapped a new coat of cheap and glossy on every square foot, the layers so thick now that the contours of the concrete were buffed out completely. But this paint job was pristine, no scuffs where boots had traveled or boxes set down, no dings from where things had been pushed into corners.

So not only was there nothing currently inside, there never had been.

Not his problem, though. If some company want to pay for the privilege of not putting a damn thing down here, that was their stupid mistake. His concern was figuring out why in the hell he was smelling something that was burning and seeing . . . absolutely nothing. And yes, he was sure he had the right space. The alarm report told him so.

Maybe he was having a stroke.

No, wait. One of the sprinklers, way in the back, was double-blinking, indicating it was the one that had gone off.

Vernon went over to it and walked around a couple of times. But nothing changed: The fire alarm continued to blink, and his nose kept talking about some kind of smoky stuff, and the storage unit remained totally empty.

Okay, this was definitely going on his weird list.

Heading back to the door, he took one last check at that which he had already checked; then he stepped out—

Vernon froze, all of the blood draining from his face.

Down at the end of the corridor, walking in the kind of flanking formation he knew from his time in the Army, there were three men dressed in black leather. Well, one had camo pants on. And Vernon did not need a metal detector to inform him that the bulges under those jackets were weapons.

All of them had dark hair, deadly eyes, and were lock-focused on him.

With a sudden wave of nausea, he realized wasn't going to make it to retirement.

Dear God . . . Rhonda. She was going to have to bury him.

Vernon closed his eyes. He had mace, but no gun.

He had no way of defending—

◆   ◆   ◆

—opened the door to the security office. Over at the console, Buddy looked up.

"That didn't take long," the kid said. "So it was just a malfunction, huh."

Vernon blinked and looked around. Buddy was the same, still bearded and long-haired, still young and bored. Likewise, the console was what it had always been, and so too the monitors. His chair was also exactly as he'd left it, swiveled around to face the door . . . yet he felt like he'd been gone twenty years. And as he went to sit down at his side of the control panel, he had some vague stomach upset and a headache that had moved in between his temples.

"You okay, Vern?"

He hated when the kid nicknamed him. Usually. Not right now.

"I'm fine." After he cleared the alarm notification, he turned his chair toward Buddy. "Hey, can you do a favor for me?"

Buddy's eyebrows popped. "Yeah, sure. You want a soda?"

"No, I want you to"—Vernon rubbed his forehead—"rerun the security tapes."

"Sure, from where?"

"Down in the—" The pain between his temples got worse and he gritted his teeth. "In the basement. Where the alarm was."

"Did you see anything?"

"No, I didn't," he said roughly. "I just want to review the tapes."

"But if you didn't see nothing—okay, yeah, sure. Whatever."

As Buddy worked the monitors and the feed was set up, Vernon opened his drawer and took out his Motrin bottle. Shaking two—and then four—into his palm, he choked the pills back dry.

He was coughing as the image of the corridor in question came up on Buddy's right-hand screen—

The second Vernon focused on that vacant, basement-level hallway of doors, his whole brain lit up with pain.

"Keep going," he groaned. "I want to see the footage from when I was down there."

As the headache intensified, he had to fight to keep his eyes on the glowing image—

The feed clicked out: Just as he emerged from the stairwell, stepping out of the fire door and into the corridor, the images went black.

"What the hell," Buddy muttered as he ran it back.

Buddy might have been a whiny codependent with his mommy, but he wasn't an idiot. He wasn't doing anything wrong with the technology. The file, for some reason or another, was corrupted to the point where it provided no visuals whatsoever.

Eleven minutes.

Eleven missing minutes.

"I give up," Vernon said as he let his head fall back.

"It happens. And hey, the alarms are off. So it's all done with whatever it was."

"Yeah."

Still, there was this nearly undeniable urge to probe his memories. Something had happened down in that basement. From the time when he'd left this office and decided to take the stairs to the—

Vernon let it all go as the agony ramped up again. It was such a strange headache, like he'd eaten three ice cream cones, one after another, a kind of sharp, cold spear right in the front of his skull.

"You want to call in?" Buddy asked in a voice that seemed worried. "You don't look too hot."

"Motrin'll kick in in a few." Vernon cleared his throat. "Tell me about the cat again, would ya?"

Buddy immediately went back into his drama. "Yeah, so my mom says he was a present from Aunt Rose, but I don't think he was. I think she needs an excuse to kick me out—"

So bizarre. As Vernon concentrated on the feline drama, the headache completely disappeared—and it couldn't be the Motrin. There was no way they were this effective this quickly.

But as if he were going to argue with what worked?

"And you can't get allergy shots?" Vernon said when there was a pause for breath in Buddy's reporting.

The kid frowned. "What are you—wait, you can do that?"

Vernon nodded and started to shrug out of his uniform jacket. "Yeah. Sure. You go in and they give you shots and then you're not allergic."

"Oh, my God, that's exactly what I'm going to do! Thanks, man."

With another incline of his at-the-moment-not-hurting head, Vernon decided to glance at the console. When the lights didn't hurt his eyes or bring the pain back, he relaxed. Who the hell knew what it was. Maybe that pinched nerve in his neck was acting up again.

Yeah, that had to be it.

Man, he was so ready to retire, he really was.

CHAPTER FORTY-SEVEN

Inside the storage unit full of designer clothes, Mae lowered the flaming purse from the sprinkler head's vicinity. The red light was no longer blinking.

"No, no . . . *no* . . ."

She turned back to the door. The reinforced panel was still shut and totally secured, but someone had been close by. She had scented them. She had heard their voice. They had been so close—

There it was again. Her instincts pricking as if she were no longer alone.

Mae looked to the sprinkler with all kinds of hope—the light was still solid.

"Shit."

As she got off the chair, she thought maybe she was just losing her mind, all fried on desperation and the terror that came with knowing your murderer wasn't going to stay away forever. And as she stared at the door again, the wave of emotion that came over her was totally not helpful: No longer scared for her life and focused on getting free, she was beyond sad. Near to the point of tears.

Mae breathed in deep—

At first, the scent did not make sense. And then she was convinced she'd imagined it because more than anything, it had been what she had prayed for.

"Sahvage!" she yelled. "I'm here! Sahvage!"

Through the connection of her having fed him, she could sense him clear as if he were standing in front of her. He was here. He somehow had found her.

Throwing the bag to the floor, she bolted across the space, shoving racks aside. Curling up fists, she pounded on the door.

"I'm here! I'm here! Help!"

As she struck the steel panel over and over again, something in the back of her mind registered—and it took some further yelling to figure out what it was. Abruptly, she stopped striking the steel, stopped hollering. Calming herself down, Mae knocked lightly.

Knocked more loudly.

Pounded again.

There was no sound.

As she made contact with the door, there was no reverberation back to her, nothing entering her ears . . . nothing that would register to anybody else, either.

Trying not to panic, she knocked on the white-painted Sheetrock by the jamb.

Nothing, either.

And even though there was smoke curling around the racks of clothes, and a stench in her nostrils, she feared, for no reason that made any logic, that no one else could smell any of it.

That Sahvage couldn't scent it.

Mae put her hands to her mouth and wheeled around to the racks and displays. This was an illusion, she realized. This whole . . . all of the clothes and the accessories, the furniture and the kitchen, that tub over there . . . it all didn't exist in the normal sense.

Which meant *she* didn't exist in the normal sense.

"Sahvage," she whispered. "Help me . . ."

How the hell was she going to breach the divide that separated wherever she was from where everyone else existed . . .

. . . before the demon returned?

Oh, dearest Virgin Scribe, if the brunette came back, Sahvage was now in danger, too.

Full-blown panic jammed up her brain, and she paced back and forth. Then an idea came to her.

Mae broke into a scramble, and as she skidded into the kitchen area, she started ripping open cabinets.

White vinegar. Thank God. Salt—yes. Lemons . . . lemons . . .

Mae tried the refrigerator. "Come on, there has to be—"

No lemons, but there was a honey-lemon vinaigrette. Turning the bottle around, she shook her head. The third ingredient was lemon. It was going to have to do.

"Candles . . ."

She opened drawers. Found pink, yellow, and blue birthday candles in one.

"Sterling silver. I need . . ."

Over on the display table, where the purses were, she nailed that one by pouring out a shiny dish that held a dozen pairs of earrings.

"Knife."

She dumped the growing pile by the door. Went back to a wooden block full of Henckels sitting on the counter by the stove. Snagged the flaming purse on the way back to her supplies.

Sitting down cross-legged, she tried to remember what Tallah had told her. What the measurements were, how much of the one and the other of ingredients. Oh, and as for the lemon-delivery system of that salad dressing? Who knew how to weigh that.

Your intention matters.

As she heard Tallah's voice in her head, she inspected what she'd put into the silver basin—as if she was going to know what was right or wrong? Then she popped the top on the birthday candles and took out a blue one. 'Cuz true blue, and all that.

What the hell was she doing? It wasn't like this had worked with the Book.

"Stop it," she commanded. "Intentions . . ."

Bracing herself, she bit her lip—and cut her palm, right over the life-line. The blood came out fast, dropping all over the place as she picked up the candle and tilted it to the still-burning purse.

The flame caught quick.

Even though Mae's heart was racing and she didn't really think this was going to work, she put her dripping wound and the burning candle over the dish. Then she closed her eyes and tried to calm her mind. Picturing Sahvage walking through the door, she—

No. If this was some kind of fucked-up, other existential plane, she didn't want to get them both trapped here.

She pictured Sahvage straddling the two planes. One foot in the realness, one foot in wherever she was.

With total concentration, Mae recalled every single thing about the fighter. She pictured his cropped hair. His beautiful, harsh face. His ob-sidian eyes. His lips . . .

But as she drew in a breath, she couldn't feel him. Even as she pic-tured him, it didn't go far enough: It was a photograph, not a sculpture. Definitely not a person.

Mae popped her eyes opened and looked around. "Think of him, think of him . . ."

Refocusing, she tried to quiet down again, and put herself inside the memories of them together—

In the bathroom. At Tallah's.

All at once, it clicked: She was so close to Sahvage, their lips nearly meeting, their eyes locked. She could scent him in her nose and feel him inside her body even though they weren't touching, her blood racing, her senses alive, the precipice she was about to jump off of leading not to a hard fall . . . but a soaring flight.

With that in her mind, she now imagined that he had one foot on the far side of the door, and one foot on her side, whatever that was. He was reaching out to her, extending his hand to her. And she was putting her palm on his. And he was pulling her . . .

Sahvage. I'm here.

She thought the words at him so hard that she began to strain, and she kept repeating them until she felt like she was going to burst. Exhaling on a great explosion, with her lungs burning and her heart skipping beats, everything went wonky.

Gasping, Mae opened her eyes and—

Nothing had changed.

Sagging in her own skin, she looked around and felt a despair that went further than even the pain she'd been carrying around about Rhoger—and that was because everything that had happened to him was wrapped up in the piercing agony now marking the center of her chest.

And she was going to lose Tallah, too.

Everything was gone. Her life as she had known it, her life as she had wished it would be.

And she would never, ever know where Sahvage's kisses would have taken her.

She was going to lose him as well.

Tears rolled down her cheeks as she regarded this strange, unholy prison she was trapped in—and the horror that there was nothing to do but wait for the demon to come back.

Which would be both a beginning and an ending.

All hope lost.

In the midst of her sadness and regret, Sahvage's face came to her mind once more, from back when he'd shown up at the cottage and they'd fought that shadow. The image of him was from after the attack, when they'd been in the kitchen. He'd been joking with her, a sly smile on his face, his black-blue eyes sparkling.

Under different circumstances, maybe they could have had a life together—

"I could have loved him!" she yelled at no one.

With a swipe of her arm, she backhanded the silver dish, the stupid, go-nowhere bullshit in it going flying—and hitting the steel-reinforced door on a splash that stuck. On account of the fucking true-blue birthday candle.

All at once, the lights flickered . . . and went out.

CHAPTER FORTY-EIGHT

While an older security guard was sent off with no memories of three vampires showing up in his building's basement, Sahvage was going insane as he walked through some kind of storage place.

That was four-thousand-plus square feet of absolutely, fucking empty.

But Mae was here.

Stalking around the pylons that were holding up the ceiling, he couldn't explain what he was scenting, what he was sensing. Mae was *here*. He could almost feel her. And yet his eyes were telling him that he was alone in this concrete four-walls-and-not-a-damn-thing.

"I don't get it," he gritted out.

Butch, the Brother who'd volunteered to tour guide him, shook his head. "This is how it was for me and V, too. We were tracking the demon on GPS, but . . . we couldn't find her even though she was at this location."

"Mae's here." He breathed in and smelled smoke, too. Along with his female's scent. "I can . . . she's here."

Faster and faster, he kept walking around. But like that was going to change anything?

"Fuck this," he said as he marched back to the steel door. "I get the fucking Book. Then I make a deal with her. She wants it, and she'll do anything to get it."

The pain of remote faces looking back at him were a loud-and-clear he was not having.

"Sorry, Mae comes first."

Tohr shook his head. "We'll get your female back. But the Book and that demon can't be reunited. It gives her too much power."

"Just so we're clear"—Sahvage leveled his stare—"I don't give a shit whether that brunette blows up half of Caldwell, the only thing I care about is Mae."

"We have other resources. We can help you."

"All I need is that fucking Book. I'll take it from there."

As Sahvage faced off at the Brothers, he recognized the screaming in his head. It took him back to all those fun-filled nights looking for Rahvyn. Goddamn, how had he gone from glancing at Mae in the crowd at that fight to this . . . hollow despair . . . at not being able to save her?

He was a simp.

"I'm coming for you, Mae," he said loudly. "You stay alive, I'm coming for you."

As his voice echoed around the gray-and-black concrete, he knew he was insane. But there was no getting off this train.

He turned and stalked out of the storage unit. Closing the door behind himself and the Brothers, he looked up and down the corridor as the other fighters continued to give him all kinds of no-go hairy eyeball.

When he walked away, he felt like he was peeling off his own skin. And the only way he could keep going was by promising himself . . . he was somehow going to find his female.

Not that she was his.

For fuck's sake, he should have listened to his gut and not gotten involved—

The clanging clatter rang out in the hallway, like something metal had hit . . . something metal. Spinning around, he frowned at the nothing-happening.

"What is it?" Tohr demanded.

"Didn't you hear that?"

"No. There was no sound."

Butch shook his head. "There was nothing, my guy."

Sahvage ignored them. But when there was no repeat and no . . . fucking anything at all . . . he knew he was just being an ass.

"Motherfucker."

He turned away—and that was when he heard the weeping. Soft. As if from a distance . . . yet the sound was unmistakable.

Gripped with focus, Sahvage walked back to the steel door, even though he didn't expect to see anything.

He was wrong.

"Mae! Holy fuck! Mae!"

The solid metal panel had somehow morphed into a screen: He could see through it now, and on the other side, Mae was sitting cross-legged on a bright white marble floor, her head in her hands, her sobs carrying through whatever kind of existential distance separated them.

"Mae!" he yelled as he dropped to his knees.

"What are you doing?" Butch said.

"She's right there! What the hell is wrong with you? Mae!"

Sahvage touched the metal—and it gave way, his fingers somehow pushing into that which shouldn't have had any give in it at all.

And as if she sensed him, Mae jerked her head up and looked around.

"I'm here!" He ripped his jacket off and held it out to the Brother closest to him. "Take this."

Tohr stared down in confusion. "What are you talking about."

"I'm going in after her. I'm going to pull her out. But I'm going to need an anchor." He didn't care how he knew this with such clarity. "Hold this!"

Tohr continued to look at him like he'd lost his mind—join the god-damn club—but the Brother grabbed on to the jacket's wrist.

"I don't know where the hell you think you're going—"

"Your opinion is irrelevant."

Sahvage braced his body, one foot planted behind him, the other set right on the lip of the door. Then he extended his arm into the steel panel . . .

The sensation was unpleasant, like he was pushing his hand through cold mud, but like he gave a shit. He just kept going, leaning farther and farther forward, his palm, his wrist, his forearm, penetrating through the door . . . and coming out the other side.

Mae reared back.

And then instantly, her expression changed. *Sahvage!*

Or at least that's what he thought she said. He couldn't hear her.

"Take my hand," he yelled. "Take it—I'll pull you through."

Even though he didn't know whether that was possible. He didn't know anything other than he wasn't leaving without her.

"I'm going in," he said to nobody.

Moving carefully, he put his boot into the other version of reality and shifted some of his weight. That same instinct that told him to make sure to keep one foot in each plane of existence, one on each side of the door, got louder and louder, so he relied on the hold on his jacket's sleeve as he tilted himself off-balance.

Penetrating the door with his torso gave him a bad case of the shivers, his skin goose bumping, his muscles twitching, his bones aching deep in his marrow. And as his head broke free of the resistance, he was hit with all kinds of sights and smells. Clothes. Something burning. Perfume.

Like he gave a fuck.

Mae was right in front of him. He could finally scent her tears, feel her presence—and hear her properly.

Oh, God, she was hurt. Her face was wounded and—

"Sahvage!"

As she launched herself at him, he grabbed on to her body, but couldn't spare even a second to check her injuries. "Hold on, my female. Just hold me tight."

Looking over her head, he had a brief, but indelible, impression of racks and racks of fancy shit. And modern furniture and a kitchen and a bed platform. There was a whole living space in the storage area, but the demon was so fucking clever, wasn't she.

"Here we go," Sahvage said.

The last thing he noticed, as he started to pull back, was the white vinegar bottle right next to the door. And the container of salt. And a box of birthday candles.

And a white-and-gray scaled purse that was on fire.

Whatever. He had Mae in his arms, and that was all that mattered.

◆　　◆　　◆

Mae had been at the end of her rope, weeping into her hands—when she'd heard something outside the door. And then an arm, a heavily muscled, heavily veined arm, had somehow, in some way, come at her. She'd been so shocked, she'd nearly bolted.

But then she'd scented Sahvage. Clearly.

And then he'd appeared, right in front of her, leaning through the door.

"Mae!"

As he'd said her name, she hadn't thought twice. She'd sprung forward and thrown herself at him—and the second his solid hold registered, she nearly blew apart from relief. She had never gripped anything so hard in her life.

Sahvage told her something about holding on to him, but that was a command she did not require as she locked on to the back of his neck and all but wrapped her legs around his waist. When he started to retreat through the door, the pulling was terrible, her body stretching until her bones were spears of agony and her muscles strings of white-hot pain. All she could do was bury her face in his thick throat and try to keep breathing.

The trembling came next, chills racing through her, chattering her teeth, spasming her legs. Just as she thought she was going to shatter apart, at the moment when she knew she could take no more, there was a release, all the drag on her body disappearing—

Mae exploded out of the lair, sure as if she were spring-loaded—and Sahvage was her landing pad. As they were thrown back against a corridor's wall, she banged into his chest, her knee hitting something rock hard, her nose registering all kinds of new smells.

"I've got you," he said in the numb aftermath. "You're okay, you're out . . . I got you."

Mae shook all over, her adrenaline ebbing and leaving her so limp, she couldn't lift her head.

"It's all right . . ." Sahvage murmured as he stroked her shoulders.

Gradually, Mae's senses came back online properly. They were in a hallway . . . outside of a steel door that was closed.

Two enormous males were standing over them.

And a demon was still returning at any second.

With panic, Mae shoved herself up off Sahvage's pecs. "We need to get out of here. She's coming back. We need—my house. Let's go there. The salt will keep her out—"

"Can you dematerialize?"

With Sahvage's help, Mae managed to stand mostly on her own, but when she lurched to the side abruptly, he cursed. So did she.

"If you have to go on foot, we'll guard you," one of the males, the stockier of the pair, said.

As she glanced at him, she realized he had a pair of black daggers strapped, handles down, to his chest. And so did the other one.

The Black Dagger Brotherhood, she thought with awe.

"I've got you," Sahvage said for the hundredth time.

The next thing she knew, he'd scooped her up and started running.

With all his strength, he carried her down the concrete hall like she didn't weigh anything at all, his boots pounding over the bare floor as the two Brothers provided cover in front and in back.

When they got a heavy door with a red exit sign over it, the stockier Brother jumped ahead and held the thing open.

"This way," he ordered.

Mae felt her awareness come and go, like it had just after she'd been in that accident. Meanwhile, Sahvage just kept soldiering on, running, running, running, as if he had endless amounts of energy and all the power in the world in his body.

Eventually, they came to some kind of delivery facility, a lineup of cargo bays and all kinds of rolling bins suggesting they were in a big building's mail processing department. The two other fighters immediately went over to one of the receiving areas and broke open a set of vertical doors, rolling the slats up on their tracks—

All at once, Mae smelled night air—that carried a hint of oil and trash. They were downtown somewhere.

"I can dematerialize," she said roughly. Clearing her throat, she spoke louder. "I can do it."

"Let's get you checked out first."

Sahvage jumped down to the pavement, and as he started running again, she realized they were heading to a huge RV . . . where a man in a white coat—a human?—was standing by what looked to be an operating room.

"No, it's not safe," Mae said as she pushed against Sahvage's shoulder. "I have to go back to my house. She's coming here any minute—"

"Mae—"

"No!" She shoved herself out of his arms and had to catch herself on the vehicle's brake lights. "She's coming!" Mae looked at all the males in a panic. "You don't understand what she is—"

"No," the stockier one countered. "We know exactly what she is. If you have a safe place, get to it now. We'll catch up with you."

Sahvage opened his mouth as if he were going to argue, but the

Brother grabbed his shoulder. "Let her go where she needs to be, we'll bring the medicine to her. You got her out once, but I will guarantee you that whatever loophole you found? That demon is going to plug it up the moment she returns. We have seconds now, let's use them."

Mae stepped forward and put both her hands on Sahvage's face. "Meet me at my parents'. Tell them where to go."

And then, even though she was still woozy, and in spite of her pounding head and the pain in her body, she squeezed her eyes shut.

You can do this, she told herself sternly. *More than that, you have to.*

Or her life, and the lives of Sahvage and the two other males, were over.

CHAPTER FORTY-NINE

He couldn't believe Mae was able to do it.

In all Sahvage's years of combat back in the Old Country, and even throughout his human fight club experiences lately, he'd never seen such an act of will. Even though the female could barely hold herself upright, she somehow managed to gather the focus and presence of mind to dematerialize back to her house.

Not only that, she made it into the garage. All the way up the door.

He'd followed her the whole time, staying right behind her. So that as she finally collapsed, he re-formed just in time and caught her.

"I've got you," he murmured as he took the keys he'd grabbed from her car ignition out of his leather jacket.

Thank fuck he'd thought to snag them. The copper lock would have been trouble.

Rushing inside, he left the door unlocked for the Brothers and headed directly for the basement with her. He did not want those other males checking out the rest of the house and finding her brother in the tub. There were too many complications already to volunteer for those kinds of questions.

"The bedroom I'm using is down there," Mae mumbled.

Fortunately, there were lights left on so it was easy to get to the modest room with simple furnishings. And as he laid her on the bed, she let out a ragged sigh—

Up above, heavy footfalls announced the arrival of the Brothers, and as Mae closed her eyes and breathed roughly, the other fighters came down to the cellar.

"Manny's ETA is about ten minutes," Tohr said.

The protective male in Sahvage wanted to tell both of them to get out of Mae's private space, but he shut that shit up quick. This was a more-the-merrier kind of situation, especially given that the merriers came with all kinds of extra guns and ammo.

As time ticked by, everyone stayed quiet as Sahvage sat on the edge of the mattress and held Mae's hand. She was so still that had she not been drawing breaths, he would have worried she had passed—

"Hello?" came a voice from up above.

"Down here, doc," Tohr called out.

The human in the white coat jogged a descent, a black duffle rustling at his side. "Hey," he said as he addressed Sahvage. "I'm Dr. Manello. We weren't introduced."

As the guy approached the foot of the bed, Sahvage looked him up and down. Handsome man. Big shoulders for a human. Seemed competent.

But Sahvage did not fucking move from Mae's side. And as the silence stretched out, the Brothers cleared their throats.

"I promise," the doc said, "this is strictly medical. I need to examine her, though. She's got obvious head trauma, okay?"

With a wave of aggression surging in his body, Sahvage wanted to tell the guy that she was just fucking fine—except he didn't really know that. Which was the point. She'd been in a car accident, gotten abducted, and then nearly been lost forever thanks to that goddamn brunette. A "strictly medical" exam was called for, especially given the fact that Mae was lying back against those pillows like maybe she needed a crash cart, her beautiful face painfully pale, her body too motionless, her chest rising and falling in a shallow way.

There was just one little problem.

Sahvage kind of wanted to take the handsome, dark-haired human . . . and put the guy's face through a plate glass window. And then maybe nail his arms and legs to a wall. And hit him with a spray of accelerant, followed by a—

"Match," Sahvage said out loud.

"What?" the human asked.

"Never mind. And you're not taking any of her clothes off."

On that happy little announcement, he glanced around Mae's bedroom for no good reason. There was a bureau, a bed stand, and a queen-sized bed with a simple duvet and a couple of pillows. Short of some books and an alarm, there was no clutter whatsoever. Functional. Non-fussy.

Barren.

And that made him sad.

"Look, I'm happily mated, my guy," Manello said. "So I know how you're feeling right now. But how am I going to examine her properly if I can't remove her tops?"

Before Sahvage had a proper thought, his dagger hand shot forward and grabbed the front of the doctor's scrubs. Pulling the human right up close, he bared his fangs.

But instead of screeching, calling for help, or shoving back, the guy just rolled his eyes. "Jesus, you people need to fucking chill. Relax, dickhead. And spare me the 'if you touch her, Ima kill you.' I've heard it a million times, and not once has anything that's six seven and clocking in at three hundred pounds had to put my face through a plate glass window."

Sahvage's eyebrows popped. "I didn't think humans could read minds."

"Wow, you went there with the glass? Really?" Dr. Manello punched

Sahvage's chest and got himself free. "Out. Now. If you care about this female at all, you'll let me do my job. I'm not fucking around with your bonding anymore—"

"Oh, no, no—you got it all wrong." Sahvage put his palms up. "I haven't bonded with her."

"So I'm smelling cologne you just decided to put on in the middle of a crisis?" The doctor tapped the side of his nose. "Niffer, niffer, dumbass. In case you've missed it."

On that note, the human planted a fairly good-sized set of payback palms on Sahvage's torso and gave things a big old push.

As Sahvage tap-danced out into the sitting area, the Brothers went with him and the bedroom door was shut.

Whereupon he just stood there. Like, well, a dumbass.

"You know," Tohrment remarked as he parked it on the sofa in the sitting area, "I'm not sure what I'm most surprised about. The fact that your coffin was full of flour, the hi-how're-ya out of the blue, the pull-a-female-through-a-steel-door . . . or this."

"What's this," Sahvage muttered as he turned around.

"The bonding."

"I haven't bonded with her, for fuck's sake."

The fact that he had to physically restrain himself from stamping his boot was something that he resolutely refused to dwell on.

Meanwhile, over on an armchair, the Brother Butch cocked an eyebrow. And didn't say a goddamn thing.

Which made it worse, of course.

As minutes stretched into three hundred years of waiting, Sahvage paced up and back. A couple of times.

Then he stopped. "So you know where the Book is?"

Butch looked at Tohrment. Who shook his head.

"We have a couple of people working on leads." Tohrment crossed his arms over his daggers. "But make no mistake, we will find it."

Sahvage thought about the summoning spell. And kept his goddamn mouth shut.

"When we get its location," Tohrment continued, "we're going to need you to help us get it. And before you try to bullshit us again that you're nothing special, you just pulled a female out of some kind of alternate reality through a steel door. We need you, warlock. Without your powers, we're not going to get to goal."

Sahvage narrowed his eyes. "Answer me this: What are you going to do with the Book when you get it?"

"Put it in a very safe place."

"You're going to destroy it?"

"It's going to be in a very safe place."

Sahvage thought about the brunette. And what that bitch had done to Mae.

Then he cursed to himself as he remembered what his Mae wanted the Book for. But maybe everything that had just happened had changed her mind—not that he knew the details of abduction yet. He sure as shit was going to find out everything as soon as she was able to tell him about it, though.

Because now there were two things on his extermination list.

"I'm staying here with Mae," Sahvage said. "You get a bead on the Book, the Reverend has my number."

"So you will help us."

Sahvage stared right into the navy blue eyes of the fighter who had once been his brother in all but blood—and lied through his fucking fangs.

"Absolutely I will."

✦   ✦   ✦

As Erika stepped off the Commodore building's main elevator, a couple of floors above where she'd been called into that scene with the murdered and desecrated couple, she was glad that short-staffing issues had kicked in once again.

Striding down, she did not miss her sleep. Her empty apartment. Her planned couple of hours off. She was firing on all cylinders.

The uniform by the door nodded to her and opened the way in. As she passed through, she nodded back at him.

"They're in with all the books," he said.

The direction was great—except for the fact that it presumed she knew anything about the layout of the rooms inside. But considering all of the balls in the air at the moment? The mystery of the body's location was the simplest one she had to solve. Besides, all she did was follow the conversation. Soft. With some weeping thrown in for tragic measure.

According to Special Agent Delorean, the wife found the husband after he'd gone to investigate a tripped alarm. And the corpse was . . . right up Erika's alley.

After she went through a room full of hunks of rock, and then one that had some pretty gruesome-looking old instruments in it, she rounded a corner—and took a memory snapshot: Nothing but shelves and books in this space, but that was not what was going to stick with her.

Over in the far corner, a very dead body appeared to have been used as a projectile against a section of shelving, all kinds of broken pieces of wood and disrupted leather covers and cracked spines around the remains.

Which were in a very bad state.

Delorean broke away from the uniforms and came over. "This has to be your boy. There's no . . . it's just like the scene at the club and the other places, as if someone waved a goddamn wand and tore him in half."

Erika went over and knelt down. Maybe it was the exhaustion . . . maybe it was the fact that her nerves were shot . . . but she was having trouble processing the victim's injuries. It was as if he had been pulled apart at the legs, the torso raggedly torn in half from crotch to throat.

A sense that she was being watched made her jerk her head back over her shoulder. But there was no one there—

Erika frowned and straightened. Inside a Lucite presentation stand with a lid, like it was something special, a book was set apart from the others and it captured her attention for no good reason: Even though she couldn't see its cover or its spine properly, and didn't have any clue about how fancy or expensive it was, there was just something . . .

Well, captivating about it—

"You okay?" Delorean asked.

"Is the wife in the other room?" she asked as she shook herself back to attention.

"Yeah."

"I'm going to go talk to her." Erika put her hand up to the special agent. "Just give me a minute with her alone."

Without waiting for a response, she followed the sounds of sniffling through a couple more rooms, and found herself emerging into some kind of sitting area that seemed big enough to be in a hotel. Over on a set of sofas, by a curving staircase, a woman with really good hair and a puffy face was wearing a bathrobe-and-nightgown set that was quite possibly worth more than a month or two of Erika's rent.

As she approached, she didn't have to ask the officer to get up and go. He took one look Erika's way and murmured something to the victim's wife before excusing himself.

"Hi, I'm Detective Saunders," she said as she came over. "I'm with homicide."

The wife patted her red nose with a Kleenex and looked up. "I just told him everything I know."

"I'm sure it will be helpful. You okay if I sit down with you?"

"I don't have anything else to tell. Herb went down when the alarm registered motion and he didn't come back. I waited about twenty minutes and then . . . I left our bedroom and found him . . ."

Erika lowered herself onto a white velvet couch that was part of an overall neutral color scheme—so that the masterpieces on the walls would show, no doubt. Jeez, the place was like a modern art museum.

"Why would someone do that?" the wife said as she stared at the wad of tissue she was holding. "Why?"

When those bloodshot eyes shifted over, Erika's heart stopped.

"I am so sorry." Leaning forward, she put her hand on the woman's shoulder. "I promise you, I'm going to find the person responsible. I will bring them to justice if it's the last thing I do."

Maybe it was the female-to-female thing, maybe it was the honest-to-God communion Erika felt with the pain the woman was feeling, but the wife's eyes watered anew.

"Do you think this has anything to do with the watches?"

Erika blinked. "The watches?"

"That were stolen." The wife sniffed and took another tissue from a white box. "We called the police as soon as my husband got home from Idaho and discovered they were missing. He went into the safe in our closet and saw they were gone. They were part of his collection. He always told me how much they were, but I don't . . . I can't remember now. But several hundred thousand dollars."

Erika glanced around at the ceiling, taking note of the pods that were mounted in the corners of the gallery space. "You have a security system here, correct?"

"There was no footage from that night . . . something went wrong."

"So you have cameras, too." When the wife nodded, Erika frowned. "The alarm was engaged when you think the theft occurred?"

"I was here alone. I swear I put it on, but I maybe did something wrong. Maybe I turned the cameras off—oh, God, what did they do to him?" Those eyes lifted again. "There's so much blood . . . and his body . . ."

As the wife started to get agitated, Erika shook her head. "Try not to think about that."

What a bullshit thing to say. But what else was there?

"I can't unsee it. Every time I blink, I see him on the floor—there's so much blood. So much . . ."

As the wife's words drifted, she stared off across the fine carpeting—and it was as Erika studied her profile that the sparkling at the woman's throat registered.

Holy . . . fuck, she was wearing a diamond necklace—and not a diamond that was on a necklace, but a collar of diamonds that glittered with every ragged breath she took. So many diamonds.

A set of blunt and buffed fingertips felt over the stones, as if the wife had noticed Erika looking at the jewels. "My husband gave this to me for our anniversary last year."

"It's . . . incredibly beautiful," Erika murmured.

"I feel beautiful when I wear it now." The woman closed her eyes. "It keeps me warm at night when my husband doesn't. Didn't."

Erika made a mental note, but wondered what kind of jealous lover had the strength to rip a grown man apart.

"No, I didn't kill my husband." The wife's stare shot over. "I would never . . . he may have been with someone else, but I loved him and—"

"You're not a suspect." Erika noted all those totally clean fingernails. "And I don't judge."

There was a moment when the two of them just looked at each other. Then the wife took a deep breath and dropped her eyes to her tissue again.

"I feel disloyal," she muttered, "even though he was the unfaithful one. Oh, God, Herb's dead."

As she started to cry again, Delorean appeared in the archway of the gallery, but Erika shook her head. When he nodded and backed off, she appreciated his discretion.

"I just want to be back in my dream."

Erika refocused on the wife. "What dream?"

"The night the watches were stolen . . . I had this incredible dream. This man came to me, and he . . . well, he told me to wear this and feel beautiful." The wife sighed. "But none of that was real, and I shouldn't be thinking about that now, should I."

"Sometimes the mind retreats," Erika said softly, "to wherever it can. Sometimes those retreats are the only reason we get through things. So if you want to remember a dream like that on a night like this? You fucking do it."

The wife turned and tilted her head. As her eyes focused, it was as if she were seeing Erika properly for the first time.

"Is the person who did that . . . going to come back?" she said hoarsely. "And why didn't they come after me upstairs?"

"Are you aware of anyone who might have wanted to hurt your husband?"

"No. He was a stand-up man. In business, at least. Am I in danger here?"

"Do you have another place you could stay?"

"Not really." The wife looked around. "But the bedroom suite is a panic room. I guess I could initiate the lockdown and stay here."

"Whatever feels right to you. If you do stay, though, how about we do a sweep up there so you're sure there's no one hiding in any of the rooms?"

"I would really appreciate that."

Erika looked at the diamonds. And thought . . . she knew what it was like to not feel beautiful. Except in her case, it wasn't because some man wasn't treating her right or disrespecting her with other females.

It was because there hadn't been a man for a very, very long time.

"I'm going to give you my private cell phone," she said. "I want you to call me anytime, about anything. Memory is a funny thing. It comes back at strange times. If you can think of something that can help us, I want you to call me."

The wife nodded. "Okay. I will."

"And keep wearing the necklace." Erika got to her feet. "It really is perfect on you."

CHAPTER FIFTY

With a groan, Mae woke up . . . and pushed herself a little higher on her pillows. As she winced, the male guard dog at her open door looked like he was ready to defend her against anything and everything, even if it was just the aches and pains she was suffering from.

The sight of Sahvage in the familiarity of her bedroom was a shock, but the fact that she was on her bed, in her home, at all?

She wasn't sure she trusted this reality.

"Did the other males leave?" she asked in a rough voice.

"Yeah. About twenty minutes ago." Sahvage cleared his throat. "Can I get you some Motrin or something? The doc said you were allowed a second dose if you're still uncomfortable."

The light from the sitting room made his huge figure seem menacing as a murderer. His scent, on the other hand, was a source of total comfort.

"I'll be okay," she said. "The doctor was really kind to me."

"I'm glad you're not hurt—I mean, not seriously hurt. Are you hungry?"

"I don't know." Mae laughed in a short rush and looked down at herself. She had some vague memory of changing into fresh clothes. Had she had a quick shower? Maybe. Everything was so hazy. "Can you imagine . . . that I don't know if I'm hungry?"

She blinked and saw those racks of designer clothes. So she tried to rub the images from her mind by going knuckle on her eyes.

"I called Tallah," he said.

Dropping her hands, she exhaled in relief. "Thank God. Did you talk to her? She doesn't know how to get into her voice mail."

"Yup, I spoke with her. I just told her we were staying here tonight. Nothing else."

"Was she okay with it?"

"Absolutely."

"Good."

As Mae shivered, she pulled half of the duvet over her legs. "I can't get warm."

There was a pause. And then Sahvage said, "I can help with that." When she glanced up at him, he put his hands out. "I'm not suggesting that we—"

With tears glossing her eyes, she extended her arms. She had no voice to reply to him.

As he straightened from his lean and came into the room, she couldn't believe what she was doing—and it was the most natural thing in the world, too. She'd never had a male in this bed, in any bed, but there was no other answer except yes.

Before Sahvage joined her, he put his hands to the front of his hips, and as she flushed and had to swallow hard—he simply removed his gun holster and placed it close by.

The entire mattress tilted as he sat on its edge, and she moved over to make sure he had enough room. But as he stretched out, she suddenly wasn't thinking about space. She was thinking about proximity.

His and hers.

Before she thought too much about anything, she curled into

him, and his heavy arm pushed under her neck. When she hissed, he froze.

"No, it's fine," she murmured. "I just have a bump on my head."

"From the car accident?"

As she settled in, she said with exhaustion, "I don't know. It could have been. I don't remember a lot."

"How did it happen?" he asked right by her ear.

"The accident?" Mae thought back to the radio report she'd been listening to. "I got distracted and hit the brakes. I was rear-ended—oh, God, she killed that nice man. Who was going to call nine-one-one for me."

As she moaned, he took one of her hands in his own. "Try not to think about it."

"I was so scared," she said as she went deeper into her memories. "In that place. She had a cage—I was in . . . a cage."

"Mae . . ." Now he sounded like he was in pain.

She lifted her head and looked into his dark blue eyes. "How did you know where to find me?"

"One of the Brothers knew where the brunette was."

"Did you call them for help?"

"They found me as it turned out." His brows dropped low. "We went there, to that building downtown—and I can't explain it. I could scent you in the space, but I couldn't see you. I walked around and around. I swear it was empty and I left . . . but then, all of a sudden, there was this clanging noise. And when I went back, the door turned into a window, into something that wasn't there in the, like, normal sense."

As he cursed under his breath, she put her arm over his rib cage—which was so broad, she felt as if she were trying to embrace a sofa.

"What if I hadn't heard that sound, you know?" he murmured. "I want to shit my pants every time I think of it."

"I summoned you." As both his brows arched in surprise, she nodded. "I used the same spell I used on the Book. At least the one for you worked."

"So that's how . . . holy crap."

There was a period of quiet. And then Sahvage rolled toward her. "You know, she'll go away if you give her what she wants."

"I'm sorry, you mean—the brunette?" When he nodded, Mae sat up. "How do you know that?"

"It's in the nature of those who covet. They acquire. You saw all those clothes."

Mae pushed her hair out of her face. "You're saying I should use the Book for Rhoger, and then just give it to her?"

"No, I'm saying to save your own life, you should just let her have it." When she didn't respond, Sahvage sat up as well. "Mae, think of where you've been. Think of what you've just survived—by a stroke of luck."

Between one blink and the next, she relived waking up in that crate. The panic of being trapped. The way it had felt being pressed up against that wall by the demon's invisible power.

She had been so terrified. So out of control.

Exactly as she had felt at the deaths of her parents. At the death of Rhoger.

"It wasn't a stroke of luck," she muttered. "I called you to me. And besides, I don't have the Book, do I."

"Mae . . ."

"No."

She wasn't even aware of having spoken until Sahvage said, "No, what?"

As Mae remembered feeling trapped and scared, she shook her head in the darkness. Then she turned to him. "I'm not going to let her win. She's *never* getting that goddamn Book."

◆   ◆   ◆

Downtown, on the basement level of the old office building, Devina clipped down the corridor to her lair, her stilettos fucking off the concrete. She could have just projected herself home, but she didn't feel like it. She just didn't fucking feel like it.

The fact that she was so enraged that concentration was impossible was a reality she refused to acknowledge. She was fine. She was just *fucking* fine—

The smell registered about thirty, forty feet from her destination, but she was so up in her head, it wasn't until she got to her door that she realized something was on fire somewhere close. And then, as she stepped into her home, there was smoke in the air. Looking around, she saw that the stupid fucking female vampire was gone—

Devina screamed. "No, no, *nonononono!*"

Falling to her knees, there was a cracking sound as she hit her polished floor, but she didn't care about the pain. With trembling hands, she reached out and tenderly cradled the innocent that had been massacred.

Her nearly priceless Birkin.

Her Himalayan Niloticus 35 with the diamond hardware.

Some absolute lunatic had burned the corner of the bag, ruining the crocodile skin, its delicate coloring and pattern of white, buff, gray, and black scales invaded by a cancer of oxidation from a flame.

Ruined. Four hundred thousand dollars' worth of Hermès's very best efforts, hours of work from a master craftsman, the very rarest and most expensive handbag in the world . . . *ruined.*

Falling on her ass, one of her ankles cranked at a bad angle, but she didn't care.

Cradling the desecrated carcass to her chest, she looked across her collection through eyes that watered. The tangled mess of the dog cage in the far corner seemed a rebuke of so much, so she willed it away, disappearing the goddamn symbol of her fucking failure.

What a night.

Everything had gone wrong.

And this was the problem with her life. When things went bad, you wanted to share the nightmare with someone who gave a shit. Somebody who could talk it all through with you, iron out the bumps, help formulate a new plan, a different approach.

A better way of getting to your goal.

Instead she was here, surrounded by beautiful things that could offer no advice or real support.

Closing her eyes, she reminded herself that her therapist, that flabby paper bag of a woman, had told her it was okay to be upset. To be disappointed. She just needed to feel her feelings—and know that, however strong they were, however unbearable they seemed, they would fade. Emotions were never permanent.

Except no, one of them was.

Though hate and anger, happiness and gratitude, jealousy, optimism, paranoia, all of the others were subject to peaks and valleys . . . love was a constant.

True love was immortal.

And when you were a demon, when there was no exit ramp for your existence, you valued things that could keep up with your forever calendar of nights and days.

Infinity was less fun than people thought.

Swamped with sadness, Devina rearranged her legs, extending them out and putting the Birkin casualty on her thighs. Running her fingertips over the matte texture, she remembered buying it at the mother ship. Twenty-four Rue du Faubourg Saint-Honoré in Paris. She had her favorite SA there, and after years of supporting the brand, and so many Kellys and Birkins bought and paid for, she had finally been invited to purchase the Holy Grail.

And she had done it the right way. Not on the secondary market, but after climbing the mountain of earning that invitation.

Four hundred thousand was what she could get if she sold it. But it hadn't cost her that much. When you were welcomed into that hallowed group who got them legitimately? You didn't pay anywhere near that reseller's premium.

But now, this symbol of everything she had achieved, of everything that she was, had been violated.

Devina narrowed her eyes at where the busted-up dog cage had been.

Payback was going to be a bitch.

A red hot ... bitch.

CHAPTER FIFTY-ONE

Outside the Brotherhood mansion, Balz lit up another one of Vishous's hand-rolls and leaned back against the still-winterized fountain. V had taken to supplying the cigs free of charge, no small giftie considering that not only was the prime ingredient very, very fine Turkish tobacco, it took a lot of fine motor skills to roll 'em up right. Lot of time, too.

It was just one of the many blessings that had rained down on a thief's head since he'd come here with the other bastards.

And he'd repaid the household how?

Closing his eyes, he hung his head and exhaled. He'd brought that demon to them. Oh, God . . . he'd brought evil to their midst.

How had it started? When had the infiltration happened? He wasn't sure. Maybe it had been that electrocution, although why that had created an opening in his soul, he wasn't sure. Yes, he had died . . . but plenty of people he knew had shaken hands with the Grim Reaper and not brought back a door prize from hell.

Like, literally from Hell.

As his antsy anxiety surged, he smoked faster, exhaling over his shoulder even though no one was around to secondhand smoke. He had been treated with nothing but respect by the Brotherhood and their community. Even, dare he say it, love.

It was in the nature of thieves to steal, however.

And apparently, he was so fucking good at the felony, he wasn't even aware of doing it anymore. Because sure as shit, he had stolen the security of those wonderful people inside this grand old mansion, and that grift was going to lead to an even larger and more dire larceny.

Somehow, it was going to kill them all.

And everything was going to be his fault—

"Let it go."

With a shout, Balz skidded around. "What? Oh, shit, Lass, what the fuck. Sneaking up on a guy like that."

On a night like this, he added to himself.

Lassiter stepped forward from the shadows, his blond-and-black hair catching the moonbeams that fell from the cold sky above. Or maybe it was just the fallen angel glowing like a night-light.

"Let it go."

Balz frowned. The male's lips weren't moving.

Let it go.

"What the hell is wrong with you?" Balz tapped the hand-rolled. "Now is not the time for some *Frozen* bullshit, okay? I'm not in the mood—"

Over at the stone steps, figures appeared from out of the darkness, the Brothers and the other bastards returning from wherever they'd been, their strong backs to him as they faced their home.

"Fucking finally," Balz muttered.

His impulse was to flick the stub, but he licked his thumb and pinched it out. And as he started off toward the other fighters, he tried to figure what pocket to put the remains in—and decided he didn't want to crap up his leathers. So he ate the goddamn thing.

He was chewing the wedge—and grimacing at the musky, burned taste while wondering why, assuming it was biodegradable enough to shoot into his digestive tract, he hadn't just pitched it on the ground and let nature run its course—as he came up to the Brotherhood.

Everyone was chatting at the same time.

". . . working with us."

"I can't believe he's actually alive—"

"—the hell he's been all these years?"

"I know where the Book is."

As Balz spoke the words, the turnaround on the stairs was such a Bob Fosse–oner, it might as well have been choreographed: Every single fighter was suddenly looking at him, and as he swallowed the wad of tobacco-flavored paper-gum, he prayed he was not making everything worse.

And not with what he'd just put into his gut.

Glancing behind to get some more atta'boy from Lassiter—

He frowned. The angel was not there.

Whatever.

"I know where the Book is," he repeated to all of them.

Tohr shook his head. And came down the steps. "This is why you told Fritz to shutter the house?"

"Yeah—and . . ." Balz took a deep breath—and coughed a random tobacco flake out of his esophagus. "I can't live here anymore. I'm infected with . . ."

Over on the left, Butch leaned in as if Balz wasn't speaking loud enough.

"You're sick?" Tohr asked as the wind blew in from the north.

Shit, what if what he was saying didn't translate again?

Balz glanced around, and there, in the back of the lineup . . . "Rehv. You can read my grid, right? I want you to tell them what you see. I'd tell them myself . . . but I'm worried she won't let me."

As the Reverend stepped around the others, the *symphath's* amethyst eyes narrowed. "Who's she?"

"Just tell them what you see."

There was a long moment, that odd wind whirling around as if it were searching for a way through clothing to direct skin. Or maybe that was what Balz was sensing as the *symphath* entered his emotional landscape.

"He's got . . ." Rehv seemed to search for words. "There's something wrong. His grid has a locking pattern across it."

Xcor descended the steps and stood right beside Balz. "Whatever it is, we are with you. We shall fix whatever is wrong."

"I'm dangerous," Balz said roughly. "I don't know how it happened—but I can't be here anymore."

"Then we find you a safe place." Xcor grabbed Balz's shoulders. "We do not desert our family."

"That's right," someone said.

"Fuck yeah."

"We gotchu."

The next thing Balz knew, all the bodies that had been at the mansion's grand entrance were down around him. And the warmth he felt was about so much more than that cold wind getting blocked.

As Xcor's heavy arm reached across his shoulders, Balz wiped off his face. Not that he was getting teary. He was a stone-cold bastion of tough guy over here. Stone. Cold.

"Tell us about the Book," Tohr said. "We need to know."

He coughed a little to compose himself. "I, ah, I went to do a little of my side hustle. Just my regular thing. I was walking through the place after I—" Did some hustle on the side with that wife. "Anyway, that's when I saw it. A book that commanded my attention in ways I couldn't—I still can't—understand. It's ancient and it smells bad, and it's like it's alive. I didn't know exactly what it was the first time I saw it, but when Syphon told me about what you were seeking, I had to go back and see if maybe . . . there's no question. It's the Book. I know it in my soul. And I tried to get it tonight, but it's protected by the brunette that Butch saw. The woman who is the new evil."

The fact that he didn't know whether his words were being heard as he intended them to was terrifying.

"Sahvage," Tohr pronounced. "We need Sahvage. Whatever meta-physical protection shit is going on, he'll handle it. And he's agreed to help."

Balz looked around at the faces that were so open, so trusting. For a thief and a liar to find this kind of love?

Well, in anyone other than a stone-cold tough guy, it would have brought a person to their knees.

"I need a cigarette," Balz muttered.

V's black-gloved hand pushed through with a hand-rolled. "Me, too," the Brother said.

As they lit up together, Balz stared at the front of the battened-down mansion and thought about the brunette. "Sahvage and I go alone. I don't want backup. If things are going to get bad, losing me won't matter."

"That is not true," Xcor interjected.

Syn, Balz's other cousin, and Zypher, his fellow bastard, spoke up as well on that one.

But all he could do was shake his head. "It is true. And what's pro-tecting it is . . . we can't take chances with that demon. Trust me." He met all the sets of eyes, one by one. "If Sahvage and I can't get the Book and bring it back, it's not get-able."

Xcor spoke up. "But how do we cure you?"

Rehv answered that before Balz could. "The Book. We use the Book to get him clean."

"That's what I'm thinking, too," Balz said on an exhale as he went back to looking at the mansion. "Or at least . . . that's what I hope."

CHAPTER FIFTY-TWO

Lying in the dark, holding Mae in his arms, Sahvage was about as calm as he was before a bareknuckle fight: He was knife-edged aware, eyes moving ceaselessly around the shadowed contours of the room, ears primed for any sound, senses reaching out. While beside him, his female—

No. She was not his.

This female, he amended, was safe. For now.

"Sahvage?"

"Yeah?" He hoped she wanted something to eat so he could do something. "You hungry? I can get you a little food?"

"I feel like I should apologize." She pushed herself up on his chest. "I feel like . . . I wish I could stop myself. But I can't. I'm hoping you can understand that, especially because you know what the loss feels like."

Without thinking, he brushed a strand of her hair back. Then touched her face. As her breath caught, he did not approve of where his mind went.

"Yeah, I know."

"I'm so grateful you're still here. Still with me."

"I'm not leaving until this is over. For better or for worse."

A ghost of a smile played over her face. "That's a human thing."

"What is?"

"For better or for worse. It's what they say when they're getting mated for life." She looked away. "Anyway, I'm grateful you're here."

"Loyalty is pretty much my only virtue." His voice grew wry. "And even so, I've managed to turn it into a sin."

They stared into each other's eyes. And then she said, "When I was trapped in that place . . . I was so angry. I felt totally cheated. I had tried to do so many things right over the course of my life, but there I was. I knew as soon as the brunette got back, she was going to kill me—and I was going to miss out on everything—which is pretty rich considering I live with a dead male and I work from home."

Sahvage thought of the wasteland of his life. "At least you know you have an end."

"The Fade again," she said with resignation. "You really need to leave that alone."

"So that advice is a one-way street with you, huh. You expect others to drop shit, but you don't have to."

"Yup." She sat up. "Kind of like you refusing to respect boundaries. No matter how many times you're told to lay off."

Abruptly, she glanced at the door like in her mind she was walking through it. And then she let her head fall back and started muttering curses toward the bedroom's ceiling.

"If you're going to yell at me," Sahvage remarked, "you might as well let me in on the lovefest. Seems only fair—and hey, I can always use pointers on how to properly use the word 'asshole.'"

She shot a look at him. "Actually, I'm yelling at myself."

"Why?"

"Because I can't believe you were one of the things I was angry at."

"Oh, come on." He laughed out loud. "That's not a news flash.

You've been pissed at me since you met me. Which is pretty rich considering you distracted me in that fight—"

"Do *not* bring up that whole cut thing again."

"Cut?" He sat up as well so they were on the same level. "You're calling that arterial bleed a *cut?* Just out of curiosity, what do you consider a wound. Total evisceration?"

"You lived!"

"I always live," he said roughly.

"Right, because you're such a hard-ass."

"Wasn't that what you were going to put on my name tag?"

"Actually, 'badass' was what I was thinking. And that was only because 'asshat' was already taken."

Sahvage started to smile. He couldn't help it. "I get under your skin, don't I."

"No." She crossed her arms over her chest and glared at him. "Not at all."

"Okay. I believe you." He put his palms out. "Honest. I'm just curious, though . . . what in particular were you so angry with me about? I mean, it can't be my charming personality."

As she turned to face him, there was a pause—and abruptly, the air in the room changed. And even though it was dim, he could tell her eyes had dropped to his mouth, and in spite of her injuries, her scent shifted. Deepened.

"G'on, tell me," Sahvage murmured. "You know how much you enjoy listing my shortcomings. There are so many of them in your book."

When she still didn't look away, even after he taunted her . . . that was when his blood started to thicken.

"Back when I was stuck in that place, I was angry . . ." Her voice broke. "I was angry that I was never going to know what it was like."

"What is 'it.'"

There was a long silence. Then she said, "Do you think we're going to survive this?"

Unlike the "it," he did not want her to struggle to define the "this." There was no reason for her to say out loud that they were facing that brunette, searching for a Book that was a black-magic catalogue, and trying to raise the dead.

Yeah, 'cuz what could *possibly* go wrong with all that shit.

"I can promise," he said, "that I will do everything in my power to get you out alive."

Like they were in a dogfight.

Like they weren't?

"Will I ever find the Book?"

"I don't know." He shook his head. "But if that summoning spell worked to bring me to you . . . I'm going to bet it's going to work to bring the Book in. It's just taking some time to arrange the handoffs."

And when it did land in her lap, he was going to save her life by—

"I was angry because I felt cheated," she whispered. "If I didn't . . ."

Now he was the one staring at her mouth. And fucking hell, there were so many reasons not to go down the road that was appearing before them, yet again. But . . .

"Say it," he commanded.

"If I didn't know what you were like."

On a surge of sexual heat, Sahvage reached out and touched her face again, letting his fingertips drift along her jaw and then travel down to the flickering pulse at the side of her throat.

"You mean, as a dinner companion?" he said. "Or were you thinking of something more . . . engaging? Like chess."

Mae sputtered a laugh. "Seriously."

"Parcheesi?" He tilted forward and pressed a kiss to her cheek. "I already know Monopoly puts you to sleep."

Mae leaned into him, and he felt her hand on his shoulder—but not to push him away. She held on to him.

"I want just want to be with you." As he went to say something, she put her finger on his lips to silence him. "I know it doesn't change anything. I know you're going to leave when this is all over. But I keep thinking . . . here I am, determined to bring my brother back—but what kind of life am I leading? All I do is work and worry. And the two people who made me swear to never have sex before I was mated have been gone for how many years? Three? What exactly am I waiting for? When is the next dog cage coming for me—and what will I be angry about not having done then?"

"I need you to know something," he said in a rough voice.

Mae dropped her arm sharply. And he put it right back where it was.

"If I could be different, I would be—for you," he told her. "And in the future, if you ever doubt how important you are, just think of me. I promise that I'll be somewhere on the planet . . . thinking about how special you are, and wishing things were different."

"You have that all backward." She cupped her hand over his own. "You're going to forget me and I'm going to be the one missing you."

As he went to speak, she shook her head. "It's okay. I am forgettable."

"Don't say that—"

"I am one of a thousand civilian females, out of her transition, but not in the decline of old age, living in a simple house, working a regular job. I worry about which day is trash day, and whether I've recycled enough. I get tangled in my own head in front of the vegetables at Hannaford when I can't figure out what to eat. My car is ten years— well, was ten years old. I snore on my back, have bad dreams if I'm overtired, and miss the feel of the sun on my face, even though it's been decades since I could go out at noontime." She laughed in a cold rush. "Even the demon said I'm not bad-looking, but hardly worth crossing the street for—"

Sahvage kissed her. Because he wanted to. Because he hated what she was saying about herself. Because she didn't get it.

Even if all those supposedly average vital statistics were true, she was still unforgettable.

To him.

When it came to being a legend, all it took was one person to recognize that you were epic. That was it.

+ + +

As Sahvage's mouth moved over Mae's with gentle demand, she knew she'd annoyed him with her reality check—except she was right about all it.

No reason to argue, though. Not while he was . . .

As his tongue licked into her, she put her arms around his shoulders, ready for so much more. Yet he eased back, their mouths parting with a soft sound.

"Mae . . ."

She rolled her eyes. "Oh, please. Spare me the I-know-best, especially when it comes to me losing my v—"

"I'll make it good for you," he whispered. "I promise. That's all."

When he kissed her again, the door to her bedroom shut of its own volition, willed by him, not her. And as her eyes adjusted, she felt like she could feel the heat in his gaze, even though she couldn't really see him. Then again, everything felt hot.

And she'd thought she'd missed the sun? Sahvage had brought it to her, not by hanging it over her head, but by putting it into her veins.

Mae was the one who lay back, and he came with her, keeping their lips together. Except as all he did was keep kissing her, she once again became impatient. So she took one of his hands and moved it onto her breast—

With a groan, she arched up to him, and he did exactly what she was hoping he would. He caressed her through her clothes, skating over her rib cage, going down to her hip, returning to where she was so sensitive. He made that route over and over again, soothing her, stroking her.

Just as she was wondering if she was going to have to take her own clothes off, he slipped his hand under her fleece, under her turtleneck. As he made contact with her skin, she groaned again. His hand was so broad, so warm, so calloused. A very male hand.

The only male hand to touch her like this.

Slowly, he moved upward, and when he got to her bra, he stopped. His thumb went back and forth a couple of times . . . and then he was under the sensible cotton cup, pushing it up.

"Sahvage," she gasped.

Her skin was hypersensitive, and he knew where to rub, what to stroke, when to pinch. Her nipples strained, the hard tips tingling for more of what he was giving her, and her whole body went boneless.

"Please . . ."

"Please what," he said into her mouth. "What do you want?"

"More."

And that was how she became half naked. With a quick shift and an up-and-over, her top layers were off—

He was the one who groaned now. "You're so beautiful."

Mae looked down at herself. Her bra was cockeyed, one cup down, the other popped over, causing that breast to puff out, the nipple so very prominent.

The front fastening popped under his fingertips, and then the con- striction was completely gone. The pink tips of her breasts were so tight, so high, and before she could get embarrassed about staring at herself, Sahvage was kissing her neck. Her collarbone. Her sternum.

Spearing her hands into his hair, she found her hips rolling, her legs sawing, her sex hungry for him.

When he captured her with his mouth, sucking, licking, kissing, he shifted so that he was lying in between her legs. Perfect. She used his body to work herself on, the pressure of him, the weight, the size, making her pant as she rubbed her core against his contours.

It was so perfect.

And if the actual moment they were joined was anything like this?

No wonder people did crazy stuff for good sex—

Abruptly, he lifted his head and cursed. "You're killing me, Mae—"

"How? What am I doing wrong—"

"You're doing everything too right."

"Don't stop."

So he didn't.

And when he lifted himself up off her naked breasts, and his hands went to her waistband, she rushed to help him, even though he knew what he was doing. The tugging and pulling as he undid the button on her jeans and unzipped the zipper moved things in a really good direction, and then he was pulling the legs down, peeling them off her thighs.

He took her panties with them as he went.

Mae had no shyness. No fear. No awkwardness. All she knew was the scent of him. And then the delicious weight of his body as it returned to her. And finally a burning anticipation that made her feel like she was on fire.

"I want to touch you, too," Mae said as he went to kiss her again.

Talk about an instant response.

Sahvage yanked his shirt off so fast, there was a tearing sound, like something had ripped—and he didn't stop to check and see what it was. He tossed the thing aside as if it were utterly disposable and went right back to kissing her mouth, kissing her throat, kissing her breasts.

"I hurt—"

The instant the word came out of her mouth, he jerked up. "Oh, God, I'm sorry—"

"No, no . . ." She was mumbling. "Not like that."

He sagged with relief. Then his voice got really, really low. "Where does it hurt, Mae."

She purred and rubbed herself against him. "Here . . ."

"Here, where?" He kissed her shoulder. "No? How about here?" He kissed her rib cage. "No . . . hmm . . . how about here."

He kissed her belly button. Then ran his tongue around it.

Mae's knees fell open. Even though where he was heading was shocking, she was so desperate for something, anything, to ease the heat and the straining and the—

"Still not the right place?"

Mae's eyes had adjusted to the darkness so as she lifted her head, she looked down her body to find Sahvage staring up at her, his enormous shoulders blocking the square of light around the door, his hulking body covering her.

Like she was his prey.

And that was fine with her. She was more than ready to be eaten.

CHAPTER FIFTY-THREE

Mae might have not had sex before, but Sahvage was the one who was unprepared for what was happening. He'd never expected to be so affected by . . . her skin, her scents, her innocent eroticism as she rubbed herself against any part of him that came into contact with her gloriously bare, beautiful aroused sex.

He hadn't meant to take things in this direction.

But here they were—with him about to put his mouth on—

"Sahvage," she moaned.

Throwing her head back into the pillows, Mae arched again and then undulated, her breasts peaking, those tight little nipples the kind of thing he couldn't not touch.

Reaching up, he tweaked one and then rolled the other back and forth between his thumb and forefinger, rolling . . . rolling . . . rolling.

And then he dropped his head and brushed her lower abdomen with his lips. "Here? Mae . . . does it hurt here?"

In a rough voice, she said, "Lower."

Fuck, he thought as he went over to her hip. Whispering his mouth on the graceful ridge of her pelvis—then he slid his lower body completely off the end of the bed. As his knees hit the carpet, he pulled her down to him by the backs of her knees, her thighs wide open, her sex glistening in the low light.

Sahvage licked his lips in anticipation. "I need to taste you," he heard himself say.

As she moaned his name, he started on the outside of one of her legs, just in case she had second thoughts.

She did not. She said his name again . . . in that rough, panting voice that nearly made him come.

Moving over, kissing his way across the top of her thigh to the very inside of it, following the crease where it met her body, where it connected to her—

He meant to stay on that soft skin, on the precipice of her beautiful sex, but her pelvis shifted without warning—

And suddenly his lips were on hers, and all his planning to be gentle, go slow, take it easy, went right out the fucking window. He sucked her in—and the instant her taste registered, his brain completely shorted out.

As Mae yelled his name and grabbed his hair hard, he unhinged completely. Locking his palms on the backs of her thighs, he widened her even farther as he pleasured her with his mouth and his tongue—lapping and sucking at her until he knew she was getting close.

With a sudden surge, Mae moved herself against his face and—

Just as he'd intended, she called out and went rigid, except for her sawing breath. And then she jerked over and over again, her body releasing as he licked at her to keep her going . . . while all he wanted was to be inside of her, feeling her contractions until he orgasmed, too.

Except he wasn't going to do that.

She deserved so much better than him for her first time, and he was not going to cheat her out of the joy and communion that would come when she gave herself out of love instead of desperation. He just couldn't do that to her.

The good news? There were a lot of other things they *could* do together.

When Mae finally went limp, her arms flopping on the duvet, her head doing the same, she was breathing hard, her breasts pumping up and down, her ribs expanding and contracting. Sahvage smiled and started planning their next position. Like her on all fours in front of him, his hand jerking himself off all over her sex so he could lick her clean—

Off in the distance, out in the sitting room, a phone started ringing.

But like he was leaving her, under any circumstances?

"Sahvage?" she asked on a mumble.

"You're incredible," he murmured as he stroked her thighs.

"What . . . what are you going to do now? What . . . what about you?"

Straightening on his knees, he went for his waistband. As he undid his combats, he realized his cock was so hard, so hungry, that he had to grit his teeth and exercise some self-control—or risk coming all over her.

Which he was about to do. He just wanted to be naked when he did it—and she was so relaxed, he decided he wasn't going to make her get on her knees. He liked this view just fine, her breasts taut and straining, her belly so smooth, her sex . . .

"You okay?" he asked her. Like the penetration that was happening in his mind was actually going on right now.

"I'm . . . oh, God, yes . . ." she said as she saw his erection.

With hands that were suddenly trembling, he did away with his pants, all but Magic Mike'ing them by ripping them off his lower body.

And what do you know, her mattress happened to be at the perfect height for him: His erection was right at the level of her core. But he needed to be sure.

"You all right?"

"Oh, God, yes . . . and I want more."

"You do?" He didn't mean to stroke himself. But he did. "Fuck, Mae . . ."

Her hands were restless, grabbing at the duvet, fisting it up . . . one of them slipping free and bumping into her hip.

Sahvage reached out and took her hand. Moving it between her legs, she gasped as he caressed her with her own fingers while he worked his cock.

As she came close to climaxing again, he said, "Mae—Mae, look up at me."

In the dimness, he caught her gleaming eyes as she followed his command. And then he lifted what she'd been rubbing herself with to his mouth. Sucking her fingers in, he was oh, so satisfied as she cried out again, his name echoing around her bedroom.

Lapping up her essence, he smiled in the darkness . . . as he realized she already was the best lover he'd ever had.

✦   ✦   ✦

When Mae's eyes squeezed shut, she couldn't make them stay open. But good God, she wanted to keep seeing everything. She wanted to watch all of it—yet there was a surprising eroticism to the darkness. All she knew was Sahvage's tongue, hot and slick, licking at her fingers . . . then his hot and slick mouth sucking her thumb in.

The smacking noises made her insane.

And a new release rolled through her.

When it finally drifted off, she opened her eyes. Her lover was a hulking shape above her and his scent was flooding her nose and he was—

He lowered her hand to the duvet. And just as she was about to ask him—what had she been going to ask?—she felt something on her sex.

It was not his fingers. It was not his mouth.

It was blunt. And very smooth. And very hot.

Mae arched again, and if there had been a way to get her thighs even farther apart, she would have done it.

Sahvage stroked her with himself, teasing the opening to her sex, then focusing on the top of her cleft. As another orgasm sprang into her core, into her blood, she knew now was the time . . . now was when it was going to happen . . .

His broad palm locked on her hip, holding her steady. As Mae was suspended on the brink, she heard hoarse words leaving her mouth and had no idea what she was saying. But he was rubbing her faster and faster, and the fact that it was his sex on her sex, the two of them so close to being joined, meant everything was magnified.

Just as she began to come again, she heard a clicking. A fast clicking. One of his arms was going back and forth—and then he was bracing himself on the mattress with the opposite palm, looming over her, about to—

The first of the hot jets lashed across her sex and the heat of them made her explode once again. As she came for—how many times had it been?—whatever, as she came again, he ejaculated all over her, covering her core, her inner thighs, her lower abdomen.

In the darkness, she could hear him breathing hard, a curse escaping what she knew were gritted teeth.

It was a while before the letdown came.

As hot as this was, as right as it felt, as careful with her as he had been . . . she came to realize that he was not going to take it any further than this.

He was not going to have her.

Not really.

Not . . . ever.

CHAPTER FIFTY-FOUR

At six p.m. the following evening, Erika parked her unmarked off to the side of the Commodore's main entrance. Putting her laminated CPD parking permit on the dash, she got out with her laptop and her bag.

Inside the lobby, there was a security guard station and a concierge desk. Both were empty, and she could hear some kind of argument around the corner, two men going back and forth about some FedEx package that had been misplaced.

Bypassing the whole check-in thing, she took the center of three elevators, and as she rode up, she stared at herself in the mirrored panels lining the inside of the car. Wow. She looked like she was a hundred and eight, the bags under her eyes dark, her skin sallow, the fact that she'd pulled her red-and-brown hair back and clipped it at the nape of her neck making every minor crease in her face like something that had been carved into her skin. And jeez, her navy blue blazer was also really wrinkly.

Maybe it was just the overhead lighting.

"Yeah, right," she muttered.

Somewhere along the line, she'd read that the manufacturers of elevators had done a study and found that if people could look at their reflection as they went up and down, they felt like they were stuck inside the cars for less time.

Well, she had to give that one a big nope.

Sick of her reflection, she looked to the seam in the doors, but because this was a fancy building, every square inch except the goddamn floor was covered with tinted reflective stuff.

"Great."

Ding!

The elevator bumped to a stop, and the double doors opened on the top floor of the building. Stepping out, she left'd and right'd it, and then went down to the triplex of Mr. and Mrs. Herbert C. Cambourg.

Which was what the engraved brass plate over the doorbell read.

'Cuz why would you put your wife's first name on her home, too.

Then again, everything was hers now, wasn't it.

Erika rang the bell and took a step back so that the peephole could do its job—

As the door opened, she braced for a maid in a gray-and-white uniform with sensible shoes and a bun. But no, the lady of the house was doing the duty.

"Detective," Mrs. Cambourg said. "Come in."

No silk robe and nightgown this time. Black leggings, black turtleneck, the brown hair long and loose and shinning. This was a woman who never looked bad, no matter the lighting. And Jesus, she was tall.

But her eyes were as bloodshot as Erika's were.

"Thanks." Erika nodded and walked forward. "I know it's late. I appreciate you seeing me."

The triplex's top floor had a foyer that was big as Erika's entire apartment building, or at least it felt like that. And there was so much marble, the browns, creams, and black separated by brass—or, shit, maybe it was even gold—curlicues.

"Would you like to come down to the sitting room?"

As Mrs. Cambourg waited for an answer, it was like she was used to holding up for the opinions of others to frame her own choices. Or maybe she was completely fried, and who could blame her.

"Sure. That'd be great."

"It's this way."

As of the night before, Mrs. Cambourg had sealed off this top floor and stayed in the panic-apartment within the condo. She'd promised not to go to the collection rooms downstairs. Then again, why would she want to?

"Here." Mrs. Cambourg indicated a silk sofa. "And can I get you anything?"

"Can," not "may." Plus no maid. This was new money—and a woman who wasn't used to it at all. Not that Erika judged. She didn't come from anything and it had never bothered her or been the kind of thing that had gotten in her way.

"No, I'm fine, thanks." They both sat down together. "How you holding up?"

As Mrs. Cambourg gathered her thoughts, Erika glanced around. Unlike the gallery below—or the collection rooms, for that matter—up here, there was a lot of color. Well, assuming gold was a color. Even the sofa was gold and black. It was like the eighties had stalked through the previous three decades and decided to camp out in the present.

Through the archway, Erika noted that even the kitchen appliances were gold.

Toilets, too? Probably.

"I didn't sleep at all."

"I'll bet. Anyone bother you?"

"Oh, no. I put the panic walls in place. They seal up the stairwell and everything, including the windows up here. Even if someone would have wanted to get in, they wouldn't have been able to . . . you, know get at me. I mean. Yes."

Erika cleared her throat. "So I have some news. I believe we've found your husband's watches."

Mrs. Cambourg sat forward. "You did?"

Erika nodded. "The insurance pictures you emailed us were really helpful, and we happened to be at another scene last night where we think they may have been fenced. May I show you some images for identification?"

"Yes. Please."

Firing up her laptop, Erika put the screen between them. "Do you recognize any of these—here, use the cursor. Yup. That's it."

Mrs. Cambourg's eyes teared up as she went through the pictures. "Yes. These are his—and yes, that's the storage case he kept them in. The one that was in our safe."

Absently, Erika wondered whether that diamond necklace was still on under that turtleneck. She was willing to bet it was. Although why that was relevant to anything, she hadn't a clue.

"And nothing else is missing, correct?" she asked.

"No, nothing else was taken."

Erika nodded. "While we were at the other scene, we found some security cameras. Their footage shows your husband's watches being delivered by a man, and I'd like to see if you recognize him? May I play you a clip?"

Mrs. Cambourg dragged a hand through her silken hair. "Of course."

"Here." Erika pulled the laptop to herself and loaded the next file. "Look at this."

As she hit play and angled things back to the other woman, she felt her lungs tighten up. And then, even though she'd watched the footage a dozen times, and had been the one to crop the file, she got lost once again . . . as the man in black walked on-screen.

He was tall, and given his muscular contours, he looked like he worked out often and intensely—and he sure as hell moved like he was in total control of his body. Up top over those big shoulders, his hair was dark and cut short, but it was his affect that really got her attention. There was such a cold, calculating calmness to his stunningly attractive face. Even as he stopped and looked at the corpse with its brains blown out on the wall behind the couch.

It was like he'd seen a lot of dead bodies.

But of course, the image of the deceased had been redacted from this cut. Mrs. Cambourg had had enough shock. Speaking of which—

Erika frowned at her expression. "Do you know who that is?"

It was a while before the other woman answered. And when she did, it was in a soft, confused voice.

"That's the man in my dream." She pointed at the screen. "That's the man I dreamed of."

◆   ◆   ◆

"Blue shirt . . . red shirt."

Nate held one in front of himself. Then the other. Both were flannel. Both had a black-based plaid. Both—

No, the red. The red was definitely better.

Tossing the blue aside on his bathroom counter, he leaned over the sink to make sure where he'd nicked himself shaving was healed. Looked good. He took the piece of toilet paper off the blood spot.

Well . . . shit. The red shirt was a good idea until he tucked it into his blue jeans. Then he looked like the Brawny paper towel man.

"Damn it." He checked his phone. "New shirt."

As he removed the offending flannel, he took a minute to study his chest. His arms. His shoulders. They were okay—by a human standard. Against someone like his father? He was the skinny kid at the beach who got sand kicked in his face.

If Elyn really needed me, could I make sure she was safe? he asked his reflection.

"Fuck."

And he wished he had some cologne.

Out in his bedroom, he went over and pulled open the closet door. Sweatshirts. More flannels. Polos that would have worked if it were May. June. July.

Unless he was Shuli, of course. And he wasn't on so many levels.

In the end, he went with a plain white Hanes t-shirt that was brand-new and a let's-be-casual Mark Rober sweatshirt. Just as he was pulling the latter over his head, there was a knock on the door.

"Yeah?" he said.

Things opened as he was back at the mirror in the bathroom, and his father walked in, dressed for war. All of Murhder's weapons were on his body, his black daggers strapped, handles down, on his chest, a holster of guns on his hips, a knife on one thigh. His red-and-black hair was hidden under a skullcap, and was that . . . yes, a Kevlar vest.

Nate swallowed. "What's happening. What's wrong?"

"I'm leaving for the night." There was a pause. "Look, I know things have been . . . weird between us. And I just didn't want to go before I told you that I love you. Nate, I couldn't love you more than if you were from my own blood. You're a good kid, and you're going to be a great male, and—"

"Dad?" Nate said in a small voice. "What's going on. Why are you wearing that vest?"

"It's just another night in the field."

No, it wasn't, but it was clear he was going to get no information on the why's.

As he grappled with a sudden terror, Murhder kept talking. "I don't even know what exactly went wrong for you here. I mean, you were happy, for a time. I'm not sure what changed, but whatever it is, we'll figure it out. There are all kinds of resources for you, and if it really comes down to it . . . we don't want you to leave, but we just—well, I said it before. We love you as our son, no qualifiers. And I couldn't leave without telling you that. Some nights, you just better say your piece because you don't know how things are going to go."

Nate's brain bubbled with so many kinds of super-scaries, he literally lost his voice.

And in the silence, after a moment, Murhder nodded and turned away.

"Wait, Dad."

Nate launched himself out of his bathroom and grabbed on to the Brother just as Murhder pivoted back around. "I love you, too, Dad. I love you."

Murhder made a choked sound, and then those huge arms were holding Nate. "I'm glad, son. That makes . . . it makes all the difference for me."

Nate stepped back. "Are you going to die tonight?"

Murhder shook his head. "Not if I have anything to say about it. And no, I can't talk about it. But you and your mom are safe here—"

"WhataboutLuchasHouse?" Nate asked in a rush.

"The—oh, yeah, no, you should be fine out there. But you know, this does make me think. Do you want to have some training—"

"Yes." He thought of Elyn. "I want to learn how to fight."

Murhder got very, very still.

"What?" Nate said. "Do you not think . . . don't you think I can?"

"I think you'll be good at it. I just didn't want this life for you, son. I'm not going to stop you, though. I'll talk to the brothers and set something up."

"Okay. Thank you. Is Mom home tonight?"

"She'll be at the training center. Are you—"

"I'm going to Luchas House."

"You be careful out there. Call me if you need me. No matter what's going down, I will always answer, I will always come find you."

After a long moment, Murhder nodded and left the bedroom, heading for the carpeted stairs that led up to the kitchen.

Some nights, you just better say your piece.

"I met someone," Nate blurted.

As he heard his own voice, he was surprised he'd spoken up. But it was something he wanted his father to know, especially if he didn't get the chance to say it to the male again.

His dad slowly turned around, and the expression on his face would have been funny. On another night. About another thing.

He looked like somebody had just told him that the Tooth Fairy was real: Wonder.

"You have?" Murhder said.

"Yeah, and I think I really like her, Dad."

CHAPTER FIFTY-FIVE

N o, cereal's fine. Really."

As Mae sat at the table in her kitchen, her bowl filled with store-brand Cheerios, the skim milk somehow passing the nose test even though it was one day after its expiration date, she was trying to hold it together. And no, not because she was about to go into a crying jag or something.

She was choking on questions she had no business asking. Mainly, like, why had Sahvage drawn that line? Two consenting adults and all that.

Except there was only one consenting adult, evidently.

As Sahvage sat down across from her with some toast and a cup of coffee, she tried to smile in a casual, no-problems-over-here kind of way. The fact that she hadn't had any eggs or bacon to offer him, and that it had been a miracle there had been enough coffee for them both to have some, was a commentary on how badly the last few weeks had been going for her.

And everything they hadn't done in bed was just the shit cherry on top of it all.

While they ate, they didn't say much . . . so all there was in the house, in the whole world, it seemed, was his crunching through the toast and her spoon hitting the side of her bowl. But the thing was, she didn't trust herself to broach the elephant in the room.

Yeah, that wasn't going to go well. She was frustrated and angry about a lot of things, and he was going to get double-barreled with stuff that didn't have anything to do with their horizontal issues—

She closed her eyes.

"You okay?"

Keeping a curse to herself, she nodded. "Oh, yes. I'm all right."

He pushed his crumb'd plate away. "So I'm going to go get some ice."

Mae looked up. "What?"

"For your brother. I need you to stay here. It's the safest thing—and I have a car I can use." He got up, his chair scraping back on the floor. "It shouldn't take me that long."

"Ah, there's a gas station not all that far from here." Except she felt a territorial urge to do the ice buying. That was her job. "But I could always just—"

"Get into another accident?" he said as he took his dishes to the sink. "Like last night? We all know how well that went."

Mae frowned. "Excuse me, as if I planned that."

Sahvage braced his palms on the counter and hung his head. As his jaw made circles, she was disappointed he was struggling to control his temper. She wanted an argument.

And that made her a bitch, didn't it.

"Is this about the Book again?" she demanded. "Because we're done disagreeing on that subject."

"You're right about that." He shook his head. "I'm not trying to talk you out of anything anymore. I never should have gone there in the first place."

"Thank you." Mae exhaled in relief. "And I'm sorry for getting so defensive. I'm glad you finally see where I'm coming from."

Sahvage nodded and then stared off into the narrow distance between him and the shuttered window in front of his face. It was impossible not to study those hard features and powerful body without thinking about what they'd done in the dark. But there was nothing sexual at all about him at the moment. He was somewhere else in his head, far away even though she could reach out and touch him.

"I won't be gone long," he said eventually. "I mean, I'll have to drive my car across town, but yeah, it shouldn't take a lot of time."

"It's okay. Like I have any kind of schedule."

Actually, she had work to do so she could keep this roof over her head. Assuming she made it through this, she was going to need to live somewhere.

"And I have to call Tallah," she heard herself say.

After a moment, Sahvage turned his head and looked at her. Something about the way he was so self-contained made her feel like—

"Don't say it," she whispered, a dull, lonely ache setting up shop in her heart. "Don't say goodbye. I'd rather just . . . have you not come through the door again than have to go through the words."

Besides, that way, she could be ever on the verge of seeing him again. A goodbye was a closed door. Nothing was . . . nothing.

"I don't want closure," she said in a weary voice. "I'm really fucking tired of closure."

"I'm not leaving you."

Yeah, sure, she thought. "I wouldn't blame you if you did." Mae smiled a little, but couldn't keep up the farce. "I would leave me if could."

"I told you, I'll be back soon. This won't take me long."

That was how he left things.

And he didn't look back as he walked out into the garage.

✦   ✦   ✦

Sahvage was way in his head as the door bumped shut behind him, but he had enough presence of mind to wait for Mae to walk over and lock the dead bolt. When she didn't, he opened things back up, intending to remind her to come across and flip the copper mechanism.

Down the short hallway, she was still at the kitchen table and had put her head in her hands. She wasn't crying; she just looked as if she couldn't hold herself up and needed her elbows to keep her face out of her cereal bowl.

It took everything in him not to go back in there, and take her into his arms, and tell her everything was going to be okay. But he didn't like making promises he couldn't keep.

So instead, he reclosed the door and reminded himself that the thing they were really worried about getting into the house was already locked out. Mae was safe.

For a moment, before he left, he stared at the spot her car had been parked in. Now there were only oil stains and marks where the tires had traveled up and back so many times, and he imagined her parents parking here in the past, too. Pictured how many times the family, including her brother, had gone in and out of the door he had just used to leave her.

He truly understood where she was about Rhoger. He'd been there with Rahvyn. And fuck, if he believed in miracles? In fate? In the universe being a right and just place? He might trust that he and his first cousin could be still reunited and if Mae brought her dead back, there would be no regrets.

But he didn't buy into that existential justice shit anymore.

And damn it, Mae was going to thank him for what he was about to do. Maybe not right away, but later . . . when nature was not interfered with and she was not in so much pain. Then, she would know he'd done the right thing.

Calming himself, he dematerialized out through the open shutter. But he didn't go back to his place to get his shitbox ride.

He went downtown.

As he'd only been in Caldwell a month, he didn't know streets' names or anything. The good news was that the Commodore was the only twenty-plus-floor residential building around, and given that it had vertical light-up letters on its flank that spelled out "C-O-M-M-O-D-O-R-E"?

It didn't take a genius to locate its roof.

And just like they'd planned, there was a lone figure waiting for him by the HVAC blowers.

As Sahvage re-formed in front of the guy, he kept his hands by his guns, but he didn't palm up. No reason not to be civil, and besides, he'd gotten a sense of the Bastard over the daylight hours. While Mae had slept, he'd gone upstairs to find out who had been blowing up his phone.

And what do you know. The call he'd been waiting for.

"So you're Sahvage, the male of the hour." The fighter extended his dagger hand. "Balthazar."

Sahvage nodded and shook what was offered. "You ready to do this?"

"Like I said on the phone, we should move fast."

Glancing around, Sahvage had the sense that the building was surrounded. *Shadows?* he wondered. No . . . he could catch the scents, even though they were distant and distilled by the cold wind, and he recognized a lot of them.

"Your backups are in position," he said. "I know we aren't alone."

"Just as we agreed, they're on the perimeter and staying put unless things get fucked. I don't want . . . well, like I told you, last night she came as soon as I got close to the Book."

"Just point me in the right direction, I'll take it from there."

The male narrowed his eyes. "That wasn't our agreement."

"Even if it keeps you from getting killed?"

"She wants the Book, not us. So if I wake up dead, it's going to be because I'm collateral damage. The same is true for you. We do this as we agreed or not at all."

Sahvage met the fighter straight in the eye. "Roger that."

As Balthazar turned away, Sahvage followed the male over to the entry to the stairwell that ran up the middle of the building. Inside, they descended the concrete steps at a jog, and when, a couple landings down, Balthazar paused at a fire door and seemed to be scenting the seam around the doorjamb, Sahvage realized something.

"You didn't make a sound," he said softly.

The Bastard glanced over his shoulder. "Huh?"

"As we went along. You didn't make any noise."

"I'm a thief." The guy rolled his eyes and punched the handle to open things up. "You think I should have a marching band plugged into my ass?"

"Now there's a Christmas card."

Out in a corridor that smelled like rich people, and had a sleek, contemporary vibe, they strode forth quickly, and Sahvage tried to take a page out of Mr. Shhh's book. But how did the fucker manage to not even have his equipment creak?

It was obvious where they were going.

The police tape gave it away.

As they came up to the door, Balthazar looked back. "Open foyer on the other side. I'm praying there's no police equipment in the way. I'll disarm the alarm and take us through the collection rooms."

"I'm right behind you."

Balthazar went in first, and Sahvage was a nanosecond behind him. No police equipment, just an open foyer as described, like the place was a museum.

"This way," the Bastard whispered. "It's down here."

The rooms were small and windowless, and contained collections of strange things. Surgical instruments. Bat skeletons? And then—

Sahvage's breath exploded out of his lungs as they entered a space filled with book displays—and his boots froze where they were. There, across the intricate floor, past a ruined section of shelving and a mess on the hardwood . . . was a clear box.

That housed an object Sahvage hadn't seen for two hundred years.

As he blinked, he was back in Zxysis's master quarters, the blood of his innocent cousin spilled on the sheeting of the bedding platform, the window open, the herbs and potions and candle wax over on the trestle table.

He had a feeling that the Bastard was talking to him.

But once again, the male wasn't making any sound at all.

Sahvage approached the display on numb legs, and he could have sworn, as he came to a halt before the ancient volume, that the pages of the open tome ruffled as if in greeting. And he wasn't the only one trans-fixed. Balthazar was next to him and staring at the Book with the same kind of captivation.

In fact, so enthralled were he and the other fighter . . . that they failed to note the blinking red light up at the motion detector on the ceiling.

CHAPTER FIFTY-SIX

I t's the alarm."

As Mrs. Cambourg stood up from the sofa with her phone in her hand, Erika was already on it, not just going vertical, but putting her hand on her holstered service weapon.

"Someone's on the second floor." The woman turned her cell's screen around. "What do I—"

"It's probably just one of the crime scene techs."

"Oh. Okay."

Or at least that was what Erika was hoping, and if it was? She was going to dress down whoever hadn't checked in properly.

"I want you to lock yourself in and stay up here," she said. "I'm going to go down and check."

"But is it safe?" the woman asked as she cradled the phone to her chest.

"I'll be right back. I'm sure there's a perfectly reasonable explanation."

"Okay." Mrs. Cambourg pointed to an archway. "You want to go through that corridor and take the stairwell down a level. Should I be calling someone?"

"I'll handle it. Don't worry. Just stay up here."

As Erika strode off down the hall, there was a series of soft shifting sounds in her wake. When she glanced back, the archway area was being closed off with a matte gold panel.

Good. That meant she didn't have to worry about anyone else.

Besides, it probably was just an investigator who had failed to check in properly.

The staircase curved around, modern art glowing on the walls. There was one painting she particularly liked, but it wasn't as if she was going to waste time checking out the chromatics of the damn thing.

Like she knew anything about art anyway.

But she sure as shit knew how to protect herself.

When she came to the bottom of the stairs, at the triplex's second floor, she unholstered her service weapon, but kept it at her side. The last thing anyone needed was her blowing a colleague out of the water. At the same time, shit was getting weird in Caldwell, so she wasn't taking chances with her own life.

All of the bodies that she'd seen with missing hearts were what was on her mind as she rounded a corner and saw, through a couple of rooms, a pair of men standing over the Lucite display box in the book room. They were . . . enormous. Dressed in black. Looking like they were capable of handling themselves in any situation.

So yeah, definitely not investigators.

They turned around at the same time.

Erika's training dictated that she was supposed to make both of them; take a mental snapshot of their features that she could use later for ID purposes. And she also needed to put in motion the backup protocol.

Instead, she stared at the one on the left. He was . . . the man from the footage from the trailer, the thief who had brought the watches there . . . the one who Mrs. Cambourg believed she had dreamed about. And God, he was still impossibly beautiful, if you could use that word on anything so masculine: His face was all perfect angles and jawline, and his eyes, as they narrowed and swept her up and down, were both cunning and . . .

"I'm almost not surprised you're here," she heard herself say. "You seem to spend a lot of time in this place."

As she spoke, he tilted his head—in a way that reminded her of a German shepherd, a predator who was curious about how fast his prey might be able to run.

"Detective Saunders, CPD." Erika pointed her gun at him and took her cuffs out. "I'm going to ask you both to put your hands on your heads and turn around. You're under arrest for trespassing—but something tells me the charges are not going to stop there."

Neither of them moved. And that was when she realized she recognized the other one as well.

The fight club, she thought with a surge of adrenaline. He was the one from the footage with Ralph DeMellio.

Holy shit, talk about your BOGOs.

Before she could repeat her commands, the one on the left, the one she really needed to stare at in a solely professional way, said softly, "I'll take care of this."

Erika deepened her voice. "Put your hands on your heads and—"

◆   ◆   ◆

As Balz went into the human woman's mind and froze her where she stood, he actually wanted her to keep talking. Somehow, she managed to turn simple words into a symphony in his ears, and that wasn't all she did.

Her scent speared into his nose and went directly into his blood.

Physically, she was not all that tall. Five six, maybe five seven. And she had a practical vibe to everything about her, from her flat shoes to the tight ponytail at the base of her neck, from her lack of makeup to her level, hard eyes. And talk about professional clothes. The shield on her dark blue blazer flashed with every breath she took, and her loose slacks gave him no clue as to what her body looked like.

But like that mattered?

It was . . . all of her . . . that got to him.

And that wasn't the half of it.

As he penetrated her mind so he could shut the present down and patch over her memories, flashes of . . . unspeakable past violence and tragedy popped up. Like even though the images, sights, and sounds were part of her long-term storage, they were always just under the surface for her.

She had faced things that no woman, no man, should ever have to survive.

And yet she was totally unafraid as she stood up to him and Sahvage, two vampires who were heavily armed and outweighed her by four hundred pounds. Then again, considering what she had already lived through? There was going to be little that rattled her.

"What the fuck's going on here?"

As Sahvage's impatience cut through the silence, Balz snapped back into action. "I got this. I got her."

"Do you? 'Cuz from over here, it looks like she got you."

In spite of the high stakes, Balz needed one more moment—and then he stripped the woman of any recollection of coming and finding them here. After that, he inserted the thought that it was just an alarm malfunction.

Alarms malfunctioned all the time.

Nothing wrong, nothing out of place.

As she pivoted around to leave and put her weapon and those hand-cuffs away, it was clear that she was comfortable with guns and confident in her ability to use them properly—and what do you know, Balz got hard in his boxer shorts.

He had to see her again.

Somehow—

A bumping sound brought his head around.

Sahvage had removed the display case's top and was straightening back up, his hands outstretched. As he moved in for the Book, his eyes were locked with total absorption, his body tensed, his—

"Oh, no you don't," Balz gritted as he lunged forward as well.

The two of them grabbed hold of the Book at exactly the same time. And as that spoiled-meat stench roiled up in the air, they both started pulling—and Balz felt like he was in a tug-o'-war for his very life. Sure, Sahvage had fronted like he was all go-team, but right now, nothing about the fucker suggested he was on board with the original plan.

He was going to take the fucking thing.

Bearing his fangs, Balz snarled, "You fucking douche."

"This is evil. This needs to be destroyed!"

"What are you—"

"You don't want this!"

"I need it to save my life!"

Somehow, in spite of the fact that both of them were leaning back, all their weight put into the pull, all of their muscles engaged . . . the Book was not torn apart. Even though there should have been, there was no ripping release of structural integrity, no break at the spine, no give anywhere.

It was like an I-beam—

Let it go.

From out of nowhere, like it'd been piped into the room—or maybe it was Balz's skull?—Lassiter's voice permeated the growling fight.

Let it go.

"No!" Balz barked. "Fucking no way!"

He refused to live with that evil inside of him for the rest of his life—

If you want to live, let it go.

From out of nowhere, the image of that detective he had just sent away came to the forefront of his mind.

But was this the evil talking to him or was this . . . actually Lassiter, trying to save him?

How did he know the difference between the brunette's seductive misrepresentations and reality?

"Fuck!" he yelled.

CHAPTER FIFTY-SEVEN

There were some battles where losing was not an option. This was one of them.

As Sahvage's body strained and sweat broke out across his chest and face, he locked his molars and kept pulling. Across the pages of the open Book, the Bastard was doing likewise, every ounce of power in that male's body and mind determined to take control as well.

There was the temptation to reach for a weapon. One bullet to the other fighter's head and this physical argument was fucking over.

But Sahvage couldn't risk having the Book ripped out of a one-handed grip. Without knowing many details about the Bastard, he had a feeling that Balthazar was fully capable of dematerializing at the drop of a hat. And if the male did?

Sahvage was not getting a second chance. In two hundred years, he hadn't crossed paths with the fucking thing. It was not happening again, and with that summoning spell out there?

Sure as shit, given his fucking luck, it would find its way to Mae—

All at once, and without warning, the Bastard released his grip. Just opened his hands and let the goddamn thing go.

With no more opposing force working against him, Sahvage's backward momentum was so great that he slammed into the opposite wall, the impact knocking him stupid for a split second.

Meanwhile, across the now-empty display case, Balthazar looked down at his hands as if he didn't understand what he'd done—or maybe that they'd acted independently.

His eyes lifted and he spoke with resignation. "Where are you taking it?"

For some reason, maybe because Sahvage recognized the numb despair in the other fighter's face, he found himself answering.

"Where no one can use it ever again."

"I need it. To get the evil out of me."

"There is no evil in you."

"You are very wrong about that, and the Book is my only hope."

If only Rahvyn were still alive, Sahvage thought. She used to take care of problems like that in their village back in the Old Country.

"I'm sorry," Sahvage said. And meant it.

With that, he dematerialized out of the room. Out of the gallery. Then it was out of the corridor and into the stairwell.

But he didn't go up. That's where the Brotherhood was—or had been. He went down, ghosting through the concrete landings faster than a heartbeat. At the bottom, he opened a fire door and expected to find all of the Brotherhood with their guns pointing to him. Nope. Just a sleek marble lobby with a couple of humans at a set of desk areas and two women coming in with shopping bags.

As he jogged across that shiny floor, he heard someone shouting for him.

Outside, in the darkness in front of the building, he expected the Brotherhood again. Or the brunette. Or shadows.

Nothing.

For a split second, he looked around and wondered what the fuck had happened to all the characters in his play. The stage was really fucking empty. But like he was in a position to argue with shit finally breaking his way?

Feeling like a bank robber on the heist of a lifetime, he closed his eyes and took to the cool spring night.

As he left the downtown, he had a bizarre thought.

It was almost like Balthazar had let him go.

◆   ◆   ◆

Up in the book room, Balz fell to the floor and put his head in his hands. "Fuck. Fuck . . . *fuck*."

When he looked up again, he was not alone. Lassiter was right in front of him, and the fallen angel slowly lowered himself down so they were eye to eye.

"Hi."

Balz swallowed hard. "I don't know what I just did."

"Yes, you do."

"How do I know this is actually you? I don't know what to trust anymore—and that includes myself."

"Give me your hand."

As the fallen angel extended his own palm, Balz had a thought that if he touched what was being offered to him, he might well be trapped forever in—

Fuck it.

Balz clasped what was in front of him and braced himself for . . .

With an abrupt surge of energy, he felt warmth, like sunshine. Acceptance, like from a *mahmen* who loved you. Peace, for a tortured soul.

You did the right thing, Lassiter said without moving his lips.

"It was my one and only chance, though." Balz wasn't sure how he knew this with such certainty. "I'm going to be eaten alive by her, from the inside out."

No, there is another way.

All Balz could do was shake his head. But then Lassiter smiled.

True love is going to save you.

Balz almost laughed. "I don't believe in true love."

When was the last time you saw the sun?

"My transition."

And yet it has continued to exist and warm the planet and sustain life, even without the benefit of your eyes. You're less powerful than that, Balthazar. True love does not require your acknowledgment to be a force in this world.

Whatever. "They're going to kill me, the Brothers and my bastards. I let Sahvage take the Book."

No, that's not what happened. There was a struggle, and you slipped and turned your ankle. As you released your hold on it, Sahvage made off with the Book—

"Ow, what the fuck?" Balz dropped hold of the angel's hand and grabbed for the bottom of his right leg—which was suddenly killing him.

When he looked up again, Lassiter was gone, but the agony was so great, he couldn't worry about the departure. Grimacing, he rolled over onto his back and wondered how in the hell the joint in question was screaming like he'd—

Well, like he'd slipped on something and twisted the shit out of it.

Fumbling for his phone, he triggered a call, and required no promise of an Oscar statue to grit out, "Motherfucker, he took the Book—I fell flat on my ass, I can't fucking walk or dematerialize . . . you're going to have to come evac me, and no, I don't know where that asshole went."

Immediately, whoever was on the other line started barking at him, and when he couldn't stand the noise, he cut the connection and squeezed his eyes shut. The only good news, he supposed, was also the bad news: With the Book gone, it was less likely that brunette was going to show up and play halfsies again with anyone who mattered to Balz.

Or himself.

Sahvage, the lying sonofabitch, had a proverbial tiger by the tail.

Chances were very, very good he wasn't going to live to see another sunset, and not because of whatever the Brotherhood was going to do to him. But his destiny was his own damn fault.

And as Balz worried about his infected soul, he heard the angel's voice in his head.

True love, Balz thought. *What a fucking crock of*—

From out of the white-hot agony claiming all of his attention, an image pierced through the veil, cutting the pain away.

It was of that human woman, the detective with the handgun and the cuffs, so orderly, so focused . . . so tired, like she'd been working a hard job for too many hours in a row. Too many years in a row.

But surely that was not his destiny.

Or hers.

Right?

CHAPTER FIFTY-EIGHT

Mae was sitting at her kitchen table, staring into space over her now soggy almost-Cheerios, when the phone started ringing. Thinking it was Tallah checking in, she took her cell out of her pocket—except no one was calling.

When the ringing continued, she got up and followed the sound to the top of the cellar stairs. Descending, she glanced around, and headed for the couch in the sitting area. Tucked behind it . . . was a black duffle. It was Sahvage's, the one that was filled with guns—he must have gone back to the cottage and retrieved it so he was well-armed over day. As she looked at the closed zipper, things went silent—but almost immediately, the chiming started up again.

Cursing to herself, she knelt down and went into the bag, rifling through the—well, rifles, as it turned out. Down at the bottom of so many muzzles . . . was his cell phone.

The screen showed the number was restricted.

With a swipe, she answered the call—

Before she could say hello, a male voice growled, "You double-crossing motherfucker. You just signed your death warrant and we know where you are—"

"Who is this?"

There was a pause. "Who are you."

"I'm a—" Friend? How the hell did she answer that. "I know Sahvage. What did he do?"

"Where is he?"

"He went out—" *To get ice for my dead brother.* "I'm sorry, but I don't know what's going on here."

And didn't that cover so much.

"Ma'am, I'm going to have to ask you to identify yourself. And you need to know that we have a tracer on the phone you're speaking into, so we are aware of your location. Sahvage is now an enemy of the Black Dagger Brotherhood. If you safe-harbor him in any way, or you attempt any deception on his behalf, you're going to be on the wrong side of the ledger, you feel me?"

Mae straightened. "What's he done."

"He has something that is ours."

Stepping to the side, she stared down at her bedroom and remembered them arguing.

As cold dread hit her head, she said baldly, "He has the Book, doesn't he."

"What do you know about the Book?"

Sonofabitch.

Hanging up the phone and keeping it with her, Mae took the stairs two at a time and went directly out into the garage—where she dematerialized free of the house. If the Brotherhood had the phone's location, she didn't want them anywhere near her home. They'd find Rhoger.

About five miles away, she re-formed behind a strip mall and tossed the cell into the dumpster in back. Then she up-and-outed once again.

Traveling in a scatter of molecules, she followed the blood signal Sahvage emitted, the kind of tracer that only she had access to. And as she zeroed in on it, she was taken to an old part of Caldwell, one that was right on the edges of downtown's urban blight. Here, the houses were three-story Victorians, of which many had been converted into apartments or were being used as dorms for SUNY Caldwell because they were close to campus.

In order to properly orientate herself, she re-formed in the parking lot of one that had been renovated and turned into a museum. As she stood in a handicapped space and looked around, she was shaking badly, but not because it was chilly and she had no coat. Closing her eyes, she fought the distraction of her anger and concentrated on where Sahvage was. When she had a precise pinpoint on him, she ghosted off again, re-materializing in a unkempt backyard that was fenced in by six-foot-tall planks loose in their arrangement.

Off in the distance, a dog barked. Then she heard an ambulance.

Surveying the back of the house, she found two back doors. One led into a kitchen, given what she could see through some windows. The other was set down at the base of a shallow set of concrete steps.

That was where she sensed Sahvage.

✦   ✦   ✦

One advantage to crashing in an old, drafty house that had been built before the turn of the last century, and that was currently owned by an old, dafty eccentric . . . was that there were a lot of old fashioned fixtures and shit in it. Like plumbing. Appliances. Light fixtures.

Heating systems.

As Sahvage walked down past his rented room, he could feel the warmth gathering in intensity, and had a thought that he was glad he'd squatted in upstate New York instead of, like, Florida or the Carolinas. No way they'd have their ancient coal-burning furnaces going on a night in April.

Pushing his way into the boiler room, he checked out the old school, fat-bellied, fed-by-fossil-fuels furnace that kept the three-story, multi-room sprawl warm.

Thanks to being a couple hundred years old himself, he was well familiar with how they worked. And yet as he stood in front of the iron behemoth, it was like he'd never seen one before.

Under his arm, he could feel the Book trembling, as if it were a small animal that was scared.

"Sorry," he said roughly. "You got to go—and you know this. You cause too many fucking problems."

As things got even more trembly, he glanced down. "Oh, come on. A little self-awareness, please."

The Book stopped with a shudder of what seemed like resignation.

What the hell was he waiting for, Sahvage wondered.

On that note, he reached out for the latch to the belly's door—

"Stop."

At first, as he thought he heard Mae's voice, he assumed it was his conscience talking. But then a red beam pierced him through the side of his right eyeball.

As he turned his head, the laser sight drilled him in the skull. And on the trigger end of that calling card? Mae was absolutely steady as she two-handed the gun he had gotten for her.

"What the hell are you doing?" she asked in a voice that cracked.

He looked back at the boiler. "It's the way things have to be—"

"Says who! This doesn't involve you—it's none of your goddamn business."

"I'm trying to save you!"

Mae bared her fangs, her face screwing tight with anger, her body vibrating with emotion. "I do *not* need help from a coward like you."

"*Excuse me.*"

"You got burned in your past, and I'm sorry about that—but you've been running ever since. No roots, no connections. Because you don't have the balls to live life. Well, that's your failing, not mine. And you're *not* going to prevent me from walking my own path."

"You don't know me," he said coldly. "You know *nothing* about me."

"I don't? You couldn't even make love to me last night properly because you can't handle any responsibility—even one that's made up in your own fucking head. You don't have the courage to be real—but whatever, I'm not going to let your failings fuck my life up. Give me the goddamn Book."

Sahvage jerked forward. "Just so we're clear, I didn't have sex with you because I knew I was going to do this." He jabbed a finger at the boiler. "And I knew you'd hate me for it. The last thing any female wants is a first time with someone she despises, so I held back for you, *not* for me."

"Well, aren't you a fucking hero."

Holding up the Book, he said, "You don't know what you're doing, Mae. I'm just trying to make sure you—"

"I'm done talking. Give me the Book. It's mine."

"It's no one's."

"I summoned it." She shook her head and lowered that gun muzzle to the center of his chest. "It's been trying to find me, and you're in the way."

How fitting, he thought. If she pulled the trigger, she would shoot him right in the heart.

"Mae—"

"No!" she yelled into the heat of the boiler room. "I don't need you to tell me goddamn anything. You have *no* right to determine the life of a stranger—especially given the stand-up way you've run your own. This is not your business! We met by mistake and you're already a regret of mine—I'm not going to add you to my list of tragedies!"

Sahvage narrowed his eyes . . . and told himself that she was right. They were strangers. Proximity and some really fucked-up shit had randomly brought them together. If she wanted to screw up her brother and herself? Why the hell did he care so much.

With a curse—at himself, this time—he tossed the Book over.

As Mae went to catch the goddamn thing, she fumbled with the gun and pulled the trigger by mistake, a bullet exploding out of the muzzle and ricocheting around the rough stone room in a series of *pings!*

Sahvage ducked and covered his head, bracing to get hit somewhere—

A high-pitched squeal, like that of a pig, marked the end of the lead slug's free-flying trip.

Lowering his arms, he looked over at Mae. She had the Book up to her chest, and as she straightened from her own crouch, she turned the tome around.

In the dusty glow of the exposed light bulb over head, the small round hole in the center of the front cover was like any other wound in flesh—but the imperfection didn't last long. As if the thing were capable of healing, as if it were alive, the bullet "wound" gradually sealed itself up.

Mae lifted her eyes, and as Sahvage met her stare, the ache in his chest was just like if he had been the one hit.

"Goodbye, Mae," he said in a low voice as he stepped around her.

In the doorway out of the furnace room, he looked over his shoulder. "And I'm saying that because I want closure. It may come as a complete shock to you, but other people make choices, too."

CHAPTER FIFTY-NINE

Balz was still crumpled on the floor of the triplex's book room when Xcor strode in. He was accompanied by a number of Brothers, none of whom really registered, and nobody looked happy.

The leader of the Band of Bastards, the one Balz had pledged his life to long ago, knelt down and took his dagger hand. As the image of that harsh face, with its cleft lip and its familiar eyes, got wavy, Balz kicked himself in his own ass. But damn, the guilt stung.

"We'll get you out of here and have that leg looked at."

God, he felt awful, and not just because his ankle was on fucking fire. "Have you found Sahvage?"

"V's tracing his cell phone."

"Okay." Shit. Shit. *Shit*— "I'm sorry. I'm so sorry—"

"You did your best. And don't worry, we're going to find him and we'll get the Book. This is nothing that's going to change our outcome. Come on, let me help you up."

Balz continued cursing for a whole lot of reasons as he got onto the vertical, and he had to rely on Xcor's shoulders to limp out of the apartment. Out in the corridor, he had to rest as the Brothers provided cover, casing the hallway.

Please don't let that brunette show up, Balz thought. And then he shut that down real quick. The last thing he needed to add to this shit show was placing a mental phone call to the bitch.

"Manny's downstairs waiting," Xcor said.

"Can we use the elevator? I can't dematerialize."

"Of course."

He had an all-armed escort down to where the arrowed buttons were, and by the time they came up to the bank of double doors, he was getting dizzy from the pain. When their elevator arrived, they shuffled into the mirrored confines. Well, three of them did. He, Xcor, and Butch made it inside. There wasn't enough room for Z and Phury.

"We'll meet you down there," one of the two of them announced.

"Roger that," Butch said.

As the panels slid closed, something moved in the corner of Balz's eye. Jerking around, he only saw his reflection, the image of his pale, pain-etched face refracted back and forth, *ad infinitum*. And Xcor's. And Butch's—

There. There it was again, something moving around in one of the sets of reflections, a shadow, jumping up a level. And another level. And another level . . . closing in on reality.

"What is it?" Xcor asked.

"It's coming for us—"

The lights flickered overhead. The car bumped to a halt.

Somewhere, an alarm went off.

"Close your eyes," Balz commanded—even though he didn't know why. "You have to close your eyes or she'll get into you! Close your eyes!"

He tightened his hold on his leader and grabbed the front of Butch's dagger holster, pulling the Brother in close.

"Don't look, don't open your eyes—"

A sound, like the hiss of a snake's tongue, came to them, surrounding them, getting louder. And through his lids, he could tell that the lighting was blinking again. Panicked, all he could do was pray the other two males were as eyes-wide-shut as he was. But there was no checking—

Something brushed his bad ankle and seemed to probe his foot, like it was searching for, and had identified, his weakness. Then Butch moved against him, like he was trying to get away from a touch. Xcor growled.

But no one said anything.

With a squawk, all three of their communicators went off at once. "Engagement! Engagement, repeat—"

The snake-like hissing got louder and snapped up to Balz's shoulder, like the entity, whatever it was, was checking out the noise.

Balz moved his hand up and silenced the emergency. As the others' units went quiet as well, he assumed they had done likewise.

It sounded as if all of the fighters had suddenly been attacked. At once.

Fuck.

◆   ◆   ◆

It was fine. She didn't need him.

As Mae dematerialized back to her house with the Book, she was totally resolved and absolutely refusing to think about Sahvage ever again. Re-forming inside the garage, she walked right into the back hall, through the kitchen, and out the other side.

"I have what we need." She ignored how her voice broke. "I'm going to take care of everything."

Opening the way into the bathroom, she caught her breath for a moment. The ice from the night before was mostly melted, nothing but a cold pool surrounding her brother's body.

"It's going to be just fine."

She had a feeling she was crying. She didn't know why else her cheeks would be wet, but she didn't care and that was the good thing about obsessions. They were utterly clarifying. Nothing else mattered, which made it all so much easier. Especially when your emotions got messy.

Kneeling by the tub, she put the Book down on the bath mat and stared at her brother's face. Then she looked at the ancient tome. Its cover was so ugly, and every time she breathed in, her nose revolted. But beggars, choosers, and all that.

"It worked," she said to the thing. "I didn't believe in the summoning spell, but here we are."

Reaching down to open it, she felt a surge of nausea as her fingertips made contact. And then, when she tried to lift the cover, she could have sworn there was resistance, as if the thing didn't want the intrusion. But it was an inanimate object, right?

As one of her tears fell on the old leather, the droplet was absorbed as if consumed. And then, abruptly, the Book opened itself, the cover thrown back without any help from her. While Mae jerked in surprise, pages started to flip of their own volition, the parchment rifling through faster and faster, until all of a sudden, the movement stopped.

Like a page had been chosen for her.

As her heart started to pound, she looked down. And prayed that whatever ingredients were required for the resuscitation, she had them in the house—

What the ... hell?

"Oh, no ... no, no, no."

There was some title at the top of the page, and there were many, many lines of brown and black ink below it ... there was even a drawing, archaic in nature—as if from the Middle Ages—illustrating a corpse rising from a grave.

So she had the right section.

But she couldn't understand the language. Whatever the spell was written in ... was nothing she had ever seen before.

"Shit!"

When she tried to see if there was a translation she could read somewhere farther along in the chapter, the pages refused to be turned, the Book becoming like a frozen block.

Mae started to breathe heavily. Then she fumbled with her phone. Her hands shook as she dialed.

"Hello?" came the elderly voice.

"Tallah, I have the Book. IhavetheBookbutIcantreadit—"

"Dearest, dearest—please." The elderly female's voice was worried. "I cannot understand you. You have to slow down."

Mae was panting, but she forced herself to get control. "I have the Book. I'm here, with Rhoger, at my house. But I can't read what it says. Can you come here and help me?"

"The summoning spell worked . . ." Tallah's voice drifted off into wonder. "And of course. As you know, I was trained properly in the traditional fashion for females so I am fluent in many languages."

"I have no car to come pick you up in."

There was a pause. "Dearest, what happened to your—"

"It's not important. Are you able to dematerialize to the house?"

"Yes, yes. Dearest, I shall be there right away."

"Thank you. Just come through the garage, the door's unlocked and one of the daytime shutters in the back has been cracked. There's nothing where my car is supposed to be so it's safe."

"Worry not. We shall work this out together."

As they ended the call, Mae sagged with relief. But she worried about whether Tallah was capable of—

Knock, knock, knock.

Her head whipped around. Getting to her feet, she stepped over the Book and got her gun out—not that she was confident about using the damn thing. She'd managed to nearly shoot herself in the heart back in that furnace room with Sahvage—

Okay, she was not thinking about that right now. Or ever again.

Dear God, what had her life become?

Knock, knock.

Who's there, she thought as she leaned out of the hall and looked at the front door.

What if it was the Brotherhood? If they could trace the phone, then they no doubt knew where Sahvage had spent the day. What if they were coming for the—

"Mae?" Came a muffled voice through the door. "Mae, dearest, are you in there?"

"Oh, Jesus—Tallah."

As she lunged through the living room, she thought it was so typical of the older female to be confused. Yanking the door open, she found the old female right on the stoop, dressed in one of her caftans, her gnarled hands gripping a small purse to her caved-in chest like she was a beggar.

"Come in, come in," Mae said as she pulled the female inside. "So you're safe."

Tallah tripped on the door's lip, and Mae had to catch her fragile body before she hit the floor. As soon as she was steady, Mae bolted back to the bathroom, talking the whole way.

"I'm praying that you can read this," she said over her shoulder.

Rounding the corner into the loo, she frowned. Over on the bath mat, the Book had closed itself up again.

"Oh, come on," she muttered as she went to pick the thing up—

"You're so fucking stupid."

Mae froze. Then slowly straightened and turned around.

The brunette was standing in the open doorway, Tallah's caftan too short in the sleeves and on the bottom as it covered her spectacular body.

"And can I just tell you"—the demon looked down at herself—"I am *so* happy to get this shit off of me."

With the wave of an elegant hand, the loose folds disappeared and were replaced by a black catsuit. Tossing her gorgeous, shiny hair over her shoulder, she smiled with those blood red lips.

"So, I think you and I are back where we started last night." One blood red finger lifted. "Well, except you owe me four hundred thousand dollars. Why—*why*—did you have to go for my Himalayan crocodile? And I'll bet it wasn't even calculated. You probably didn't even know what you were burning, did you. You are such a stupid, fucking cunt."

"I don't ... understand."

"Of course you don't. I swear, you're that line out of 'Thirty Something.'" As Mae blinked in confusion, the brunette well-duh'd her. "Jay-Z? Jesus Christ, you probably listen to folk music, and you definitely don't shop at Bergdorf's. Fine, you want to know what purse is that? Birkins are a handbag made by the Hermès company. They are the most coveted bags on the market, and each one is made by a single craftsman who takes—"

Mae shook her head. "Not about the purse."

The demon seemed surprised her lecture was being interrupted. "You know, this could be a real learning opportunity for you. Then again, you're not going to be alive for much longer sooooooooooooooooooooooo . . . yeah."

"How are you in this house?"

"You invited me in, dummy." She smiled some more. "And no, the fact that you didn't know it wasn't Tallah doesn't count. An invitation is an invitation. You should have been more careful—oh, and I was in the cottage before your boyfriend with the salt went to town. All he did was close the door with the wolf already in the hen house. Or something. I've never been very good at animal metaphors. Sorry."

"But ..."

"Oh, for fuck's sake. Do I have to draw a diagram? You summoned the Book, and as soon as you did, I felt the spell. The goddamn thing is mine—and some asshole stole it from me, but that's another story. That shithole cottage was not protected, so I just waltzed right in— and Tallah—"

"Where is she," Mae demanded. "What did you do with her—"

"Sweetie, she's long gone. She had nothing left to fight me with. It was like pulling off a wet Band-Aid. Work of a second."

Mae moaned and weaved on her feet.

"Puh-lease." The demon rolled her eyes and stomped her stiletto. "I wasn't *that* bad as a roommate. I even cooked for you and your BF—and you liked that stew. Then again, it was really good. I put a lot of heart into it, I really did."

As Mae's mind struggled to catch up, she wanted to fall into her emotions, but knew that that was a death sentence. She had to think. Think. *Think*—

In the silence, the demon's eyes shifted to the tub. And then she did a double take.

"Oh, my God." She glanced at Mae and laughed. "Of course. I was wondering why someone as straitlaced as you wanted my Book, but I should have known it was for a sappy reason. Who is he—"

As the demon stepped toward the tub, Mae threw her arm out. "Don't you hurt him!"

The demon froze. Looked at Mae. Looked back at the tub. "Holy fuck . . ." Then, "He's your brother? That . . . that virgin, *my* virgin, the one who got away, is your brother?"

Mae felt dizzy as she remembered Rhoger coming through the door and collapsing into her arms. Dying . . . from his wounds.

"You killed him," she breathed. "You are his murderer."

The demon whispered a couple of curses. "Man, fate is so fucked up sometimes, it really is—and that explains why I recognized you back in the cage he'd been in." She drew a hand through her hair, as if in frustration. "And yeah . . . even though I mighta let you use my Book, you know, 'cuz I'm such a nice girl, now it's a case of over my dead body you're bringing that thief back. And considering I'm immortal? You're going to have to wait forever before I keel over."

Instantly, the demon's affect changed.

Gone was the breezy conversation bullshit.

"Now give me my fucking Book," she gritted out.

Mae grabbed the tome and held on to it with both arms crossed over her chest. "No. You're not taking this from me."

Black eyes glittered. "Give. Me. My Book."

Mae shook her head slowly even as she started to shake. "You're going to have to take it from me. Go ahead. You're so much stronger than I am. You're so fucking powerful. Come and take it."

The demon's beautiful face grew ugly with fury, and the air around her warped. "You don't know who you're fucking with."

"Yes . . . I do."

Even as she wondered what the hell she was doing, Mae unfurled her lower arms and laid the Book out to the demon.

"Take it."

The snarl that vibrated into the tension between them was that of a predator, low and deadly. "You fucking—"

"Mae," came a deep voice.

The door into the garage closed with a bump at the other end of the house.

"I'm just here to get my guns," Sahvage called out. "And then I'm gone. Don't frickin' worry."

The demon straightened. And cocked a delighted smile.

Then she whispered, "Looks like I've got a little leverage all of the sudden, don't I."

In a louder voice that sounded exactly like Mae's own, the demon said, "I'm down here. And I need you."

As the demon winked, Mae tried to call out. Tried to warn him. Screamed as loud as she could. But she couldn't seem to make a sound.

It was as if her voice had been stolen.

Natch.

CHAPTER SIXTY

I t was like a nightmare.

As Mae heard Sahvage's heavy boots come down to the bathroom, closer and closer, she desperately tried to warn him. But then
he stepped into the open doorway.

As he stopped short, tears fell from Mae's eyes. *I'm so sorry,* she
mouthed.

"Hi, honey," the demon pronounced to him. "Evidently you're
home."

Before Sahvage could respond, his body was slammed back against
the hallway wall, the same kind of invisible-hand pressure that had hit
Mae back in that underground lair making him strain and fight to
breathe.

"So," the demon said to Mae in a reasonable tone. "Here's how this is
going to go. You give me the Book, and I give you him. And before you
go-off-sis with a bunch of exit demands, yes, I'll leave. No offense, but
this house, just like you, isn't my style at all. Frankly, it needs a good
goddamn fire. Do we have a deal? You give me what's mine, I give you
what's yours. Even, Steven."

Over on the wall, a good foot off the floor, Sahvage's lips peeled back off his fangs from the agony, and the veins in his neck stood out in sharp relief.

"Oh, and P.S.," the demon pointed out, "his life is your *Jeopardy!* theme. So when it runs out, you run out of time, and though I have other options to work with, he'll be dead as a door handle. Or is it knob? I think it's knob."

Mae looked to the tub. Looked back to Sahvage.

As she met his eyes, she knew what she was going to decide before she was even aware of making a choice.

Standing in the face of such a source of great destruction, Mae recognized how destructive she herself had been. In her desperation, she had sacrificed too much; in her grief, she had taken herself over the edge . . . in her refusal to accept tragedy, she had brought so much of it to herself. To others.

Sahvage wasn't the coward. She was.

"Have the Book," she said loud and clearly. "Just have it. I never should have gone down this road to begin with."

As she tossed the heavy weight over, the demon had a Christmas-morning expression on her face, all fury gone, nothing but delight. And then she was the one clasping the old, ugly thing to her perfect breasts.

There was a moment where her black eyes closed, as if in relief.

And then her lids popped open.

"Thank you," she said with a strange sincerity. "You did the right thing. And I'm sorry about your brother. But honestly, you're better off not fucking with death. It's the one thing even I am careful about."

Out in the hall, Sahvage's straining body was slowly lowered back to the floor. And then he shook himself, as if he were casting off shackles.

"Mae," he said as he reached out his arms—

Without warning, his head spun on the top of his spine with a sickening *crack!* and his body dropped to the floor in a heap.

The brunette went saucy-hip and forefingered the air. "Psych."

"*Sahvage!*" Mae screamed at the top of her lungs.

CHAPTER SIXTY-ONE

OMG, the night was *so* picking up, Devina thought as she delicately sidestepped out of the female vampire's way. She'd been in a really bad mood to begin with, but this display of tragic emotion? Come on.

It was better than sex.

Well, the meh sex she'd been having lately, at any rate. *And* she had the Book.

"Although you and I are going to have words," she muttered at the thing. "Bad Book. You are a very, very bad Book."

Out in the cramped hallway, the female vampire was gently rolling her stud over, the male's loosey-goosey head flopping around, his sightless eyes staring at the floor, the wall—oh, and now the ceiling.

"You could try mouth-to-mouth," Devina suggested, "but I don't think it's going to help."

The female collapsed on that big, immobile chest, and positively wailed. And for a moment, Devina thought about making some wisecracks, just to cut the tension. 'Cuz this was getting a little intense.

And then it dawned on her.

No one was ever going to mourn her like this. No one was ever going to care whether she lived or died. Nobody was ever going to . . . love her like this.

Just as the pain shot through her chest, the female wrenched around.

With a gun in her hand.

As a wobbly red dot skated into her eyes, Devina recoiled—

The female screamed in fury as she pulled the trigger over and over again, the sound of the gun going off competing for airtime over the roaring grief.

And Devina had to give the bitch credit. She was a helluva shot.

The bullets ripped through flesh and bone, blowing chunks out on the tile, the floor, even into the tub with the female's dead brother, all kinds of perfect features getting ruined as Devina was thrown back—

Click. Click. Click.

Devina opened the one eye that was still working. The female still had the gun straight out in front of her, and she was compulsively squeezing the trigger, even though nothing was coming out.

Lunging forward, she grabbed the female by the throat with one hand and took her careening down the hall into a pathetic little kitchen. As the vampire tripped and started falling, Devina gave her a shove—and a table with a cereal box and a bowl full of milk caught the scramble, everything splintering, chairs knocking over.

Devina kept the Book in her other hand as she went over and dragged the female up again and then pitched her against the counter. Against the cupboards. Against the stove.

And in proof that she was the superior entity, she managed to do all of that ping-pong'ing while she reknitted the gunshot injuries.

By the time the female slumped to the floor, things were back to rights.

Devina took the front of that throat one last time and tossed the piece of unresisting meat back against the empty wall by the door into what had to be the garage.

Holding the female in place with a spell, Devina fluffed her hair. "Well. That happened. And I'm going to settle a score now. You ruined my bag by fire. So I'm going to burn this piece-of-shit house down with you and your corpse boyfriend and your soggy, dead-ass, motherfucking thief of a brother in it." She glanced around. And then stamped a heel with frustration. "Damn it, I don't have marshmallows. Do you have— oh, never mind."

She walked in a little circle and wondered where to start. "You know, I've always wanted to have my Oprah moment. Here it is! You have a flame . . . and you have a flame . . . and you have a flame."

All around, little bursts of yellow and orange appeared on things: The back of the sofa and the corner of the carpet in the living room. The cupboard over the refrigerator. The archway into the hall. And there were more in the back bedrooms, too. Down in the basement as well.

"Phew." She took a break and fanned herself. "Is it me or am I hot in here. And by the way, you still owe me at least two hundred grand. There's no way this hovel is anywhere close to the cost of my bag."

◆   ◆   ◆

Up against the wall, Mae was losing consciousness—at least until the house burst into flames around her. As smoke and heat began to thicken the air, and her skin prickled in warning at the flames, a wave of adrenaline whipped her brain back in order.

But there was nothing to be done. Just as Sahvage had been held in place before—

Moaning in her throat, Mae squeezed her eyes closed. She had killed him. Not intentionally, but her actions had created the situation that had led to his demise.

This was all her fault. And she'd never had a chance to apologize . . . or tell him that she loved him. She had ruined his life all because of her selfish quest for power over death.

Lifting her lids, she focused on the demon. The brunette was smiling as the smoke swirled around her, the Book that had started it all clasped against her—

From out of the billowing gray swirls, a figure emerged.

A figure that made no sense.

Sahvage? Mae thought. How was this possible?

But it was him—although maybe he wasn't real. Maybe he was just a figment of her desperate, dying brain.

"Well, my job is done here," the demon said. "And as much as I'd like to hang around and watch the barbeque, I've got spells of my own to—"

With a battle cry that shook the house, Sahvage—or the mirage of him—threw his arms around the demon. Before the brunette could react, he bared his fangs and sank them into the side of her throat.

As the demon screamed, the flames that had found purchase around the house exploded into full-blown fires, the inferno redoubling.

Still latched on, Sahvage dragged the demon back to where the flames were the strongest, the fire burning the brightest. The brunette, meanwhile, fought and kicked, clawing and biting at the hold that was upon her.

Just as Sahvage disappeared into the blaze, his eyes locked on Mae.

"I'm sorry!" she screamed. "I love you!"

And then he was gone.

"No!" Mae cried out. "Sahvage!"

As she started to weep, she tried to peel herself free of the hold. But there was no budging, no getting away, as the house became an oven and every breath she took burned her lungs.

She was going to die.

Even if the human fire department came, it was going to be too late for her. Too late. Too late—

Mae.

Just as she was losing consciousness, she heard her name. Forcing her lids up, she—

"Rhoger?"

The fire was loud now, the crackling and popping and creaking of beams and walls so deafening that she didn't know whether her voice carried. Then again, like the image of Sahvage, was she really seeing her brother right now? And he was not alone.

Tallah was standing right next to him.

The two of them were holding hands, and the yellow and orange flickering cast them in a strobing light that was, in a strange way, heavenly. In the face of the heat, they were somehow unaffected, their clothing unburned, their hair not on fire.

They just stared at her, their expressions saintly with peace.

All will be well, Rhoger said.

Okay, not that she wanted to argue with the ghost of her brother during her last moments on earth—but they did not agree on the definition of that term. Nothing was well—

The vision of the pair of her loved ones was shattered, the mirage broken apart by a male dressed in black.

Her first thought was that her fantasy Sahvage had come back again, but then no, it wasn't him. This was a fighter, though.

A goateed fighter with a pair of black daggers strapped, handles down, to his chest.

"I've got you," he said in a commanding voice.

"No, no, I'm trapped—"

All at once, the hold on her disappeared, and as she dropped forward, he caught her and swung around.

"Sahvage!" she yelled over the din. "Sahvage is down there!"

The soldier glanced to the hall. "No one can survive in there! I have to save you!"

They were both having to scream to be heard, and as he started rushing them away, she clawed to get free. Even though she knew he was right. Nothing could live in that kiln, and her love had been dead before it started.

Even a demon couldn't survive back there. Which had to be why her body was no longer imprisoned.

"Sahvage," she moaned.

As all of her strength left her, the Brother broke out into the garage, nailed the opener with a punch, and the instant fresh air barged into the concrete space, she saw the other males who had lined up in the driveway.

She tried to focus through her sudden delirium.

"He took the demon," she told the Brother with the goatee. "Sahvage came back to life somehow, and he took the demon into the flames. He saved me . . . he saved all of us."

Sirens now. Loud sirens.

Humans were coming.

"We're going to take good care of you," the Brother told her. "Just stay with me, true?"

Staring over her shoulder, she saw her parents' house on fire, the flames spasming behind every window there was, the smoke curling out of holes that had formed in the roof.

Utter destruction.

Nothing left behind.

Just as she was put into the RV she recognized from before, she saw the red bubbling lights of the first of the fire trucks.

The double doors were closed, cutting off the sight of the humans come to rescue that which could not be saved.

As the RV's engine roared and things lurched forward, she realized there was another male sitting off to the side on a bench. One of his ankles was bound in an Ace bandage, and he had the whole leg elevated up on a wad of white blankets.

He was staring at her.

"What happened?" he said as the male with the goatee secured her body on the table with a series of straps.

"I lost the male I love," she mumbled even though he hadn't been talking to her. "I lost him before I ever got to tell him how I feel."

And that was the last thing she remembered.

CHAPTER SIXTY-TWO

At Luchas House, Nate was lounging next to Elyn on the sofa. His laptop was open on her—well, lap, as it were—and she was searching a names database of the species. Across the way, up on the TV mounted over the fireplace, *Stranger Things*, season two, was playing.

As Elyn shut the computer sharply, he looked over. "Nothing?"

She didn't answer. She just stared at the floor.

When he breathed in and smelled fresh rain, he frowned and sat up. "Elyn, you're crying."

She put her hands to her face. "I'm sorry. I'm sorry . . . I'm sorry . . ."

"What? Tell me. Tell me what's going on."

With a shudder, she seemed to try to pull herself together. And when she looked at him next, her silver eyes glittered in a way that made him sit back.

The light in them was . . . shimmering. Like they were basins of illumination, rather than anything conventional that the female simply looked out of.

"I've lied to you," she said quietly. "I haven't . . ."

"What."

"I don't belong here."

"Luchas House is meant to help people just like you—"

"No, that's not what I mean."

"Caldwell, then?"

"This present time. This was all a mistake. A huge mistake."

Elyn put the laptop aside and got up. Pacing around, she looked into the kitchen.

"We're alone," he said roughly. "You can talk freely. Shuli and the others won't be back for another half hour."

"I'm sorry, Nate."

Her words were spoken absently, as if she were unaware he was still in the room. As if she were unaware of where exactly she was.

"I have to go," she blurted.

"Go where."

"Out for a walk. I can't stay inside right now—I need some air."

"I'll come with you."

"No, I have to be alone. I won't go far, I swear unto you."

With rough kicks, she pushed her feet into the boots she'd been given by the Luchas House staff, and then she walked to the front of the house. After a moment, he heard the door open and close quietly.

"Shit."

Nate looked around, and wondered if he should call the social worker. She was due back along with Shuli and two potential boarders to the house. They'd gone to stock up the cupboards and the fridge.

Anxious and unsure what the hell to do, he pulled his laptop over. Signing in, he went into the search function. He told himself he was violating her privacy, but he couldn't stop himself. Something was up. Something . . . had probably been up the whole time. He was just a simp, though, and he worried that he—

The name she had searched came up right away because she hadn't closed out the database.

Sahvage.

Sahvage was the name she had looked for.

✦   ✦   ✦

Back at the Brotherhood's training center, Rehvenge pushed his way out of the office and strode down to the clinic. There were a lot of people gathered outside one of the exam rooms, and no one was saying much. Then again, there were a lot of injuries, all kinds of bumps, bruises, and welts marking the faces of the Brothers and other fighters.

"Jesus, you guys got tore up," he remarked.

Their grids registered one by one for him, and the sorrow was so overwhelming that even though he was a *symphath* and had sociopathic tendencies, it was impossible not to sink into the suffering.

Well, and then there was the fact that these were his people. His community. His . . . family.

The door opened and Vishous stepped out. "Smoke inhalation. But she's going to come through. She's conscious and we're trying to get her to stay, but she's insisting that she wants to go home."

"I thought her house burned down," Rhage said as he rolled his bandaged shoulder.

"'Nother one. There's a cottage somewhere."

"What happened to Sahvage?" Rehv asked.

V lit up a hand-rolled and on the exhale said, "He saved the day— night, whatever. That female in there said the brother somehow came back from a catastrophic neck injury, locked onto the demon, and dragged her right back into an inferno. They died together in the fire."

"Fuck," someone said. "Guess he wasn't a warlock after all."

"And the Book was with them," V concluded.

"Thank God." Butch made the sign of the cross. "We don't have to worry about either of them anymore."

Rehv glanced to the exam room door. "Is it okay for me to go talk to her? I won't upset her or anything."

"It's okay with me." V took another drag. "There's no medical restrictions, and anyway, Ehlena's in there right now."

Rehv pushed his way into the exam room. The instant he saw his *shellan*, he felt his body respond, and his female smiled from over at the sink where she was washing her hands.

"Mae, this is my *hellren*."

From over on the bed, the soot-covered female was in sad shape, the oxygen mask obscuring a lot of her face—but none of her emotions.

He read those all too easily. And that was why he'd wanted to see her.

The suffering was so awful, so deep . . . it reminded him of himself.

After he greeted his *shellan* with a kiss, he looked at the patient. "I'm sorry I lied to you," he said roughly. "About what I knew."

Over on the gurney, the female nodded. Coughed a little. Kept her bloodshot eyes on him, and yet she was not angry at him. Then again, she wasn't feeling anything but the pain.

"I just wanted you to know that," he said. "And I wish there was something I could do."

Ehlena dried her hands. "She would like to go home. Maybe you could drive her where she'd like to go? There are so many injured here."

The female on the hospital bed pulled her mask down. "What happened to them?" she asked in a hoarse voice. "The Brothers."

Rehv answered that one. "The shadows came for them. It was an epic fight downtown, like the demon needed them to stay where they were at the Commodore. Fortunately, there were no casualties. There might have been, though—except all of the sudden, it stopped. The enemy just up and disappeared."

"Sahvage," she said in that rough way. "When he pulled the demon into the fire. As soon as she was killed, her power disappeared. He saved the Brotherhood."

Rehv nodded and glanced back at the door. "Well, that explains it."

"Explains what?"

"Why all the fighters in this household are outside your hospital room."

"I'm sorry, I don't understand—"

"You're Sahvage's female. So they honor his memory by taking care of you." Rehv lowered his voice. "You're not as alone as you think you are. Not anymore."

There was a long period of silence. And then she said, "You are so wrong about that. Without him? I will always be alone."

CHAPTER SIXTY-THREE

Two hours later, as the Mercedes's headlights washed across the front of Tallah's cottage, Mae felt the agony in her chest ramp up again—and she had a thought that her pain was like that house fire the demon had started, suddenly exploding in intensity.

She closed her eyes and wondered if she would be able to go in at all, much less spend the rest of the night inside.

"You know, you can stay up at my lake house instead," the Reverend said next to her. "It's safe. There are Chosen there. It's a good place to heal."

Mae refocused on the front door. "No, this is my new home. I might as well get used to it."

And yet she didn't get out of the warm car. Instead, she stared at all the darkened windows, the overgrown bushes, the ragged trees.

"A wonderful female lived here once," she remarked sadly.

And now she could see the pathway to her becoming what Tallah had been, an old female who lived in those four walls, tottering around the oversized furniture, forever resolving to tidy things up a bit better.

"Thank you for the ride," she said as she popped her door.

As she went to get out, the Reverend touched her arm. "You can always call the training center. There are resources there for you. I gave you the number."

"Thank you," she said, even though she knew she would never phone in.

"Anything you need, you come to us."

She nodded, but only to get him to stop talking. She honestly did appreciate what he was saying, but she couldn't think about anything other than the aching present and the four hundred years in the future when all this was done. All the suffering over. When she finally died herself.

Getting out, Mae said some stuff to the male, and he nodded like whatever it was had made some sense. Then she walked over to the cottage's front door. As she opened the way in, she took a deep breath and only smelled smoke.

It was going to be like that for a while, they'd told her. Her sinuses had captured, and were going to hold on to, the acrid scent for a number of nights.

Like she cared, though.

Mae waved over her shoulder and closed the door. Then she leaned back against the cool panels and looked at the back of the hutch that Sahvage had moved out of place to protect them. Memories of him picking it up were as sharp as knives, and yet she couldn't avoid them even as they sliced at her heart.

To try to get her attention elsewhere, she took another inventory on how her body was doing. Not too great: Her skin was hot, but more than that, her inner core was overheated, as if her body temperature had been permanently raised by the fire.

Like she was a roast beef in a restaurant, just out of the oven, throwing off her own BTUs.

Wonder how long that will last, she thought listlessly.

Staring out through the contours of all of Tallah's too-big, too-fancy furniture, she listened to the silence and wanted to cry. But there were no more tears left.

God, every time she blinked, she suffered another image from the bathroom at her parents' house, the demon in her face, her brother under that cold water, Sahvage's neck breaking—

Mae moaned and resolved to never, ever blink again. Even if her eyeballs turned into marbles in her skull.

Straightening, she went down to the bathroom and stared at the shower. She could picture Sahvage standing there in front of it, his body so magnificent, his eyes boring into her, his scent deep in her nose.

With a sad capitulation to reality, she stepped in, shut the door behind herself, and started the water. As she took off the hospital scrubs she'd been given, she glanced down at her body. Lots of bruises. Patches of red, angry skin. Scrapes.

Looked like she had been through a war.

Getting under the warm spray, she hissed as stripes of pain registered all over the place—and the soap stung, as did the shampoo. But by the time she got to the conditioner part of things, she was doing better with it.

She couldn't smell any of the familiar stuff she used. Just smoke. As if the fire was a pursuer who was not giving up the chase.

When she was clean—or as clean as she could get—she stepped out and shivered. Pulling a thick terry cloth bathrobe on, she wrapped her hair up in a towel and rubbed the condensation off the mirror.

A stranger stared back at her.

And all she could think of was what she would have done differently: Talk about a list that was going to get her nowhere.

Food. She should try and see if there was any food around.

Like in the refrigerator that was still pressed up against the back door.

As she thought of Sahvage once again, she still didn't understand exactly what had happened back in that fire. How he had gone from a broken neck and dead in her arms . . . to coming back to life. Then again, heroic things happened to the dying, and when it really counted, he'd obviously been determined not to let her down.

Shaking her head, she opened the door and—

Screamed her bloody lungs out.

CHAPTER SIXTY-FOUR

Okay, so as romantic reunions went . . . it was not exactly what a male hoped.

But as Sahvage put both of his hands up to his ears and winced, he wondered exactly how he could have made this easier on Mae.

"I'm sorry," he said into the din. "I'm sorry!"

Mae stopped screaming and started to hyperventilate. "What-what-*what* . . . ?"

She was dressed in a robe, her hair in a towel, her too-pale face marked with all kinds of bruises and soot smudges that were going to take multiple showers to get rid of. And what do you know, she was the most beautiful female he had ever seen. Would ever see.

But she looked like she was going to pass out.

Sahvage jumped forward and caught her arm as she listed. "Here, come here, let's sit down over here." He drew her over to the kitchen table and sat her in a chair, because he wasn't sure she was going to remember how to do it on her own. "Take some slow, deep breaths with me. That's right. That's—"

"How are you alive?" she said hoarsely. "Again?"

As she panted, he sat back and rubbed his thighs. "I need to tell you everything. And I should have before . . . but I just didn't know how to."

"P-p-please." She reached out and touched his face. "Is this really you? How is this possible—"

"I can't die."

Mae frowned. Blinked a couple of times. Then put her palms up to the sides of her face. "Oh, my God, you're a warlock—"

"I'm not a warlock."

"But—"

"I'm not. My first cousin Rahvyn, she's the magic one. And two hundred years ago, I died trying to protect her during that attack on her life. I was struck by arrows and laid out in a coffin. It took me decades to figure out what had happened, to put the pieces together, and I'm not sure I have it all correctly. But what I know for certain is that she brought me back using a spell from the Book, and then she . . . disappeared. That's why I didn't want you to bring back Rhoger. Mae, my existence is terrible. Everyone thinks they want to be immortal, but it's . . . hell. You belong nowhere, with no one, because the only thing that exists for you is time. It's a nightmare. Friends, family, lovers, they're all gone, everyone I once knew . . . except for a handful of the Brotherhood who I saw last night . . . are gone. It's an endless mourning."

"Sahvage . . . how is this possible?" she asked with wonder.

"The Book." He shook his head. "It was a spell in the Book. And Mae, I just didn't want you to do the same thing to your brother. All he would know is the deaths of those he loved, including you. I've had to separate myself from everyone, because how could I possibly explain my situation? Who would believe me? And as for destroying the Book—it was my only option to help you. Or at least . . . that's what I thought at the time. You were right, though, and I'm sorry. I didn't have the right to take your choice away, even if I was worried about its implications."

Mae rubbed one of her eyes and then winced like it hurt. "So back at the parking garage . . . that first night, you were going to live anyway. I didn't save you, did I."

"Oh, Mae," he said in a voice that cracked, "you *have* saved me. In all the ways that matter, you absolutely have saved me. My heart was dead, and then you came along—"

Without warning, Sahvage's female launched herself at him, throwing her arms around him, pressing her lips to his.

"I love you," she said as she pulled back. "And I'm the one who needs to apologize. I was just so tunnel vision'd about Rhoger that I was destroying everything—"

"Wait, what did you say?"

"I was destroying everything with my single-minded—"

Sahvage shook his head. "Before that."

There was a pause. And then she stroked his hair. "I love you. And I don't care about what comes next. All I know is that you belong here. With me."

On a shudder, he closed his eyes. And remembered standing out on the lawn of the little cottage, thinking he would love to be able to clean the place up.

Because it was where Mae lived.

Now? It was where they would both live.

Slowly lifting his lids, he stared into Mae's face. There were so many things he didn't know. So many veils obscuring the future. So many things left to question and talk about.

But he knew one thing for sure.

"I love you, too," he said simply. "Forever."

✦   ✦   ✦

Up in the cottage's second-floor bedroom, Mae lay naked in between cool sheets, her head on a plump pillow, her breathing deep and easy. Downstairs, she heard heavy footsteps moving around . . . and then they started up the stairs.

The weight ascending was so great, the old wood creaked, but it was a cozy sound.

Because she knew who was coming up to her bed.

In the open doorway, Sahvage appeared, his huge body resplendent, powerful, naked as well. Light from the fixture overhead bathed the cuts and valleys of his muscles, and when he came forward into the room, she saw his massive chest tattoo clearly.

Except now the finger pointing to her felt very different.

She felt like it was the answer to the question . . . of who he loved.

Mae smiled as she moved the bedding aside, revealing her body.

"Oh, Mae," he sighed.

"Come to me, my male."

Sahvage prowled his way up to her, and when he started to roll to the side, she shook her head.

"I want to feel you on me," she whispered.

"I'll be gentle."

"I know you will. You will never, ever hurt me."

"Never." He started to kiss her. "My love."

The contact of their lips was sensuous, and she had the sense that he wanted to take it slow. But she was too hungry—and so was he.

"Mae—"

"Please," she begged. "I just want you inside me. I've waited so long. I've waited a lifetime."

He groaned, and then she felt one of his hands between her legs. When he brushed her sex, she purred in anticipation.

As Sahvage started stroking her, and she felt her pleasure rise, she shook her head. "No, I want to be with you."

"You will."

Just when she was on the cusp, his hand disappeared—and she felt the blunt head of him right where she wanted to.

"I love you," she breathed.

Sahvage dropped his head in her neck as he repeated the words she was never going to tire of hearing or saying. And then he moved his hips forward and there was a brief flare of pain—that was instantly forgotten as a miraculous feeling of fullness and stretching carried her over the brink of a release that brought tears to her eyes.

As Mae started to orgasm, she called out her love's name, scoring his back with her nails, her body arching into his.

And he did the same, joining her in all the pleasure.

It was so beautiful, so perfect, she cried tears.

Of joy.

CHAPTER SIXTY-FIVE

N o known cause," a man's voice said.

"They haven't figured out how it started?"

"Nope. But the fire inspector is coming back for a second look."

"So weird. The witnesses said it went up like a match strike."

There was a series of crunching footsteps. The sound of one car door shutting. Then another. And finally, a pair of vehicles crackling over some debris and taking off down the street.

Silence. Well, not exactly. There was dripping everywhere, water falling from places all around, like it was raining. And then, from the other houses that were close by, distant sounds of people taking showers. TVs with early-morning news reports. Parents yelling up the stairs to children to hurry, it's getting late, the bus is coming.

Predawn had come to this stupid, fucking middle-class neighborhood, and the only good thing about any of it was that shit was still mostly dark.

The demon Devina sat up out of the pile of ashes. Looking down at herself, she had to shake her head. She was nothing but flesh and bones. Literally—

"Oh, shut up," she snapped. "I know I need a shower, and anyway, this is all your fault."

She glared at the pile of burned shit next to her. "You know, you can play hard to get all you want, but you need me. Without me, you're nothing."

A wad of wet soot hit her in the boob as the front cover of the Book whipped open. And when pages shuffled in anger, like she cared?

"Fuck that," she said as she got to her feet. "I should leave you here, you know that. They're going to bulldoze this whole site. You'll end up in a landfill, which is better than you deserve."

As a section of pages stood erect out of the spine, she gasped. "Are you flipping me off? Seriously? How rude!"

Trying to make her way through the debris, she slipped and caught herself on a still-steaming beam. But eventually, she got past all the ashy crap and stepped onto the singed lawn. Shaking herself, she gave the raw meat of her corporeal body a sad eye.

It was going to take a while to get her strength back. Her looks, too.

"Whatever." She started to walk off, and then realized how badly she was shivering. "Goddamn it."

She needed to be back in her lair.

On that note, she opened up a tear in the fabric of reality, her comfy little home appearing in front of her so that all she needed to do was step through to be in it. And she did put one foot into the other side.

A plaintive whimper turned her bald, open wound of a head back to the fire site. The whimper was repeated.

"I don't know why I should bother. You treat me with no respect. You're always leaving."

Whimper.

Rolling her eyes, she was about to leave the Book behind when she had a memory of that female vampire bent over and weeping across the chest of her dead male.

With a curse, Devina minced her way back into the fire damage.

"You better apologize." She leaned down and glared at the fucking piece of shit Book. "And courtesy of me taking you right now? You're going to do me a favor. You now owe me."

Grabbing the thing out of the mess, she marched back to the tear in reality.

She was due her true love.

And this ungrateful bunch of parchment was going to give it to her. Or else.

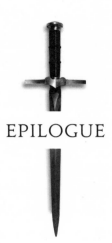

EPILOGUE

I don't . . . I don't know how this is possible."

As Sahvage spoke the words, he had a thought that he'd been saying them over and over again. Like since he had hung up his phone at the cottage and stared across the kitchen table at his Mae.

"I don't know . . ."

Good thing his female was driving his crappy junker of a car.

Trying to get a grip on himself, he took her free hand across the worn seat of his beater, and reviewed the fact pattern with himself again: *Phone rings. It's Murhder. He says he has something he needs to talk about.*

Annnnnd it was right about then that things went totally off the fucking rails. Which considering what the last twenty-four hours had been like was really saying something.

". . . how this is possible." He looked over at Mae. "Thank God you're here. I couldn't possibly do this without you. Do you know where you're going?"

Mae glanced across the interior with a smile. "I do. And it's not far now."

"Okay. Good."

Sahvage swallowed through a tight throat and tried to distract himself. And hey, at least the latter got him grinning. He and Mae had made love all through the daylight hours in their big, creaky bed, the two of them learning each other's bodies, loving each other, being close and finally falling asleep together. It was the single best day of his life.

So in a way, having that phone call come through about thirty minutes ago? Kind of felt like overkill.

Then again, he'd been overdue for some dumb luck, he supposed.

"Here we are," she said as she got off onto a county road.

The lane took them up to what he was determined to turn the cottage into: A farmhouse that had its trim freshly painted, and its shutters restored, and its chimney stick straight, the whole lot of it sitting pretty in a yard that was well-tended and thriving.

"This is so lovely," Mae murmured as she turned off the engine and looked out to a meadow that was off to the side. "I'll bet it's beautiful when the leaves come out and the grass is green."

He nodded. And then said, "I can't feel my legs."

Immediately, his female was focused on him. "I'll help you. We're going to do this together."

"After all these years . . ." On an impulse, he went in to kiss her briefly. "Thank you."

She stroked his face. "We're in this together. Whatever happens."

They opened their doors at the same time, and that was when he scented the Brotherhood—and the other males who had been in on the infiltration the night before: From out of the garage, the big bodies came, and he was surprised as they approached him with smiles and words of welcome.

One by one, they shook his dagger hand. Patted him on the back.

Greeted him. Or introduced themselves if necessary.

More than one of them said something like, *Glad you're back.* Or, *We're going to really need you.* Or, *Let's meet at the mansion.*

Whatever that was.

And then . . .

"Shit," he said. "Wrath . . ."

In the midst of all the Brotherhood and the fighters, the great Blind King was unmistakable. Literally nothing had changed about him—except for the dog at his side. He was still tall as an oak, still with the black hair falling from a widow's peak, still with that cruel, aristocratic face.

"My brother," Wrath murmured as he came forward. "Good to see you safe and sound. You did the race a great service last night."

Sahvage swallowed. *Was he back in? Was he rejoining?*

"I . . . don't know what to say."

"Good. Too many idiots with opinions in this group anyway. And yes, if you want back into the Brotherhood, we're glad to have you."

Glancing around, Sahvage saw all kinds of nodding faces. And with Mae at his back? Was it possible . . . that the male who could not die had a future he no longer dreaded?

And then he didn't hear anything anymore.

A diminutive figure appeared in the doorway of the garage.

Everyone stopped whatever they were doing. Time seemed to stop as well.

"Mae?" he said as he reached out blindly. "Mae, I need you . . ."

Instantly, he felt his female's arm shoot around his waist and she steadied his balance. "I'm right here, Sahvage. What's wrong? Do you feel sick—oh."

The crowd parted as the little female came forward, and Sahvage was vaguely aware there was a male hanging in her background. He was young, though. Just out of his transition.

Nothing that could hurt her.

God . . . she looked different. No more the black hair, no more the dark eyes. She was silver now. She . . . glowed now.

"Rahvyn," he heard himself say.

With a strangled cry, his long-lost cousin launched herself across the distance that separated them. "*I am sorry, Sahvage! I am so sorry!*"

As she burst into tears and kept speaking in the Old Language, he caught her and held her up.

While Mae held him up.

After he was sure Rahvyn was in fact, yes, actually *alive*, he set her back down, and a cold shiver of sadness went through him. Her hair was so very different—a gray so pale it was white—and yes, her eyes were in fact silver now, too . . .

In his mind, he went back to that bedchamber. The blood. The violence.

Sahvage touched her face. Even though she was still young in appearance, she had aged a hundred thousand years—and he hated that for her.

As talk bloomed among the Brotherhood, like the fighters were trying to give them privacy, Sahvage cleared his throat.

Before he could ask, she said, "*I am alive, yes.*"

True enough, but he of all people knew that that term was very relative—and utterly unrelated to respiration and heartbeat.

Was the pain worth it, he wanted to ask. *The power you sought, was it worth it?*

Instead, he switched into English and said, "Where have you been? I looked for you throughout the Old Country for two centuries. I crossed the globe trying to find you."

"I was not here."

"Yeah, I know—when did you get to the New World?"

Rahvyn switched back to the Old Language and dropped her voice so that only he could hear her. "*I have been in time, dear Cousin, not location. I have traveled through the nights and days to meet you here, at this moment, in this place. My beloved cousin, my protector, I told you your job is done. I just had to find you to let you know that all was well.*"

Sahvage blinked—and realized her mouth was not moving. She had somehow put the thoughts into his mind.

But all is not well, he thought with a shiver.

"*You have been reborn,*" he choked out. And thought of the headless guards. Of Zxysis. Of . . .

"*Yes,*" she said. Out loud? Maybe. He wasn't sure.

"Would you like to introduce us?" Mae prompted. Like he and Rahvyn had been standing there, not talking out loud, for a while.

Refocusing, Sahvage drew his female toward his cousin—and wondered if he had to protect Mae against the female he had sworn to defend. Except that was crazy . . .

Right?

He tried to stare through Rahvyn's eyes and into her soul, but he had never been a warlock. The magic had always been hers, and hers alone, to command.

"This is my Mae," Sahvage announced. "Mae, this is my first cousin, Rahvyn. I've been looking for her for a very long time."

He felt a little better as Rahvyn smiled shyly and bowed low; it was like some part of her still remained who he had once known.

"Greetings," she said. "It is my honor."

As Mae smiled and they started chatting, as if it was a normal first meet-and-greet of in-laws, Sahvage told himself not to worry. He needed to focus on the miracle, not worry about what any of it meant. Or where they were all going to go from here.

And yet . . . as happy as he was to see his blooded relation, he found himself frightened of the female.

Fuck it, though. His nerves were just shot, and why wouldn't they be. He'd had enough near-misses with bad news in his immortal lifetime, and now that he finally had found his female?

He wasn't into taking chances anymore.

Glancing around at his brothers, and then staring down at his beloved, he decided . . . well, maybe the universe wasn't as unjust as he'd thought.

◆　　◆　　◆

Off in the corner of the garage, standing apart from the crowd of fighters and females congregating on the driveway, Lassiter frowned. And frowned some more.

As he watched the two females embrace, and Sahvage, the missing brother, looked like he was worried he was about to wake up from a very good dream, Lassiter shook his head and tried to reframe the last week and a half.

The trouble was, the film reel kept with its final edit, none of the scenes altering, the soundtrack of conversations and inner thoughts remaining the same, the script evidently not subject to alteration.

"What the fuck is your problem, glow stick," came a dry voice.

Great.

Vishous.

Exactly the brother he didn't want anywhere near him at the moment. 'Cuz really, why bring a matchstick to a gas party.

"You look like someone broke all the remotes in the house." There was a *shcht* of a lighter firing up. And then the scent of Turkish tobacco. "Come on, angel, this isn't like you—and I can't believe I'm jumping into your pool of weirdness, here."

"I didn't see her," Lassiter murmured as he stared at the female with the long silver hair and strange, glowing silver eyes.

"Huh?"

"In all the visions about this . . . I never saw her." Lassiter focused on the brother. "I don't get it. I saw everything . . . the demon, the Book, Sahvage, Balthazar, Rehvenge . . . all of it. Even down to this scene here, although I couldn't figure why it would be here and not the mansion. But I never saw *her*."

He went back to staring through the crowd of familiar bodies, people blocking his view and then revealing her when they stepped aside. One young male in particular seemed to dote on her, bringing her a glass of milk from inside the house, but she seemed suspended and unconnected in the midst of them all.

Ethereal.

Beautiful—

Her eyes shifted around as if they were looking for something to light on, as if she were starting to feel overwhelmed and maybe wanted to escape—

See me, he thought at her. *I want you to see me.*

Her stare continued on past him. And then promptly doubled back.

As their eyes met, a shimmer of awareness, of heat . . . of purpose . . . went through Lassiter's entire body.

"Well," V said, "all I can tell you is that I never saw anything that was meant for me, true?"

Lassiter looked back at the brother. "Huh, what?"

"My visions. They've only ever been about the destinies of others, never my own." The brother shrugged and started to walk away. "So good luck with that, angel. Or should I say, good luck with her."

With a knowing look, the brother wandered off.

Leaving Lassiter with the strangest sense that the Gift of Light wasn't an object at all . . . and that he and this silver-haired female were just getting started with each other.

ACKNOWLEDGMENTS

With so many thanks to the readers of the Black Dagger Brotherhood books! This has been a long, marvelous, exciting journey, and I can't wait to see what happens next in this world we all love. I'd also like to thank Meg Ruley, Rebecca Scherer and everyone at JRA, and Hannah Braaten, Andrew Nguyen, Jennifer Bergstrom, and the entire family at Gallery Books and Simon & Schuster.

To Team Waud, I love you all. Truly. And as always, everything I do is with love to and adoration for both my family of origin and of adoption.

Oh, and thank you to Naamah, my Writer Dog II, who works as hard as I do on my books! And to the Archiball!

5/5/21